A BLOODSTONE SERIES COLLECTION BOOKS 1-3

SEVEN SINS

USA TODAY BESTSELLING AUTHOR

J.R. THORN

Cover Art by Sanja Balan
Title Page Cover Art by Jennifer Munswami
Line-Editing by Kristen Breanne

ISBN: 978-1-953393-01-2

Published in the United States.

RECOMMENDED READING ORDER

All Books are Standalone Series listed by their sequential order of events

Elemental Fae Universe Reading List

- Elemental Fae Academy: Books 1-3 (Co-Authored)
- Midnight Fae Academy (Lexi C. Foss)
- Fortune Fae Academy (J.R. Thorn)
- Fortune Fae M/M Steamy Episodes (J.R. Thorn)
- Candela (J.R. Thorn)
- Winter Fae Queen (Co-Authored)
- Hell Fae Captive (Co-Authored)

Blood Stone Series Universe Reading List

Recommended Reading Order is Below

Seven Sins

- *Book 1: Succubus Sins*
- *Book 2: Siren Sins*
- *Book 3: Vampire Sins*

The Vampire Curse: Royal Covens

- *Book 1: Her Vampire Mentors*
- *Book 2: Her Vampire Mentors*
- *Book 3: Her Vampire Mentors*

Fortune Academy (Part I)

- *Year One*
- *Year Two*
- *Year Three*

Fortune Academy Underworld (Part II)

- *Episode 1: Burn in Hell*
- *Book Four*
- *Episode 2: Burn in Rage*
- *Book Five*
- *Book Six*

Fortune Academy Underworld (Part III)

- *Book Seven*
- *Book Eight*
- *Book Nine*

Dark Arts Academy

Crescent Five: Rejected Wolf Shifter RH

- *Book One: Moon Guardian*
- *Book Two*
- *Book Three*

Unicorn Shifter Academy

- *Book One*
- *Book Two*

- *Book Three*

Non-RH Books (J.R. Thorn writing as Jennifer Thorn)

Noir Reformatory Universe Reading List

Noir Reformatory: The Beginning

Noir Reformatory: First Offense

Noir Reformatory: Second Offense

Sins of the Fae King Universe Reading List

(Book 1) Captured by the Fae King

(Book 2) Betrayed by the Fae King

Learn More at www.AuthorJRThorn.com

AUTHOR'S NOTE

This is a fast-burn reverse harem romance. Mature scenes include F/F, F/F/M, F/M/M, and F/M. Two of the four-man harem are introduced in Book 1 with the the rest of the relationships developing through books 2 and 3.

SEVEN SINS

SUCCUBUS SINS

USA TODAY BESTSELLING AUTHOR

J.R. THORN

CHAPTER 1

SEVEN DEADLY SINS

Darkness has chased me all my life. It's not tangible, and Sarah thinks it was all in my head, but the painful seven runes on my stomach aren't part of my imagination. Four of them cluster together around my navel, each with a distinct pattern as if representing a different piece of my soul. Three more runes wander on the outside, only one glowing with a soft pink of satisfaction and giving me enough power to stay alive. I feel like if I'd never met Sarah, I most certainly would have died.

Even now, as I lay awake in my bed with Sarah sleeping peacefully at my side, I run my fingers over the slightly raised scars. They hum with a need I can't explain. Anyone lucky enough to have seen them thinks they're tattoos, but I was born with them. The top one just above my navel has a maddening itch and my nails go to it, softly scratching, which doesn't award me with any relief. I don't want to turn on the lights and look at it. I know it's only getting worse, darker and angrier as if I am supposed to be doing something to stop the darkness from coming. It's trying to urge me, but to do what... I don't know. My heart quickens with fear. If I don't figure out what it means soon... the darkness will find me. Of that much I'm sure.

The rune. I feel like it's supposed to help me, but at the same time, I know that it's a beacon to a force I can't even begin to describe. I've seen it in my dreams. I don't dare close my eyes and face the nightmares again. When I do, dark claws rake the skies of my dreams. It's a horrifying cloud of glittering blackness and it's coming after me. It's always been coming after me, but now time is running short. The edges of my vision are weakening, and no matter how many times I rub my eyes, I can't shake the feeling that I'm slowly dying and the rest of the world will come tumbling after me.

SUCCUBI DEN

Sleep so wasn't happening and there was one thing worse than an insatiable itch across my abdomen, and that was the gnawing hunger that was making me see red. I found myself wandering the streets heading to the one place that could offer some small sense of relief to a succubus such as myself. If I didn't get the sexual nourishment I needed soon, I *would* die. It was kind of ironic. A part of me felt like I was meant to be loyal to a select few, yet my nature compelled me to seek nourishment and filled me with a lustful need that pushed away any rationalization. My fingers slipped under the low hem of my shirt and scratched at the blasted runes that wouldn't leave me alone with their incessant itching. I cast a glance at the sky, almost expecting the claws from my nightmares to streak through the low, sleepy clouds and come after me, but nothing happened.

Even if the nightmares were all in my head, I was still a succubus, and the starvation I'd been subjecting myself to was very real, and very dangerous. Sarah would find me in the afterlife and kill me all over again if I allowed myself to starve when all this time she was convinced that she could satiate my magical, sexual nourishment needs.

The last place in the world I wanted to be was a slum like Seattle's Succubi Den. The tattered awning peeked through the foggy horizon surrounded by slanted buildings. Approaching it, I pulled my hoodie closer around my face, but my sensual gait betrayed what I was. I couldn't hide my nature, and I hated how I was growing nauseatingly accustomed to handing over a hundred dollar bill to a round-faced succubus who leaned over a polished counter.

Fucking paying for it. So humiliating.

She'd started the business to help succubi and incubi who'd run into unique difficulties with their life-sucking magic, but finding enough willing participants to donate their life-force didn't come for free. She probably thought I was sick, because I kept coming back. Sometimes the magical wells got clogged, be it a magical manifestation or an emotional one. We needed sex to survive, or at least we needed to feed off sexual energy. Pain tingled along my fingertips and was the first warning sign that I was getting close to my own mortal limit of enduring abstinence.

"Why do you keep coming back, hun?" the succubus named Lucy asked with a concerned knit to her brow. She gave me a once-over, noting my fingers still under my shirt scratching away like some kind of drug addict. Aside from my quirks, I was the perfect succubus. Her eyes roamed over my voluptuous boobs that only got in the way, and noted my plump lips. She sighed. "I know there's nothing wrong with your magic. I just can't work out why you need a Den."

I glared at her until she produced a golden key to my assigned bedroom. It was none of her business. When I took the key, I decided to humor her this time. Maybe she'd understand. "I've got a girlfriend," I muttered.

She painted on a fake smile, but homosexuality in the succubi community was widely frowned upon. I didn't expect judgment from a do-gooder like Lucy, but there was pity in her eyes.

By our nature, we could only feed on those of the opposite sex. To maintain a relationship with a same-sex partner was both unfair and unsatisfactory on both sides. Most succubi enjoyed the occasional orgy or threesome, but a one-on-one relationship with a same-sex partner just wasn't done, even in a community designed around sex.

"That's a shame," she said as I walked away. "We have a program for that."

Bristling, I shot back, "I don't need fixing. I just need breakfast."

"Well hello again, sweetheart," a handsome incubus greeted me as he lewdly stretched over silk bedsheets. I didn't know his name, and I wanted to keep it that way. All I needed to know was that he had enough power to keep me alive without making me break my promise to Sarah.

A hundred dollars bought me ten minutes with the den's most powerful incubi, and even if ten minutes wasn't much, it was all I needed not to fall over and wither into a pile of Sonya-shaped dirt.

Without wasting time, I crawled over him and bit his lip hard enough to make him flinch. "No talking," I reminded him of our golden rule. It was bad enough that I had to do this. I wanted to get what I needed, and then get out of here, wiping my memory clean as best I could.

As his hands wrapped around my hips and grated me over his stiffening erection, separating us only by a thin layer of sheets and my own clothes, his fingers squeezed as I began the feed.

The soft magic of his life-force bled into me and I gasped with slight relief. Knocking my head back, my eyes fluttered closed as he kissed his way down my neck and peeled away my shirt. I flinched when his fingers ran over the raised scar of my runes and I pushed his hands away. He wasn't allowed to touch me there. Something deep within me knew that those runes weren't meant for him. He obeyed, his touch and kisses going to the soft skin of my neck and the taut skin around my thighs. Numbness fled from my extremities and a satisfying warmth curled in my belly. The itch from my rune still persisted, but at least it was more manageable when I had the energy to ignore it.

"It's been months of foreplay," he complained. "You only tease me, succubus."

I jerked and wrapped my fingers around his neck. He only grinned at my anger. "I said no talking."

He offered me a slow nod of agreement and shifted me over him, rubbing through my jeans with his erection that was now in full force.

His arousal gave me a surplus of energy and what I couldn't feed on filtered through the air in an unused hint of sweat and sex. I wanted to go farther, to give into the temptation to sheath him and ride out this aching need inside of me. I could survive with these snacks, but every time, I grew just a little bit weaker when I denied a climax my body craved.

"I see it in your eyes," he purred, his grin coming back to taunt me. "You're going to need to feed soon, really feed, not just these little snacks, and if you don't give in, you're going to harm yourself." He lifted me with an ease that pissed me off. He flipped me on my back and gave me a deep kiss. Part of me wanted to toss him off, but I reminded myself that I was still halfway clothed. I was still protected by fabric that stretched its restriction across my hips and kept him from pushing me to do something I knew I'd regret.

When he went for my zipper, I snatched his fingers in the strongest grip I could manage. "No," I told him. "You know the rules."

He sighed, because even if he was a powerful incubus, I was still his client. "Very well," he said, and leaned in to graze his lips across my neck. "When you're ready, I'll be here, and what you really need will be on the house."

Shivering, even though Seattle was humidly hot during the day, I wrapped my fingers around my elbows and marched away from Seattle's Succubi Den as the sun banished most of the fog. This was the moment I painfully wiped away my memories of kisses and teasing at the hands of an incubus I'd paid to be with. Sarah didn't know, couldn't know, that I had to resort to a Den to stay alive. She believed that I could feed on her, and because she was a muse, she was strong enough to survive me.

I couldn't tell her the truth. Not yet.

But this time, the need inside of me hadn't relaxed. I'd banished only the worst of the pains that came with starvation from abstinence. But even though I still tasted the musky delight of an incubus on my lips, he'd been right. I couldn't keep this up for much longer. I doubled over when my rune changed its reminder from an itch to a stab of pain, just like I'd been gouged by a blade. I groaned and lifted my shirt, cursing when a drop of blood squeezed from the center of the rune that had turned so black it was in danger of scabbing over.

"Damn it," I spat, and marched back home towards Sarah.

What the fuck was I going to do now?

HOME SWEET HOME

Sarah wasn't home when I returned, which wasn't until the day was almost over. Let her think I went to work. That sounded a lot less pathetic than wandering Seattle trying to get an incubus' sex scent off my body.

"Sonya!" Sarah squealed as she burst through the door. A sports tank clung to her sweat-glistened body and she wrapped her arms around my neck. I smiled against her teeth as she gave me a sweet kiss. She leaned and gave me a smug grin. She knew the effect she had on me made me crazy. "What's for dinner?" she asked.

I gave her a raised brow. "Pizza?"

She laughed with delight. "Perfect!"

"Didn't you just work out?" I asked as I poked her perfectly flexed abdomen.

She smirked and detached herself from me before waltzing down the hall. "Working out is just so I can eat all the pizza I want, duh." She gave me a wink over her shoulder before she disappeared upstairs. I stared after her until the sounds of a shower running intertwined with the pounding of my heart.

I loved life with Sarah, at least when it was like this. She was always happy and giggling, and a little hole inside of me welled with guilt knowing that I was lying to her. If the truth came out, she'd be broken.

That guilt nagged at me as I slumped on the couch and flipped open the laptop to order pizza.

I picked out our standard, two medium pizzas and a liter of soda, but just as I hit the confirm button, tiny zaps jolted up my fingertips. I hissed and tried to make a fist, but a fresh jolt of pain went through my temple and I jerked, sending the laptop careening to the floor. "Damn it!" I yelled as the screen swept with white lines before losing power altogether. Sarah and I were both bartenders, and even though we were both holding Seattle's record for tips per night, things were running tight. Sarah didn't know that half my tips were going to a Den's incubus down the street. I couldn't explain why I couldn't afford to fix a laptop.

Sarah rushed to the top of the stairs with wet strands of hair clinging to her face and a towel clutched to her chest. It twisted, in danger of falling off her body. "Babe, you okay?"

She frowned as I swayed on my feet. "I'm—" I tried to say, but the world spun and the next thing I knew Sarah was screaming my name as I fell into the cackling blackness of my nightmares.

When I finally awoke, it was to Sarah's deep frown. She towered over me and tiny droplets fell from her curls. Okay, that was a good sign. I hadn't been out long. "You had me worried sick!" she snapped.

I gave her a wry smile. "You're going to give yourself wrinkles with a frown like that," I croaked.

Unamused, she gave me a nudge. "The hell is going on?" She

surveyed me, as if looking for what had caused my episode. "I didn't think succubi were supposed to get sick."

Easing up, I clutched my pounding head and ignored the urge to scratch the enflamed rune at the apex of my stomach. I didn't want to admit what was wrong. I hadn't had sex with a male in six months and my body was starting to rebel. I couldn't keep this up for much longer. "It's nothing," I murmured.

Her frown deepened with a vengeance. "Don't make me read your mind. Because I will!"

Black dots sprinkled across my vision as I forced myself to stand. Sarah shot up to guide me, still only wearing her pink towel.

"Don't threaten me with your mighty muse ways," I teased and pinched her chin. "I'm just hungry, that's all."

She narrowed her eyes. "But we just had sex last night." She pouted. "Am I starting to bore you?"

I huffed a laugh and kissed her cheek. "Of course not, my beautiful girlfriend. I'm just having trouble feeding. I'll go see a doctor first thing in the morning."

She frowned. "A doctor, or a *doctor* doctor?"

I snickered. "What other kind of doctor is there?"

She frowned. "There are doctors, and then there are those creepster voodoo witches you call succubi doctors. I don't trust them." She turned over her palms and looked into them as if she could read her own future. By the lines on her face, she didn't like what she saw. "They'll tell you that you need a boyfriend."

Easing back down to her side, I took her face in my hands. "That's not going to happen, okay? I'd rather die than cheat on you."

Her glittering eyes found mine, instantly glassy with emotion. As a muse, Sarah could be extreme when it came to passion, but that's what I loved about her. "Then prove them wrong. Feed on me, and don't hold back."

She pressed her warm lips to mine and the sweetness of her magic filled my senses. I couldn't feed on her, no matter how much I wished I could, but there was so much power that her presence still made me drunk. I didn't fake the impact she had on me.

"We don't need to—" I began to protest.

Sarah eased her fingers over my breast and nipped my lip with her teeth, making me flinch. She licked over the small hurt. "You need to feed. I'm always hot for you, babe. Take what you need from me."

I needed to feed, and as much as Sarah aroused me, and I aroused her, sex with her wouldn't fix what was wrong with me. "Okay," I said with a grin, in spite of the emptiness of her offer to most succubi. "But the pizza guy is going to be here soon and I'm not going to fuck you through dinner again."

She sighed and pressed herself to me, fitting her curves perfectly into mine. "We'll see about that." She flashed me a smile that was full of mischief and tugged me to the stairs. "I still need to finish my shower."

Reluctantly I allowed Sarah to drag me through our bedroom and into the confined space of our apartment's stand-up shower. She curled her fingers under my shirt and I lifted my arms to allow her to peel it off. She glanced at my angry runes. She ran a finger around the top one that had turned black. "Is that normal?"

I grabbed her fingers and brought them up to my lips for a kiss. The worry lines across her face smoothed as she smiled. She knew I didn't like to talk about it, and she appeased me, giving me what we both wanted instead.

This was what I enjoyed with Sarah. She was so strong and dominant. I never got to experience that with men who were enthralled to me the moment I even thought about spreading my legs. But Sarah? I could never tell her no, and it felt nice to be wanted for me instead of my magic.

After I'd stepped out of my jeans, I squeezed into the shower with Sarah and wrapped my arms around her. I smiled as she kissed my neck. I squeezed her perfectly formed butt cheeks in return. "You're working out too much," I teased. "I think you could open a beer bottle with these."

She growled as she slid her fingers into me, sending my breath hitching. "You don't want to tease me," she warned. "I'll make you suffer and then we'll miss dinner for good."

I rolled my eyes into the back of my head as pleasure wafted through me. When I gave in and moaned, she spread her fingers apart, making my knees buckle. "You need to feed," she insisted.

I'd always told her that my own arousal wasn't enough, that I needed to give her pleasure. Had she been a man, that would have been true, to an extent. But the truth was that I felt guilty, and giving Sarah orgasm after orgasm was my way of making it up to her.

She took my hand and guided me over soft flesh. When my fingers rolled across her hard nub, she gasped and I took over, rolling in soft circles and pressing her against the tiled wall.

I took her breast in my mouth, syncing the rolling of my tongue with the swirl of my fingers, bringing a sweet musk of Sarah's magic and arousal into the steaming air. When the doorbell rang, I ignored it, accepting that we'd both be going hungry tonight, but comforted by the soft moans of Sarah coming to climax because of my touch. Not my magic, not because of what I was, but because she wanted me for *me*. It was almost worth starving for.

Sex with my muse was always dynamic, even without the curling warmth of feeding on sexual life-force. But this time I was weak, and even though we'd brought each other to climax more than once, I lay awake and hungry as she slept curled up next to me with sheets wrapped around her like gift paper. Not to mention the rune across my stomach burned with renewed fever and the skin was starting to peel. It hissed a need inside of me that I was missing something important and it was time I stopped ignoring it.

I didn't want to deal with my nightmares right now and I laced my fingers behind my head and sank deeper into the pillow. Sarah's soft sounds as she slept next to me gave me a mixture of comfort and guilt.

I'd spoken the truth when I told her that I'd rather die than cheat on her with a man, even if I needed to feed. The last time Sarah had caught me with a guy she'd disappeared for two years. It didn't matter if she knew what I needed, it still hurt her. That heartache had been a dagger that dug a little deeper every time I came home and found our apartment empty.

Then, one day, Sarah was there, and I'd made a promise not to have sex with another guy. I'd thought that I could feed off of her, for a little while. Since she was a muse, there was a magic to her that I could taste. But it took a dangerous night where I'd almost died to realize that her magic wasn't something I could live off of. I'd been two blocks from the Succubi Den and that's when one of the regulars had found me and paid for me to have a night with their most powerful Incubi. Even then, I hadn't let him take off my clothes, but I'd fed off his kiss and the pressure of his skin against mine. It was just enough to keep me alive.

Now that I was starting to black out again, I had a decision to make. Either I was going to cheat on Sarah… or I was going to die.

I forced myself into a fitful sleep hoping I could run away from my problems by getting some rest. That's not how it worked and I knew that, but I was good at denial.

My standard nightmare of the end of the world raking death across the horizon took a back seat and something else took its place. There's only one thing worse than a nightmare... and that's a memory of my mother's death.

It was the last memory of my mother I only seemed to be able to recall in my dreams. She was speaking to a tattooed woman who I could only remember as a shadow. The tattoos wound around her with black wisps, blocking out her face. It was magic that I remembered and that kept drawing me back to this place. Magic that didn't want me to recall what had been done to me. Magic that had come from a witch.

My mother clutched at me as if the woman might take me away. "No!" she shouted.

The sharp tone of her voice brought tears to my eyes. She'd never told me what would happen when I turned sixteen.

"Who is this, Mama?" I asked.

The witch's voice never did come through quite right in my dream-memory. The words came out as broken, garbled sounds, like pieces of glass falling down a metal tube. "You made a deal," she hissed and reached for me.

That's right. I always seemed to forget this part when I woke up. My mother had sold her firstborn child in exchange for power over a Blood Stone... over the force of hell itself. Anger burned in me that she'd have been capable of such a thing, but the way that she bravely stepped between the witch and me said how much she regretted such a bargain and she was going to fight to have it undone.

Perhaps she imagined she'd never get pregnant. Perhaps I was a mistake and I was never supposed to have been born. Regardless of her intentions, here I was, payment due, and the Witch of Shadows had come to collect her debt.

"I curse you, witch," my mother spat, even as the witch's magic ripped her out of the way.

I screamed as an invisible force dragged me to the witch's feet. Even in my dream-memory, I couldn't make out her features. Tattoos and shadows spiraled around her, but the magic couldn't wipe out the scent that filled my nostrils. Sulfur. The stench of hell wrapped around me and made me gag. This was a Witch of the Shadow Coven, one of the dark arts and old ways. Blood magic was the darkest of them all and even though I knew what was coming, I was horrified when its burning magic tingled through my veins.

I turned to look at my mother, my vision blurred as tears welled in my eyes. I hated this part, not because of the pain that came next, but because I would have loved to have seen my mother again. Even through the splotchy limit of my sight I knew she would be stunning. Sharp, angled cheekbones set on a stern face, currently tilted up in determination to use the power the witches had awarded her against them.

There was only one thing a Witch of the Shadow Coven could want with a virgin—a succubus virgin, no less.

Sacrifice to redeem a sin.

I was to resolve one of the cardinal sins. Each supernatural was capable of this twisted purpose. I sensed the sins the witch had already quelled. Four. Four sins were missing from her rotten soul.

Greed.

Envy.

Gluttony.

Anger.

That left three left to be resolved. Sloth. Pride. Lust… I knew which one I was for.

The witch raised her ceremonial dagger and moonlight glittered on its dangerous edge. I opened my mouth to scream, but no sound came out.

"You will redeem me," the witch said as shadows writhed over her face, forming a malicious grin.

I was the innocent daughter of a succubus. I could redeem a witch's sin—lust, in particular.

Witches who dabbled in dark arts eventually went to hell. There was a loophole, however. Sacrifice could get them off the hook, but not just any sacrifice. The seven cardinal sins had to be redeemed.

I buckled over when a sharp warmth spread through my belly just before the witch struck. Her blade bounced off an invisible wall with a loud *clang* that echoed through my chest and made my teeth clack.

Her eyes went wide as my mother chanted. She was the one who'd given a succubus magic, and now she dared to use it against her. My mother stretched out her hands and her mouth moved as she spoke words I didn't understand. Power hummed in the air and her necklace gleamed with ruby malice.

Her eyes found me, just for a moment, and my vision cleared just long enough to see the panic and dread that would crush my heart to pieces so badly that I'd only ever remember this moment in the depths of my worst nightmares.

"Take the power," my mother insisted as she crumpled to her knees. My mother snapped her fingers and the witch screamed, but I didn't dare turn around. I kept my gaze pinned on my mother who wove her own magic through the air. I'd never seen her do that before and I traced the gleaming red lines as they spidered and flicked the expanse between us before finally reaching my feet.

The process was slow, as was the pain. It started as a twinge deep in my belly, then a throb, and then it twisted and I whirled to find the witch contorted with it. Her shadows writhed around her as if enraged as my mother's ruby magic ripped at her.

Each sin she'd appeased filtered through the air.

The golden scale of a dragon's greed pierced the spot just above my navel and struck like the bite of a tiny but vicious insect. I cried out, but the magic held me tight as it continued its work.

The second sin came next, envy, a green and twisted rune that screwed into my skin to the right of my navel. My mother bellowed over my cries with encouragement, but I'd never been prepared for this sort of pain.

The third sin came at me, ruthless in its rage. Anger. It burned hot to the left of my navel.

I didn't have time to rest as the fourth sin, gluttony, oozed low on my stomach, dark and swollen red with blood that a vampire could gorge on for days.

Black dots sprinkled my vision. Those were the sins the witch had managed to redeem, and so those were my only guaranteed gifts. One day, I would find mates that matched those sins. The strongest of their race that would help me get revenge on the Shadow Coven for what they did to my kind, for what they had forced my mother to do to me.

The final three sins marked my body and I slumped to the ground as the world around me leapt into flames. Four sins with forgiveness, three unresolved. It would have to be enough. I would have to find a way for it to be enough.

As my dream ended, the world around me burned, and my mother took the witch with her to hell.

The memories faded of a nightmare that burned hot and made my runes itch all at once. I hated that I couldn't remember it. It was as if my mind rejected any attempt at recalling the vile dream no matter how hard I tried.

It didn't matter. I was awake and I certainly wasn't getting any sleep now. Guilt stabbed harder than ever as I slunk through the midnight streets. Once again, I was drawn back to the one place that could give me some sense of reprieve.

Every step made me anxious. What if Sarah woke up and found me missing? What excuse was I going to tell her this time?

No matter how much failing Sarah terrified me, I still found myself staring at the inconspicuous Succubi Den wedged between two buildings masquerading as a massage parlor.

The round-faced succubi gave me a beaming smile as I dragged myself through the foyer. "Oh, honey, you look like you need more than a snack tonight."

I slammed all the money I had onto the counter. "Don't rub it in."

She pushed my life's savings back towards me. "He said this one would be on the house."

She dangled a familiar golden key and I growled as I shoved the money back into my pocket. I glared at her before I took her offering.

She ushered me inside and allowed me to make my own way down the hall lined with red velvet. When I unlocked the suite on the final row and swung the door open, *he* was waiting for me, and this time there weren't any sheets to obscure the view.

He leaned back against the headboard with his hands clasped behind him. His body twined with muscles and the lines at his hips pointed to a perfect cock already hard at my arrival. "I've been waiting for this," he said.

I frowned. I didn't know if it was the smug tone of his voice, or how trapped this life made me feel, but no matter how helpless I felt, there was always a choice.

With a growl I hurled the key at the ground. It clattered across marble floors as my vision wavered with red. "No," I snapped. "I'm not going to live like this."

He launched to his feet and his gaze burned with need and anger. I saw now why he'd offered a session for free. My magic had affected him just as much as he'd affected me. He needed me, wanted me for what I was. That only made me clench my jaw with determination that I wasn't going to go through with this.

"It's the rare succubus that lets herself starve." He tilted his head. "Madame said you have a girlfriend. Would she really want you to die over fidelity?"

I pinched my lips together. He was probably right. If Sarah knew I needed sex with a male to survive, she'd tell me to do it.

But her heart would be broken, and damned if I was going to be the one to break the tender heart of a muse.

"I can't do this to her," I said through clenched teeth as tears stung my eyes. "I just can't."

He crossed the room and gripped my shoulders with a strength that made my knees buckle. He pulled me close and let me rest against the hard warmth of his chest. "Madame said you're not welcome back after tonight."

I stiffened. "What?"

He tucked a strand of hair behind my ear. "This place is for those who need help. The King doesn't support what you're doing, and if word got out, the Den would be forced to shut down." He cupped my chin. "This pain you're causing yourself is pointless. After tonight, you're going to have to go back to the way it's meant to be." He leaned in and grazed his lips across my neck. "You're going to have to prey on men again and do what you do best. What you were made to do."

Pain splintered through me as I shrieked. "No!" I cried. "I won't kill to survive! I'm not a monster! Not like you."

He didn't seem hurt by my outrage. Instead he gathered the bedsheets and wrapped it around his waist. "I'm sorry. I can only hope you'll come to your senses and accept what you are, even if your *girlfriend* can't."

As pissed off as that incubus made me, he'd struck a nerve. Sarah loved me, but she'd never been able to accept me for what I was. The runes across my stomach were just an oddity, not a prophecy. That wouldn't change now, not even if I ever grew the balls to tell her the truth.

I was a killer. And if I wanted to survive, I was going to have to kill again, and the runes across my stomach were trying to tell me something important. When I looked up at the sky, those dark claws were there. I blinked twice, and then they were gone.

Perhaps it was the starvation making me see things, or perhaps it was a prophecy that I'd better start listening to.

I knew what I needed to do in order to survive. I was supposed to kill. Sarah would find out and see me for the monster than I am.

I clenched my fingers into fists and growled at the mocking sky. "I'd rather starve."

The second I arrived home, I curled into bed with a still-sleeping Sarah and let the sobs take me.

She roused from a deep sleep, her eyes still heavy with satisfaction. That only made me cry harder. "Babe," she said, wrapping her warmth and sweet magic around me, "it's okay. I'm here."

I cried into the curve of her graceful neck, and was surprised that she didn't try to pry into my head to find out what was bothering me. She was a powerful muse, capable of ripping my mind apart if she so chose.

The reality struck me like a dagger. Maybe she was afraid of what she'd find.

Forcing myself to sit up, I took her hands in mine. "Sarah?"

"Yeah?"

"Let's go to the bar tomorrow. There's something we need to talk about."

A NIGHT TO DIE FOR

Walking to the bar, Sarah noticed something was off. She wrapped her fingers through mine and gave a light squeeze. "You doing all right?"

I grit my teeth together. No, I wasn't fucking doing all right. The rune across my stomach was bleeding again, but I'd worn a bandaid this time. There was no working around what it meant. I was dying.

"I'm fine," I snapped and wrenched my hand free of hers.

She pouted before crossing the street and pushing her way into the bar. Men parted the instant she got near them, likely not even knowing that they'd been influenced by magic beyond their comprehension.

Frowning, I disapproved of how Sarah blatantly used her powers just because she was mad. I didn't want to see what she was going to do when I broke up with her in a public place, but I'd decided this would be the best way. I wanted her to think that my starvation was because I'd left her, not because I couldn't feed on her. I'd much rather her hate me… than hate herself.

"Hey!" David shouted, beaming a smile as I caught our

favorite human's gaze. He waved and propped the door open. "You coming or what?"

Giving him a smirk, I waited for a motorcycle to careen by before crossing the street and brushing past David's broad chest. "Thanks for coming," I told him, honestly grateful that he'd shown.

David's beaming smile dimmed when we made our way inside and he saw that I'd brought Sarah. "Oh," he said, his disappointment obvious.

I rolled my eyes. "You're going to play the buffer, okay? We're breaking up again."

His eyes went wide, this time sparking with excitement. But he had the grace to give me a sympathetic pat on the shoulder. "Don't worry. I've got your back."

My stomach twitched, and I scratched at the rune, wondering if his touch had somehow eased the pain.

Breaking up with Sarah had been one of the hardest things I'd ever done in my life. Not just because I didn't want to do it, but because my whole body screamed with agony, telling me to turn to the nearest man and take what I needed. The sheer number of penises in this place was making my jaw twitch.

The second Sarah had gotten the message that I was serious, I stormed out behind the bar, more for the relief of getting away from all the testosterone than Sarah's sad eyes. She probably thought I just wanted to get away from her, but the truth was that my world was spinning and I couldn't keep a straight face with the pain anymore. If I'd stayed in there, I'd have taken what I needed from anyone whether Sarah was watching or not.

My watch buzzed and told me I had ten minutes left to live. I turned my wrist to glance at it. Yep. This sucked.

The dark alley was hardly my first choice of where I'd die. I'd always imagined I'd go in blood-red velvet sheets stabbed with a knife from a victim who'd finally overcome my compulsion. I'd always hated what I was. This wasn't life.

Stretching out on the pebbled asphalt, I found my only bedmates were twittering mice and three empty beer cans.

I stared at the moon and contemplated if I should be doing something monumental with my last minutes. Sarah would still be inside the bar, probably wondering where I was. I could see her now, twirling a straw in a strawberry daiquiri with a pouty lip and adorable scowl. We'd broken up what, five times now? Did she even believe I was serious this time? I'd meant it. I was going to leave her for good. Not because I wanted to, but because she deserved better than me. And I deserved what would happen to me when I didn't screw men to death, literally.

And David would be next to her, telling her I wasn't worth it. Even though I knew how he felt about me, he wouldn't let Sarah think she deserved a broken heart. That's just the kind of guy he was. I'd invited him to be the buffer, but also to keep her occupied long enough to let me die in peace.

As if on cue, the wooden door creaked open and I rolled my head across the pavement to see if my angel of death had arrived.

"What'cha doin' down there, gorgeous?" David gave me a winning smile and he seemed like an angel for sure. The moonlight was drawn to him and illuminated the dark locks framing his face. The runes across my stomach twinged with pain as if recognizing him as something I needed. Perhaps it was a sin to take what I needed from him, but all sins could be forgiven, couldn't they?

I tore my gaze away. Those had been my mother's words. *All sins could be forgiven.* Had that been a lie just to try and make me feel better about myself? "What am I doing?" I muttered, trying to focus on the present before my memories ruined my last minutes alive. "Waiting to die."

He laughed and skipped down the three short steps to the street, oblivious to my torment. "Aren't we all?"

My heart skipped when he slid down beside me, not seeming to care that we were lying on a grimy street behind an even grimier bar.

I blinked a few times before thinking of what my monumental last words should be. The world was already warping and turning grey. It was difficult to breathe and I scratched my nails across the ground, barely able to feel the pain. I'd hoped there would be a near-death experience, or something astounding to give me some miraculous insight of the world before I died. But all I could think of was the innocent girlfriend I was about to leave behind. "Do you think Sarah will be okay?"

"Sarah..." He said her name with a curl to his lip in distinct distaste. "I know you care about her, but it feels like there's something more ahead for you." He propped up on his elbow. "Have you ever considered that your feelings for Sarah are misplaced? I mean, there's something different about her that anyone would be attracted to, but you two have never been that compatible."

My eyes went wide. The runes across my stomach all twitched in agreement, as if I'd been using Sarah as a crutch to avoid facing a future that terrified me. "What makes you say that?"

"It just, it seems right, for some reason." He sat up and pulled me with him. His strong fingers wrapping around my arm made me want to forget what I'd resolved to do. I forced myself to bring up every victim's face in my mind. Terrifying memories were always stronger than the good ones. I could still see each pale face staring back into mine, that blank look of poisoned desire masking the horror of their own death.

He tucked a lock of hair behind my ear and pulled my chin to look at him. "Are you crying?"

His blue eyes locked onto mine and I gulped down my pride. "Yes," I whispered.

His fingers trailed down my neck, extracting a sliver of my magic that wanted to wrap around his cock and lure him into giving me what I needed. He shivered as if I'd stroked him.

I squeezed my eyes shut and wished it would all be over. My watch buzzed again. I had one minute left.

His breath puffed on my lips. I couldn't open my eyes. I couldn't let him fall under my spell. David deserved better than my sins. He was kind, sweet, and had been the only human not to immediately throw himself at me. I didn't know what had made him change his mind, but I was close to taking him up on his offer. A succubus only has so much willpower.

"Sonya..." he whispered. His voice dripped with longing and desperation.

My eyes shot open and I had nowhere to look but his concerned and adoring gaze. My tongue shot across my dry lips and hesitation tugged at my heart.

He leaned in, and fuck, I didn't pull away. I couldn't.

His lips met mine and pure ecstasy shot through my limbs. His kiss made me feel whole and I only wanted more. Any reservations I had for propriety or phantom loyalty were overwhelmed by the magic that demanded my survival. The ache deep in my bones finally sighed in relief from the sexual nourishment that flooded my senses. As if I had been wandering a desert and found a drop of life, I thrust my hands under his shirt and dug my nails across his skin and drank it all in.

How I wished I could just be human and feel the magnetizing pull of sex without the need to feed. Then again, if I was human,

I wouldn't be slipping my tongue over David's. I'd be with Sarah, happy and oblivious to what it felt like to be on the brink of death when I didn't feed.

When David's stiff arousal grated against my hips through our jeans, it was impossible not to drink his lust. I didn't have to open my eyes to know my nails were going from corpse-blue to radiant-pink. Knowing that David was literally giving me life itself only made me want him more. This was the part I couldn't fight. This was when my instincts as a predator took over.

He must have felt the drain, for his breath hitched and his eyes went wide. He stared at me, his lust clouding over with confusion. My powers kicked in out of reflex, wafting an invisible scent that made him smile as if he'd forgotten what made him startle and he groaned with pleasure, no longer able to feel the pain I was causing him. I wished I knew how my powers worked. How could something that made him look at me like that eventually kill him?

He licked his lips as if he could taste the poisonous nectar and growled as he ripped off my thin sweater, nearly tearing it in half. He didn't even notice the bandaid still plastered over the top rune that had finally staunched its throbbing ache, as if satisfied with the sexual nourishment running freely in my veins. I couldn't help but feel the rush too, some unexplainable need to have him even here, on this grimy street, even now, when Sarah could walk outside and find us together.

My heart raced as I clawed at his zipper. It didn't matter how many times I'd had magical sex. I was the most clumsy, uncoordinated creature to exist. He huffed a short laugh as he popped off the button on his jeans and slipped down the zipper with ease and his erection escaped from the confines. It was bigger than I'd imagined, and my desperate hunger paused to admire his pulsing cock.

"Like what you see?" he asked. He didn't look me in the eyes, but cupped a hand around my breast and squeezed, his face lighting up with a smile.

"Yes, I like what I see, and yes, they're real," I said with a laugh.

"I knew it!" he exclaimed. Then we laughed together, half-crazed with the disbelief of touching each other's bare skin.

Humored by the moment, and the draft of nourishment I'd already absorbed, I wiggled out of my jeans while he groped and kissed my breasts. I tucked the fabric underneath my bare ass and hoped he'd be gentle so the knobby ground didn't tear through the clothes and into my skin.

David pushed my legs apart and tested my neck with his teeth. He didn't wait for my permission and rammed into me. The thrust made me cry out with pleasure. His flesh wasn't the only thing that entered my body. The magic of his desire came in too. The two pleasures battled with one another until they combined, bringing me to climax and blossoming me back to the fullness of life.

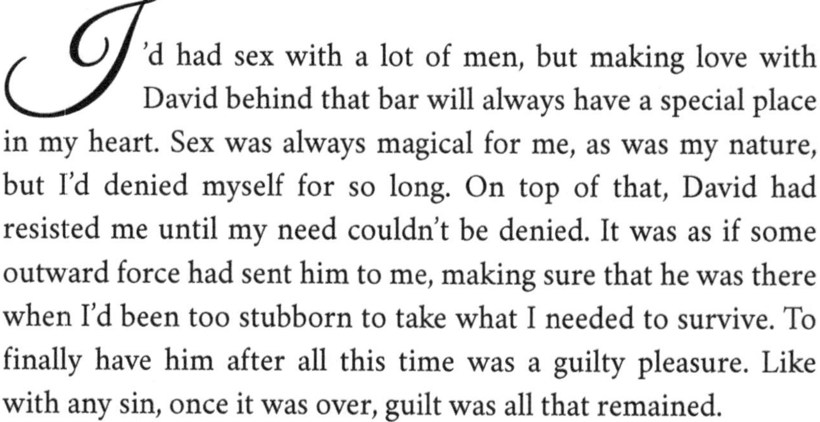

I'd had sex with a lot of men, but making love with David behind that bar will always have a special place in my heart. Sex was always magical for me, as was my nature, but I'd denied myself for so long. On top of that, David had resisted me until my need couldn't be denied. It was as if some outward force had sent him to me, making sure that he was there when I'd been too stubborn to take what I needed to survive. To finally have him after all this time was a guilty pleasure. Like with any sin, once it was over, guilt was all that remained.

I could sense David's life dwindling. His skin had greyed just a shade paler than the moonlight should have made it seem, and there could be no doubt the deterioration had already begun.

Yet, he couldn't sense his own life leaving him. His blue eyes remained sharp and pure, as if they held his very soul and would never let go.

I wished that were true.

I shifted my gaze away and lingered on the gold chain dangling from his neck—the only article of clothing that still remained.

I slipped out from under him, grimacing as the protruding rocks speared through our pile of clothes we'd used as bedding. David had not been gentle whatsoever and my backside and shoulder blades burned with tiny cuts. I ran a finger over the rune that had lost its bandaid, but it was smooth as if soothed by the romp. I looked down at it, and even though it was still angry, it had definitely calmed. Then a voice filtered into my mind. *He's not one of the seven, but now you will survive. Find them, Sonya, find the other pieces of your heart that your mother scattered into the world. Reunite with them and fulfill your destiny.*

I froze, staring at the rune that had just fucking spoken to me. Okay, now I was really losing it.

"That was..." David said, his words drifting off with a sense of wonder. He clearly hadn't heard the voice, meaning that I was definitely losing my shit.

Trying to calm the shakes that rippled over my fingers, I focused on my watch. It'd been buzzing for the better part of thirty minutes and it was time to reset it to 730 hours—one month until I had to take what I needed again.

"That was wrong," I finished for him. David wasn't who I needed, but the prophecy had just revealed itself a little bit more to me. There were men out there who could survive sex with me, and I could survive with them. I just needed to find them.

He snapped his gaze up and I ignored him, pulling on my jeans and fighting with the button that seemed too big for the loophole.

"Wrong? That was amazing."

I tugged at the button and the wretched thing wouldn't go through. I jerked left and the threading caught my nail, tearing it the wrong way. "Damn it!"

David scrambled to his feet and stepped through one leg hole of his jeans. "Is it Sarah? After all those things you said to her—what she said to you. It's over for good, right?" He turned somber. "I've seen you two breakup before. This time seemed different. It seemed real. That's why I..." He features took on an aura of pain as he stared at me. I knew he was waiting for me to tell him he was right. But I'd meant to die. He'd given me a second chance and I didn't know what to do with it.

Not meeting his gaze, I searched the ground for my bra. A cool breeze drifted through the alley, bringing with it a sense of relief under my sweat-dampened hairline and the faint smell of garbage.

I'd get the button-hole later. At the very least, I could cover my breasts. I looked down at them and sighed at the lasting red marks of David's teeth.

The bar's door creaked open and I threw my arms over my chest. Not that I'd expected privacy in a bar's back alley, I just didn't want to entice any further victims.

"Sonya? You out here? I—" Sarah sounded as if she was about to make an apology until she scanned the scene and drew in a deep breath as if to scream.

I threw my hands out, waving in defense of whatever accusations she was about to throw my way. Not that I had any sort of defense prepared, I just couldn't fathom Sarah being witness to my crime.

David shoved his other leg through his jeans and battled with the zipper. "Sarah, it's not what you think."

Her mouth bobbed open and closed like a fish stuck on dry land. Her pink skirt flirted with the wind, flapping around her thighs until she pushed her white hand-purse over it. Her gaze fell to her feet and she shifted, looking unbalanced on her ivory platform heels.

Then I saw what she was staring at. A black laced bra.

"God sakes." I scrambled to the steps and snatched it up, wrapping it around my chest and pulling the straps over my shoulders.

"I'm sorry, David," Sarah whispered. "You don't deserve to die."

I staggered. How dare she frighten him? Never mind if it was the truth. He still had months, if not years. I hadn't taken more than I needed...right?

She clenched her purse, as if debating to say something else before shaking her head and scampering back into the bar.

David rubbed his neck and gave a nervous laugh. "Uh, did I hear her right?"

I stiffened and bore my gaze through the closed door as if I could will Sarah to come back. Not that my powers worked that way—at least, not on women.

A cold hand on my shoulder made me jolt. "Cripes, David."

He chuckled. "Cripes? Does sex transform you into a British chick?" He smirked. "I could dig that."

"Look, I need to go after her, all right?"

His face fell. "What? Why?"

"She thinks..."

He rose one eyebrow. "That you're going to kill me?"

I scoffed and jerked away from his touch. He couldn't find out. Not so soon. Not like this in a back alley of a bar with mice, and empty beer cans, and—where was that god awful smell coming from?

A tiny flash of light caught my eye. If I'd been angled the other way, I would have missed it entirely.

I froze. *No, it can't be...*

Another flash of light and an unmistakable, audible, *click*.

"What is it?" David asked.

I pushed him and hoped he didn't notice how my legs wobbled. "You're stepping on my sweater."

He murmured an apology as I tugged the dirtied blouse over my head.

David's skin still left its scent on mine, and somehow, someway, Mr. Anderson had caught me in the act.

JUDGMENT

I'm not one for indecision, but the overwhelming desire to make David *mine* battled with the hope that Mr. Anderson could actually save him. I'd been given a second chance at life, and David deserved one too.

The breeze drifted a can across the alley and I knew Mr. Anderson was waiting for me to make my move. If the rancid smell was any indicator, he'd probably been hiding in a dumpster. He'd definitely watched too many bad detective movies…

With one last defiant glare into the dark alley, I hopped the three steps back to the bar and ripped open the door.

"Stay with me," David pleaded. My skin tingled with the desire to make him surrender completely. It'd only take…

I glared at him over my shoulder, feigning disgust. "I didn't mean for this to happen. Let's pretend it didn't happen and you let me go after my girlfriend." Even as I said the words, I knew they were empty. The rune across my stomach that she'd activated when we'd first met was now dormant. It didn't burn, it didn't sting, it didn't do anything. Whatever my prophecy needed from her, it'd already gotten it.

She's one of the seven... but she's not one of the four.

His eyes followed me with a sad puppy stare as I turned away. I escaped into the drunken laughter and droning music that pounded against my chest and hesitated once the door had closed. Searching for Sarah, I ran my thumb across the small ring around my pinkie finger before blundering through the crowd.

"Sarah!" I shouted, ignoring my reflection in the bartender's mirror that showed my hair spiked out at the ends like a crazed lunatic.

We had to get out of here. We had to get some distance from Mr. Anderson before he cornered me and slapped on those handcuffs he was so fond of. In any other case, handcuffs sounded like a good time, but not when it came to Detective Anderson. He was not only immune to my powers, but now he had his evidence. Real pictures of me leeching David's life. I might as well have thrown my hands up and said, "You got me!"

David's garbled cry cut through the closed door and I cringed. It took all my willpower not to go after him, but he was safer with Mr. Anderson, wasn't he? If the Detective had figured out how to thwart my gifts, maybe that meant there was a cure for the deterioration. Maybe David wouldn't have to die.

However, I didn't trust the bastard to help David on his own, even if he had the means. I'd need some backup to make sure he kept his priorities straight.

"Sarah!" I shouted again, this time more frantic.

A blonde head bobbed at the entrance and I launched myself, putting my palms together like I was going for a swan dive in an ocean made of unshaven men and whiskey. My nose pinched and I wondered how starving I'd been to have been attracted to anyone in this place.

Sarah's eyes locked onto mine a split second before she bolted outside. I knew that look. That's the look she had the last time I'd failed her. The last time someone had to die.

And she'd disappeared for two years.

I shoved my way to the front and ignored elbows stabbing my ribs. I didn't have two years this time. Mr. Anderson was right outside and he had David. I needed someone to watch him. Someone to guide him in the right direction without them knowing they were being influenced. Someone with skills I didn't have.

By the time I made it out onto the dusty street, Sarah was gone.

I was on my own.

Disbelief rooted me to the spot. How could Sarah abandon me? Not now, not when I needed her most.

"Move, wench!" A drunken man shoved me from behind and I stumbled.

I turned and glared at him. When his eyes met mine he locked into my spell. I slipped into my magic so easily. I couldn't resist. I'd just fed and the sexual energy made me giddy and spontaneous.

He stiffened and wavered as the wall of desire hit him. His eyes grew wide so that they looked like yellow orbs protruding from his leathery face. His tongue flicked across his dry, cracked lips.

Taking one empowering step towards him, the man faltered back with one hand pushed out in defense. A gold ring glinted against the bar's neon light.

I shoved an accusatory finger in his face. "You're going to go back home, tell your wife you're sorry, and not touch a drink again for the rest of your life. Got it?"

He swayed side-to-side, fighting against my compulsion.

I smiled sweetly, leaning in and grazing my nail across his cheek. "You understand?"

Skin contact made it solid. His shock melted into a goofy grin. "Yes, but me wife's dead."

"Do you have anyone at home?"

He pondered for a moment. "No, but me boy's struggling down in Texas. He's the only family I gots left."

"Why's he in Texas?"

He grinned as his eyes searched my face. "You're so beautiful."

"Answer me."

He blinked as if he couldn't focus. Alcohol always messed with the interrogation side of my powers. Something to do with the brain synapses not being able to connect fast enough. At least, that's what my mom had told me.

"Drinking," he answered after a moment. "I can't keep a steady job 'cuz me drinking. I drink away any money he sends me. Texas is far enough he don' have to see it. But he sends me money anyway." His gaze grew distant. "Maybe he hopes I'll use it to visit him someday."

I pressed both hands against his cheeks and resisted a gag against the sour plume of alcohol. "Then get home. Rest. And go to your boy tomorrow. Work hard and don't touch the drink again. Pay him back and earn his respect. Got it?"

He nodded against my grasp. I released him and he stumbled down the street mumbling, "Me boy, me boy."

I took in a deep breath. That inner voice tried to justify what I was. *See? You do good with your gifts. You may take a life, but how many do you save? Imagine what you could do with your four...*

I stomped my foot. It wasn't a matter of mathematics. I couldn't just justify infidelity, rape, murder...no matter how much good I did. And four? What was this damned four my nutty voice kept going on about?

I scanned the street. Parked cars judged me with their

frowning grills and broken headlights. Even a few toothless hookers added their own oppressive stare for good measure.

Refocusing, I pushed away the judgment, self-hatred, and regret. That wasn't going to help David.

I wavered on my feet as I considered my options. If I couldn't find Sarah, I needed the next best thing. Maxine.

Stomping down the street with clenched fists didn't stop the fluttering in my chest. Maxine wouldn't appreciate a visit from a succubus, especially one being tracked by a detective. But I didn't have a choice. I needed help. Even if that meant getting help from a nun.

THIRD SIN'S A CHARM

My vision blurred as the sidewalk faded in and out of sharpness. Spaced-out street lights left long lengths of darkness for me to slink through like a thief in the night. Budget wasn't an issue. Seattle had more than its share of city money. Unfortunately, the crime-ridden south side of Seattle, dubbed "White Center," was known more for its bars, porn shops, and crime… None of those things enjoyed being in the spotlight.

I wrinkled my nose at a leering pair of men with hairy arms hanging out of their car window like they owned the place.

I didn't have time for this. Sister Maxine was where I was heading, not trouble.

Their beady eyes flickered with interest and I sighed. Fine. Let them try and bother me on a night like tonight. Let's see how that worked out for them.

The clicks from my heels echoed out and preceded me down the street. I shouldn't have come down this way, but I'd been preoccupied. I'd lost my girlfriend, stupidly dumped her thinking that would finally allow me to let go and die of starvation. Dumb. My aura of temptation must have been strong, strong enough to lure David out and fuck me right there on the street. And I let him. I was a fucking monster.

"Where you off to, sweetheart?" said a burly man who slinked from the beat-up Cadillac.

His buddy with a half-showing beer belly shuffled to my side and inhaled. "Smells like dessert." He grinned, giving me a bird's eye view of his row of yellowing and cracked teeth.

Being a succubus didn't mean I was blind. The drunken old man had been spontaneous. I didn't care how ugly they were when it was spontaneous. But this? The burly man stroked his beard, and I could swear there were dried pieces of meat still stuck to it. *Gross.*

I squeezed my eyes shut and leaned, holding my arms out and letting them drape over each hairy neck like I was hugging mangy dogs.

"Fellas," I breathed in my most seductive voice. I remembered David's lips on my neck and heat swept through my chest. I let the memory engulf me until the yearning returned. I sighed and pushed it through my palms and into the men's bodies.

To control them I needed to feed them.

I screwed one eye open and their tongues were already lolling. Their eyelids fluttered and they staggered under my slight weight. Maybe I was laying it on a bit too thick.

Then I saw the fresh bloodstains on their boots.

I stumbled back and they toppled over onto the ground, wobbling around like overthrown turtles. While they were drunk and disoriented on my power, I shifted to the car and peered in.

Two women.

Dead.

Once the bastards righted themselves, they crawled to my feet and I forced my lips into a smile, focusing on the lust I tasted on my breath. A succubus' lust for vengeful death... That was a compulsion I rarely had the chance to use.

"You know what I want?" I asked sweetly.

"A spanking?" the bearded man barked.

I huffed a laugh. "Ah, yes! What a great idea. Except..." I ran my finger across his chin and ignored the nausea rolling in my stomach. "Why don't you spank your friend? With your fist, of course. Over and over again, right in his face. Do it until he stops moving. I would *love* that."

He blinked, and there was a flicker of fight in his eyes. I pressed in closer and exhaled.

He breathed in the fine dust of my power and trembled. "And then?" he asked. There wasn't a shred of disobedience left in the man.

"And then, I want you to drag him—" I pointed to the belly-man, "to the police station. Tell them what you did. Everything... you've ever done. Would you do that for me?"

The belly-man clapped his hands together like a bumbling idiot. "What do I do?"

I swept my hand over his face and purred my next words. "You die."

The thumps of fist against flesh matched the steady beat of my heart and clink of my heels as I made my way to the West Seattle Bridge.

Bam.

Bam.

Crunch.

A grin smeared across my face.

I didn't mean to enjoy it. Yet, how I loved the sound of flesh on flesh. A little voice told me just to relish my handiwork. Those two murderers deserved what was coming to them.

I turned my wrist to reset my watch timer. The purple numbers pleasantly glowed as they counted down in a rush. I didn't mind taking off three hours for this. One hour per man I'd fed enough sexual energy to overcome their will. Two murderers and one dead-beat dad dealt with. Worth it.

The thought of Sister Maxine's judgmental frown splattered across my vision.

One violent shake of my head and my thoughts flung her out as quickly as they'd materialized. No sense getting myself riled up. There was only one thing I needed from Sister Maxine, and then she'd never see me again.

Cars rushed on the wet pavement as I crossed the lower street to the better part of town. This side had lights all over the place and I squinted—no, not lights. The sun was rising.

An orange glow bled above that cathedral's pike and I hurried my gait. The morning's heat and nighttime's events had made me work up a sweat and I looked forward to the cool air of the cathedral. Whoever came up with that phrase "sweating like a whore in church" clearly didn't realize they had the best air-conditioning in Seattle and the most expensive insulation to keep it in. None of that cheap crap for God.

Even if I was enthusiastic to escape the heat, I couldn't help but slow to a saunter as my gaze was drawn to the bursts of broken reds in the stained glass. I desperately tried not to think of belly-man's face.

Calling upon my skills of suppressing emotion, which were probably extremely unhealthy, I shoved the discomfort deep into my chest and assured myself that I'd feel better once I was inside. My mother had said it was the only place you could truly come to an understanding with sin, and one day, I'd have to face mine if I wanted to survive, all seven of them. I'd never paid much attention to her back then, but as I absently rubbed the runes through my shirt, I wondered if she'd been more literal than I'd realized.

My free hand's thumb twirled the small ring on my finger, reminding me my mother was gone, and all I had left of her was this silver band, along with an abandoned mansion I refused to recognize, and far too much pornography she'd promised was just for research.

The church's shadow was already cooler than the humid air drifting in the street. I gratefully took shelter and breathed out a sigh of anticipation. How would Maxine react to seeing me again after all these years?

The massive oak door rimmed with engravings was already cracked open and I slipped inside, expecting to hear the rhythmic chanting of the nuns or a boys' choir practicing their song. Instead, I heard Zack yelling at the top of his lungs.

"Sonya's out there right now fuc—" He cleared his throat, remembering he was talking to a nun. "Sonya's *killing* people! Are you going to let one teensy tiny itty bitty technicality get in the way?"

Sister Maxine's unmistakable no-nonsense voice boomed through the foyer. "Technicality?" she screeched. "That's hardly a *technicality.*"

Tugging off my shoes, I shifted against the wall and peered around the corner.

Zack crossed his arms and stared down his nose at Sister Maxine with smoky eyes. I swear, I wish he'd stop using eyeliner. Though… it did kind of make him look sexy. Like some sort of exotic rock star.

"Sonya can't just go around killing people. When she was finding douchebags to feed off of, that was one thing. At least she was subtle. But now she's after random blokes behind a bar? No. This is the only solution."

Sister Maxine thumped her rosary beads against his chest. "Does the Lord's word mean nothing to you?"

I balked. Don't tell me he came here to…

Zack weighed both hands down on Maxine's tiny frame. "If it held any weight in my heart, do you think my first girlfriend would still be alive?"

I buried my face in my hands. Fornication. He was talking about fornication, and more importantly, the first fornication I'd ever had. Sure, great conversation with a Nun.

THE FIRST OF FOUR

Luke

So many sounds escaped my body that made me feel like some kind of beaten animal. I couldn't help it. The pain tore out of me and became a creature of its own.

"Shut it, freak! Or I'll come down there and knock your teeth out!" Detective Anderson yelled down the dank stairway.

Why couldn't he ever use my name? And it wasn't just him, it'd been the kids at school, strangers on the street, heck, even my own family members. No one ever called me Luke. Well, except my mother. Though when she called me Luke it came with my middle name "Mitchell" and a twitching left eye.

Sadly, even memories of my mother couldn't bring me out of my misery. I writhed on the grimy floor and my cheek slid against caked dirt and unpolished cement. The pain tumbled its way through my stomach and ripped out of my throat with a primal release of agony.

Detective Anderson yelled again, but I couldn't make out what he'd said this time. He was probably upstairs in the lab, either studying the blood he'd taken from me, or cleaning up the mess of it off that damned pristine floor. Not sure why he always cleaned it up if he was just going to rip me open again.

Thinking of the lab made me relive the last five hours of torture. It blurred together with my weekly episode of agony. Pain, I've discovered, is a sentient thing. It's alive, and it can take over your body in ways you'd never thought possible. Pain made me screech, or cry, or even defecate. A year of this shit has made me appreciate pain for what it is. My body was punishing me for being unable to protect myself from harm. Every nerve that lit up under my skin with a razor blade of fire was the cost of my own stupidity. I can't do anything about it now. It's just the price I have to pay.

Pinching my fingernails into my palms added an indecipherable sensation to the symphony of agony. I reminded myself I needed to save it all up. Keep all of this pain for myself, because when I finally got out of here, I was going to give it *all* back.

For now, I closed my eyes and drifted into the bittersweet relief of unconsciousness where only my nightmares could rival reality.

When I'd woken, the pain had retreated to a dull ache and I could only tell it was still there if I tried to breathe. Unfortunately, I'm no different than other humans in that I do actually need oxygen to some extent, so when I tried holding my breath and pretended everything was back to normal, reality came rampaging back with a fit of wet coughs. Twinges sparking through my chest reminded me where Anderson's knife had slid through my ribs. Each breath brought a fresh pinch biting through my skin. I shifted, trying to find a more comfortable position and my leg throbbed, still healing from the pieces of bone fusing together in my cracked leg.

This wretched body needed eight hours to heal. The level of pain told me I had two or three more hours to go.

I eased my way to the corner of my cell. Pressing against the damp cement made me feel like there was something solid to hold onto. Floating in a nightmare wasn't how I'd keep sane. A year of perpetual darkness can make a man go mad. But my mother had done this to me sometimes too, so maybe that's why I was used to it. Not the torture or anything like that, but the isolation. A man didn't need training to handle torture. People are born with a certain pain tolerance, and either they can take it or they can't. Pain is just a biological response, but being left alone with your senses deprived tricks a person into thinking they're already dead. To survive isolation isn't innate. It's trained.

Only a fortune teller could know I'd need such insane training. Unfortunately, or fortunately, depending on how you looked at it, my mother was a bonafide psychic. She'd tried to tell me that her destiny was linked to three, which meant I was next in line. There would be three others I was linked to as well, all for the purpose of the girl I had to save. I never knew what she meant by that.

Until Detective Anderson had locked me down here, I'd thought my mother a bona fide psycho as well. When I'd turned eight she'd begun my "training." She'd throw me in the basement and let me scream until I fell asleep, and wouldn't come back for me for a whole day, sometimes two.

She always cried every time she brought me back into the light. I remembered how even the soft living room lamps burned my retinas and looked like tiny suns casting beams across the room. I'd tremble and cling to her, even though she was the one who'd left me all alone. She'd just stroke my hair and tell me that I needed this, and one day I'd understand.

When I'd turned thirteen, I'd gotten enough sense to alert the authorities. Of course, she'd seen that too. And through the tears she'd told me to forgive myself for doing it to her. She'd understood, and it was a small price to pay for keeping me alive.

I clung to the hope that one day I *would* forgive myself, because ever since I realized what she'd sacrificed for me, still rotting away in a cell, forgiveness seemed impossible. The only comfort was that I was in a cell too, and could live out my term just as she was now.

She'd been right about everything. Once I'd learned the truth, I'd wracked my brain trying to think of any wisdom she'd offered from her visions through the years. Which was difficult when at the time, I'd thought everything she'd said was psychotic rubbish. All I could remember was the last vision she'd given me, and her assurances that even though I'd reach the limits of my endurance, I *would* survive. Given my manifesting powers of regeneration when I was a teen, I didn't need a psychic to tell me that.

I pressed my fingers into my eyes as I tried to recall anything useful. The motion sent pain jabbing through my cheek and eye socket as I snagged dried blood. With a short chuckle I couldn't believe I'd forgotten he'd taken the eyeball during this torture session. What did he imagine he could do with it? Was there some black market for creepy grey eyes? Sure, my eye had already grown back. My broken bones always healed, my plucked organs regenerated, but it didn't mean he'd learn anything from taking them out. My regeneration wasn't fucking *scientific*. It was supernatural, and he knew it.

After I'd peeled off the scab, I crawled and roamed my hands across the floor hoping to find a bottle of water. If it was past evening, I wouldn't always get dinner, but I'd get water. I couldn't regenerate my own fluids, and my new left eye felt like some kind of deflated leather balloon.

My fingers struck the soft plastic and the delightful *swoosh* of moving water made me crack a smile. That was the trick in isolation. Make tiny goals, and when you can accomplish one, enjoy the shit out of it.

As slow as physically possible, I relished each finger that wrapped around the bottle. The cool water stole my heat without adding more dirt to cake onto my skin, and I reminded myself to enjoy the small reprieve.

I set the bottle upright and ran my finger around the lid. It was rimmed, and the shape of it meant it was a Dasani bottle. Damned Anderson, why'd he have to buy water with sodium added? I didn't need more salt. That was for sure.

Closing my eyes, I chided myself for not fully appreciating my water. It was water…with *minerals* added. Don't think about the sodium. Appreciate what you've got, Luke.

Just as I was about to take a sip, a searing beam of light cascaded down the stairs, and my right iris desperately retracted. My left eye wasn't as functional and sent shooting pains through my skull as it absorbed every bit of luminescence before it sluggishly shrunk.

"Looks like you've got a new roommate, freak. Isn't that nice?" Anderson sneered as he dragged a body down the steps. "Been a while since you've had any company."

My vision finally adjusted and I leaned against the iron bars. Anderson let the body thump down each step while he sauntered with an unceremonious stagger.

"What's the problem, no muscle to do your dirty work?" I retorted, my voice coming out hoarse from all the screaming I'd done.

Anderson shot me a glare. "For someone in your position, your consistently cocky attitude amazes me."

I pressed my face against the bars and tried to look bored, but in reality, the pits of my stomach were desperately trying not to retch bile.

Anderson had some unconscious guy rolling down the steps, and I pitied the poor soul when he woke up. His pale face was marred by a streak of red where he'd been struck on the temple. But I knew that color of pale. It wasn't from blood loss. His lips were white, and his cheeks were sunken in. This guy had been fed on by a fucking succubus.

FORNICATION

Sonya

"Zack!" I shouted as I spun around the corner.

Both Sister Maxine and Zack turned their startled stares at me, and then their shoulders eased as if they'd been expecting my arrival.

Zack offered me a devilish grin paired with a flirtatious wink. "Since when do you attend Mass?"

My lips puckered. "Funny. Look who's talking."

We matched each other's glares until I decided I didn't want to play this stupid smoldering-gaze game. He always won, anyway.

"Did Sarah put you up to this?" I asked.

"She didn't put me up to anything. She told me about David." He rubbed his neck and his loose shirt draped, giving me a glimpse of the perfect arch across his collarbone. "After something like that, where else would you go?"

I sighed and slunk up to Maxine's side. "Long time no see, Sister."

Sister Maxine narrowed her gaze and set her bony fists on her hips. "You can't just come barging into the Lord's house justifying your sins." She thrust a pointed finger at the confessional. "You're supposed to admit all wrongdoings! Not arrogantly wave them in my face!"

I perched my hands on my hips and desperately tried to ignore Zack's crude inspection, looking me up and down and offering approving nods at my tight sweater. "Look," I said. "Just hear me out."

"Is it true? This..." She twirled her hands as if at a loss for words. "David...business?"

"Yes, yes. I slept with David."

"More fornication!" Maxine bellowed and threw her hands up in disbelief.

"Hey! I had one minute left to live. That's sixty seconds. You can't suggest I just let myself die."

"That's your own fault," she countered. "You're more than capable of finding a husband with your looks and... skills... and not break any of the Lord's laws. Why'd you let time run out and resort to sin?"

"Seriously? You're going to sit there and turn a blind eye to seducing someone with supernatural gifts, as if it's not against any of these so-called laws."

Maxine straightened. "Who am I to question the Lord's creations? If he created you, then you have a purpose." Her eyes narrowed to slits. "But it's your responsibility to keep your abilities within the law."

Zack slipped his arm around my waist. "Don't be so hard on her. She was just trying to be loyal to Sarah. Right, love?"

Maxine buried her face in her hands. "Homosexuality? That's even worse!" She thrust her hands to her sides and balled them into fists. "Don't you think there's a reason your gifts don't work on women?"

"Sure," I bit out, the word bitter in my mouth. "Because I need a relationship where my mate doesn't *die*," I sneered and wriggled out of Zack's grasp.

"Enough bickering, ladies," Zack said. "Let's—hey, is that blood?" he asked, pointing to my jeans, then tugging at my sweater where my rune had started to bleed again.

Attention span of a moth…

I sighed. "Cripes. Whose side are you on?"

Zack chuckled. "You sound like Mom when you get all flustered." He ran a finger under my chin. "It's cute."

"Is it David's?" Maxine's quavering voice asked, her eyes glued to the bloodstains on my clothes.

I rolled my eyes. "I'm not a vampire. The blood on my boots is just from some thugs. Unfortunately, it's not their blood. They killed these girls and—"

Maxine turned green.

Zack chuckled. "C'mon. Don't get her all worked up. She *is* a nun."

"Then help me get my mom's necklace and get out of here already!"

Maxine blinked. "If you think your mother entrusted me with that necklace just so you could—"

Zack draped an arm over Maxine's shoulder. "Now, now. That's why I'm here, all right? It's either give Sonya here the necklace, or I'm going to have to get her some power another way." He leered at me. "I believe you said it broke some law in the good book? I can survive her, you know. One night with me and—"

"Yes," Maxine confirmed, cutting him off, then sighed as her arms hung in defeat. "Fine. Come with me."

Maxine shuffled away.

Before I could follow, Zack wrapped both arms around my waist and pulled me in close, pushing his lips against my ear.

"Looks like you're finally getting that blasted necklace 'cuz of me." He groped his hands across my breasts and squeezed, filling me with desire mixed with mortification. I'd only slept with Zack once, and as fun as it was, he rubbed me the wrong way. His voice caressed me anyway, building a heat between my thighs. "I think I deserve a reward," he purred.

If I hadn't just fed, I would have fallen lips-first into Zack's influence. I may be a succubus, but he's an incubus... and much more powerful than I at the art of seduction. When I was sixteen, I had troubles unlocking my powers and had almost starved to death. I couldn't feed on humans. I tried—my lucky prom date didn't die. Only an incubus could trigger my powers to their full potential. He'd been one of the incubi to hang out with me when I was growing up. He was my friend, not my lover, but that night, I'd needed him. Ever since then I'd craved what he had to offer. But other than unclogging the succubus plumbing, I couldn't live off him forever. Screwing him was just a quick fix. It was like swapping spit. Kind of gross and left foreign bacteria in my mouth that'd just linger for days. Does that sound disgusting? Because it is.

I threw his hands off. "Enough. I'm here for the necklace and I'm going to save David with it. I can't let Sarah think I meant for this to happen."

Zack chuckled. "If you say so. But," he thrust his finger in my face before curling it around my collar and tugging me close. "One night with me and you won't need a lay for a year." He tilted his head with amusement. "Imagine what you could do in a year not spent finding some poor sod to fuck? You could even scurry back to Sarah for a little while."

Why was he toying with me? The lust lingered in the air

between us, and I knew he could taste it. That just made it even worse.

I jerked away and resumed walking towards Maxine's stiff frame. She may be old, but she wasn't deaf.

"I don't need you," I said over my shoulder. "Once I have my mother's necklace, I'll have all the power I need."

"You'll see," he called as I walked away. "You're going to need to charge that thing. Then you're going to be begging for me!"

I clenched my fists and didn't turn around, keeping my eyes fixed on Maxine's steady gait as we headed deeper into the cloister.

I was glad Zack didn't follow and the heat on my skin cooled as I focused on Maxine's bulbous black habit rolling around on her behind. What could be less sexy? Perhaps that was the point.

"Here we are," she said as we reached the end of the impossibly long hallway.

I huddled up behind her shoulder and peered at the ancient door. It felt like I was in some Merlin movie and was about to gain entrance to the hidden treasure everyone was trying to get. The door even had handsome engravings of runes in the wood that made it seem mystical and surreal.

Maxine pulled a rusted key from her pocket and fiddled with the lock. The mechanism gave a reluctant *click* and the door creaked open.

Maxine stepped inside and flicked the light switch.

The small room didn't disappoint. Thick velvet drapes framed massive oak chests, making it look like we were inside a monastery that housed the most precious of religious artifacts. The lights glimmered with the soft glow of modest chandeliers covered with frosted glass. The way the lights flickered made them seem like candles and added to the ambiance that I'd walked into a Merlin movie.

"Where's the necklace?" I asked impatiently. Every second wasted was a second less David had to live.

"What made you change your mind?" Maxine asked, placing both hands on the smallest chest perched on the room's only table. "Your mother entrusted it to me for a reason. She said it was dangerous until you had completed the destiny you were born into."

It was strange for a Nun to prattle on about Succubi magical destinies, but she was one of our allies. She knew all about the supernatural community, and that was saying something. There were few humans who'd been accepted into the fold.

My gaze swept over the room, taking in other locked boxes that contained supernatural treasures. Holy ground was the only place we'd store any sort of relic and it took a strong woman like Maxine to guard it. I knew under the frowns and stern face, there was more than met the eye.

I frowned and resisted scratching my runes that had started to bug me again. "It's time."

"Anything in particular bring you here?" she asked, still pressing for more answers I didn't have.

I'd known about my mother's necklace, that it could give me exactly what I needed to survive. With the power of a Blood Stone, I could swear off men and be with Sarah without any problems, but there had to be a catch. The dark magic lingering inside my chest roiled just being close to it. There would be a price to pay for such a prize and I'd never been brave enough to test it.

I rotated my watch around my wrist, not looking at the timer. "Because, now it's just not about me," I admitted. "I fed on David. He's a human. If there's anything I can do to save him, then I must do it."

She offered me a sad smile and a nod. She cupped a box that hummed with familiar power and creaked the small box open, revealing the necklace my mother had always worn around her neck. The chain had always been just long enough to rest it in her cleavage; a silver locket with mesmerizing swirls encrusted along the edge.

Maxine stepped aside and I faced the powerful relic, taking one trembling hand and grazing my finger across the metal. I should have been able to feel the leftover sexual energy still trapped inside. My breath caught in my throat as I took the treasure in my hands and forced myself to pop it open.

A single red gem, a lost precious stone to the history books cradled in the locket's setting. Some would mistake it for a ruby, but my mother had taught me what it really was. A Blood Stone.

A tear rolled down my cheek. It should have been bright red, yet the Blood Stone had lost all its color and was completely white, looking like a cloudy diamond. A human would call it a moonstone, not really knowing what it was.

The Blood Stone was empty, and if I wanted to save David, I'd need to charge it...

I'd need to fuck Zack.

SPEECHLESS

Luke

I'd grown so accustomed to silence during the spanning hours in-between Anderson's torture sessions that it was unnerving to hear my cellmate's breathing. But after a while, the sensation grew on me. The soft intake and exhale drew me in until I measured each one, marking its minute difference from the last. His breaths came in long and deep, holding for a second before releasing. He seemed so calm, and somehow it made me feel safe.

When the breath stopped, my heart flung into my throat. I rushed to the bars and beat my palms against the slick iron. "Hey. You okay, dude?"

His sharp intake of breath followed by a ragged cough sent relief flooding into my chest. It was just human sleep apnea.

My panic had woken the poor guy from his slumber. He groaned and scuffled across the ground. It was pitch black and if I were him, I'd be freaking out right about now.

"Hey. It's all right. Over here," I offered.

An incoherent grumble preceded dragging steps towards my location. Finally, a warm hand fumbled against mine. I stiffened, not used to physical contact that wasn't followed by blinding pain. But I kept my hand where it was. For once, someone needed me. Someone innocent who didn't deserve to be here. The least I could do was offer comfort.

His hand slid around mine, as if there would be Braille on my skin to explain where the heck we were. "Who's there?" he asked.

I plastered a smile on my face and even though he couldn't see it, perhaps the gesture would seep through my words. "My name's Luke. I'm a prisoner here, just like you."

The grip tightened around my fingers. "Prisoner?"

"Yeah." I shifted uncomfortably, my hand growing sweaty under his clammy touch. Damn, the guy's skin was freezing. "What's the last thing you remember?" I asked.

A moment of silence. Then he said, "I'd finally got my shot with Sonya. But then it all went wrong, and some bum must have attacked me from behind. I don't know how I got here."

I finally couldn't take it anymore and withdrew from the bars. "Sonya? Is that the succubus?"

A short chuckle. "What makes you call her that? Though she is damn irresistible. I know I couldn't keep my hands off her."

Shit. I'd hoped he'd been simply fed on, maybe she got in a lick or two. But if he'd gone all the way, he was a dead man walking. I tried to keep the panic out of my voice. "Did you fuck her?"

"Excuse me? What kind of question is that?"

I crossed my arms, now getting annoyed. "You're in a pitch-black cell, talking to a fellow prisoner, and you find my *question* odd?"

As if it hit him this wasn't a dream, he rushed to the bars. The sound of metallic jewelry clanking against the metal made my ears hurt. "Where the fuck am I? Who are you?"

"I already told you, I'm a prisoner, just like you. If you slept with this Sonya girl, and she's a succubus, then that's why you're here. Anderson must think he can learn something from you, or use you to get to her somehow." I shifted my weight and grunted. "He's obsessed with supernaturals."

A moment of silence, then he asked, "What are you?"

"Ah," I said, spearing my finger up in the darkness, "now you're asking the right question. Too bad even I don't know what I am. I just know what I'm not, and that's human."

A sea of fluorescent lights blinked across the ceiling. Out of reflex, I snapped my eyes shut. But I'd still been too slow. Black dots sprinkled my vision when I tested my sight again, revealing the abhorrent contents of my cell. Anderson hosed it down once in a while, but man, I was starting to feel like a cat stuck in a litter box that never got emptied. Except I had way more than nine lives, which Anderson loved to remind me.

I tensed, expecting to see Anderson and his tools of torture. He favored the good ol' hammer and nails, but to extract my eye he'd used only a spoon. When I got out of this place, I'd never be able to have tea again.

When my vision cooperated and revealed a petite blonde instead, I blinked in confusion. I was about to say, "My, Mr. Anderson. You've changed," which I found quite witty and chuckled to myself, but when I opened my mouth to impress the pretty lady with my mad joke skills, complete gibberish came out instead.

I coughed, rubbed my face, and tried again. "Blurg mangaravatah!"

She blinked and tilted her head. "Uhm, excuse me?"

What the hell was that? I'd heard of an attractive woman rendering a man dumb, but this was ridiculous.

My cellmate pressed his face against the bars. "Sarah! What're you doing here?"

Relief flooded her face. "David!"

I passed my gaze between the pair. "Humaga?" I blurted, which was my attempt at asking if they knew one another.

They both turned to consider me. "He was speaking fine a minute ago. Maybe he's been locked up too long." David shivered. "What the hell is this place?"

After taking a glance at my cell, Sarah seemed to have dismissed me as unimportant and focused on David. "So, are you hurt?"

David rubbed the back of his head. "I got a nasty hit by some bum or something, and woke up in a fucking cell. I wouldn't say my day's going so great."

Sarah backed away and hovered her fingers over the light switch. David's eyes widened. "Hey, what're you doing?" He rushed to the bars again. "Look, I know you and Sonya had just broken up and I'm sorry to make a move so fast. But you should have seen her. She was devastated. She *needed* me."

Sarah scoffed. "You're right. She did need you. But you have no idea what for."

The lights clicked off.

$10,000 WHISKEY

Sonya

I snapped the locket closed and headed for the door.

"Where are you going?" Maxine asked.

I paused at the doorway, leaning on the frame to prevent myself from falling over.

"I'm sorry." It was all I could say before breaking into a sprint and leaving Maxine behind.

I couldn't get out of this place fast enough. The clicks of my heels beat against the walls as if the very sound waves wanted to escape. Each corridor led to the next and I started to worry I couldn't remember the way out on my own.

I practically grew up in this damn place. Could I really not remember how to get out?

Finally, I made it to the dimly lit foyer and burst through the doors in a whirlwind of exasperation and relief.

Zack was waiting on the stoop staring at his phone and I tugged his shoulder after catching my breath. "C'mon. Let's go."

He huffed a short laugh and draped his arm around my

shoulder as we walked away from the cathedral. "So, is the necklace empty?"

I nodded.

He sighed. "Look. I didn't want to be right."

"Yes, you did," I snapped. He'd been trying to get back into my pants ever since prom.

He chuckled and motioned me to follow him down the street. "You're going the wrong way."

"Huh? But my place is that way."

He shook his head. "We're not going to your place," he said before stuffing his hands in his pockets and following the sidewalk.

I'd never seen Zack like this before. His shoulders drooped and he kept his eyes cast down at his feet. Even his usual cocky "I know I'm hot" strut had transformed into a solemn shuffle down the sidewalk.

"So," I ventured, "if we're not going to my place, which has unlimited Oreos and beer, by the way, where are you taking me?"

He chuckled. "I don't know if it beats that but," he patted his back pocket, "I texted Derek while you were with Maxine. Luckily, he's in town."

I balked. "*The* Derek? Since when do you *text* with the oldest incubus on the planet?"

"Since he found out that you had a Blood Stone."

I clutched the necklace now hanging around my neck. It was cold and lifeless. "Well, he's not getting his mitts on it."

"Relax. It's not like that."

"Then what's it like?"

He swerved and glared down at me. "Trust me this once, will you?" He grasped my necklace, pulling my body close to his. "You know how I feel about you," he whispered, placing a soft kiss on my forehead and my ears went hot. "But your mom told me about your destiny long before you ever accepted it. I'm not one of your four, hell, I'm not even one of your sins." His thumb ran over the cool metal of my necklace. "I'm not capable of changing this for you, but I have a feeling I know who can."

He pressed his lips lightly against mine, briefly letting me taste the salty residue of his lust, and then spun around, stomping off down the street, leaving me gasping for breath.

I huffed and clamped my mouth shut, trailing after him and pushed down the butterflies fluttering in my stomach.

After a few moments of hearing nothing other than Zack's shuffling feet and my own clicking heels, we finally came to a halt.

"There we are," Zack said.

There was nothing other than a limo with its headlights still on.

Wait.

"Are you shitting me?"

Zack smiled and crossed the street. I tried not to let my jaw hang open as I followed him and stared at the glistening paint job before he opened the door.

We were really going to see the freaking Incubus King.

Zack loved luxury, especially the overindulgent, expensive kind. His radiating smile filled me with warmth and when he opened the door and I slipped inside, I saw how indulgent the limo really was.

Sheer silk curtains draped across the tinted windows, bubbling champagne and bottles of whiskey were hooked into the upper cabinet, and a massive TV hung where a sunroof should have been.

I swallowed and settled across from two well-dressed security guards that blended in with the luxurious interior.

I'd always gone through life just as any human would, never using my ability to wrap any man around my little finger to an unfair advantage. I'd had a weak moment once or twice, but how could I be selfish? Any moment of weakness meant death. *David...*

I scooted down the long seat and Zack slipped in behind me.

"So," I asked the statuesque guards, "what're you, FBI agents or something?"

The one closest to me pulled off his glasses and leaned an elbow on his knee. His piercing blue eyes bore into mine and I wondered if he was really human. My insides lurched as our gazes met and a rune among the four blazed with heat, making me buckle over and grab it. It wasn't pain, but an intense pleasure that took me off guard.

"Better than the FBI," he said, his voice husky as if he sensed the impact his mere presence had on me. "We're the King's Guard," he replied with a sidelong smirk.

I rolled my eyes as the sensation faded. My runes were just confused. This guy was not one of the seven I was looking for.

One of the King's guard, hmm. Even if that was true, he didn't have to make it sound so ridiculous.

The human leaned back in the leather seat, spreading his legs like men tend to do when they think they have ten pound balls that can't be bothered to be grazed by their supposedly massive thighs.

Zack cleared his throat and shoved the guy down a few inches so that he could sit across from me. "Who's the incubus here? You or me?"

The guard frowned and crossed his arms. "My father's an incubus," he muttered.

Zack chuckled. "It only carries down from the female gene. Tough luck, bro."

I smiled at the guard in spite of the revelation. At least I knew where his good looks came from, and perhaps why he'd confused my prophecy. Depending on the lineage of his father, he might have some relation to the pull of the dark magic I'd been running from.

The guard winked at me and tapped the window. The limo eased into motion and pop music began to play. The TV overhead blipped on and displayed a bunch of attractive dancing girls rubbing up on each other in a club.

Zack breathed out a sigh and leaned over to run his fingers across the array of bottles. "What's your poison?"

I smiled. "Whiskey, please."

He nodded and plucked the largest bottle from the selection. The second security guard popped open a shiny black compartment, revealing dazzling crystal glasses I'd only seen in magazines.

As Zack poured me a drink, he flashed my necklace a glance, his eyes lingering there for a while.

My hand shot up to it, and I realized the necklace was neatly tucked in my cleavage, just like it always had been with mom.

"It's bad enough you want to screw me. Don't get hot on me because I remind you of my mother," I said.

He laughed and handed me my drink. "Relax, will you? I wasn't thinking of her, and I never slept with her. Don't be gross."

I snorted a laugh. Oh, so *that* was the line he wouldn't cross.

The heavy aromas from the golden whiskey drifted up and kissed my nose. *Oh man.* I brought it to my lips and ventured a sip. My eyelashes fluttered and a moan escaped my throat as the delicious silk slid across my tongue.

Both security guards fidgeted, but Zack leaned in with a

smile, his own whiskey on his breath. "So," Zack said, "you like ten thousand dollar whiskey. Why am I not surprised?"

I glared and finished off my glass, enjoying the creeping warmth that spread through my chest.

Zack offered me a refill, but I declined. No one was sexy plastered—not even me.

I leaned my head back on the cold headrest and watched the girls dance on the TV. The whiskey burning in my belly made it seem as if the cabin swirled and I was dancing with them as I rolled my head side to side with the beat.

The moment burst as Zack's phone buzzed obnoxiously against the seat, sounding like a dentist's drill searing into my brain.

I lifted my head to glare at him, but he was staring at the screen as if he wasn't sure if he should answer. Then he bit his lip—cripes that's cute—and tapped the screen before pressing it to his ear.

"Yeah. She's with me," he said and shot me a glance.

"Who is it?" I mouthed.

He shook his head and swatted me away.

"Really?" he asked the caller, his eyes going wide.

I pinched his knee and he flicked off my fingers with an agitated glare.

"Should I tell her?" he asked.

"Tell me what?" I snapped and Zack pressed the phone against his chest and shushed me.

He lifted the phone to his ear again. "Okay. No. I'll text you the address. Yeah, we'll meet up tomorrow."

He tapped the side of the phone and it offered a click. Then

Zack considered his glass, took a generous sip, and slouched into his seat.

I narrowed my eyes to slits. "Who was that?"

He tossed his phone, letting it somersault before catching it in mid-air. "Sarah," he said casually.

I lurched across the short expanse of the cabin and latched onto his knees. "What'd she say? Where is she?"

He chuckled. "Wouldn't you like to know?" He swiftly spread his legs and I tumbled face-first into his groin.

I lurched back with a snarl as he bellowed with laughter and sloshed his whiskey. "Aw, don't make me spill this liquid gold, girl. If you wanted a taste all you had to do was ask." He offered me a sly grin and even the security guards smothered their laughter.

"This isn't a game," I snapped and glared at all of them.

Zack wiped the tears from his eyes. "Relax, all right? Sarah is working her magic until you can get the Blood Stone."

I crossed my arms and slumped. "If Anderson can resist me, what makes her think he won't resist her?"

Zack shrugged. "Your powers aren't always reliable." A mischievous glint sparked in his eye. "Perhaps I need to help sort you out again."

Ignoring the tempting invitation, I rolled the empty glass across my palms. "I already have the Blood Stone," I said, changing the subject. "You didn't tell her it needs to be charged?"

"Hell no. She'd just run off and leave David to die rather than let you charge that thing on your own."

I swallowed the rising bile. "She's that against it?" I was going to have to give in and sleep with an incubus to charge it, and I guessed King Derek would know who'd be strong enough to help me. Not that I knew what he wanted in return, but one night would be worth it to help David and be with Sarah guilt-free, right?

Zack's eyes softened before he looked down at his half-emptied glass. "That's between you two."

I stuck out my lower lip in a pout and pushed myself further into the leather seat. What was Sarah thinking? The only reason I'd gotten Mom's necklace in the first place was because I'd thought she'd abandoned me. If my powers were really going wonky, I needed the boost to take on someone as dangerous as Anderson without her.

I ventured a gaze to Zack. "If Sarah is with Mr. Anderson, does that mean she thinks she can save David?"

Zack scoffed. "You know what? You and Sarah are perfect for each other. You're hopeless romantics." He clicked his tongue. "As if there's a cure for the deterioration." His eyes locked onto mine. "Don't you understand what you do when you feed? Your powers have a cost to maintain."

I frowned. "What if I don't want these stupid powers?"

He gave an exasperated sigh. "Sonya. Just accept what you are already. Get with the program and use your powers for once. You need to take out that Anderson bastard. Don't make Sarah do your dirty work."

I frowned. "Is she safe on her own? Should we send someone?"

He chuckled. "There you go, giving her too much credit for one thing and not enough for another. She's a muse. Nobody's going to touch her if she doesn't want them to." His eyes narrowed. "You just better hope what she wants is still you. Nothing worse than a pissed off muse. That's how the Dark Ages got started."

NINE LIVES

Luke

That Sarah chick was a muse, wasn't she? There was only one supernatural in the world who can fuck with someone's brain other than a succubus, and if my mom's mad ramblings had taught me anything it was to stay the fuck away from a muse. Too bad I was in a locked cell with nowhere to go, stuck with a fucking brain-killing muse just two feet away.

"Sarah, you still there?" David's voice pierced the darkness.

The door to the security room creaked open, shedding a faint red light across the cement floor. "Will you shut up?" she hissed. "I'm trying to help you. Which is going to be tenfold more difficult if you let Anderson know I'm here."

I rubbed my temples. She wasn't going anywhere soon. That was for sure. And every second she stayed, her aura burrowed deeper into my skull like one of those brain-sucking monsters I'd seen on Saturday cartoons. Except, instead of a purple cloud with fangs teething at my brains, a gorgeous girl hid in the shadows and wouldn't… fucking… leave.

"Blargalargalarg!"

"Will you tell Luke to shut it, too?" Sarah asked.

We all fell silent when the door two floors up slammed shut. That was the lobby, and there were only two kinds of people who came into the lobby: corrupted police officials and the psycho detective.

Unfortunately for me, it was the latter.

I recognized his gait by now, the way he slunk down the steps like a drunken raccoon. The *swish, swish* of his faux silk pants made the hairs on the back of my neck stand on end. It didn't really matter if I had a day or a week to prepare myself for this moment. The promise of torture always made my knees go weak.

As I curled into a ball, the lights blinked on. Anderson pranced across the floor and seemed to enjoy the fact that his collection of prisoners had grown. "Let's see. Who gets to play first?"

David slammed against the bars. His cheeks were sunken in and his muscles trembled. The deterioration was slight, but it was there. "Who the hell are you?" David demanded. Even if his body showed all the signs, I was struck by the intensity of his ice-blue eyes and his demeanor that he'd rip Anderson apart the second he got a shot.

Anderson slunk to the cell. "Detective Anderson. Pleased to meet you." He extended his hand for a handshake, then chuckled. "Ah, right, you're my prisoner."

"And why, exactly, am I your prisoner?"

Anderson rubbed his stubbly chin and cast me a glance. He was putting on a good show, but he always shaved. Something had him rattled. "You're going to help me," Anderson growled in response to David, "just like my freak here."

David snarled. "Why would I help you? You're a fucking maniac!"

Anderson smiled. “It’s cute that you think you have a choice.” He reached into his coat pocket and pulled out a small gun with a plastic tip. The tranq. I hated that thing.

One silent *plup*! and David was out on the floor with a dart sticking out of his chest.

Anderson cast me a glance as he unlocked David’s cell. “You’re quiet. No jokes today?” He grinned. “Cat got your tongue?” He loved that joke. Cats have nine lives. Haha. Hilarious. It’d lost any humor it might have had once I’d gotten through enough mortal wounds to vastly surpass nine lifetimes.

I frowned and cast a glance to the security room where Sarah’s blue eyes peered through the darkness. I flicked my gaze back to Anderson.

Anderson hesitated, and then looked to the security room.

I wasn’t sure if Sarah was friend or foe. History didn’t favor the muse as a species. They were just too strong, capable of burrowing into people’s brains and seeing whatever they wanted to see, and making people do whatever they wanted them to do.

Though, seeing her triggered my mother’s vision. At the time, I’d thought my mother had drugged me and I was having one hell of a trip. The vision had said I would have to wait in this cell until a woman came, and only I could help her embrace the fate of four. If I didn’t intervene, then supernaturals would overrun the world. And not the good kind, if there was such a thing.

But Sarah, she couldn’t be the girl I was waiting for. I was waiting for someone pure of heart. If Sarah was friends with the succubus, that made it pretty clear she was no friend of mine.

Sarah’s eyes widened as Anderson approached the darkened doorway. She reeled back into the shadows, but it was too late.

Anderson snatched the door open. “Who’s there?” he roared.

Going on the offensive, Sarah pounced like a lion. Her aura brightened the room as she reached into a supernatural territory of power I barely understood. Its effects made me waver and my eyelids felt like hundred-pound weights suddenly hung off them. I staggered and marveled how Anderson straightened, completely unaffected by her aura. Sarah snarled and the air shifted like oil, sweeping out in a shockwave.

"Sleep!" Sarah shouted.

Anderson laughed. Damn it, he just stood there and laughed at a muse. "How kind of you to deliver yourself to my lab. You were never my main target, but since you're already here, you'll get to help me nab that succubus bitch too."

Sarah launched herself at him like a wild animal. Anderson sidestepped her attack and she landed face-first into the cement. Her lip busted and a splotch of bright red blood smeared across her cheek.

Anderson took out a pouch of tranquilizers and picked the smallest one. He kneeled over her and pricked her in the neck.

Sarah yelped and reached for the dart, but it was too late. She slumped over, completely paralyzed. But her eyes darted, still awake.

Anderson grinned and pointed his dart gun my way. The last thing I saw was Anderson dragging Sarah into my cell.

24 HOURS UNTIL I LUST AGAIN

Sonya

Being reminded that Sarah wasn't human wasn't what I wanted to hear right now. Nothing about my life was normal. Zack was only trying to assure me she could take care of herself, but when it came to my life, nothing ever went as planned.

I sighed and thrust out my empty glass. "Fill 'er up."

Zack smiled and popped the whiskey bottle open and poured me another drink. The wafting scent of ancient oak and orange peel tickled my nose and I brought the heat to my lips, letting it slither down and calm the butterflies in my belly.

I clicked my tongue and eyed the security guard who was pretending not to watch me. That pull between us was still there and I did the best I could to brush it off. Whoever held this connection to my runes, it certainly wasn't a human. "We almost there?" I asked the mortal, hoping to jar him out of his blatant staring.

He started and cleared his throat, then elbowed his

companion who shifted to the window, pulling the drape aside. "Yes," his smooth voice replied. "We're pulling into the driveway now."

I shifted to my own window and peered outside. The limo bumped over a rail for a security gate and eased through popping gravel. Even through the heavy tinting of the glass, the array of floodlights lit up the mansion like a beacon. A Queen Anne style home blocked out the moon, and I bit my cheek in revulsion that I knew what the style was called—Sarah always said I spent far too much time watching "Million Dollar Homes."

When the limo slid to a halt, I realized I felt weak and dizzy. It wasn't the alcohol, although that didn't help. This would be the first time I was meeting a man who I not only couldn't control, but could possibly control *me*. Even Zack I could overcome to some degree. But this wasn't just a powerful incubus. This was *the* incubus. Not having my powers of seduction to fall back on made me feel more naked than if I'd dropped all my clothes and walked down a crowded beach.

Zack nudged me in the ribs and I yelped. "C'mon, succubus. It's time to get that necklace charged and get your girl back."

Once I took three steps down the grainy path, I paused to marvel at the modern castle towering over me. The mansion was just like any I'd seen on "Million Dollar Homes," and it was even more breathtaking in person. The symmetrical walls made it look like a fort, but the twirling iron bars kept it elegant. And no castle would be complete without a moat. The only way to get to the house was a narrow path flanked by a still mosaic pond on each side. As I picked my way across the stones I felt as if I'd been teleported to some outlandish Japanese garden.

A shiver of delight sped up my spine as Zack slipped an arm around my waist and guided me down the trail past the water's edge. I welcomed his warmth and was too drunk to resist pulling in the lust lingering on his skin. He only pulled me closer to his side in response, not seeming to mind that I was stealing his energy.

Zack's sexual power sobered me up just enough to keep me from staggering to the massive oak door.

"Do you think he likes blondes?" I ventured, hoping my question didn't sound as pathetic to him as it did in my own head.

Zack gave me a smile and guided me to the small screen to the side of the building. "Why don't we ask?"

I clutched his arm. "Wait. I'm not ready."

He sighed and wrapped his fingers around my hand. "What are you so nervous about?"

He drew my hand to the necklace at my chest and I let his weight linger on my breasts. Even from the minute dust I had drained from his skin, the necklace remained cold and lifeless. I wished to feel it burn again, blazing with life as it had on my mother.

I realized suddenly that I wasn't doing this for David, or Sarah. As selfish as it was, this was my chance to accept that I was a succubus. To embrace what I was, wholly and completely, and finally let go of the guilt that tormented me.

My gaze fell to my feet and I stared at the ground lamps' glow cascading across my red heels, choosing to ignore the dull bloodstains smeared across my jeans. Even if I never had to kill anyone again… could I really accept what I was? Could Sarah?

Beeps sounded as Zack plucked away on the keypad and I cried out in horror. The screen blipped on and the most beautiful creature to grace the planet smiled directly at me.

Even through the filter of pixels and the dilution of a speaker, I was instantly trapped in an iron web of magnetic desire and fascination. I could feel his heat through the screen. It didn't matter if he was a hundred feet away, at that moment I would have done anything he asked.

"Hello, you must be Sonya," he breathed and I staggered to Zack's side, grabbing onto him for stability.

So this is what my victims felt when I controlled them with their own desire.

"Would you please come in?" Derek asked and his liquid sex voice was followed by a mechanical click at the door.

I stared at the bronze handle, frozen in place.

"This place's got remote control locks. How sweet it that?" Zack declared and gave me a hearty slap on the back and I stumbled into the screen, realizing I was pressing my breasts against the camera a bit too late.

"Oh my, aren't you friendly?" Derek's voice caressed me from the speaker.

"E-excuse me!" I launched back from the screen and gave Zack the best death glare I could manage.

"Make yourself at home," Derek continued. "I'll be down in a moment."

The screen went black and I stared at it until Zack tapped my shoulder. "You heard the man, let's go."

Zack tugged the door open and waltzed inside as if he visited the ancient, all-powerful, all *sexy* Incubus King every day of his life.

Then again, since he was just another incubus, he was unaffected by Derek's magnetism, wasn't he?

I swallowed the dry lump in my throat, wishing I'd stolen that whiskey bottle from the limo and could down it before going inside. Instead, I shook myself, fluffed my hair, and followed Zack through the doorway.

The cool air kissed my cheeks and I sighed, not realizing how warm it'd been outside. Plus, Derek getting me all riled up and the remnants of alcohol with the buzz dried out made everything uncomfortable...and sticky.

I pulled down on the leg of my jeans as Zack disappeared around a corner.

"Hey, where you goin'?" I shouted out after him.

His voice echoed down the wide hall in reply. "He said to make ourselves at home. I'm hitting the bar!"

I snickered, and pranced across the plush maroon carpet in anticipation and my eyes scanned the massive paintings decorating the foyer. "Do you think he has more of that whiskey?"

A promising clink of glasses told me it was a good possibility. I smiled and was about to speed around the corner until the most breathtaking painting caught my eye. I enjoyed art just as much as the next girl, but something about this piece was absolutely enchanting.

A naked woman lay across a couch, and the setting seemed antiquated with long beige drapes framing a Victorian style one-armed chair. The woman, though, was draped over it as if she was absolutely timeless. The paint strokes were so intricate I could even see the wave of goosebumps across her flawless skin. She leaned on one hand staring out into the mansion—staring straight at me.

"I see you've found Silvia," a voice breathed behind my ear and I squeaked in surprise.

Derek smiled back at me as Zack sprang into the room. His jolly gait slowed to a halt and he rubbed his neck. "Hey, man. It looks like you're out of the—"

Derek flashed Zack a wicked smile and pulled out a thick glass bottle he'd been hiding behind his back. It was even bigger than the one I'd had in the limo.

Zack laughed and produced a glass, giving me a sympathetic glance. "She's not looking too good."

I swayed, not sure what he meant. The room was a little fuzzy, and I couldn't quite focus on anything with the exception of Derek. He stood out like a beacon of clarity, as if he was the only object worthy of my attention.

Derek uncorked the whiskey bottle with his teeth and I nearly fainted with how hot *that* was. Before I fell over, he poured and offered me the glass. "Nathan said you liked this one."

"N-Nathan?" I asked. How could he just stand there, in his half-open shirt with that massive bulge begging at the zipper of his tight jeans, and speak of someone named Nathan? Shouldn't he be wrapping his arms around my waist? Telling me I was the most beautiful creature to walk the earth, and if he didn't have me right this very moment, he'd die?

His smile broadened. "Yes, my son who you met on the ride here. He seems quite taken with you, even if he won't admit it."

I staggered against the wall, pressing myself up against Silvia's painted breast. "Your son?"

"Yes. Silva and I have had a few, actually. Too bad we haven't had a girl yet. For the boys, she can't pass on more than good looks, but," he smiled and took a white pill out of his shirt pocket, letting it *plunk* into the whiskey glass, "her looks are pretty damn good, wouldn't you agree?"

I took one long gaze at the woman in the painting peering over my shoulder. Even she seemed entranced by the Incubus King. Jealousy surged a sour taste in my mouth and I clenched my fists.

"You'll feel better after you drink this." He stretched out his arm, offering the spiked drink as I blinked furtively, battling between my desire to rip off all my clothes and ask him what the hell he put in my whiskey.

He bobbed the drink in my face. "Take it."

The Incubus King's words held a command I couldn't deny and I snatched the thick crystal from his grasp, draining the spiked drink in seconds. The whiskey burned deliciously down my throat and the knobby pill went with it.

I choked, stumbling and pressing against the painting, watching Derek suspiciously and cradling the cold glass to my breast.

Zack jolted forward. "Dude. Is she all right?"

Derek held out a hand to keep Zack quiet. "Just give her a moment."

Zack growled. "If you're messing with her I swear—"

Derek glared, sending Zack into silence.

The world spun, and it made me nervous that even Zack was worried about me. But the fact that I could even focus on him was a good sign.

After another few heavy breaths, everything became clear—the grand hall of massive paintings, the dangling crystal chandeliers, and a black-haired woman peering around a white-washed corridor who looked suspiciously like Silvia.

As if I'd imagined her, she vanished.

What was in that drink?

I shook my head as the heat in my loins abated to something less than an inferno, and my mind stopped drowning trying to imagine what was beneath Derek's pants.

Derek tilted his head with an attractive smile. "Feeling better? More..." his tongue flicked across his lips, "yourself?"

I sighed and put my face in my hands, rubbing my temples softly. "I think so." I remembered walking inside, but it felt as if I had just woken from a dream. I opened one eye to look up at him. "What'd you give me?"

"A resistant to my influence. It'll last for twenty-four hours."

I shot my head up and stared at him. "There's a drug against our powers?" I blinked. "No, more important question: Why the hell did I need a drug to think clearly around you? I'm not human." I straightened, for once indignant that my heritage didn't make me special in this situation. "I may only be twenty-two, but my mother was over five hundred years old when she had me. I should be able to resist an incubus."

Zack smiled and pulled me away from the painting and into his grasp. "He's a lot older than five hundred years. He's not called the Incubus King for his good looks alone."

With a growl I twisted my watch, fiddling with it to figure out how to set a second timer. I always felt at ease when my life timer was in the hundreds, and 724 hours and 28 minutes shown pleasantly back at me with the familiar purple glow. Managing to pop up a second timer, I set it to 24 hours before I'd be Derek-goo again.

Derek peered over my shoulder and his scent tasted like roses and sex. Even with the resistant, he exuded everything I desired.

I flicked my gaze back at him. "You don't have one?"

He hummed in response. "Can't say I've ever needed to monitor my feeding." He rested a warm hand on my shoulder and it sent butterflies fluttering back to life in my stomach. "Only those of us who deny ourselves need such devices."

Zack pulled me away from Derek and closer into his chest. "That's my sister. She cares about the humans, you know." He kissed the back of my head. "She waits until she finds someone willing to die for her rather than simply take what she needs."

Derek chuckled, but it wasn't in a mocking way. "I admire that."

I wriggled out of Zack's grasp, even though it felt familiar and safe. I needed to focus on my mission. Charge the necklace. Save David. Win Sarah back.

My manicured hand shot to the lifeless silver around my neck. "I'm here to charge this. Zack said you knew an incubus who could help."

Zack offered a muffled chuckle and I glowered at him. What was so damn funny?

Derek's eyelashes lowered and considered the locket. He drifted his fingers over it, and a soft warmth encased the metal at his touch. "I believe I can help you with that." Just when I caught the gleam in his eye and realized he meant *he* was the one who was going to charge my necklace, his smile turned wicked. "You'll need to do something for *me* first."

I narrowed my gaze and glared at Derek. I needed the necklace charged. I needed to save David if I was ever to live with myself, or see Sarah again. "What do I have to do?"

He bent down to press his lips against my ear. "Fuck my wife."

USA TODAY BESTSELLING AUTH
J.R. THORN

ANDERSON'S TRUTH

Luke

When I woke, Sarah was seething in the corner. Anderson had left the lights on and looked far too smug slicing his apple while lounging on a puke-green chair.

Anderson narrowed his eyes at his newest prisoner. "I'm not quite sure what species you are yet."

"Doesn't much matter." Sarah glared. "You resisted my powers, not that it should be possible."

He shrugged. "I have a knack for supernaturals. It's the same way I can resist your succubus friend, I suppose." He leaned on his knees. "Look. I don't think I'm human either, but unlike you two," he pointed the knife, "I don't have any nifty powers to separate me from the rest. I just… resist." His palm layed out flat, as if that wasn't any sort of personal achievement.

Sarah rolled her eyes. "That's a damn good power, if you ask me. So, what do you want with us?"

He glanced at me. "I need all the power I can get to rescue my daughter."

His daughter? The psycho had offspring? What an unfortunate blight on the world. I hoped I'd never meet the she-beast.

"You could try asking for help," Sarah suggested.

He frowned, and then stood. He unbuttoned his suit and pulled his shirt until we were plagued with the pasty white of his ribcage. A nasty red scar lit across his side. "This is what I got when I tried asking." He tucked his shirt back in.

I couldn't take it anymore and beat my fists against the bars. One puny little scar and he'd justified kidnapping and torture? Just because I didn't keep a scar didn't mean I didn't have a vendetta too. He'd sliced me up like an onion on a daily basis and I was going to kill him one day. Nice and slow.

"Calm down, freak," Anderson barked. "I know you don't have any sympathy for me. But I don't need it. Once I get the succubus, you're free to go."

That was news to me. If he thought I'd just shake his hand and be on my way, he had another thing coming.

Sarah frowned. "What's Sonya got to do with this?"

He smiled. "You know, freak here never asked. But I think you'd appreciate what I'm trying to do." He settled himself into his chair like a fluffed out hen. "A succubus can extract power, right? And I resist it." He leaned, his eyes growing wide and intense. "She kissed me, once. When she thought her powers worked on me. Do you know what happened next? I realized I wasn't human, because I woke up ten years younger and my wife was dead." A moment of rage passed his face. "Unfortunately, by the time I figured it all out, the succubus was long gone and so was my daughter." His eyes narrowed. "I've been tracking her ever since. The Black Widow. That's what I called her when I saw what she did to men." Anderson went quiet and his gaze drifted to David.

Sarah turned somber as we considered his slow-rising chest.

"She can't just get away with this. I'm going to take her abilities again, and I'm not going to take life with it. I'm going to take power." His eyes met mine. "I'm going to take every supernatural's power I can and save my daughter."

Sarah scoffed. "Take a supernatural's power? Sonya can't do that."

He popped a slice of apple into his mouth. "I can do it. I just need a boost." He eyed me like a hungry beast. "Infinite regeneration would be a pretty convenient power to have. It'd get me a long way towards rescuing my daughter if I could recover from dagger wounds." He shrugged. "I'm not the best in a knife fight."

Sarah glanced at me. "Regeneration, huh?" She searched my eyes, and then her own went wide as if a memory had been triggered. Shit. She knows what I am?

She coughed politely, turning her head away. "Never heard of a supernatural who could regenerate."

Anderson waved his knife. "No matter. I just need to get the succubus to turn herself in and then my real experiments can get started."

I scoffed. Anderson shot me a glare. "Aw, don't be jealous. I'm not done with you yet." His grin turned sinister. "You still have your role to play."

Anderson glanced at David and frowned. The poor guy had deterioration something fierce, and being locked in a cell without food wasn't helping matters. "First one to let me know when he finally wakes up gets dinner."

With that he switched off the lights and left the room.

I shivered in the darkness. I'd gotten used it, but now there were two other people in the room. I didn't like being unable to see them, especially when one was in the same cell as me. And she also happened to be a muse.

I jumped when her hand rested on my shoulder.

"Hey," she said. "Sorry. I just..." She went silent. I pulled away but then she grabbed my shoulder again. "Hold still. I feel something."

My whole body went rigid as a surge of power bit into my skin. The bitch was strong. I'd give her that. Her aura seeped into me like a cold shard of ice. I'd never felt anything quite like it. I wanted to say, "Get off me, bitch. I get enough stab wounds from Anderson." But nothing other than a pathetic groan came out.

The razor retreated and she pulled away. "Holy shit."

I backed into the bars and slumped. If she wanted to tell me what she'd found, she would.

Her breaths went heavy. "I see why your mother didn't tell you what you were. You weren't ready." She sighed. "You're still not ready. But you will be when this is all over."

There it was again. Everyone else seemed to know so much about me, yet I was kept in the dark. Anderson's cell was just a metaphor for my life. When would the lights turn on? What was this promise of "when it was over?" Would it really ever end?

"You have a key to this cell," she whispered. "You can leave whenever you want."

I stiffened. Yes. I did have a key to my cell. I kept it hidden under a loose stone in the back wall. One of the police officials who was not as corrupt as Anderson had thought had given it to me. But I couldn't leave, not until I'd fulfilled my mother's vision. I had to endure this until the woman came to me.

I expected Sarah to rush to the back wall and undo all my work. If she used the key to escape, Anderson would know and I'd never have an escape plan for when it was time to leave. I crouched, ready to stop her and do whatever I needed to do. I'd already endured more torture than any man alive and I wasn't going to let a muse fuck this up.

"I understand," was all Sarah said. I relaxed, but still didn't trust her. I ran my hand against the bars and made my way to the wall, slumping down against the loose stone. If she was trying to trick me, she'd have to get past my body first. But she didn't make a move. Instead, I heard her make her way to the opposite corner of the cell and sit down. And then we drifted off into sleep, listening to David's slow breaths engulf the silence.

A DOUBLE-D COCKTAIL

Sonya

"Excuse me?" I asked, a bit surprised by his request. Incubus or not, what kind of man asked someone to screw his wife?

He tugged at my sleeve and Zack reluctantly let me go.

"Aw, don't look so glum, my friend. I'm not going to take Sonya without leaving you something in return." Derek clapped his hands twice.

Movement caught my eye down the corridor where I thought I'd seen Silva.

Three girls wearing bikinis covered in sheer pink dresses flounced out of the hall full of giggles and smiles. "Derek!" they squealed in unison.

I rolled my eyes. Nothing I hated more than mindless thralls.

Zack, however, perked up. "Hey, chicas!" He spread his arms as if he expected the girls to frolic into his embrace, scantily clad boobs and all.

Instead, they flounced right past Zack and draped over Derek, pulling at his already half-open shirt and revealing a set of six-pack abs that just wouldn't quit.

Zack's arms fell and his mouth drooped into a pout.

A red-head stood on her tippy-toes and flicked her tongue against Derek's earlobe. "What can we do for you, master?"

Derek shrugged the girls off as if they were pests. "You're for Zack."

They frowned, and the blonde hugging his waist scrunched her nose. "But we want *you*."

Zack sighed. "Man. I can't compete when you're in the room."

Derek laughed. "They'll be fine once I leave." He peeled the girls off his chest. "Okay, ladies. Wait here and I promise you'll find Zack more appealing once I'm gone." Derek winked at me and took my hand. "I have something else on the menu tonight."

I swallowed. I'd never had a threesome before. Not that I was opposed to the idea, but it was bad enough I'd kill one person, let alone two. Needless to say, I'd never found an Incubus King and his wife for such an opportunity to present itself.

I let Derek lead me away while the other girls gave me angry stares. Their interest waned once we'd made our way down the hall and they investigated Zack with increasing cascades of giggles. He offered me an encouraging wave as Derek swept me around the corner.

"I imagine you've never done something like this before," Derek said. I nodded and he squeezed my hand. "I'm not going to make you do anything you don't want to do. That's why I gave you a dose of Silvia's blood." He bobbed his head to the side, as if to admit that was only a half-truth. "Well, that and I need you capable of looking at Silvia instead of me."

I blinked. "Silvia's... blood?" A wave of queasiness swept through my stomach. I'd told Maxine I wasn't a vampire. I wasn't... right?

"It's not easy to make a dose. But I won't get into the technicalities of how it all works." He pointed to a door at the end of the long corridor encrusted with silver. "Those are my bedchambers."

I blinked and reluctantly tugged away from him. "Look, I'm sorry but I'm confused." I wrapped my fingers around the cold necklace. "I need to charge this. Someone's life is on the line and it's my fault. I can do whatever you want later… but first, please, help me charge this and undo my mistake."

He chuckled, running a finger under my chin. "My dear, you and your necklace can have all the sexual energy my wife has to offer. I don't need it." His finger ran down my throat and traced a circle around the locket across my cleavage. "My wife isn't human. I don't know what she is, actually, but she can charge this without even breaking a sweat." He bent, placing his lips on the locket and warmth pressed through to my chest.

Even with the resistant, my knees turned to Jell-O and I couldn't help but bite my lip in anticipation, my eyes glued to his hairless pecs.

I forced myself to match his gaze, and he smirked. How could a smirk be so damn hot? His skin reminded me of silk on marble and I couldn't help but graze my finger across his collarbone. I'd never wanted something so bad and wanted to run away at the same time. Derek was a "double D" cocktail: delicious… and dangerous.

What the hell am I getting myself into?

"I'm not sure what to expect," I said.

"Come with me and you can see for yourself."

I suddenly felt anxious and unsure. Is this something I really wanted to do?

"Why don't you tell me a little bit more about your wife first?" I leaned against the wall and crossed my arms. "She's got to be something special if you've got a giant ass painting of her naked for everyone to see in your living room."

Derek chuckled. "She's not shy." He straightened, tucking the tips of his fingers into his waistband. "She's the mother of my children. She's an endless supply of love, life, and sexual energy."

I cocked my head to the side. A sense of hope swept over me. "Endless? She doesn't experience deterioration?"

"No. I've never seen anything like her in all my years." His gaze grew distant and my hope dwindled. It was too good to be true. I'd have to continue to kill to survive, unless I found someone like her. He said she could charge the Blood Stone. Did that mean I could feed off her? I couldn't simply start up a tryst with the Incubus King's wife… or could I?

As if he sensed my malicious thoughts, he leaned in with a growl in his throat. "Let's get something straight. You're just here to do what I need you to do. When the night's done, she's mine."

My knees went weak and I swallowed a dry lump in my throat, wishing I had more whiskey to endure the fire burning in Derek's eyes. "You're pretty good at reading body language," I said with a weak laugh, hoping flattery would buy me some kudos. His stare continued to bore through me. "If you're so protective, why do you want me to sleep with her? I don't get it."

He sighed, rubbing the back of his neck. I relaxed, feeling as if he'd lowered his hackles. "She's kind of...more into chicks." His face went red-hot.

I blinked. "What?"

He looked down the hall at the silver encrusted door, his face drooping. "I know she loves me. And she wants children just as much as I do, which is probably why she stays with me at all." His gaze drifted to the necklace resting atop my breasts. "But the way it works is she can't become pregnant if she's not aroused. I'm not sure why, or how, but that's just the way her body is built."

I choked on a laugh and rushed a hand to my face. “Sorry,” I blurted the apology and turned sober. “You have no effect on her?”

He eyed me as if he was tired. “Her blood makes the resistant, remember? And if she’s a lesbian at heart, it’s not easy for me to get her blood pumping.”

I hummed. I may only be twenty-two years old, but I’d never once heard of a creature, human or otherwise, who could resist the Incubus King.

“So, why do you need me?” I peered down the way we had come. "What of those thralls?"

His eyes went dark. “Do you really think I want to conceive my child by taking someone else’s life? No, I need a succubus. And there aren’t many of your kind left, nor many willing to take the risk.”

I jerked upright. “What risk?”

He waved the air as if my question had no merit. “Your necklace will protect you from that.”

I pulled the collar of his shirt, hearing a slight rip of the silk as I pulled him to look me in the eye. “What…risk?”

He smiled, his hot breath puffing on my face in a short laugh. “Have you ever heard of a succubus overfeeding?”

I released his collar. “No.”

He placed one hand against the wall next to my head and leaned in, and I suddenly became aware of his hard chest so close to mine. “I learned it the hard way. Our first try with a succubus left her mad with the surplus sexual energy. I’d been so afraid of depriving her that I’d given her too much, and she drowned in it. A bit ironic, wouldn’t you say?”

I swallowed and averted my eyes, then flicked them back when I’d registered what he’d just said. “What do you mean *you* gave her too much? It’s your wife’s sexual energy, how is it yours to give?” I shifted my weight and tried to ignore Derek’s hot breath tickling my neck. “It’s one thing to push sexual energy onto humans, but it’s quite another to transfer it to another succubus. I should know, trying to feed off Zack is like getting three drops of water from a stone. Is that some Incubus King perk or something?”

Derek pushed in closer with an impatient growl, groping across my flat stomach. I froze when his fingers grazed mercilessly over my runes. They awoke under his touch, blazing with heat and he flinched. His hand groped until he reached the rune that seemed to blend with his warmth on the far left of my ribcage.

He tried to lift my shirt to get a better look, but I gripped his wrist and widened my eyes. He was one of the seven, somehow, just like Sarah had been. I felt a kindred strength and his link to my destiny—but not one of the *four*—whatever the fuck that meant. There was something sinister there, too, but I needed to explore why my prophecy included him. I needed to know why my body sang under him. “Do you feel that?” I asked, both hesitant and hopeful.

His fingers continued to stroke and he leaned in until his breath caressed my skin. “What is it?” he asked, sounding curious now.

“You and I…” I breathed, “we share a destiny.”

He laughed—actually fucking laughed at me—then his teeth bit into my neck and I held in the moan of pleasure. “I don’t believe in destiny,” he growled.

I straightened, pushing him back and stepping purposefully for the bedchambers. "All right. Let's get on with it then, shall we? I have a human to save and you have a wife to get pregnant." He might not believe in destiny, but my stupid ass runes didn’t just light up for anyone.

He gave me a wicked smile, seeming pleased with my eagerness. "Am I wrong, or are you more into women yourself?"

I offered him a dry chuckle, wrapping my fingers around the silver handle. “I suppose we’ll find out.”

SILVIA

Sonya

If I'd thought the painting in Derek's foyer was breathtaking, then seeing Silvia in the flesh was like a 3D hologram on the sexual equivalent of steroids. She rose from the bed, her flawless skin covered only by a skimpy nightgown and a layer of lace ribbing across her chest underneath. Only a perfect figure could pull off such a tight stretch of fabric. Derek had said she wasn't shy, but damn, I wasn't sure even I could wear a getup like that.

As she glided across the room, her shadow crawling across the beige marble and curling about my feet, I wondered if she was ever allowed outside. The moon formed a halo around her head, making her look like Lilith, an immortal succubus I'd heard about in fairy tales. And if I'd seen Silvia on the street, I'd think her Lilith incarnate.

"You must be Silvia." I extended my hand in greeting. "I'm Sonya. Pleased to meet you."

Her plump lips curved into a wry smile. "Aren't you formal?" Her words held a mysterious accent that melted my heart.

She bypassed my hand and swept into my chest, wrapping her arms around my torso and pressing her lips against my cheek. I chuckled, folding my arms around her body and letting my fingers tease the curled strands of the midnight-colored locks bouncing all the way down to her waist. Her scent enveloped me, springing up images of fresh peeled oranges and orchids.

But I couldn't ignore a cold sensation that filled my heart. Like any other woman on this planet, I couldn't feel any of her sexual energy.

I pulled away, feeling naked even though I was fully clothed. She smiled, her cheeks flushed and her long eyelashes drooping over her emerald eyes in a flirtatious flutter.

"How do you like her, my dear?" Derek asked his wife, his words dripping with lust and hope.

Silvia giggled, and the sound chimed against my ears as the most pleasant sound to have ever existed. "She's perfect."

My thumb ran around the ring on my pinky out of habit. While her words were kind, I couldn't sense any energy on her skin. Even with Sarah I felt *something*. "She doesn't seem to like me."

Derek chuckled knowingly, draping his arms over the both of us and pulling me into his chest…and closer to Silvia's lips.

"I assure you," Derek said, "you're quite mistaken."

I'd never seen sexual energy as a visible aura before, but in my gut I felt Derek do something and the air around us snapped. His right hand glowed blue as it squeezed Silvia's shoulder, the light crawling through his veins until it made its way to the other side…and into me.

I gasped with the sensation of Silvia's desire. Silvia moaned and the sexual energy burned through my skin where Derek held on tight. I leaned in, placing my lips against hers, and reveled in the burn of her lust and the silk of her skin. Now, I understood. I could never feed off of a woman. It was a limitation spun by the cruel gods who had created my race. But with Derek as a conduit, I could bend the rules.

Like a funnel, the sexual energy saturated my skin and bones until it migrated into my necklace, filling it like an endless reservoir.

My hands groped across the tight lace binding her abdomen and pulled at the strings. The bodice loosened just enough for me to reach my hand in-between her thighs. Still locked in a kiss, I grinned against her teeth when I felt the moist welcome of my touch.

A pulse ran through Derek's hand and he staggered. His stiff erection rolled against my leg and suddenly I was very aware of the magnitude of his presence. Silvia was no succubus, but her allure was fascinating. Thanks to Derek, I could feel it for myself. He'd opened a whole new world to me and my hand fell to his erection, wishing to show my gratitude.

Derek chuckled and removed his grip. My body went cold without access to Silvia's lust and I cried out. "No, please. Don't take it away."

Derek gave Silvia a fond smile. "All yours, my dear."

Her hands caressed my breasts and ran down to the rim of my shirt, tugging it off my body. I complied, wishing only to feel her desire again. She paused as she examined my runes. I kept a hand on the one Derek had activated and its heat threatened to burn me, but I kept my grip. She finally smiled, appeased with what looked no more to be than tattoos, and she pushed down my pants. Now naked, I shivered in the cool air. Silvia led me to the bed as Derek disrobed.

She lay down on her back and pulled me on top of her, safely hiding the rune between the shadow of our bodies. As my tongue danced with hers, a shock of heat hit me from behind. Derek's erection fit between my butt cheeks and Silvia stretched her hands around my neck. When Derek and Silvia grasped wrists, any contact with Derek's skin set me on fire. I gasped and lowered my hips, grinding against Silvia. Her moan was intoxicating. Derek eased inside of me carefully, as if he was afraid to break the fragile connection between the three of us. I pushed my hips back and he slid in farther. I gasped again, feeling Silvia's stimulation against mine, and Derek filling me up from the inside. We all moved together as if we were one. My necklace burned hot with the rolling waves of sexual energy bursting through my body.

The rocking escalated, forcing me over the cliff of an orgasm that threatened to take me under. Derek only kept moving, easily taking my contractions and pounded into me without relent.

Silvia was about to reach her climax, which through our connection I knew was a rare occurrence. Every thrust sent me rolling stimulation over her. Yet it wasn't just the touch, but the sensation of oneness we had with each other. It was only amplified by the power of the rune across my side that recognized Derek as a piece of my destiny, one of the seven, and a sin that would help me avoid the looming darkness that had haunted me all my life.

Her eyes fluttered closed and Silvia bit her plump lip until her lips parted in a soft gasp. Derek felt it too. With one swift motion he pulled out of me and thrust into his wife. I was pushed into her breasts and could hardly endure the level of sexual power radiating through Derek's hard grip against my shoulders.

As she cried out in climax and he came into her, I felt the explosion as if I were him, leaving my seed and my hope for a future inside her womb. I felt her wish, and his, as if they were my own. There would be a child. The knowledge of the power of our union brought me to tears and I cried out with them, feeling the full effects of their euphoria. When the tremors slowed, I slumped over Silvia's heaving body, and Derek rested over mine, not pulling out of his wife. I wanted that moment to last forever, and so did they. And when I managed to open my eyes and look down, Silvia's sweat-glistened breasts were pressed against mine, illuminated by the intense glow of the locket containing the Blood Stone. We'd done it. I now had enough power to save David, face the truth of my prophecy, and live my life without feeding… for now.

SARAH'S SACRIFICE

Luke

David's bloodcurdling scream sent shivers down my spine. Where was his succubus now? Did she even care what he was going through because she'd spread her legs?

"Stop moving," Anderson chided. "Freak doesn't put up such a fuss."

I rolled my eyes and tested my wrists against the straps. I was lying flat on the good ol' torture table. Just one of those cold metal gurneys you'd see in a morgue. It made me envy a corpse.

Anderson patted me on the shoulder and his fingers stuck to my skin, glued with David's blood as the adhesive. I jerked away, as much as I could with my body strapped to the gurney.

"Stop it!" Sarah shrieked. She wasn't laid out like David and me. Anderson had tied her to one of those puke-green office chairs supposedly to keep an eye on her. Though if you asked me, he just got kicks out of having an audience.

Anderson waved the scalpel at her. "He's dead anyway. No

sense letting him waste away when he could do some good in this world."

David moaned, all sense torn out from him after Anderson had sliced open his chest. He should have passed out by now, but there was magic in his veins to dull the pain. I couldn't imagine how much the deterioration would hurt otherwise without the magical numbing. I would have appreciated the succubus not leaving her victim to suffer, if I hadn't been pissed at her for making David a victim in the first place.

Anderson picked up the rib spreader. Thanks to this place being some kind of bioresearch center, he had all kinds of tools to rip a body open. He fumbled with the crank, holding it up to the light. Did he even know how to use the damn thing?

"You're going to kill him!" Sarah shouted and clanked against her chair. It fell over and she cried out.

Anderson laughed. "No. I won't be the one to kill him." He tilted the rib spreader and the sheen of metal glinted against the fluorescent light. A cruel grin spread across his face before he lowered it into David's open chest.

David gasped in panic, his fingers trembling and his eyes locked on the crank. I wished he'd just pass out already.

Anderson's face turned hard. I knew that look of determination. It's how he looked every time he maimed me. My supernatural "gifts" rarely let me pass out either.

When I heard the sickening *crack* of David's ribs being spread, I turned my face and vomited. Anderson could do all kinds of shit to me, but I would heal. What he was doing to David was permanent.

Sarah began to sob and hot tears pricked my eyes. I didn't know David very well, but he seemed like a half decent guy. He didn't deserve this.

When the screams stopped, I turned back to see if David was dead. He'd passed out, thankfully, and Anderson had his hand *inside* David's chest. But that wasn't the worst part. Anderson was glowing.

At first, I thought it was a trick of the light. But his skin had an unmistakable red hue, and blue streaks were spidering up his veins.

"It's working!" Anderson shrieked.

Once the blue essence had run all the way up to Anderson's shoulder, he took out his bloodied hand. The maniac was actually onto something. Our powers were kept within our hearts. Or at least, the succubus's curse had settled there in David.

He grinned and his wild gaze caught mine. "Time for the real test."

As he reached for me, lust for power filling his gaze, Sarah thwacked him from behind. Anderson yelped out in pain. "Bitch!"

Sarah's wrists dripped with blood, the result of yanking herself free of the plastic ties. She balled her hands into fists, ready to fight. "If you think I'm letting you steal Luke's powers, you're insane."

Anderson laughed. "Ah, told you his name did he? You two getting chatty? Close?"

Sarah swung with an impressive right hook with a grunt and Anderson leaped out of the way. The air shimmered as she delved into her powers.

He laughed. "Your powers don't work on me."

But her powers hadn't been aimed at Anderson. Strength surged through my arms, enough to break my binds. I'd never imagined a muse was capable of anything like that.

I burst off the gurney and pummeled towards Anderson. He swiveled and reached in his pocket for the tranq gun. But I dove on him and began beating him in the face. Blind rage overtook me. I didn't care about my mother's vision or saving the world. I didn't care if I lived or died. All I wanted to do was beat the shit out of that man.

Then Anderson pierced me in the chest with a cold iron rod. It went straight through, nearly grazing my heart, and I doubled over as I vomited up blood. Then a cold chill swept through me, not from blood loss, but Anderson's stolen magic seeping into my skin, looking for my powers to drain.

Sarah swept in and pushed me off. The rod yanked out of my chest and I gasped. Through bleary eyes I watched in horror as Anderson took a dagger and plunged it into Sarah's bosom. Anderson smiled as her ice-blue eyes turned dull and grey. Her eyelids fluttered and I knew he'd taken her powers instead of mine.

Anderson grinned and looked my way. "Get back on the table." The command hit me hard. And before I knew it, I'd done exactly as he'd said.

TAKES ONE TO KNOW ONE

Sonya

Waking up in the king-sized bed wrapped in maroon velvet sheets gave me a terrifying jolt of panic. This was exactly how I'd imagined I'd die. I froze, sure that the wet warmth running down my lips was my own blood. Everything felt hot and slick with my own sweat. With a stab of fear, I groped across my stomach, looking for the protruding hilt of a knife impaled by a retaliating lover. Instead, I found Silvia's warm hand draped around my waist just above the rune that had stitched over with cool, pink skin. Whatever Derek had given me, my runes were satisfied.

With a sigh of relief, I wiped the drool from my mouth and peeled off Silvia's fingers, surprised at the weight until I realized Derek's arm was on top of hers. Both stirred, smiling with half-closed eyes as I crawled out of the bed.

Silvia, with her long gorgeous hair sprawled across the pillow, was the most beautiful creature I'd ever seen. Her breasts bunched up like they were stuck in a corset made by Derek's weight, the good bits hidden by his muscular arm. I'd gotten more than an eyeful in the mystical aura of the Blood Stone, but craved to see if she was really that perfect in the stark reality of dawn.

Derek closed his eyes, settling around his wife with a satisfied sigh and his arm slipped. My heart leaped and I bit my lip. Yep. Definitely perfect.

Silvia didn't mind me looking at her. She seemed to enjoy the scrutiny as my gaze lingered on her skin. But when I met her gaze, I couldn't look away. Her eyes were so grey they seemed silver, and she hardly looked human by the way her cheekbones arched a bit too high. She kept her magnificent eyes on mine, and her mouth formed a silent "thank you."

A blush rose to my cheeks. How was she the one thanking me? But as she groped across her stomach and held it there, I realized. Last night I was hit so hard with their elation of a child. But with a heritage like that, what kind of child would it be, especially if it was a girl?

Silvia glanced at my necklace just for the briefest of moments, her face becoming a rainbow of emotions I couldn't decipher. Then she reached for the nightstand, tugging open the drawer. She flashed me a smile and gestured to it before settling back into the sheets. She pulled her husband's arm around her body and tucked his hand under her ribs like a child's blanket and closed her eyes.

Free from the magnetizing hold of Silvia's gaze, and afresh with curiosity, I peered into the open drawer. A simple purple drawstring pouch was the only object, and when I opened it, a single white pill rested inside.

It was one of Silvia's blood pills, a resistant, and for some reason… she wanted me to have it.

I wrapped my fingers around the prize and gave the sleeping couple one more glance. Last night had been draining for both of them; and I was the only one left with energy. And damn, there was so much energy! My limbs tingled and I wanted to do a hundred jumping jacks and then run twenty miles. And it wasn't just from the sheer amount of energy I'd been fed, but the realization I was waking up and the person next to me wouldn't have to die.

Resisting the urge to clap my hands like a delighted child who'd learned not to kill caterpillars, I drew a deep breath and took in the luxury of the bedroom. The morning light revealed ridiculous amounts of crystal absorbing dawn's rays, only to spit them out again in blinks of white. The ceiling dripped with glass like we were inside a cave with stalactites that grew nothing but jewels and diamonds. Even the walls glittered, and I became dizzy with the richness of it all. Who had the kind of money to bedazzle their entire room?

I supposed an Incubus King, and his succubus-feeding wife.

Finding my jeans draped across an oak chest, I snatched them up and grimaced at the sight of the dried blood across the denim. I really needed to get home and find a change of clothes. Did I have enough detergent to get day-old blood stains out?

The reality of life hit me then, thinking of laundry and my apartment and such regular things. Sarah was out there… and David could be saved.

My hand shot to my necklace, finding it scalding hot. The skin around my cleavage had grown accustomed to the warmth, but my fingertips were cold and clammy from lying on top of the covers, exuding the heat from the night's exertions. I bounced the locket from one hand to the other until my hands warmed, and popped it open.

The Blood Stone radiated as if I'd set a ruby on fire. The energy in the gem swirled, roiling like a gleaming whirlpool. I'd never seen a Blood Stone this alive.

I clicked the locket closed and the moment of awe passed.

Nausea set in, thinking of what Derek had said last night of a succubus dying from overfeeding. What would have happened to me if I didn't have an empty Blood Stone for protection? Did Derek fear for his own life? Is that why he didn't hold back, and gave me all Silvia had to offer?

Questions for another day. I had a man to save, and sins to amend with Sarah.

I donned last night's clothes, slipped on my heels, and eased out of the room.

Clicking my way through the empty hall, I realized I wasn't exactly sure where David would be. Of course, he'd be with Detective Anderson. But where was that pest hiding now? He wouldn't still be at his old rundown office. I'd had Zack ransack that place more than once.

Turning around the last bend of the hall, I found Zack wearing nothing but his jeans. He teetered on the edge of an enormous leather chair, failing to procure any of the expensive comfort as he leaned on his elbows and stared at his phone. He balanced on the balls of his feet, bouncing his heels on the ground, never taking his gaze off the screen.

"Shouldn't you be in bed with a bunch of thrall girls or something?" I asked, pinching my cheek between my teeth.

He glanced at me. "It's not polite to speak of the dead."

I balked. "What?"

He shrugged and looked back at his phone. "What can I say. I was hungry."

There was a certain fondness for Zack in my heart. But it was times like these that I was reminded how true he was to our race. He saw humans as food. Nothing more. Nothing less. I could never truly love anyone who felt that way.

As always, I attempted to divert my feelings with humor. "Waking up next to a corpse is the least sexy thing I can think of. Much less three."

He glared. "You're one to talk." He thrust the phone at me like a spear.

Blinking, I took it and stared at the screen.

A message from Sarah. My heart lifted, until I read what it said.

I have my evidence, and the freak of a girlfriend.

The Black Widow has 24 hours to turn herself in, or the girlfriend's next.

- Detective A.

Two pictures were attached, and I tapped the screen while my heart fluttered its way up my throat.

The first image was a close-up of Sarah, gagged, with one black eye, and a frightening patch of red around her chest, holding up a note that read, "4112 Lance Street. Come in 24 hours or I die."

The second image was loaded off the screen and my finger trembled as I scrolled to see what came next.

Bile rose in my throat when I saw David had fully deteriorated. His pasty grey skin was taut across his cheeks and his cloudy eyes stared back at me, full of judgment and terror.

David was dead.

The phone clattered to the ground as tears welled in my eyes. "D-David. How is he dead?"

Zack wouldn't look at me. Rage filled my chest and I stomped towards him and shook a clenched fist. "Don't you sit there and judge me. You just killed three innocent girls. *Three*!"

"Thralls choose their fate, David didn't."

There was truth in that. A selection of humans learned what we were, and what would happen to them if they slept with one of us. There was nothing short of a cult, full of an endless supply of men and women who thought it an honor to give their life-force to a supernatural. They told themselves that they'd be reborn as a succubus or incubus themselves, but that's not how the curse worked. There was no rebirth. There was only death.

Zack had the nerve to roll his eyes before he stood. My fist went flying of its own accord, aimed straight at his face.

Zack could have dodged, but he didn't. My knuckles cracked against his cheekbone and a shockwave rippled through the air. My ears popped and the hairs on my arms singed from the heat.

How dumb could I be? I'd just filled a Blood Stone to the brim. My locket and body burned with more sexual energy than I'd ever had in my life, and Zack had just devoured three thralls. No way would we be able to hurt each other.

A breath shuddered into my lungs and I shook my fist as if it hurt, but it only felt hot.

Two knuckle marks seared red across his skin before vanishing. Zack watched me, his own fists clenched and his lips curled over his teeth in a snarl. He was always laughing. I wasn't used to seeing him this way. I tensed, waiting for him to retaliate, but he relaxed his shoulders and waited for my heaving breaths to slow before he spoke. "Sonya," he whispered my name. "How much time did you have left when you slept with David?"

"What?"

He glanced at my watch. "You always time your starvation down to the millisecond. How close was it?"

I swallowed. What did that matter?

His eyes went wide. "How close?"

"Seconds," I spat.

He clicked his tongue and looked away. "The fuck, Sonya."

"That shouldn't have mattered. I was with him for not even half an hour. There's no way that was enough to kill him, no matter how hungry I was. He should've had months left." I crawled my fingers through my tangled hair and growled with frustration. "How is he dead?"

Zack's hand rested on my arm and I flung him off. I couldn't stand for anyone to touch me right now. I shouldn't have left David alone with that madman. While I was having orgasmic, supernatural sex… David…

"Detective Anderson must have done something," Zack blurted.

I matched his gaze and held onto it, searching for some grain of hope that this wasn't all my fault.

His hand hovered over my arm, but then his fingers retracted, curling into a ball. "If he's got Sarah then we were wrong about everything. Your powers aren't to blame."

I swallowed. Sarah was still in danger. But she was a muse. She should be able to protect herself. My mind reeled back to the image of her with a black eye and that blood spot pooled just above her stomach. It didn't seem real.

"Look," Zack said, splitting into my thoughts again. "This is bigger than Sarah. If that detective has got something that can mess with our powers, we need to find out what it is. This puts our entire race in danger. You understand what that means?"

I'd never heard of anyone finding a way to mess with our powers. But the few times I'd come face-to-face with that damned detective, he'd been unaffected by my touch. I'd just assumed something was wrong with me…

My gaze fell to the floor. The phone was still laying there like road kill. Its black screen reflected the image of the paintings lining the wall. Silvia's was right in front of us, and I hadn't even noticed the shockwave had dotted it with bits of smoldering embers. *Derek is going to kill me...*

Zack's hands wrapped around my shoulders and I squeezed my eyes shut.

"Get ahold of yourself. You have a *Blood Stone*. We can save Sarah, and stop that stupid human."

I wriggled out of his grasp with a snarl of anguish. "We? There is no 'we' here. You don't give two shits about humans, probably muses either. I'm going to save Sarah, and I'm going alone." I whirled and stomped for the massive double-doors. Placing both hands on the oak, my rage exuded through my skin and seared burn marks on the wood.

"Sonya." Zack's voice was hardly above a whisper.

"What?" I snapped.

Zack's heat lingered at my back, but he didn't attempt to touch me. "Be careful."

There was no way I was going to respond to that. If I wasn't a succubus, he wouldn't have cared what happened to me. His love was hollow, and *wrong*. I deserved better than that.

Rage swelled in my chest, turning my locket molten hot and jolting energy through my fingertips like lightning. Spider cracks flew through the doors, the wood turning black before splintering under my weight. Sunlight poured in, far too cheerful for my mood. I snarled at it before walking outside, and head towards 4112 Lance Street.

BROKEN HEARTS

Luke

My own screams reverberated in my head. Sarah sobbed somewhere in the background, yet at the same time it was as if she was here, right in front of me.

Anderson poised the scalpel before slicing and plunged his fingers into my chest. The agony reverberated through my body and burned like fire. Then I felt what I had hoped was just my imagination. Anderson had Sarah's powers. They'd altered, and weren't as strong, but I could feel the magic within him. The magic whispered to me, urging me to hand over my powers to Anderson. Even if I wanted to, I couldn't obey. My powers weren't something to trade. They were simply a part of me.

Anderson snarled. "Dammit!"

I gasped when he jerked his hand out and blood trailed down my ribs.

Through my bleary vision I could make out Anderson waving the bloody scalpel at Sarah. "I only had enough to absorb one supernatural's power! I didn't want yours. It's useless!"

Sarah spat.

Anderson sneered and turned back to me. "Come on, freak. Give me your powers."

I'd do anything to make the agony end. I babbled incoherently and Anderson didn't bother to try and understand. He went straight to work plucking out bits of my body, forcing it to scramble into regeneration. I jerked and the IV sticking out of my vein tugged at my wrist. The cold fluid seeped into my body, replacing the blood I was losing by the pint. Anderson gave me a short reprieve as he replaced the bag, tossed it to a building pile on the floor. The damn guy wouldn't let me wither up and die. He'd keep this regeneration going on forever.

He continued his work, slicing off my ear and holding his hand over the flesh as it grew back. Magic tingled across my forming veins, and added its own burn to my plethora of pain. Yet I kept regenerating, which meant Anderson wasn't getting any closer to absorbing my powers.

Anderson tossed the scalpel and it clattered across the floor. "There must be a way!" He stomped his foot like a child having a tantrum. "I have to be able to replicate it! I can't risk the bitch getting the best of me. Just one fuck up and I'm done for." For the first time, he hesitated. Desperation flashed across his glassy eyes and then all the color drained from his face. He stepped to the tool table and took the rib spreader once again, still stained with David's lifeblood.

I strained against my binds. But I was so weak and so cold. Anderson had taken off all my clothes just so he could slice up every inch of my skin. The small slits had already sealed. But the larger gash running up my chest strained to close. Anderson forced the rib spreader in before it could.

He pumped the crank once and a crack reverberated through my chest. I screamed, but the mere sound of my own voice could hardly express that sensation. I'd never been so horrified in my life. He was literally ripping me apart.

Another pump of the crank sent me into manic cries for the pain to end. For the sweet darkness of death to finally take me away.

I wished I had blacked out, but my own body seemed to want me to witness whatever horror was about to transpire. I didn't want to know why Anderson needed to crack open my chest. He'd taken so many organs out of my body, but it'd always been a kidney or bits of my liver. Never anything that I couldn't have lived without anyway.

But now Anderson bridged that gap between insanity and reality. He reached inside my chest and the burn radiated to my left side. His grip tightened and I sucked in a breath.

No. Surely he wouldn't go so far.

The thump of my heart strained against Anderson's grasp. He leaned in, squeezing as a tremor overtook my body. "Forgive me," he whispered.

My tongue rolled as I tried to speak. I couldn't. The muse effects were too strong and the pain swept up and down my limbs like lightning.

Anderson closed his eyes and pulled my beating heart from my chest.

SUCCUBUS ON STEROIDS

Sonya

Never before had I felt so powerful and yet at the same time, on the verge of losing control.

Emotion overpowered my senses, and at first I thought it was fear. The image of David's pale corpse blocked my vision and I shook my head, struggling to breathe. When I let the tears come I realized it wasn't fear constricting my throat, but the reality of my failure.

With a growl of frustration I ripped off my heels and tossed them into the road. Let them be destroyed, blasted things. My bare feet couldn't feel the pain of the jagged street as I broke into a run. I jerked my phone out of my pocket and took a sharp left to follow the bold green line. I didn't fail to notice my walking icon had been replaced with a bicycle. Stupid Google. Doesn't have a "Succubus on Steroids" setting.

Anderson was going to regret messing with me. I didn't care if he had something to block my powers. He couldn't block my fist. Even if he wasn't human, he wouldn't come back from a smashed-in skull.

After jogging for fifteen minutes, my breath still came slow and easy. My heart retaliated against my raging emotion and thumped with a steady beat. The power bubbled from my necklace and merged into my soul, giving me a bottomless source of energy. No matter how upset I was, my body wanted to act as if I was lounging on a beach basking in the sun.

The faster I ran, the more I realized I was bringing attention to myself. Cars slowed. Strangers walking on the street jerked to a halt to stare, men with lust and women with awe. Was I glowing? Maybe. But it didn't matter. I'd failed David. All this time I'd entertained the fantasy I could save him with a fully charged Blood Stone. My mother had told me of its regenerative powers. Although, she'd never specified if those powers could be gifted to another. It was a faint hope I'd clung to in order to justify what I'd done to David. My selfishness was almost crippling. Why hadn't I just let myself die?

Tears evaporated off my cheeks and hoarse sobs scratched in my throat. My legs pumped and I pushed myself into a frantic run as my face scrunched in pain.

Why was I born this way? I shouldn't be on this planet, plaguing men with my poisonous kisses. Being an unfaithful girlfriend to Sarah, who only deserved the best. But it was too late for that now. My mother didn't drown me when I was born as I would have, had I been her. Instead she raised me with the knowledge of what I was. How cruel was she to teach me the difference between good and evil, when I was doomed to sin?

An ancient medical building loomed when I rounded the last bend and I snorted a laugh. Of course. The sign read:

Seattle Biological Research Center

I should have known. This place was the highest running rumor in Seattle for the creepy, haunted bio center that was all but shut down, yet still accepted cadavers and experimental medical patients, and the best possible place Anderson could hide. I'd been dared more than once to brave the mostly-abandoned research center at night, although the dare had always come from an infatuated stranger who wanted to flatten me against a dark wall. Little did they know the favor I did them by declining.

I drew in a deep breath and approached the building. This time not for fun, but for redemption. And as if to encourage why I was here, my necklace sizzled, as if sensing my need and dousing my body with energy. There was no doubt I was glowing now. My skin burned hot and glinted red off the lamp poles like tiny embers.

Four pristine cameras clashed against the medieval, mossy exterior of the research building. Their dark lenses stared at the abandoned parking lot with dead vulture eyes. I rolled my shoulders back and took three more steps. The cameras swirled onto my face and I thrust my middle finger in the air.

"Fuck you, Detective," I snarled. "I'm coming for you!"

SHE'S HERE

Luke

I was alive, which meant two things. One: Anderson hadn't been able to take my powers, even when activating them to peak performance. And two: I could fucking regenerate my own heart. Holy shit.

I crawled in the darkness towards a dull red light. Anderson was in the security room. That meant he was expecting someone.

"Luke? Is that you?" Sarah whispered.

I crawled to the bars and peered at her, letting my eyes adjust to the dim light. She had a nasty gash across her cheek and was bound to a chair. A strange hiss sounded every time she breathed. She wasn't doing so good.

She softened when she saw me. "You really are one of them." Her voice held marvel and awe.

One of what? What the fuck did that mean?

Sarah smiled, a friendly kind of smile that said everything was going to be okay, even if I didn't understand. The kind of smile my mother had given me right before she'd been taken off to prison.

"Luke," she pressed.

I pulled myself closer to the bars and rested my face against the cool metal, sticking my nose through the cell like a hound stuck inside a car.

"She'll be here soon. The one you're meant to protect."

I was so weary of this prophecy. Would this mystery girl really come into my life? How was I supposed to protect her? The second Anderson got ahold of that succubus and gained her soul-sucking ability, he'd be unstoppable.

Then I felt the boom. It was just as my mom's vision had described. Her presence would hit me and the need to protect her would overpower my senses.

The room remained dark but light flashed across my vision like exploding stars. I scrambled to the back of the cell and fumbled against the loose stone, getting my hidden key.

It was time to get the fuck out of this God-forsaken place and save the world.

MYSTERY MAN

Sonya

The cameras followed me as I stomped to the front double doors. Expecting resistance, I pushed as hard as I could to break the hinges. Yet the doors weren't locked and flung across the room at my touch, crashing into a stack of chairs, reducing the pile to splinters. I couldn't help the grin that spread across my face. It was damn nice having real power for once.

The lobby looked just as I'd imagined it would, full of draped waiting chairs, minus the stack I'd destroyed, and an old reception desk covered in a thick layer of dust taking up the majority of the lobby in a wide arc. Cheap paintings lined the walls depicting research scientists nobody knew or cared about. I stepped inside and ignored the splinters crunching under my feet.

There wasn't a single light on in the place, not that it mattered. I glowed brighter than ever. The amulet around my neck burned hot and I gripped it for reassurance and strength. It was like holding a piece of red-hot coal, but one that fed me its warmth. Its stored power seeped into my hand and bled through my skin, muscles, and bone, empowering me like I'd never been strengthened before.

"Careful," said a voice from the loudspeaker. "Don't waste all your magic. I'll be needing it."

I jerked at the sound, but no one was in sight. The only sign of movement was a glistening camera straining against cobwebs as it followed my movements.

"Seriously?" I shouted. "You're going to talk to me from an intercom? Don't hide from me like a coward!"

"I'm not hiding." Detective Anderson's calm voice echoed through the room. "I'm documenting this moment for the judge." He snickered. "Thanks for glowing and removing all doubt of what you are."

I scoffed. "Even if I'm revealed to the humans, what kind of judge would side with you? What kind of justice system lets you go free and puts me behind bars?"

He laughed, and continued to laugh until the point of almost becoming hysterical. "Put you behind bars?" His voice went up a pitch as if I was being ridiculous. "Demons don't get put behind bars. They get sent back to hell."

I stomped towards the camera and growled. "I'm not a fucking demon! If anyone is a demon around here, it's you! You killed David!"

He chuckled, this time sounding as if he pitied me. "We both know you're at fault for his death, as you are for countless others. And now is a chance for your redemption. Come inside."

The camera swerved to the reception desk and a light blinked on from behind the fogged glass of the employee entrance.

I glared. "Why the hell would I go in there?"

Sarah's frantic voice burst through the intercom. "Sonya?

Don't listen to him! Get the fuck out of here! He has—" Her words were cut short by a soft thump and muffled cry.

"Trade yourself for your girlfriend," said Detective Anderson, "or there'll be more blood on your hands."

My eyes went wide. "What's to tell me you won't kill her anyway? I'm not going to walk into some trap. Just let her go!"

He laughed and Sarah's whimpers lingered in the background, both from the intercom and some faint echo from behind the door. "What choice do you have?" said Detective Anderson. "Either enter into my care, and your girlfriend goes free, or cause trouble and I'll release my evidence to the government." His voice tinged with a sneer. "Every black-tied oaf will be after you then. The Black Widow in the flesh. Imagine what kind of reward there would be—"

The intercom released a rush of static before blipping off into silence. I crouched, waiting for the Detective to pounce from the shadows. But no movement came.

There was a crash from somewhere behind the door, sounding almost like it came from below ground. I straightened and stared at the fogged window, waiting for signs of life. What came next was a scream of rage. A man's scream, but it wasn't Detective Anderson's. The sound rolled through the hall and found its way into my chest and settled there like living thunder. I gripped my heart and cried out, not at any sort of pain but the shock of this feeling of invasion. What the heck was this? No… Who was this?

The scream was followed by the frantic slap of bare feet hitting the ground, and whoever it was, was heading straight for me.

Curling my fingers into fists, I prepared myself for whatever monster Detective Anderson had set loose. Perhaps this was his secret weapon, how he'd subdued my powers and Sarah's. Whatever it was, it sounded big.

The gorgeous naked man who burst from the employee's entrance was not at all what I'd expected and the undeniable connection of his magic hit me straight to the gut.

I balked. This... *man,* was one of the four? He held a piece of my heart and was a piece of my soul that would determine my destiny?

He stared at me, likewise taken aback as our connection sizzled through the air like fire. He was covered in dirt and blood, but that didn't diminish his exotic beauty. His wild eyes caught onto mine before lowering to the hidden rune astride my navel that sang for him.

I relaxed my shoulders. "Are you okay?"

I'm not sure why I asked such a silly question. There he was with his willy swinging away and his six-pack abs covered with nasty looking scabs and caked layers of dried blood. Whatever he'd been through, he was far from okay.

He just stood there and stared. His eyes were such a wild blue that I wanted to coax his gaze back to me.

Spreading my fingers and holding out my palms in what I hoped was a non-threatening motion, I slowly approached him. "You're safe now, okay?"

He cocked his head and peered into my face, but then he flinched when his eyes fell onto my amulet. Without warning he released a sound unlike any I'd ever heard from any human. His scream pummeled me from all directions and unseen splinters shoved into my brain. I cried out and felt that invasion of *him* once again, but this time the rage was directed at me. I crumpled to the ground, unprepared for the onslaught from someone who was supposed to be one of my four.

My amulet lit up like a firecracker and a shockwave bellowed through the hall. By the time I regained my composure and could stand, he was gone.

My hands drifted to my side and I stared at the wide open

door. The only thing that moved me from my shock was one more scream... Sarah's.

I burst into the darkened hall of the employee basement. A wall of shit-scented air hit me in the face on my way down, but I didn't stop to gag. Sarah was still screaming.

"I'm coming!" I shouted. Her heart-wrenching wails wound my stomach into knots.

Stampeding down the dark staircase I bypassed a freakishly bloodied lab and continued my descent until I finally entered into a room with one bright bulb gleaming over my girlfriend bound to a chair, not by chains, but by fucking plastic zip ties. There were all kinds of odd paraphernalia filling the room, including grey jars with floating body parts and a small prison cell that reeked of feces, yet there was no Detective Anderson in sight. The only evidence he'd ever been here at all was a trail of blood leading to a cracked door at the end of the hall. The coward had escaped.

Sarah continued to scream as if she'd been stabbed. Her eyes were squeezed shut and she shook her head, tossing her sagging blonde curls into her face and strained against the binds. It didn't make sense. A muse was strong enough to get out of that and even if the telling bloodstain at her chest suggested she'd actually been stabbed, she should have convinced her body to heal by now.

I rushed to her side and shook her by the shoulders. "Sarah! I'm here. Why are you screaming?"

Finally, she stopped thrashing and blinked. I expected her familiar striking blue eyes to greet me, the same color eyes that had attracted me to David. But just like David, dead, grey eyes stared back at me. It was as if Sarah's soul had been ripped out, leaving nothing but an empty husk that still breathed. "My God. What did that bastard do to you?"

Her lower lip trembled and tears streamed down her cheeks. "He took my powers!"

I froze, unable to register what she'd just said. Was such a thing even possible?

She sniffled and her gaze drifted to my necklace, still burning red-hot. "But it seems you've enough power for the both of us."

I clutched the Blood Stone, and even from its exuding, never-ending warmth I didn't think power was the fix for this. Sarah was human now.

Frowning, I rested my fingers on the plastic tie binding her wrist to the arm of the chair. It melted, and she yelped as her skin turned bright red. "Sorry," I whispered. She bit her lip and held still as I melted the other one.

Rubbing her wrists, she slumped and whimpered. I was accustomed to pain. I suffered through the ache of starvation on a regular basis, but Sarah was a muse. She wasn't used to it. What was she going through right now?

She whimpered, holding onto her chest and wheezing. "Can you… Is it possible to heal me?"

I'd never tried using my powers that way, but damn it, the Blood Stone had to be good for something. I pressed my palm against her chest and willed energy to go into her. It funneled without protest, seeming relieved to find an outlet in its ache to be used.

Sarah sucked in a breath and trembled. Her black eye turned pink and her breath lost its wheeze.

After a moment she seemed to compose herself. She rolled her shoulders back and straightened. "Sonya," she whispered.

"Yes, are you all right?"

"I'm fine." Sarah ran her fingertips across the hollow of her chest. "That man. Did you see him?"

"What, the hot, naked one?"

She smirked. "Yeah, that's the one."

I shifted, resting on my knees. "What about him?"

She leaned in. "He can't die."

My heart skipped a beat. "What do you mean, he can't die?"

"I mean exactly what I say. I saw Anderson do things to him that should have killed a man. But whatever he cut out… it eventually grew back." She rubbed her wrists and stared into the dark depths of the cell. "I don't know how long he's been here, but I think it's been a long time. Anderson was trying to figure out how to take his powers, too. His gift of regeneration…immortality."

I wavered, unable to think of any supernatural who could regenerate, much less live forever. Even my kind had a limit to their lifespan. Sure, we could live for hundreds of years, but if you ripped out our heart it wouldn't grow back…

"Did Anderson keep him in there?" I asked, following Sarah's gaze to the iron bars.

Sarah nodded and drew in a deep breath before she continued, keeping her gaze on the cell floor. "His name's Luke. He had a key to his cell this whole time. He could have left whenever he wanted. I wasn't sure what he was waiting for until I touched him." She tilted her head and finally looked at me. "When you arrived in the lobby, he sniffed the air like a dog. He turned all frenzied, burst out of the cell and attacked Anderson. Bit him on the neck like some kind of maniac, and then ran upstairs." She looked me over head to toe. "You're who he's been waiting for."

"What do you mean, I'm who he's been waiting for?"

Sarah offered a weak smile. "You'll find out, I'm sure."

I rolled my necklace across my fingers, remembering Luke's bewilderment turning to fear. "I think this frightened him."

Shaking my head of thought, I stood, bringing myself back to my priorities. The mystery of the hot, naked man would have to wait. I'd saved Sarah, and now I needed to protect myself.

"There's got to be a security station around here. Sounds like Anderson didn't have time to make off with the footage."

Sarah staggered to her feet and fell on my arm. She was so light and tiny, like a finch I could crush by accident if I wasn't careful.

She pointed to the end of the hall. "There. That's where he was before Luke scared him away."

Dragging Sarah along, we teetered our way to the door. Inside were two monitors showing the entrance hall and what must be the secondary exit Anderson had used to escape, but he didn't escape on his own. A stream of blood led to the curb before vanishing into a line of blackened tire streaks. He was long gone.

With a sigh I eased Sarah into a rickety green office chair and investigated the dusty equipment. There was only one box blinking a green light, and after a few button-jabs a tape popped out. Damn thing was ancient, but this meant there was only one recording in existence. I weighed the plastic in my hand before tossing it to the ground and grinding it under my naked heel. Detective Anderson just lost his evidence.

It was too hard to believe that this was all over. Was I safe? I looked back at Sarah and she shivered as if she couldn't get warm. No, it wasn't about me anymore. Maybe it never was. Detective Anderson was trying to figure out how to extract powers… He wasn't trying to stop me from murdering men. I scoffed. There was nothing honorable about his work.

Even though Sarah was the one who needed comforting, she knew me better than I knew myself and wobbled to my side. Without any concern for herself, she wrapped her arms around me. "You have to go after him," she whispered into my neck. My skin was hot and I knew it burned her to touch me, but she didn't pull away.

I stiffened. "What about you?"

She shrugged. "I'm human now. I can't be your girlfriend anymore."

I wrapped my arms around her body and hugged her tighter. "Sure you can."

She shook her head and pulled away, but I kept my hands bound behind her back. "No. Even as a muse, I couldn't give you what you needed."

"How can you say that? I starved myself for you. I almost died. That's why David—"

She jerked out of my grasp. "I didn't ask you to starve."

Tears pricked at the edges of my eyes. "How else could I be faithful? By asking me to be exclusive, you were asking me to die. Even so, I tried…"

Pain and guilt warmed her pasty cheeks. "I thought you could feed off me. You acted like you could." Trails of wet tears streamed down her face again. "You *lied*."

Rage heated my chest and my skin sparked to life like a flame. Sarah stepped back when I thrust a finger in her face. "You don't know what it's like to love someone but never be able to be faithful. You should have known what it'd take." I pressed both hands against my chest. "I'm a succubus!"

Hurt spread across her features and no matter how angry I was, I knew I wasn't truly angry with her. As always, I blamed myself for ever being born.

"Sonya, I lied to myself too, okay? I let myself believe I was enough for you. But I wasn't."

"I'm sorry," I whispered, my rage evaporating. "I didn't mean to mislead you."

She smiled then, her features going soft. "Look. I understand now, okay? And that man, out there," she pointed to the door, "he's someone you're meant to be with. Before I lost my powers, I *felt* you inside of him, and now, I feel him inside of you." She grabbed my arm and her voice turned urgent. "Don't you know what that means? He's a part of your destiny. You need to go find him." Her fingers went lower, ghosting over my runes. "I didn't want your tattoos to mean anything. I avoided it as long as I could, just like I knew you couldn't feed off me. It's time I stopped lying to myself and face the truth. I'm not the one you're meant to be with, and that's okay."

I huffed a short laugh. "Seriously? And this guy you think is part of my destiny, or whatever, what do I have in common with him? He doesn't know me like you do."

Sarah flashed me a sad smile. "Maybe you have more in common than you think. You've both had your hearts ripped out." And then she walked out the door without looking back, leaving me alone with the glowing monitors. I clutched my chest that ached with pain that confirmed her words.

Sarah had ripped out my heart, and left me to bleed. I sure hoped she was right, and that man I'd met was one of my four, because the gift of his powers was the only way my heart would ever grow back.

PUBLIC TRANSPORT

Sonya

I'd saved Sarah and it didn't feel right to head to our cramped apartment and pretend nothing had happened. We were no longer together, no matter how much I wished it to be otherwise. There was a chasm between us and I couldn't even focus on it. An aching need pulled me in two different direction. I'd met two of the men who were part of my four, but there had to be some sort of mistake.

Zack was waiting for me when I returned to Derek's mansion. It should have startled me to find Sarah already in the living room drinking away her memories, which now that she was human, would be an effective means of treatment. But where else did she have to go? She needed help, and in Seattle, the Incubus King was where you found it.

Zack crossed his arms when he walked in. The tick in his jaw revealed he was relieved I'd come back, but he was still pissed off. "The King wants to talk to you two," he snapped, then promptly led me to what I could only describe as a throne room.

Derek lounged in a red velvet chair complete with spires and jewels. He wasn't just a king for show, but I knew this was a reminder of who I was… and who he was. I was just some random succubus he'd fucked, and now that he'd gotten what he wanted from me, he held my fate in his hands. The rune he'd activated on my ribcage was cold and silent. I slipped a hand under it and scratched at the smooth skin.

He might think he was done with me, but I wasn't done with him.

Derek motioned for Sarah to approach him. He would be gentle and polite with a muse in the room, especially given who Sarah's father was. One of three powerful male muses who held the fate of all supernaturals in their palms was a force to be reckoned with. "Tell me what has transpired, muse, and I will aid you with all the protection I have to offer."

She flinched at the term. He hadn't realized that she'd lost her powers. "Sonya thwarted a supernatural I haven't come across before." She paused, as if debating to offer up Detective Anderson's unique power, but then continued. Wise girl. Don't ever give the Incubus King everything he needed. "He was holding a prisoner," Sarah continued. "I want Sonya to find the fugitive that has fled and I will return to my father and seek out the perpetrator."

Derek rubbed his chin. "I see. Sounds like you have it all planned out. Well, I shall gladly offer my assistance. I have airlines and private jets—"

"I can take care of myself," Sarah said and propped a hand on her hip. She did that when she wanted everyone to think she was confident, but she was actually about to fall apart. I didn't know how she planned on getting to Miami, but she wasn't going to give Derek a chance to find out she'd lost her powers. "Give Sonya public transport," she added. She glanced at me as determination and rage glittered in her eyes. "He'll be heading to New

York, so you best send her in the morning on the next flight out. We don't want her to draw attention. The supernatural is skittish, but I want Sonya to find him and bring him back to me as soon as possible."

I suppressed the growl that threatened to emanate from my throat. Public transport my ass. She just wanted to punish me.

"Very well," Derek said with a nod. He slipped his hand over the arm of the chair and leaned, the folds of his shirt opening to reveal the hard lines of his chest. His gaze met mine and he grinned. "I'll send two of my men to escort her, if that is permitted."

Sarah glanced back at me and my eyes widened. No. C'mon, Sarah, no. He just wants to capture me like a toy and he's going to send his goons to bring me kicking and screaming back to him.

"Very well," she agreed.

Damn it.

FIRST CLASS

Sonya

The strawberry daiquiri left a wet drizzle against my palms. The ice was nearly melted, but I couldn't bring myself to raise the drink to my lips. The cabin interior was sweltering and all I wanted to do was get out of this stuffy airplane filled with sweaty men who seemed to be incapable of anything but leering at me.

"Excuse me, Miss?"

Wearily, I peered at the fidgeting flight attendant. By the way her knuckles went white as she gripped the headrest, I guessed she'd been standing there for some time trying to get my attention.

She swallowed. "Would you like me to get you a new daiquiri?"

My fingers tightened around the drink. "No. I'm fine, thank you."

Her lashes lowered as she considered the slush once more.

Her lips forced into a tight smile and she bobbed her head before heading back down the aisle.

This stupid drink was all I had left of Sarah. I was pissed off at her, but at the same time my heart ached. Thanks to the Blood Stone that had saved her, humans acted bizarre around me. Men openly stared and rolled their hips in their seats and I sighed dejectedly. I was a living ball of lust and I couldn't help how I made them feel. I didn't ask for this curse.

The women were even worse. I avoided their gazes as best I could. My powers never had an effect on women before, but now it seemed I'd changed. I caught them staring just as much as the men, if not more. Often their gazes lowered to my chest. My leather jacket plumped with my breasts and my pendant resting on my bosom. The Blood Stone was quiet, but constantly warped the air around me like a sexual forcefield. I exuded with its power. It hadn't been phased by the juice I'd taken from it to heal Sarah from a bullet wound.

A jab in my ribs made me jolt and my drink toppled over my tray. Pink slush splattered in all directions and I cursed, turning to investigate the source of the disturbance, only to find a small boy pushing his nose between the seats like a hound.

"Jeffrey!" his mother cried. "I'm so sorry. I don't know what's gotten into him." She peeled the boy away from the seat and offered me an apologetic smile paired with a blush.

The attractive flight attendant reappeared with cocktail napkins and began dabbing away at the mess. The useless bits of paper greedily sucked up the slush and only served to smear the sticky ice across the plastic. She kept her fretting over the tray and didn't use the excuse to clean my jacket and cop a feel, which I found odd.

"Penny!" An elderly man with slicked-back grey hair and the biggest Adam's apple I'd ever seen pushed her aside. "Allow me to take care of this."

Penny frowned down at the sad little napkins and moved out of his way.

The man smiled and wiped the slush into a bucket. "I'm terribly sorry for this, Miss. Please, let's get you out of this seat. We have an opening in first-class. Please relocate to the front as our apology."

I balked. I'd gotten a cabin ticket for a reason. If I'd wanted first-class I could have simply asked for one. Heck. If I wanted this man's kidney he'd cut it out right now if I told him it'd make me happy.

But as I stared into his eyes, I saw a flicker of concern. I'd expected knee-buckling lust, which is all I'd ever gotten from men as of late. But this one seemed unaffected. I squinted, trying to make out any supernatural features. Aside from the piercing blue eyes, he seemed unremarkable. His friendly face was framed by kempt white hair, and his outstretched hand, waiting to guide me to my upgraded seat, was accented by wrinkles. An incubus didn't age, so that meant he was something I didn't understand. I frowned. I didn't like not understanding anything.

I pressed my lips together and squirmed out of my chair, trying to avoid the trickling pink droplets. The elderly man trailed behind me as I picked my way through the narrow aisle to the front of the plane, passing through multiple drapes as I escalated through economy and business class until I reached the front hatch where I'd entered. I glanced at it before considering the over-exuberant drape running past it, shimmering with different shades of blue as it moved with the subtle rolling of the plane that would take me to first class.

I peered over my shoulder and the elderly man smiled warmly and nodded. "Your new seat is 2B."

I swallowed hard. That was really their only seat left? That was right across from...

With a sigh, I broke through the fragile curtain, sending the metal rings clanging against the rail. A few passengers turned to glare at such a rude intrusion, until they saw who had entered. Even without the Blood Stone, I was my mother's daughter and could command a room with ease. Or in this case, a class. But with the Blood Stone, my power seeped through my skin and wafted over the crowd like noxious gas. Shoulders rolled back, backs straightened, and all eyes locked onto me.

All eyes…except for the guy sitting in 2A.

Nate, one of the many sons of the Incubus King, and my unwanted escort, took a long swig of his whiskey before exhaling with satisfaction and swirled the gold-tinted ice in his glass. I frowned, not because he was pretending not to notice I'd been forced into first-class, but because he drank whiskey like I did. Why'd he have to ruin a good thing with that smirk?

Finally, he acted surprised to have realized I was standing there while everyone continued to stare at me. He smiled his obnoxious, boyish smile and I returned his unspoken gloat with a glare.

Without a word, I stomped to my seat and plopped down with as little grace as I could muster, crossed my arms, and set my mouth into a pout.

"What's wrong, babe? Do I get under your skin?" he asked with a wicked grin that matched his father's, except I'd been fighting the fact that Nate stirred the prophecy within me. He didn't know that a rune across my stomach burned with need every time he was around, screaming at me that this insufferable human was one of my four… no. No fucking way was I going to accept that.

I glared at Nate, and then transferred my rage to the elderly flight attendant who seemed to be quite pleased with himself.

I crossed my arms. "Don't tell me you got that little boy to poke me?"

The old man bowed and offered me a cup of ice water in a

much nicer cup than what I'd received in economy. "Dear me, no," he said. "I can't control children any more than I can control anyone else." His eyes crinkled in another smile, this time hinting at some hidden joke I didn't get, before he shuffled to the back of the cabin and disappeared behind the curtain.

An exasperated sigh escaped my throat as I jerked down my armrest and glared at the unnecessarily large cup holder which had something still inside. I fished out a wadded piece of paper. Well-written calligraphy swirled through the scented paper with my name on it. Inside, the note anonymously invited me to dinner, followed by an address which I knew far too well. Ever since I'd inherited the d'Ange mansion, my grandmother's, then my mother's, and now mine. The handwriting suggested someone in my family was still here, but who? Dammit, I had to find out now.

This sucked. Just because I was going to New York didn't mean I had any intention of revisiting my inherited home. If I went there, I'd have to finally admit my mother was dead and I was ready to move on. I wasn't.

I glanced at Nate and he shrugged before turning back to his tablet and pulled a black headset over his tousled hair.

With a growl I crumpled the note and shoved it into my pocket. Dammit. My plan had been to go straight to Queens and look for Luke. Luke, the only reason I hadn't split in two when Sarah left my life for good. Luke… one of my supernatural four who deserved a place in my soul.

I gagged on the thought. How pathetic was I? Maybe going to a party in my own house would be a good idea. I glanced again at Nate, trying to see him as his father had asked me to. *A needed distraction until you find what you're looking for.*

He was hot, there was no doubt about that. But he was constantly joking and acting like he was twelve. Hardly my definition of sexy. But at this very moment he seemed almost serious as he focused on the movie playing on his tablet. His jaw went firm and his amber eyes remained steady on the screen until they flashed at me and I drew in a quick breath before looking away.

Maybe this wouldn't be so bad after all.

Nate didn't say a word when the elderly flight attendant followed us from the gate and crammed into the mid-sized elevator with us and twenty other people.

To my surprise, both the flight attendant and Nate positioned themselves as a barrier between me and the elevator's jittery passengers. Given that I literally oozed sexual energy, it was a much-needed precaution. Though the humans couldn't see it, a soft red glow hissed off my skin like steam and tickled their noses. They would twitch and flick their eyes, unaware of what was bothering them.

Three men closest to me started to arch their necks, trying to peer over my guardian's broad frames. The flight attendant sputtered a wet cough, driving the men back in disgust. He politely covered his mouth and excused his outburst while Nate wedged himself even closer to me.

I became acutely aware of Nate's body pressing against my chest. His warmth radiated through our clothes and joined with the ever-present radiance of my Blood Stone resting on my bosom. It felt right, somehow, even though it shouldn't have. Nate was one of the King's sons, and not Luke. Not the man Sarah had said was my soulmate and "reason to be." I shook my head. Both men sounded like a ridiculous fit for me.

Then I realized what felt so different about this moment. Nate wasn't his jolly, bad-jokes self. When the other passengers leered my way, his body would go rigid and he crossed his arms, trying to make himself as big as possible like a peacock. His head swiveled side-to-side, inspecting the crowded elevator for any sign of danger.

Likewise, the flight attendant set his jaw and widened his stance, as if he was readying himself to spring into action.

In spite of his age, the old man's broad shoulders and even wider forearms assured he was stronger than he seemed at first glance.

My hand rose to my chest, subconsciously pressing against the lump that was my locket resting underneath the leather, searching for comfort and strength. If I was in danger, I could protect myself.

The elevator released a loud screech and my skin went white-hot with fear. Sure, I could protect myself from a lust-crazed human, but I couldn't stop an elevator if it decided to go into free-fall.

The lights flickered and between the moments of illumination and darkness, I jolted upright and my chest went tight with fear. There, a woman in the very back, had her eyes locked on me and didn't seem the least bit concerned about the jerky up-and-down of the elevator. Instead, she waited for me to notice her gaze, and then she smiled, and *vanished.*

WELCOME HOME

Sonya

"Did you see that?" I hissed into Nate's ear.

The only indication that Nate had heard me was the slight twitch of his gaze. But he remained fixated, scanning the elevator for the threat.

Although what he could possibly do if we were in danger, I had no clue. How could we protect ourselves from a woman who could vanish into thin air?

I unzipped my jacket and let my naked hand scramble through the fabric to take the Blood Stone in a solid grip. The heat against my fingertips was soothing, but for some reason, it didn't feel like it was enough.

The passengers murmured and fidgeted, casting wary glances in my direction as the lights dimmed and the elevator screeched to a halt on the ground floor.

The second the doors opened, Nate took my wrist as if I were a child who he might lose at any moment and jerked me outside.

I suppressed a yelp, but didn't resist. Whatever was going on was way above my pay grade.

Nate continued to drag me along and I tripped at his heels while the elderly flight attendant silently followed. In a moment of wistfulness, I'd hoped we'd stop to get our suitcases, but Nate sped right on by the carousel with the bright blue numbers flashing our flight number and jerked me outside. Whatever had them so spooked, we couldn't stick around, especially not for my suitcase filled with my favorite heels and sad little mementos of Sarah which mainly consisted of strawberry daiquiri shakers.

Nate sped over the crosswalk and into the parking garage, only stopping when we arrived at what was apparently our ride. I stared at it. Really? A Chevy? One of the mighty incubus princes, human as he may be, wouldn't be caught dead in such a piece of junk.

To my surprise, Nate shoved me into the backseat like a piece of baggage and nodded to the flight attendant to take the driver's seat. Nate slipped in beside me and continued to scan through the windows as if he was a guard dog on high alert.

When the car gurgled to life and we puttered out of the terminal entrance way, everyone seemed to relax.

"Would someone mind telling me what the hell is going on?" I blurted.

The car jostled over a speed bump and Nate cast me an apologetic glance. "I'm not sure how she found us." He looked at his hands curling into fists in his lap. "You're not supposed to know about her."

I narrowed my eyes. "About who?"

He drew in a deep breath, held it as if whatever he was about to say was difficult to admit, and then expelled it with the words, "Your daughter."

I balked. A hundred thoughts flew through my mind, but none of them helped that statement make any sense. I'd never given birth, and if I did, I'd certainly remember it. "What the hell are you talking about?"

The flight attendant caught my wild gaze in the rearview mirror. Towering buildings cast us into a shadow, blocking out what little light the overcast skies offered. "There's a reason I look so old," he said. His eyes went hard and a flash of anger crossed his face. Then it transformed into resignation and he looked back to the street. "The price for your Blood Stone wasn't just a night with the King. You affected others, too."

I blinked, my chest constricting and my breath coming in short gasps. My eyes followed the wrinkled lines on his face. "What do you mean?"

Nate waved a hand dismissively. "You'll learn about it soon enough. For now, know that when you slept with my father and mother," he said with a surprisingly straight face, "you helped them create something they've been after for a very long time."

Something. Not someone, but something.

I knew that I had helped Silvia and Derek conceive, but that had been barely a few days ago. And last I'd checked, it took nine months to have a baby, and the girl we saw in the elevator had to have been at least sixteen.

"But—" I began, but Nate cut me off.

"It's not a *natural* birth, by any means. You are her mother, just as much as Silvia is."

Whoa. That was far too much to take in. I shook my head and groaned, leaning into the cigarette-scented seat.

The car eased to a stop and waited at one of the many traffic lights. There seemed to be a new light every two feet. I gazed out the window, hoping to be calmed by the sight of a tree or friendly face, but all I saw was a blinding sea of yellow paint. We were surrounded by an incessant number of taxis and I numbly wondered why they couldn't use a more attractive color.

"We'll make it on time," the flight attendant announced.

I shifted in the seat and peered over his shoulder, trying to match his gaze in the rearview mirror. "On time for what?"

He grinned as the arrow turned green and he rounded the corner, revealing a mansion in the middle of Manhattan. It towered over the street and I'd completely forgotten the bronzed statues decorating each pillar, each boasting stone women dancing around the edges of the roof, holding only bits of cloth and leaves to cover their bodies. Their grey eyes peered down at the street and glittered with joy as if they could see me. I scanned the clouds for rain, but couldn't see a drop.

Nate nudged me with his elbow. "Welcome home."

A DISTRACTION

Sonya

The second I walked inside the d'Ange mansion, I was hit by the scent of lilac potpourri. It was so much like my grandmother's perfume. I couldn't help but draw in a deep breath and let my memory spiral back to when she would greet me in the doorway and I'd run into her arms, wrap my legs around her waist and my tiny arms around her neck.

When I opened my eyes, my memory had become flesh. My grandmother stood in all her glory, even though she was well into her six-hundreds, she boasted the body of a twenty-year-old and a skimpy silk dress with a floral pattern complete with a slit running up her thigh. She smiled and spread her arms wide. "My Sonya," she purred with her familiar British accent.

Tears filled my eyes as I realized I somehow wasn't hallucinating, and my grandmother hadn't tragically died in the fire that killed her and my mother six years ago. My breath hitched. If my grandmother was alive, did that mean my mother had made it out too?

I staggered towards her and resisted the urge to fling myself into her arms as if I were a child again. Yet, when I saw her same healthy blush and her nonchalant smile, anger bloomed and found its way to my fists, curling them into balls as my shocked cry turned into a snarl. "Where have you been?" I hissed. "All these years, I thought you were dead!" My voice went shrill and my vision blurred with salty tears.

My grandmother's face softened and an array of regret and pain swept across her features. "I'm sorry," was all she said.

Nate rested a warm hand on my shoulder. I snatched away from his touch. "Where's mother?" I demanded. The impossible hope choked the breath from my throat and I staggered, waiting for an answer.

My grandmother crossed her arms over her chest as if to protect herself from the anger rolling off my skin. Because of the Blood Stone, my rage was a tangible thing sending waves of heat billowing through the room.

"Her death wasn't a lie," she whispered. "Please, Sonya." Her lips tugged into a forced smile. "Come inside. We've made a welcome party for you." Her smile widened, gaining confidence. "We should celebrate our reunion, my Sonya." When I didn't respond, she added, "It's what your mother would have wanted."

Jazz music lingered in the background and glasses clinked together like rain droplets hitting a tin roof. But I couldn't celebrate, not when the hope of my mother's survival dangled in the air, only to be snatched away again. "No," I said.

My grandmother pinched her eyebrows together and opened her mouth to speak. But I didn't want to hear her excuses. She'd lied to me and let me believe I was alone for six years. She didn't deserve a chance to explain herself. "Enough," I snapped. "I'm not joining your stupid party. In fact, I'm not going to be staying very long." Without a moment's hesitation, I rushed past her and resisted the magnetic pull of her lilac perfume. It sent comfort and warmth tingling through my chest.

Thankfully, the scent faded as I rounded a corner and stomped down the hall. Nate's soft footsteps followed and I didn't protest. I didn't really want to be alone, I just didn't want to face my grandmother. Not now, not like this.

When I didn't snap at him to leave, Nate quickened his pace so that he was only one step behind. I led us to the only place I knew to go: the library.

Once inside, the tightness binding my chest loosened and I could finally draw in a deep breath. The rows of ancient oak shelves housed hundreds of books and towered all the way to the ceiling. Cathedral arches with glossy, dark wood accented the trove of musty treasures and I couldn't help but smile. I took off my heels and let my toes curl in the softness of the plush rugs, heirlooms from Persia.

"Nice racks," Nate said, breaking the comforting silence with a crude joke.

I cast him a mournful look. "Really, Nate. Not now."

He quirked a smile. "Just trying to lighten the mood."

I rolled my eyes, but appreciated his effort. In spite of myself, I felt better already.

As I ran my hands across the shelves, drawing comfort from the long-seeded memories of my early childhood, Nate followed like a shadow. "So," he whispered, his voice sounding huskier and sexier than usual. "Why are you so interested in finding this man you know so little about?"

My heart skipped a beat. "My so-called-dead grandmother comes back to life after six years, and you want to know about Luke?" It made sense. Even if Nate couldn't feel it, if he was really one of my four, he was bound to Luke too.

He chuckled. "I'm not looking to dredge up family drama. But I *would* like to know why you've come to New York."

I could have told him to go screw himself, that it was none of his business, but the honest curiosity in his voice only made me want to open up. "Luke and I are connected," I said. "Sarah told me I should find him, and when I lost her, it felt like she'd died. It felt like…that was her last wish." I left out the part where my rune stopped responding to her. Whatever connection her and I had was now severed. It was time for me to find my four, but I wasn't sure if I was ready.

He scoffed and irritation prickled down my spine. "She didn't die," he pressed. "She lost her powers. That's all."

"You're human; what would you know of it?" I closed my eyes and leaned my cheek against the shelves for strength. "Becoming human is just as good as dead for a muse."

He sighed and came dangerously close. Just when I thought this was another joke, his warmth encased my body and he ran his nails over my arms, sending goosebumps over my skin ending with his fingers lacing over my knuckles. "And what do you think will happen when you find your mystery man?" His voice was a challenging whisper, daring me to say this was anything but a foolish errand. "What will you do then?"

What *would* I do? I'd hope for the impossible, that's what. I'd hope that this damn prophecy was true. That Luke was my a piece of my soul and could absolve me of my guilt and torment. Only true love could redeem someone like me, and how desperately I longed for absolution.

Nate's whisper sent shivers through my body. "I can't pretend to know what it's like to be a succubus," he said, "but I think what you need is to stop being so hard on yourself."

I shivered, unable to turn and look at him. Ignoring the growing tension, I shrugged him off and plucked a book from the shelf, pretending to be fascinated, even though I couldn't force myself to read a single word. I went stiff when Nate's warm hand fell on my shoulder.

"I don't need to feed," I said. "And even though you might think I'm worth it, I assure you, I'm not worth dying for."

He wrapped an arm over my collarbone, letting his fingers drape across my breasts and caress the Blood Stone. "That's why this is such a special opportunity. You can enjoy what I have to offer without damning me to death, all because of this delightful, red gem."

I blinked and peered up into his face. He smiled, and it wasn't that boyish smile to which I'd grown so accustomed, but the confident smile with perfect lines that could only come from being a son of the Incubus King.

"I hadn't considered that possibility," I admitted.

His finger ran up my throat and traced my lips. "Not even once?"

My lips parted of their own accord as his breath on my face sent goosebumps spreading across my arms. He tested my neck with his teeth and instead of pulling away, a delicate moan escaped my throat.

His tongue found my earlobe and then he whispered, "I may be human on the outside, but there are supernatural qualities I still inherit from my father."

My eyes grew with curiosity and a yearning inside of me responded to his promises. I pulled away, only to be secretly delighted when he grabbed my waist and forced me close. His stiff erection pressed into my hip and my breath hitched with anticipation.

Growling with victory, he laced his fingers through mine before taking me with a hungry kiss. The sweet taste of his tongue sent chills through my chest and made me yearn for more than just his mouth.

Then, at the worst possible moment, Luke's face popped into my mind. I jerked away from Nate and the lust in the air turned cold.

"What is it?" he whispered. His eyes glazed over with concern, but as he searched my face, he smirked. "You're thinking about Luke, aren't you?"

I expected him to be hurt, or perhaps jealous, instead he seemed to relax. "What is it?" I asked.

He grinned. "There's something… I don't know. This is going to sound weird, but it feels like it makes sense. I mean, you're a succubus. You're not supposed to be with just one guy." He shrugged. "Maybe I'm okay with sharing, as long as you can handle me when it's my turn."

While I was distracted by his honesty, his mouth ravished mine with new vigor and I squeaked in surprise. "No, Nate I—" My words were cut short as he thrust his hand down my pants and sent a surge of pleasure through every nerve ending as his fingers thrust inside. I should have resisted, but my disloyal body bucked underneath him and wanted more. The rune that responded to him, just astride my navel, burned with hot need. He was one of my four, one of my men that would fulfill my every need.

I closed my eyes, giving into the waves of hot bliss running through my insides. Nate gave a husky growl against my neck, sensing my acceptance, before sinking his teeth into my skin again, this time harder than before. The flash of pain was a delightful contrast to the pleasure and mixed its sweet tones in my body.

I hadn't even touched him, but the taste of his arousal wafted against my senses. My instinct screamed to drink it in, but instead, I redirected my focus and drew on the power of my Blood Stone. It ignited under my command, sending a bright flash and warm glow wafting through the room. My own cry of victory shuddered on my breath as I delighted in the assurance that I could have this, I could have him, without consequences. Without regret.

Nate ripped off my pants and pummeled me into the row of shelves and I grappled my fingers behind me for a handhold. Books toppled out of their organized piles and tumbled to the ground as Nate lifted me off my feet. I wrapped my legs around his hips and realized how badly I wanted a guilt-free night with someone who only wanted to take all my cares away.

He didn't hesitate. The elastic of my already thin thong broke as he clawed it aside. Likewise, I fumbled at his jeans and was delighted to see they were already unbuttoned. One pull on the zipper and his thick erection made a brief appearance before disappearing between my thighs. The supple skin found its target and thrust inside. I arched my back and hit my head against a shelf, but the pleasure slamming through me dwarfed the pain. Nate's desperate thrusts pummeled into me and didn't stop; it was as if he needed me right now as much as I needed him. Even when the pleasure spiked and I couldn't hold my orgasm any longer, and I quivered and contracted hard around him, he didn't cease. He kept going and flashed me a pleased grin at my shocked face, as if this was just the start. His mouth found mine and he continued to pound into me as he muffled my cries with his tongue.

A memory of his father taking my orgasms with ease streaked through my mind and I realized this is what he'd meant. His heritage. He could fuck me as long as he wanted, make me orgasm until I was screaming, and not even break a sweat.

He was definitely one of my four.

His lips broke away from mine as he watched my face, seeming to enjoy the expression of ecstasy and shock I couldn't control.

I hung onto him for dear life with one hand, and brought the other to my mouth for a firm bite. I'd already hit my climax three times, and he showed no signs of slowing. A deep ache I'd never felt before burned in my stomach and threatened to overwhelm me. I bit down harder and hoped I could muffle my own screams.

"Tonight, you're mine," he whispered confidently as he pulled my hand from my mouth. "Tell me that you're mine."

When I didn't respond, he slowed his thrusts to a soft in-and-out, giving me blessed relief, but keeping me on the edge of another cliff.

My lips parted and I realized it was true. In this moment, I'd do anything he wanted. "I'm yours," I breathed. The rune across my stomach hummed in approval.

He grinned and ran his fingers through the roots of my hair, just enough to get a good fistful before gripping and exposing my neck as I arched into the pull. He knew how to grab me without hurting me, and that just turned me on more.

"How do I make you feel?" he asked.

I closed my eyes and focused on the soft gyrating of his hips. My insides were so swollen and my wetness ran down the arch of my butt. Thankfully to be absorbed by my shirt instead of my poor grandmother's book collection.

"You overwhelm me," I admitted.

I forced my eyes open to blink at him through the red haze of my Blood Stone's power, and basked in his stamina. I didn't have to explain that as a succubus, men didn't last long with me. This was an entirely new experience.

He slowed his movements even more, just barely moving and forcing me to push my own hips to keep the sensation of his lust going. I'd never been pushed this far, and I didn't want it to stop.

His tongue slid across my neck until it reached my earlobe. Chills ran over my arms as it briefly went inside my ear canal. "Do you want me to keep going?" he asked.

Words were beyond me now. I gripped the shelves and pressed my thighs against his hips as I lifted myself up and down on his crotch. A pathetic whimper came out when I couldn't replicate the intense thrust he'd been doing to me a moment before.

He smoothed my hair and forced me to look into his eyes. "I want to hear you beg."

The bastard. But I wanted him, so I parted my lips and forced the words out. "Please," I whispered.

Nate leaned in closer, running his hand to the arch of my back and pulling me into his hard chest. "What was that?"

"Fuck me as hard as you can," I pleaded. "Fuck my brains out."

He smiled. "Yes," he said. "You understand now, poor succubus. You've always been the seductress. You've always melted men and given them what they needed so you could have your small bit of nourishment." He tilted his head sympathetically and pulled me up far too effortlessly. "But what have you ever gotten other than survival? What about overwhelming pleasure? What about being *taken*? Don't you want that?"

My eyes searched his, pleading for him to give me everything he'd just said. "Yes." I wrapped my fingers around his neck and hovered my lips over his. "Please, take me."

An evil smile spread across his face as he lowered me to the floor. I trembled as he pulled off my shirt, stopping only for a moment to rake his gaze over my runes. His eyes widened when he spotted his, the one that resonated with his own sexual energy he'd drilled into me. He reached out and grazed it with a gentle touch, making me shiver. "What is that?" he asked.

I smiled. "That... is a long story."

We didn't have time for long stories. Both of us panted with need and he twisted me onto all fours.

Nate thrust into me without warning and my insides exploded with the force. I cried out and didn't care anymore if someone heard. I'm a succubus. I have sex. My grandmother and her guests shouldn't be surprised, right?

Nate grabbed onto my hips and I knew I was in for the night

of my life. He pounded, going faster and faster as the slapping of my ass against his thighs told me I was going to be either raw or bruised by the time he was done with me. Each thrust sent a cry of agonized pleasure shuddering through me as I clawed my fingers through the plush carpet.

Then he leaned over my body and groped his fingers across my flat stomach, running across the runes before settling onto the one that pulsed with his heat, then instead of going for my breasts, his fingers ran down until they reached my clit. He circled the swollen flesh, sending flurries of fresh pleasure through me as he continued to move his hips, but gently, letting me savor the graze of his touch.

"Delicious," he whispered into my ear. "I want a taste."

To my shock, he pulled out and rolled me on my back, his kisses following the same path his fingers had taken until his tongue found my swollen folds. It felt so good it hurt, and I cried out when he kissed and rolled his tongue across my flesh.

I tried to squirm away, embarrassed by how engorged I was. So much raw pleasure, so much blood all in one place, it was unfathomable that he would find it attractive.

His hands latched onto my hips and kept me where I was. I was drained and unable to fend him off, and instead let my head fall to the carpet in defeat. I gripped my Blood Stone for strength, drawing in the power to help me survive this pleasure. He was so turned on by me; I could feel it lingering in the air and plucking at me like short electric sparks. But what amazed me most was how much sexual energy *I* was exuding. My necklace drank it up and fed it back into my core, as if repulsed I would waste it into the air.

Heat ran through my skin and when I saw the room was beginning to take on a blue hue, I looked down to Nate doing unimaginable things with his tongue. His eyes softly glowed with sexual energy, azure, like his father's, and it swarmed in his gaze as he pushed me to climax. It was so hot, to see him watching me while I exploded in his mouth.

He wiped his chin and grinned, satisfied with his handiwork. I, on the other hand, heaved, barely able to hold my head up.

"You're even more delicious than I imagined," he whispered as he drew himself over me. Gently, he pressed his erection into me, being careful not to overstimulate my impossibly swollen pussy.

He didn't look away as he gyrated. As his features softened I knew he was allowing himself to come to climax. It felt so intimate, far more than a fling with what was only meant to be a distraction. I couldn't pull myself away as he began to moan, the sound such amazing music to my ears. I felt so grateful for everything he'd given me that it made my heart pound to hear his pleasure. I latched onto his biceps and squeezed myself around his cock, hoping to strengthen his orgasm. I wasn't sure if I'd feel his ejaculation, everything was so hot already. But as he sped up, I knew there could be no doubt. I'd feel this one.

His eyes fluttered closed in bliss as he reached his climax. The veins on his neck bulged and heat exploded through my insides. I couldn't help but climax with him, the sensation and mere sight of him driving me to new heights of pleasure.

When the moment ended, I knew everything had changed. I wanted what I'd said in lust-drunkenness to be true. I wanted to be his. Not just tonight. For good.

Nate

Second of Four

Fucking Sonya had been a job, but after I'd done the deed, damn, she was more than a job to me. She'd unhinged something in me and I wasn't sure how much of it I could handle. As the son of an incubus, I could have sex as long as I wanted, control my orgasms with precision. Sonya was a new challenge, a succubus used to being the seductress. To see her vulnerable and the *need* in her eyes had made me feel something I'd never felt before. Not to mention, what was that damned rune? The moment I'd touched it… something in me had locked into place.

"And, what have you learned?" my father pressed, impatient to hear more of the triumph.

"Look, she's vulnerable right now," I snapped. "I don't want to do this anymore. Send someone else."

My father's deep chuckles filled my ears and I had the urge to jerk out the earbuds attached to my cell phone. But I needed him to agree with this. I had to get him to understand that I wasn't the right guy to find out Sonya's secrets… even though I was already too close to uncovering them all.

"Nathaniel," my father purred with mock concern, "is that guilt I hear in your voice? Or satisfaction?" He gave a soft mock-gasp. "Both?"

The moonlight trickled in my window and I stared at the motes dancing in the streak of light. "Send. Someone. *Else*," I said through gritted teeth.

"Look, son. You have a job to do, and you're going to put your sister above your unfortunate human conscience. Find out if Luke is what we think he is, and then we'll go from there. Got it?"

Right, Luke. He was another one, someone like me bound to Sonya and a power that was something so much greater than the Incubus King's plans for this world. I softly hit the back of my head against the wall in frustration. *No.*

"Sonya will understand," he continued. "This is for her best interest as well, you see? She'll be grateful when this is all said and done. If you care about her, you'll do as I say."

"Are you serious?" I said, not listening to the tiny voice in my mind screaming at me to shut up. Reminding me that my father was not *just* my father, but the most ancient Incubus on the planet and the King of a race I could never inherit. In his society, he didn't have to recognize me as his son. He could have just as easily killed me at birth rather than honor me with tasks, must less the task of seducing a succubus like Sonya.

"Tell me, son. What did one good fuck with her do to give you such ideas?" His voice turned mocking once again. "Did she laugh at you? Oh, is it better than that? Right when things were getting good, did she scream my name?"

I suppressed the growl rolling in the back of my throat and took a deep breath. It hadn't bothered me that he'd fucked Sonya first. But now, damn, it got under my skin. I didn't mind sharing her with men who deserved her, but my unholy father was not one of them. "Hardly," I said, trying to sound nonchalant. "I just —" I clenched my fists and squelched the tiny voice that was now shrieking like its life depended on it.

I knew I'd given Sonya the night of her life. I'd seen it in her eyes. That surprised me, knowing my father was literally the king of sex. I was human, and even if my Incubus heritage did wonders for my dick, there was no way I could have been the same. Realization wafted over me that for Sonya, she wasn't just turned on by a good lay. She'd felt my desire for her, my genuine concern. That's what she wanted, and there's no way in hell my father could ever have given her that.

I cleared my throat and tried to give my father something close enough to the truth to get him off my back. "I just don't want Sonya to get hurt."

"Touching," my father said. "Why don't you get some sleep and we'll talk about this when your head's screwed on straight. One of them, at least."

I gave one glance to the doorway, waiting any moment for Sonya to step through. I could feel her down the hall just three rooms away. I'd tasted her and her Blood Stone connected me to her desires, and right now, all she could think about was me. My dick got hard just thinking about it. With a blush, I realized my father was still on the phone. "Sure, *dad*," I said, making sure to emphasize in no way did I feel he deserved the title 'dad.' "Sleep sounds like a good idea."

The call ended with a click and a fluttering heartbeat approached me through the halls. I held my breath, waiting for the door to open, and to my surprise, it did. Sonya basked in the moonlight, already peeling away her silk robe. Her skin beckoned me, moist with her desire and her tongue flashing across her lips.

No way was I getting any sleep tonight.

THE DYING BLOOD STONE

Sonya

Waking up next to Nate was the best sight I'd had in many-a-morning. His naked chest gently heaved as he drew in deep breaths. I curled into his embrace, taking comfort in the strong, steady beat of his heart. It was different than when I'd awoken to his father and mother, and a part of me felt guilty to even be thinking of that now. But when I got past the perversion of it, I had to admit this was so much better. Nate had emotion and passion. My night with his father had only been lust and a touch of desperation.

I traced the arch of his nose, so like Silvia's, and drew a line down his solid jaw, a perfect resemblance of his father. His features held the best of his parents, and yet, as he drew his eyes open and sleepily blinked at me, I realized he was something they weren't. Was that his humanity?

His gaze held such softness I'd never noticed in him before. He was always turning things into a joke, never taking me seriously, and seeming to generally be a giant pain in the ass. But now, as I matched his gaze with an affectionate smile, I realized he hid behind those jokes because his father didn't approve of his humanity. How sad, to have to always hide who you were. I could relate.

"Good morning," he breathed. Then he slid his thumb across my cheek. "You shouldn't sleep with makeup on. I thought you were a clown for a second."

I glowered and pulled out of his grasp. Way to destroy the moment. "I'll get washed up," I mumbled, keeping the sheets tight to my body and taking them with me to the bathroom. Nate's chuckles followed me like gnats and I slammed the door to keep them out.

Sunlight streamed in through the glazed window and sent the luxurious features of the oversized bathroom into a scene of stark reality. The light revealed the stains from standing water across the delicate marble countertops, specks of ingrained dirt in the tile's grout, and my own makeup-streaked face staring back at me in the fogless mirror.

"What you lookin' at?" I snapped at my reflection and frowned. I snatched a pristine towel and began scrubbing my face.

"What was that, babe?" Nate's muffled voice sounded from the other side of the door.

I rolled my eyes. "Nothing!"

When the skin under my eyes retained the dark hue from my makeup, I lathered the damp towel with soap and went at it again. What was I thinking getting so close to Nate? Was I really that fucking desperate?

I sighed and drew back the stained towel, successful in my mission to scrub my skin raw. Fresh pink glittered at me in the mirror and a small wave of satisfaction warmed my chest. Then I looked down to my necklace. The Blood Stone's power swirled, but seemed different than before. I grabbed it and yanked the chain over my neck to get a better look. I popped the locket open and gasped.

The stone had turned blue.

"What the fuck is this?" I demanded as I burst out of the bathroom.

I hadn't bothered to put on a robe that was hanging on the back of the door and instead of answering, Nate smirked and eyed my naked body. "Looks like somebody wants seconds," he tilted his head. "Or to be more accurate, sevenths."

I yanked him out of my way and pushed him back onto the bed. "I'm fucking serious. Look at this." I dangled the Blood Stone in his face. "What did you do to it?"

He blinked, looking genuinely surprised. "What did *I* do?" His wide eyes rolled to look at me. "Are you serious? You know I'm human, right?"

I released him and he rubbed his arm as if I'd bruised him. When I saw the yellow hue bloom across his arm, I realized that I actually had. "Sorry," I muttered.

He shrugged. "Comes with the supernatural territory, I suppose."

Feeling silly, I slunk back to the bathroom and pulled down the robe to wrap myself. Having nowhere else to go, I went to the bedside and slumped beside him.

Nate wrung his hands before speaking. "So, what do you think that means?" He looked down at his hands, his voice turning guilty. "Do you think it takes so much power not to feed on me?"

I froze. Did I seriously just drain my Blood Stone for a single night with a human? My eyes widened as I cradled the gem in my hands. Its light clearly was waning. This was all my fault.

"I could have used this to say goodbye to Sarah," I said, more to myself than to Nate. "I'd planned to, actually. When some time had passed and she'd grown used to…"

"Being human?" he finished for me.

I nodded. Tears sprung to my eyes. "I didn't know this would happen. I've lost my chance to say goodbye." The thought of never being with Sarah again broke my heart into a thousand tiny pieces.

As tremors began to overtake my body Nate wrapped an arm around my shoulders and pulled me in. "Hey now, it's all right. It's like those fancy batteries you get at the specialty store, it recharges, right?"

"Regular stores sell rechargeable batteries," I mumbled.

He chuckled. "Okay then. Bad analogy. But still, don't sweat it, okay? If it's all out of juice, you can just go talk to my dad and—"

I arched my neck to stare at him. Even he seemed to realize what he was saying and clamped his mouth shut.

I looked away as my cheeks began to burn. "Yeah," I said. "Great."

DEMONSPAWN DAUGHTER

Sonya

The one nice thing about being back home was that there were random closets filled with adorable outfits just my size. All the women in my family were five-foot-five, busty blonde beauties. I don't know if our race came with some kind of precoded DNA for what is supposed to be the sexiest womanly form, or if Hitler's Arian fanatics had a play in our creation—I wouldn't have been surprised. Either way, it felt damn good to take a steaming shower and open the closet in Nate's room, pull out a red skirt to accent my hips, a puffy white blouse to show off my cleavage, and red shoes to draw the eye down my long legs.

After slipping into the outfit like a favorite glove, Nate offered an approving appraisal before I went for the door.

"Babe," he said, waving his arms out in amazement. His outfit consisted of tousled hair and the sheets I had thrown at him, all too thinly draped over his perfect body. "Seriously, you can't dress all cute like that and then just leave."

I offered him a wry smile. "Really? You want to go again?" I popped open my locket and let him have a long look at the withering stone. "You want to test how much more it can take? I'm in if you are."

He stared me down, and for a moment I wondered if he was seriously considering the risk. Then he put on his classic jokester smile and crossed his arms, letting himself fall back into the bed with a dejected sigh. "Sucks to be human. You have no idea."

I chuckled and gripped the doorknob, feeling a mixture of pity and longing, which was an odd combination. When I closed my eyes, I saw images of Sarah, my past, and Luke, my future. Nate wasn't in there, and shouldn't be. There was no room for a human in my life. Especially not one who was the son of the Incubus King, the only person I knew who could help me recharge the Blood Stone. Talk about your fucked up love triangles.

When I slipped outside, Nate didn't protest. One quick glance before the door closed showed me his eyes closed, looking asleep in his bed. I wondered if this was as hard for him as it was for me. But as I clicked my heels down the empty hall, it felt silly to believe this was anything more than a stroke of good luck for him. How many humans got to fuck a succubus and live to tell about it? I was probably going to be the topic of his boyish bragging many drunken nights to come.

The best way to get over a guy, especially one who was just intended to be a one-night stand but had somehow turned into something more, was to have a distraction. I chuckled, realizing that Nate was *supposed* to have been my distraction. Well, it had worked far too well.

I still needed to get to Queens, but first I needed to deal with my grandmother. I turned a corner and found myself walking to the sunroom, knowing that's where she would be spending her morning tea if she was still the woman I remembered.

Sure enough, there she was sparkling like an orchid misted with morning dew sipping from a darling porcelain cup.

Her eyes crinkled with delight when she saw me approach. Nothing about her seemed aged except for her eyes. They were blue and bright, but ancient and ever-so-slightly wrinkled when she grinned. "Sonya, my sweet," she said, putting her tea on the table with a soft *clink* and rose to embrace me.

I couldn't resist falling into her arms, enveloping myself with her lilac scent and letting myself be lost in the embrace of a loved one. I didn't have any left, except her.

She nuzzled my face like a kitten. "I'm so glad you could find it in your heart to forgive me. I have missed you so much."

I squeezed her tighter. "Why did you do it?" I wanted there to be a good answer to the question. Why had she let me believe she'd been dead? I'd not only had to grieve my mother all alone, but grieve my grandmother too even when she'd been alive all this time.

She pulled away, her face scrunching with regret. "I hated not telling you. But there was no choice. You never would have met *him* if I hadn't let you find your own path."

It was hard to swallow the lump in my throat. "What do you mean?"

She smiled, and then drifted about the sunroom trailing her fingers across the flowers. "Would you believe me if I told you?"

I frowned. "I've seen a lot of things. There isn't anything you could say that would surprise me."

She chuckled and wrapped her fingers around a rose just about to bloom. Her sparkling eyes found mine. "Your mother had a vision. She sacrificed herself to make that vision a reality, and if I had approached you before you met him, her death would have been for nothing."

Tears threatened at the edges of my eyes, burning like tiny

embers. I swallowed and kept them in. "How could my mother have a vision? We're succubi. We don't have such gifts."

Her eyes drifted to the necklace about my neck and she said, "There are exceptions."

My hand went to it instinctually. The locket hadn't gone completely cold, meaning it still had some power left. What warmth I could feel spreading through my fingers made me feel solid and in control. "You're talking about Luke, aren't you?" I clenched my jaw. "Why does everyone think he's so damned important? I've tried looking for him, and he's supposed to be somewhere in Queens. Instead of taking me there, Nate and the random flight attendant dragged me here." I growled and stomped to a wicker chair, ignoring the small snaps as I jolted into the seat. "Why *deter* me from such an important task, as it were?"

She shrugged. "Your mother's vision made it clear the path would be set once you had met. After that, making it come true would be entirely up to you. Nothing I could say or do could interfere." She pointed her index finger in the air. "However, I'm not going to let a demonspawn drain your soul before I've had a chance to make amends."

I scoffed. "That sounds like you. Who cares about my safety, as long as you've made amends?" I narrowed my eyes. "Demonspawn," the word trickled off my tongue. "I thought they'd gone extinct."

She shrugged. "It was bound to happen again. They usually appear after the Blood Stone is recharged. I'm not sure why, though. It is odd." Her ancient eyes locked onto mine as if searching for answers. "You wouldn't know anything about it, would you?"

I froze into the best poker face I could pull off. I loved my grandmother, don't get me wrong. But I certainly didn't trust her farther than I could...well, farther than a human could throw a boulder. If she was talking about my daughter, I certainly wasn't looking to give away that secret.

Instead, I shrugged and reached for the pot of tea. An empty cup with two cubes of sugar was waiting for me. I cracked a smile. My favorite.

After pouring myself a steaming bit of tea, I swirled the mixture with a miniature metal stirrer and took a sip. I sighed. Absolutely heavenly.

My grandmother frowned. "Those monsters in Seattle obviously haven't been taking good care of you. When's the last time you had a decent cup of tea?"

I shrugged. "My whims have centered more around Oreos and beer, to be honest."

She drew the back of her hand to her forehead in a mock swoon. "My poor dear. What have they done to you?"

Cradling the warm cup in my hands, my mood turned somber. "If Luke is so important, what happens when I find him? Won't he just run from me like last time?"

"Is that his name?" She smiled as if I'd told her a dirty secret. "I'd always wondered."

"Seriously, Grandmother. He's not affected by my powers. What should I do?"

Her gaze fell to my locket again. "It seems the source of his fear is dwindling."

With my hand warmed from my cup of tea, I drew it up to the locket and was shocked that the metal felt cool and smooth against my touch. I arched my neck down and popped the locket open. It was nothing but a weak glimmer and the edge had turned white like an infection.

I swallowed hard against the lump in my throat.

One last rush of power, and my Blood Stone would be completely emptied.

I'd grown accustomed to the ease of which the Stone let me forget the price that came with being a Succubus. I could use my powers to excess, go months without feeding, and generally just live my life. But without it, I'd have to go back to how things used to be.

That thought rolled dread through the pit of my stomach which was already cold and heavy as I wandered New York's streets. The sun beat down, all too cheerful and the crowds of teeming people all too energetic for my melancholy mood.

The blood continued to drain from my face, making me feel faint as I thought about having to go back to my old life. How could I live like that again? Killing innocent men who'd pledged to die for me? No matter how I tried to justify it, pretend they were willing sacrifices, my powers took out all choice. They were nothing more than thralls, and I was no better than the Incubus King or Zack who threw away women like empty Cheetos bags.

The lust-filled glances ushered my way from more than a few men purposefully bumping into me down the street made me wonder if I should take my grandmother's advice to heart. Her words tore through me, "Live as you're meant to live. In the midst of life, and the only one who can drink the nectar." She didn't understand why I'd retained my brief whiff of human morals. She assured me it was youth holding me back, something I'd outgrow. She'd always touted morality to me, but that meant feeding on those who were willing victims. Old enough to know what that meant, it didn't seem so moral anymore.

As I wandered the streets, I realized I was approaching a familiar sight. In my mindless meandering, I'd come upon a church like the one in Seattle where I'd spent so much of my childhood.

There was one paramount reason I had any sense of morality, I realized with a wry smile. That darned nun, Maxine.

Still, I couldn't tear myself away from the magnetizing pull of the deep reds and blues of the stained-glass windows. Maxine had been a mother to me even more than my own had been. All I wanted was to feel safe and secure like I had with her.

Without thinking, I wound my way up the stairs and swept into the shadows of the church.

A sharp snarl sent my teeth clacking the moment I stepped inside, followed by a pained shriek just behind my ear.

I twirled and my skin went hot as I drew on the Blood Stone out of reflex. The girl who Nate had said was my daughter was just beyond the doorway and clutching at her hand which was already scabbing over with oozing blisters.

"Damn it, mother," she hissed. Her voice hardly seemed to match her teenager's body. The rumble of it was deep and angry, as if from a much older woman who had been screaming for hours on end. "Of all places, you decide to wander into a church?"

I stared at her, waiting for her to make a move. She retreated a few steps and the bubbles across her arm sizzled as a fresh layer of pink webbed over it. The wound completely disappeared and the pained lines in her face eased.

"Who are you?" I breathed. My senses were on full alert. My instincts screamed that this was a wild, cruel creature I had no business being around. No way should I let my guard down or dupe myself into believing I was safe. I gripped my locket and readied myself to drain the last of its power if necessary.

The silver shimmer of her eyes reminded me of Silvia, but there was a red tinge that burned around her irises that weren't from Silva, Derek, or myself. I realized there was only one place she could have inherited such a flame, the Blood Stone itself.

"Mother," she said again, as if I were being ridiculous. "You don't recognize me?"

She straightened as if she'd been sitting too long and rolled her eyes in a way that reminded me of a bored teenager. Yet, those red-ringed irises belied any sort of innocence.

When I didn't respond, she jerked her chin at the Blood Stone in my hand. "You clutch at that as if it's not a parent to me too. Do you really think it'd ever hurt me?"

My blood turned cold as she smiled. It wasn't the sweet smile of a young girl I'd expected with a face like hers. The pointy, slightly upturned nose and dimpled cheeks made her seem like a doll. But there was an ancient, evil element that seeped through her pores like a nightmare. I swallowed hard and took a step backward into the church.

She rolled her eyes again. "You can't stay in there forever."

"What do you want?" I snapped. "Why are you following me?"

She feigned a hurt expression by plumping out her bottom lip. "I wanted to see my mommy."

"No," I said, taking extra effort to make sure my voice didn't shake. "You aren't human. I didn't know what I was bringing into this world, what Silvia really is."

I could no longer deny what this creature was. This was a Demonspawn. A tremor rattled up my spine as I realized what Silvia must be in order to birth a Demonspawn. Where there are spawn, there are fallen angels.

"Fuck," I whispered under my breath. I slept with an angel? No...nothing so awe-inducing. I'd slept with a *fallen* angel.

Just as my Demonspawn daughter was about to make a witty comeback, she recoiled with a hiss as if she were a vampire exposed to sunlight. Not that vampires existed. That's ridiculous.

With a snarl she fled, the loops of her sleeves flinging with her as she vanished into thin air. I landed my hands on my hips and tilted my head with confusion.

"Your daughter seems lovely," a smooth voice caressed me from behind.

I swirled and was face-to-face with the object of my desire for the past three months. My eyes bulged and my jaw fell open. "Luke?"

He grinned and his whole face lit up in a way that made me want to grin too. His body was covered this time by a loose shirt, but the ripples of his abs were insinuated as a breeze flirted and tousled his hair. "You know my name," he said, sounding pleased.

I numbly nodded. "Of course. I've been looking all over the country for you."

For a moment, I just stared at him. His face wasn't flawless, as I'd expected. There were tiny scars that lined around his eyes and his lips, as if he'd been cut as a child. My fingers went to them of their own accord. "Why have you been running from me?"

"I wasn't running," he said, his eyelids lowering. His hand drifted over my fingers. "I visited my mother and then she told me to lead you here. So that's what I did." His gaze went distant and wary, staring where my daughter had just been. "Now I see why."

I blinked a few times. "That doesn't make any sense."

He shook his head and wrapped his fingers around my wrist. "We shouldn't talk about it here. Come with me."

My instincts told me not to trust him, but a rune that had long been cold ignited to life, reminding me that this was one of my four. I could trust him with my life. Sighing, I followed him into the shadow of the church.

Luke took me into the depths of steep halls that bent low into the ground, leading us down into the crypt where I expected creepy skulls and skeletons. It was New York, they liked those kinds of things.

We were stopped by a guard on the way down, but when he saw Luke's face, he nodded knowingly and let us pass.

"What's down here?" My voice came out hushed as if we were in a haunted place and I didn't want to disturb the spirits. It was a church, but it felt like something else altogether. It felt like we'd stepped out of reality and into a whole other realm.

Luke had no such apprehensions and his voice boomed, echoing down the corridor which looked suspiciously modern. "We're on holy ground," he said as if he'd invented the place himself and spread his arms wide.

I stifled a giggle and found myself already liking him. "Is that so?"

He nodded matter-of-factly and led me to a steel door which also looked terribly modern and ruined the creepy, ancient vibe of the place I was jiving with. "Didn't you see how demon-chick couldn't come inside?"

I narrowed my gaze. "Sure. But I also saw her run in terror when she saw *you*." A hint of distrust found its way into my voice. "Why was that?"

He shrugged as if women ran in absolute terror from him all the time. "Beats me." Without another word, he turned to the pad next to the door and pressed his thumb against it. The door unlatched and eased open with a hiss as if the room had been pressurized.

"Where the hell are we?" I demanded and resisted against his tug to pull me inside.

He gave me a sideways grin. "It's much easier if I just show you."

Curiosity battled with fear of the unknown. It hit me that no one knew where I was. I hadn't brought my phone. I was underground with my supposed soulmate, trapped inside because my Demonspawn daughter could be waiting to rip my throat out if I tried to leave, and now I was about to walk into a pressurized "holy" room with who knows what the hell else trapped inside.

Curiosity won and I found my feet echoing Luke's steps into the room which smelled like honey and roses.

ANGELSTONE

Sonya

A small crew greeted us once we'd made our way deeper into the bunker. They seemed familiar with Luke and didn't give me more than a curious glance. Half of them played cards while the rest exchanged glances over the tops of dusty old books, their phones lifeless black bricks on the granite countertops. I guessed bunkers didn't make good wifi hotspots.

Then I realized what was missing, what was striking me as odd and *wrong*. I wasn't sexually attracted to Luke, and nobody was even a little bit interested in me. They were all young men with thin t-shirts straining over bulky muscles like they were in some kind of photo shoot for hunks'a'licious. Which was immensely odd, because the stronger the male, the more he should be attracted to me, but after one look they'd all but lost interest. I jerked my locket from underneath my blouse and ripped it open. The stone still pulsed blue as it had before. It wasn't drained.

I closed the locket, still perplexed. Even if it had been

drained, I was still a powerful succubus. These were all men ripe for the taking. What the hell?

"We can talk in here," Luke informed me. He waved me inside a dim room and seemed completely oblivious to my dilemma.

Unease sent bile up my throat. I slipped inside and was strangely grateful when Luke closed the door and we were alone. It unnerved me being around so many strong men I couldn't control with my pinky.

He gestured to the sitting area which was complete with decadent fruit and cubed cheese. I popped a grape in my mouth and tried to relax.

"I don't know what I am," he began, "but I'm not human."

"No shit," I murmured. "Sarah said you'd had your heart ripped out and it fucking grew back. I sure hope you're not human. Otherwise you're Frankenstein's monster."

He snapped a grape from the vine and offered it to me, for the first time giving me a glimmer of attraction behind his sparkling eyes. "Do I look like a monster to you?"

I refused to take the bait and plucked my own grape from the platter, popping it into my mouth and chewing defiantly. "No. But I have a question," I said after I'd swallowed the morsel and deliberately ignored his question, "why lead me on a chase? You knew I was looking for you, right?"

He nodded. "You and everyone else. I couldn't trust you not to turn me over to that bastard you call your king." He snorted with disdain. "If you saw what he really looked like, you'd be fucking disgusted with yourself for ever sleeping with him."

"How do you know I slept with him?" I asked defensively.

He grinned. "I didn't until now."

I scoffed and leaned back into my seat. "Why'd you bring me here?" I demanded, flustered.

"I told you. My mother told me to lead you here. I didn't understand why until now. That daughter of yours had nothing good planned for you and it's my job to protect you from her."

"You didn't lure me here. I came on my own."

He chuckled. "Oh, really? I'm sorry, but no. I lured you with this." He held up a silver chain that glittered in the light. "It calls your destiny to you. I figured the muse would pick up on it. I made sure it knew I'd be heading to New York."

I went silent. So he knew our destinies were intertwined. Hearing him say it aloud was odd and personal, yet he didn't seem perturbed in the least. His eyes watched me, patient and kind. It wasn't as if he wasn't attracted to me. I could sense something there. But without the assistance of my powers, it was all a mystery.

"Why aren't my powers working?"

He shrugged. "There's no sex in heaven. It's a mortal's gift. It's meant to be fleeting and precious, just like any other mortal pleasure." He nodded to the walls. "This is a piece of heaven. A very tiny, minuscule piece, but enough to change the supernatural laws once you're inside."

I followed his gaze and scrutinized these so-called heavenly walls which were lined by seamless mirrors. Seeing nothing out of the ordinary, I bounced to my feet and made my way to the mirror. I grazed my fingers across the surface and gasped at the realization. It wasn't a mirror. It was a sheet of pure crystal, or was it diamond?

"What the hell is it?" I breathed.

He chuckled. "You're brazen to curse in the presence of angelstone."

"Angelstone?" I repeated the word as if that would help me wrap my mind around it. Then I registered that I'd just been insulted. "Who cares if I curse? It's just a word. Just a sound humans created to express distaste. It holds no meaning."

His jaw went taut. "Words are the most powerful thing in the universe. The entire cosmos was born by a single word. The stars, the ocean, life and death, were all born of *words*."

I had no response for such philosophy. What did I know of the creation of life and the universe? What did I care?

My fingers grazed the cool, silk sheet of angelstone. I found myself dropping my hand to my skirt and clutching the trim-line, my fingertips feeling chilled. I was never chilled.

I turned and shot him a playful grin. "A gentleman is supposed to offer his coat when a girl gets cold."

Luke peeled off his shirt without hesitation and offered it to me. I chuckled. "I didn't mean the shirt off your back. That's a whole different level of sacrifice."

He grinned and dangled the cloth between his fingers. Even amidst the presence of angelstone, seeing his body again shot pleasure through me. Whatever had kept the air cold between us slowly melted, leaving something sweet and delicious on the tip of my tongue.

I approached to take his offering, grateful to have an excuse to examine his muscular physique. He was an amazing specimen. Most supernatural men had an agonizing level of perfection. Even Nate. I thought I liked that, until now. Luke's skin wasn't porcelain like a doll, but rough like a human's. The hairs on his arms were white as if he'd bleached them, and tiny scars lined his whole body. I found myself unable to resist the urge to trace my finger across some that were still pink, as if trying to heal.

"Detective Anderson's handiwork," Luke admitted.

I jerked my hand away, not realizing that I'd been stroking the outline of his abs. "I thought you healed?"

"I do. But a small mark always stays behind." His hand drifted to a red line up the center of his chest. "I prefer it that way. I never want to forget why I want to kill him."

Realization hit me. "Why are you on some blind mission to lead me to 'holy ground' by your prophetic mother? You should be tracking that bastard after what he did to you." And Sarah, I added in my thoughts.

He smiled. "Because the end of the world takes precedence."

"End of the world?"

God. I sounded like some blonde bimbo. Which in this case, I was.

"Yeah. It's real." His eyes fell to my Blood Stone. "And you're going to have to get rid of that, for starters."

My hands clutched it defensively. "Are you kidding? Do you know what this is?"

His cheeks pinched as if he'd tasted something bitter. "I know exactly what that thing is. It's entombed evil. It needs to be destroyed."

I shook my head. "Hell no! This is the only thing that keeps me from killing people. Without this, I'm just a walking murder weapon and I can't do anything about it." My cheeks flushed with the unspoken certainty that I never would have experienced Nate without it, and he'd opened up a whole new world. One that questioned my desire to be with my so-called soulmate.

Luke's eyes narrowed, but he didn't make a move to snatch it from me. Instead the tension in his shoulders eased. For some reason, the pretense of "not giving a damn" made me bristle. I crossed my arms and shifted my weight to my hip. It probably made me look even more the blonde bimbo, but I was past the point of caring.

He snorted a laugh. "Look, don't get all prissy on me. We've got a lot to do."

"Like what?" I snapped. "All I'm interested in is making sure I don't need to kill people, which means either you help me or I go back to Derek and Silvia."

I wasn't sure what I'd expected to happen when I met my soulmate, but it wasn't this. He was supposed to fall madly in love with me, sweep me off my feet and nourish me with as much sexual energy as I could want. I wasn't supposed to have to go back to killing, or go back to bartering with the Incubus King to screw his wife and spawn demon babies.

Luke openly laughed at me, making my blood boil. "You already gave Derek what he wanted. You tipped things over to some dangerous dark scales by unleashing a Demonspawn on earth. Now they'll want your head on a pike. Your daughter is the first on the list who wants you dead."

Did he mean that literally? I sure hoped not. "Why would my own daughter want to kill me?" My words came out defiant, even though I'd seen the cruel gleam in the Demonspawn's eyes. She didn't look like she'd blink twice to lop my head right off my body.

Instead of responding, he gingerly sat on the plush sofa and reached under the maple table. A soft rustle sounded as he drew out a small box and cradled it in his lap. His face rose and his eyes met mine. The expression made me soften. There was something in his eyes I hadn't expected. There was hope, but also fear and dread. "It's better if I show you," he said, seeming to force the words out.

Suspicious, but curious, I eased into the seat beside him. "And that is…?"

His hand caressed the silver box as if it were the greatest treasure in the world. "Some would call it Pandora's box." He flashed me a grin. "To me, it's just the place I keep my soul."

My eyes dashed away from his magnetizing gaze. There was definitely attraction in it now. Electricity zinged in the air between us and my cheeks burned with the inappropriate thoughts that were springing into my mind. For some reason, I felt like Nate would approve of this. I could almost hear him in the background, telling me to get it over with so I could go share his bed again. "Sounds mysterious," I said.

He eased the chest open and my eyes were glued to the lid,

dying to know what someone's soul would look like. To my surprise, a diamond rested inside. I chuckled. "Your soul is my new best friend."

He reached for me and my curiosity made me still. He took my hand and he guided my fingers to the stone's surface, closing his eyes as my skin grazed the glass. Emotions and memory surged after a moment of contact. I jerked, but his grip tightened, keeping my fingers pinned.

Memories infused me like a hundred ghosts taking claim of my mind. Images of a woman, fleeting feelings of being trapped in the dark. Crying. Torture. Detective Anderson ripping out my heart and then I was looking into my own eyes, frozen in a loop looking into my eyes, into my eyes, into my eyes...

The world snapped back to reality the moment my hand was freed from the diamond. I gasped for air and crawled to the other side of the sofa. "What the hell was that?" I squeaked. The memories continued to flood. They were incoherent and massive. My eyes darted as fleeting glimpses of shadows sprinted across my vision. My head jerked at every new voice that droned in the distance, every sharp cry of Luke's suffering at Detective Anderson's hands.

Then a deeper memory unfurled, one no human would ever remember. At first I thought it was one of the memories of Luke as a child, trapped in the basement when his mother had locked him away for "training." But Luke was much younger than that. Much, *much* younger.

I was inside a womb, just conceived by an angel father. No, not one... but three. Two angels and a... some supernatural I couldn't name. Conceived with the power of a prophecy's blessing to combat the reign of terror that would come for this world. To save a conflicted succubus from darkness. To save the world from destruction. To save *me*.

The small room came back into focus. My eyes found Luke's

and blurred with tears. "You're…" I couldn't say the word. It wasn't possible.

His eyes went wide and hopeful. "Did it work?" he whispered. "Only you can see what I cannot. Please, tell me what you saw."

I realized now why he wanted me to be linked to his destiny. It had nothing to do with romance or love. He simply wanted to know what kind of supernatural creature he was. He had no idea. Angels who hadn't fallen didn't breed, so how could he know he was one of them? How could he know that all the rules of natural order had been broken to conceive him in order to save the world?

Rage filled me the moment I realized his selfishness. "How dare you!" I snarled and slapped my hand across his face as hard as I could. His face lashed to the side and his lip burst open, spraying blood across the floor. Being a succubus at full strength, he was lucky I didn't break his neck.

The sight of blood didn't deter my rage. I slapped him again, sending him sprawling to the floor. "How dare you force such magic on me without my consent!" I was angered he'd done something like that to me, but the truth was I was hurt. I had wanted him to love me. I'd wanted this fairytale of intertwined destinies to result in absolution and explosive, magical sex. I was wrong.

He groaned and tenderly wrapped his fingers around his dislocated jaw. He squeezed his eyes shut as he popped it back into place with a muffled cry.

I snorted. Served him right. The angelic bastard.

Without giving him a chance to recover, I stormed out of the room and down the hall back the way we'd come.

The men outside shot from their chairs the moment I smashed the final door open. I probably could have walked out without a fuss if I hadn't made such a scene, but I was pissed off.

A small glimmer of glee spread through my chest when they

went for their weapons. They wanted to come at me? Fine, let them try. I needed an outlet for this rage.

My vision tinted in red as I drew from the Blood Stone. It was low, but it had plenty left to deal with these punks. Inferno spread through my limbs and filled me with energy.

The humans' eyes went wide.

One reached out his hand with disbelief. "This is holy ground," he said, as if to himself.

"So?" I smiled and drank in their delicious fear. "I'm not a demon. Just a succubus."

Recovering from their shock, the others readied their weapons. I crouched before launching myself at them like a bowling ball going head-first into a bunch of plastic pins. They scattered the moment I blurred into them, but not fast enough. I caught two by the belly, my fists putting the full weight of my momentum and force into the blows. They crumpled and I swiveled to deal with the last four.

Luke's lip curling into a snarl and a steel bat filled my vision before it bounced off my head and the world went black. The almighty succubus, wielder of the Blood Stone, soulmate to angels, taken out by a freaking *home run.*

IT'S NOT OVER

Nate

"What do you mean you don't know where she is?" my father's voice on the other end of the line roared. "Go find her, you idiot!"

If I'd thought the King's voice had been deafening, then hearing the silence engulfing me while knowing his unending rage was about to meet my face in a few hours was far worse. I couldn't do anything but keep the phone pinned to my ear as sweat ran down my neck long after the call had ended. The King was coming to New York? What would happen to me if I didn't have Sonya when he got here?

Panic rose in my gut like a swarm of bees and I forced myself to lower the phone and tuck it in my pocket. The room was dark and empty without Sonya in it, and I cursed myself for getting so attached to her after one night. But *damn*, what a night.

I readjusted my pants which strained at the zipper just thinking about it and began gathering my gear. I grabbed my heat-sensing goggles, my GPS tracker, and a small golden cross.

Because, couldn't be too careful when a Demonspawn was on the loose.

A sharp knock at the door made me gasp and I clutched my chest. "Damn. What?"

The door cracked open and Sonya's grandmother peered inside. I narrowed my gaze. I'd much rather be talking to Pete, the Incubus who'd gotten too close to the Demonspawn and aged like a mortal. He at least knew what we were dealing with. Not this ancient succubus who probably didn't give two shits about her granddaughter.

"I just wanted to check if you'd heard from Sonya," she asked. She was a powerful succubus, as any of the d'Ange family were, and I shook off the effects of her powers with a degree of effort. "How the hell should I know? Sonya and I aren't that close."

She gave me a knowing smile. "My destroyed library would suggest otherwise."

Heat ran up my neck. "Yeah, well. She's not here."

She eased inside the room, shutting the door behind her. "I can see that."

Still organizing my gear, I retrieved my last but most important piece of equipment. My pistol.

The cool metal gleamed in the retreating sunlight from the draped curtains. I popped open the barrel and checked the rounds.

Sonya's grandmother didn't seem affected. If anything, she was more intrigued. I inwardly cursed myself. Of course a succubus would like a bad boy with toys.

"Calm down," I said with a smirk and kissed the pistol. "If a succubus is going to take my life, it's going to be your granddaughter."

She winked. "Of course. Let's go find her."

BAD LUCK

Lilith

The first time I'd seen my mother and that damned angelic bastard had ruined it.

"She hates me," I said to myself and pounded the heel of my palm into my forehead. "She fucking hates me!"

I allowed myself to scream with angst, then tried to rationalize my emotions. "Give yourself a break," I said into the mirror. "You're only three days old."

My green eyes and red-rimmed irises stared back. No way could I pass as human, no matter how I'd tried to change my appearance. I was a Demonspawn. What use were my powers if I couldn't even decently hide effectively in public?

There was no way I could contain my rage, so I shoved my knuckles into the mirror and shattered it into a thousand pieces.

"That's bad luck for seven years," my father's voice said.

I rolled my eyes. "Shut up, *dad.*" I turned to glare at him. "What the fuck are you doing here?"

He clicked his tongue and eased into the room. "Such language. Don't be a bad girl."

I crossed my arms and glowered. "I'm a demon. I'm entitled to be bad."

He stroked my cheek and smiled. The fondness in his gaze melted away my rage. I knew he'd been desperately doing all he could to conceive me. My mother meant the world to him, and my father had done some pretty terrible things to make her his. I knew he'd do anything for me as well. "Sorry," I said, my shoulders lowering. "I'm just frustrated."

His thumb continued to stroke my cheek, but I saw his jaw tense. "Is it about Sonya?"

I nodded. "The angel's got her."

His hand fell and his flush of rage wafted through the room. My shoulders shot up to my ears again, but this time out of fear. I may have been a powerful and feared Demonspawn, but I was just a newborn. The Incubus King created me and could smother me out of existence with a snap of his fingers.

He must have gotten ahold of himself, because the room cooled and he shot me an apologetic glance. I relaxed. "That's all right," he assured me. His gaze turned to the window and he peered out over the city. I had a perfect view of the cathedral from here, the place where the angel had taken my succubus mother. I wanted to meet her, and I'd tracked her all the way here trying to do just that, but she was never alone.

I pressed against his shoulder and stared with him. "Do you think she'll come out?"

His arm wrapped around me and made me feel safe. "She has to, my daughter."

I didn't know his plans, but I imagined we had very different reasons to see Sonya again. My cheeks went hot and I refused to look up at him. He wanted something from her, and I was afraid it wasn't anything good.

HELPLESS

Luke

I felt like the biggest asshole to walk the earth. Sonya's limp body sprawled across the white marble floors and my uncles all watched me with expectant stares. They knew I was bringing a succubus into their territory, which was why they'd insisted I bring her here, to the fucking bunker of angelstone. But now, seeing the purple bruise forming at her brow, I knew it'd been a mistake. She meant something to me that I couldn't explain. A connection stronger than heaven or hell spanned between us and stretched fingers out into the world calling to other pieces of my soul I'd thought lost. I couldn't let anything bad happen to her, but I was doing a bang-up job of that.

"What?" I snapped and rested the bat across my collarbone. "You wanted me to just let her beat you all to death?" The truth was, I'd been afraid for *her.* I kept my chin raised in defiance, hoping my uncles couldn't sense the truth. She was powerful, but the Angelstone would have drained her too quickly. My uncles were stronger than they looked. Even if she'd caught them off guard, they would have won in the end… and then she'd be dead.

"She needs to trust you," Uncle James said, breaking from the row of his brothers. They all looked my age, and if my mother hadn't warned me that they weren't human, I wouldn't have believed we could have been related.

"Yeah," I said, "you should have thought of that before you made me bring her here. The angelstone messed with her head."

Uncle James stomped up to me and laid a heavy hand on my shoulder, making sure I was looking him in the eye before he spoke. "Do you understand what's at stake, nephew?"

Before I could retort, the damn devil himself waltzed into the room.

"Well, well, well…" the Incubus King said as a smirk played across his flawless face. "Looks like you've made this easy for me."

My uncles reacted before I could, blurring and drawing the powers of the angelstone into their movements. I still didn't know what I was, if I was capable of more powers than just regenerating my flesh. I could do nothing but watch with awe as they did what they couldn't do with Sonya and went full-force against the Incubus King. His life wasn't important, and in fact, he was the enemy.

The angelstone affected him, but not enough to keep him from moving so fast he was a blur. He snatched Sonya from the ground and then a painful snap sounded as he broke my wrist.

"You're coming with me," he commanded.

I fought back with a snarl, trying to yank my limp arm free. Pain shot up my elbow but I ignored it, having been well trained by Detective Anderson's torture.

My uncles came after us, but they weren't fast enough. Pain blurred my vision as I was sped out of the cathedral's bunker and into the sunlight.

Away from the holy suppression of angelstone, the pain melted away and all I could feel was the intense desire to please the man with a death grip on my wrist.

He flashed me a smile, and glanced at my uncles swaying at the cathedral's doorway.

"Remember, Luke. Remember who you are!" Uncle James shouted.

The Incubus King hefted Sonya over his shoulder and I numbly followed. A part of me wished I knew who I was so that I had something to hold onto. Instead, the city's sunlight seemed to dim around the Incubus King and all I could do was follow in his footsteps, somehow feeling that my life was about to change in a terrible, amazing way.

CAPTIVE

Sonya

Raw desire woke me from my concussion-induced coma. Luke, naked and beautiful, peered down at me through the canopy of his eyelashes. His lust hit me like a blow and I curled onto my side, trying to douse the awakening of the second rune that recognized Luke as one of the four… but something was wrong.

We must have moved out of the range of angelstone, for the force of his lust pushed all thoughts out of my head. I'd never felt this drunk on lust before, except maybe when I'd been around the Incubus King.

I curled deeper into myself. Luke righted me and pressed my shoulders to the ground. He eased himself against my underwear. "I want you," he breathed. He moved, his erection rolling over my clit, sending pleasure awakening between my thighs. "I need you," he corrected.

A part of me liked being woken up like this, but it was strange. The Luke I'd gotten to know, however briefly, was in full control of his body. This one groaned like a madman, unable to think of anything but shoving himself inside me. Images flitted into my head, a rare extension of my powers when a man was fully invested in having me. It usually took weeks of preparation to get a man this engrossed into the fantasy that I could read his thoughts. Something was definitely wrong.

I battled against the force of lust, and his physical weight. He refused to lift away from me and his fingers grappled at my underwear. "Wait," I said, hesitating to enjoy his unexpected pleasure.

I held power over men, and their lust gave me life. Luke and I were meant for one another, we were meant to have sex that sent the stars reeling, but as his dick slipped under the fabric and squeezed through my body, I knew it wasn't supposed to be like this.

My head ached from the metallic bat that had rung my skull, the one that *Luke* had beamed me with. But I recovered from injuries with impressive speed, and sex only made my recovery faster. But this time, I wasn't able to drink in his lust. The sweetness of it kissed the air, but it lingered, as if it was something foreign and I had no knowledge of how to take it in. It slithered until it found my necklace and the heat of it burned my chest. Relief pricked my thoughts, glad that at least my necklace could drink what I could not.

Luke rocked against my body and I closed my eyes. I didn't know what would happen to an angel who fucked me. But why was he taking me? Where were we, if not in the bunker lined with angelstone?

I forced my eyes open and tried to gather a sense of my surroundings. Luke continued to groan on top of me, grabbing my breasts and squeezing. He was lost in the ecstasy, and a part of me wanted to join him. But there was no way I could shake the feeling of wrongness that lingered like a stench.

Then, I realized what it was. We weren't alone. My eyes found their silhouettes in the darkness, and I knew, without a doubt, that Derek, the Incubus King, was here. The form beside him I thought might be Silvia, or even my Demonspawn daughter. But when the light shifted and Nate's furrowed brow came into view, my breath hitched.

They watched in silence as Luke pummeled into me. I glared at the Incubus King, knowing that somehow he was manipulating Luke into doing this to me. Why would he want Luke to have sex with me? And why was he freaking watching?

When the Incubus King smirked, I shifted my gaze to Nate. His cheeks burned red and he cast his gaze to the ground, as if ashamed. Here was one of my four... standing by while Derek used me... used us. We were supposed to be a team. I didn't know how I knew that, but a voice inside of me screamed that Nate shouldn't just be standing there.

I thought they'd watch us the whole time until Luke was done. But Luke slowed, his eyes glazed over as if he didn't even know where he was anymore.

Derek scoffed and approached, resting his hands on Luke's shoulders. "Stop resisting. Finish it," he commanded.

The blue haze that drifted from his lips tinged Luke's nose. Luke's whole body convulsed and his dick throbbed inside of me, growing even bigger than before.

I hissed and snarled at the Incubus King. "What are you doing to him?" I demanded.

Derek ignored me, leaving us and Luke resumed his thrusts. I'd gone raw and groaned at the ache. I wasn't turned on by this; I was pissed off. My body wasn't complying to the supple wetness of enticement I usually enjoyed.

"There's got to be another way," Nate insisted, for the first time taking a step into the light and making my heart skip a beat that perhaps he hadn't abandoned me completely.

"You're the reason this is necessary," Derek retorted with a sneer.

I snapped my gaze to Nate and hoped that the question mark was painted across my face. What did he mean he was the reason?

The answer came with a burning heat that spread across my chest. Luke's passion flooded into me and this time, I couldn't help but groan with the sensation of his pleasure. His lust, no matter how forced, still found its way through my body and filled my Blood Stone, bringing it back to the fullness of life. Luke could power my necklace, and for some reason, the Incubus King wanted that to happen.

After a shower and a very, tender, moment of healing my raw skin with power borrowed from my Blood Stone, I wrapped a towel around my chest and made my way to Nate.

He was waiting for me in the bedroom, his face red with shame and anger. I'd never seen him like that before, and for a moment lost my resolve to rip him a new asshole.

"What the fuck was that?" I demanded.

Nate refused to look me in the eye. He stared at a spot on the wall and the muscles on his jaw rippled as he clenched his teeth.

I stomped to his side and gripped his chin, forcing him to look at me. His eyes were pained and it was difficult for me to keep his gaze. "Nate, I need to know what's going on." To my surprise, my words were softer than I'd intended.

He peeled my hand from his face and wrapped his fingers through mine. His gaze fell to my necklace. "The angel would never have charged the Blood Stone for you without our intervention," he whispered.

I stiffened. "You know what he is?"

He nodded. "Derek told me."

Which meant he'd known all along who and what Luke was.

I growled and curled my arms over my breasts as I sat beside him on the bed, taking my turn to stare at the wall. "Why didn't Derek just charge it himself?"

Nate scoffed. "He'd need Silvia for that. And she wants nothing to do with him until Lilith has returned."

I peered at him from the corner of my eye. "The Demonspawn?"

He nodded. "Yes." He lowered and stared at his hands. "Your daughter."

I sighed. "Look, I don't know why he found it necessary to *force* Luke to fuck me. That was just messed up." I narrowed my eyes. "He's... important to me. I'm supposed to have sex with him, but not like that. I didn't like it."

He rubbed his forehead. "I'm sorry, Sonya. If there'd been another way—"

I punched him on the arm and he grunted. "Another way? There *was* another way! And why does he give two shits if I have a charged Blood Stone or not?"

He growled and shot to his feet. "Look, you proved that you can help him create Demonspawn. He wants more." A shiver overtook his body. "He wants a fucking army."

END OF THE WORLD

Luke

Pissed wasn't a strong enough word to describe how I felt. After finally gathering my uncles and luring Sonya to the bunker, I'd still lost everything.

I rapped the chain of my handcuff across the bed frame and tried not to let the rising panic take hold. After years of torture and imprisonment by one certified nutso named Detective Anderson, my mind was having a field day sending memories fluttering through flattened scars. I couldn't help but relive the agony of Anderson's blades slicing me open, his forceps ripping out my organs… his hand extracting my heart.

A soft hand brought me back to reality with a jolt. "Hey," a female voice whispered, soothing me.

I blinked and thought it'd be Sonya standing over me. The soft, sensual voice was so much like hers, and her touch genuine and kind. But when I saw those red-rimmed irises framed with green staring back, I reeled against my chains.

She lurched away from me, hurt flashing on her face. "Hey,"

she said again, this time the lilt in self-defense. "I'm not going to hurt you."

She hadn't sounded like this at the church. Perhaps the holy ground had damaged her voice box just like it'd sent boils across her skin. Or, perhaps, it exposed what she really was.

I snarled and she backed all the way to the window. "I'm not going to fall for your tricks," I snapped. She was going to curl her fingers over her elbows and act all innocent?

"There's no trick," she insisted. The sun supported her argument, filtering in its rays and making the green overtake the red in her eyes. With her round face, midnight curls, and bombshell boobs, she could have easily been a girl to fall in love with, not a hell-bound demon.

Sympathy filtered into her gaze. "I'm sorry for what my father is doing to you. I'd hoped to get Sonya away from him before he came." She frowned. "I didn't know I'd need to protect you, too."

I strained against my constraints and my wrist fought against the blister trying to form, my body continually healing. I wasn't going to question why this demon seemed to be on our side. Perhaps it was a trick, perhaps not. Regardless, she could give me answers. "What's the Incubus King planning?"

She shivered, but didn't leave her place at the window as the cold draft poured in. "The end of the world," she said flatly. And I believed it.

STAY ALIVE

Nate

"You've proven yourself untrustworthy," Derek declared.

I didn't want to hear it. This had been humiliating enough and I hated how powerless I felt. I'd seen the runes across Sonya's stomach and I'd been around supernaturals long enough to know a seer's prophecy when I saw one. No one liked to talk about it, but before I was born there'd been a disturbance strong enough to shake the supernatural community. Actual angels had come in legion, fought off some great darkness, then left as if nothing had happened. The story made its way around occult circles, which was one of my specialties. I learned things. Even as a human, I'd earned a name among supernaturals as someone who got shit done, who knew things I shouldn't know, and could keep a secret even if my life was in danger. I hadn't thought much of it until I'd felt the surge of power on Sonya's skin… power I was not supposed to have. I was human, or at least, I was supposed to be.

"Do you hear me, *boy?*" Derek spat.

I jerked my head up and met his glare. Let him think he had me. Even the Incubus King couldn't overcome destiny once it was activated. "What the fuck do you want from me, then?" I spat. "You have the angel. You have the succubus. Why are you even wasting your time berating me?"

Derek growled with warning and I took an involuntary step back. Pissing him off was probably a bad idea, but I was pissed off just as well.

"You, my son, are too attached to the succubus. I see the judgment in your eyes. Don't you know that a darkness is coming? There's only one way supernaturals will survive the coming wave."

I knew what he was talking about. The cycle of death came every thousand years and it took a psychic and her protectors to stop it. This time, something different had happened. An echo had broken through the realms, warning that something bigger and more terrifying was coming. There were more worlds than just the human world. There was heaven, hell, and the ghost realm. Rifts had started springing up all over the place, letting creatures in that weren't supposed to be here.

Derek knew all this, but what he didn't know was that Sonya was the prophet meant to stop it all from coming to fruition. She held the seven runes of power on her body... and one of them was linked to me, which meant I'd better stay alive.

"I'm well aware," I said, clenching my fists to keep the rest of the words from spilling out. I wanted to curse the Incubus King from here to Seattle and back. My fists shivered at my sides instead. "Just tell me my punishment so we can move past this."

Derek grinned, and it was never a good sign when he grinned.

Just hold on... just a little longer. There were other runes on

Sonya's body. Other souls that would make her unstoppable once she completed the unity of four.

I just had to hold on… and stay alive.

SEVEN SINS

SIREN SINS

USA TODAY BESTSELLING AUTHOR

J.R. THORN

A TODAY BESTSELLING AUTHOR

J.R. THORN

Muse No More

Sarah

Life without superpowers sucked ass. I'd lived my whole life as a muse with the power to bend freewill, among other things. I could convince anything or anyone to do what I wanted—or at least I used to.

"Sorry, Miss," the teller told me as she scrunched her face as if I smelled worse than her armpits, "but a flight to Miami costs five hundred dollars." When I stared at her blankly, she added, "This isn't a charity."

Fucking charity, you kidding me? Charity was what I'd done for Sonya. I'd let her seduce me, lie to me, use me, and what thanks did charity get me? A loving relationship? A girlfriend who finally loved me for "me?" Wrong, it cost me everything.

Instead of spouting my sob story to a human that didn't care, I cursed my lack of powers and tried to talk some sense into the woman. "It's not charity. This flight isn't booked and the plane leaves in an hour. You're really going to just let a bunch of seats go empty when someone is asking you for help?"

She narrowed her eyes and chewed on the end of a pen already riddled with tiny teeth marks. "How about this," she said as she leaned in and glanced around the room. Other passenger hopefuls glowered as they shifted baggage across their shoulders.

I likewise pressed against the counter, hopeful that the teller's conspiratorial tone meant I'd talked some sense into her.

Instead, she slammed her hand against the counter so hard that I jerked back with a yelp. "How about I call security so you get out of my line and I can help the real customers?"

Spitting every curse I knew, I dug out my limited supply of cash. The flight would cost me the last of my dwindled savings since Sonya had made us go broke with her secret trips to the local Succubi Den. I shoved the money across the counter.

"Fine. Here. Give me one ticket to Miami."

If I'd thought that losing my precious supply of cash was bad, the flight was even worse.

An attractive flight attendant gave me a fake smile. She was so skinny I wondered if she was starving. Taking a look at what the other passengers were eating, I didn't have to imagine why.

"Turkey or Cesar salad?" she asked with her body contorted like she wanted to forget about me and my lunch and just catapult herself to the back of the plane.

Without thinking, I wrinkled my nose at the bundles of wrapped plastic and said, "I'll have the special from first class." They'd have plenty of meals ready to go just in case anyone wanted seconds—or thirds.

The woman bit back a laugh. "I'm sorry, Miss, but those meals are reserved for *first* class."

Putting down the faded magazine I'd found crammed in the seat pocket, I took another look at the cart and sighed. "Okay, fine. Turkey."

She handed me the ugliest wrapped box I'd ever seen and tottered off to the next row of passengers.

It took some fiddling to peel away the clingy layer of wrap, and I regretted it as soon as I did. A plume of gravy-scented heat burst into my face. After I blinked my watering eyes, I discovered that the "turkey" was a spongy type of mystery meat soaked in brown liquid—definitely not gravy.

I suppressed a gag and turned to tell the flight attendant that she'd made a terrible mistake, but she was already rolling down the row as the new set of victims picked at their own boxes restrained with wrap.

As a muse, I'd always gotten what I'd asked for, and no one *ever* left me alone unless I dismissed them. To see the flight attendant completely unaware of my misery made it click for me that this was real. I'd lost my powers, but that wasn't the end of it. I'd lost everything that I knew about how the world worked and how to live in it. As tears pricked in my eyes and I stabbed my mystery meat with a plastic fork, it sank in how real this was.

"Pull yourself together, Sarah," I chided myself and took a determined bite of my food. I ignored the turning of my stomach as I chewed.

I was human now, which meant that every meal was a means of survival and I'd take what I could get. I only had fifty dollars to my name after having to pay for the flight. The fact that I was on my way to voluntarily track down deadly sirens meant that my human life very well could be a short one.

I vowed to survive, but I also vowed to use my last bit of cash on a real meal once I got to Miami. If I was going to die at the hands of a drowned freak of nature with freakish magical powers, you could bet your ass I was going to blow my fifty bucks on a lobster lunch.

Even though I'd choked down the entirety of my turkey lunch and washed it down with ginger ale from a plastic cup, the nausea in my stomach couldn't entirely be contributed to airline food.

Miami's humidity slapped me in the face the moment I stepped into the walkway that was small enough to make even me claustrophobic. Everyone seemed to love the idea of Florida and living close to the islands that hung from Miami like a tail—everyone except me.

I hated tropical weather. As a Muse, I worked best in conditions that fostered passion and creativity. That usually meant being cooped up indoors with nothing to do. I preferred art, books, music and late nights with my girlfriend.

Thoughts of Sonya made me growl as I stomped past guys ignoring me. I wasn't one of the many scantily clad girls skipping about in layers of strings they called bathing suits. Sonya had helped me with my overly modest side. I still wore the dangling silver earrings she'd bought for me that were spotted with little red jewels. My fingers went to the long slip of cold metal at the mere thought of her. The kiss of metal was a relief against Miami's sweltering heat.

But Sonya was my past and the past was best forgotten. She'd been my biggest mistake, even if she'd helped me crawl out of my shell. She was so exciting and fun. She was the first relationship I'd had where I didn't read her mind or impulsively force her to do things. She was a strong supernatural in her own right, and it's why I'd naively thought that she had been able to feed off of me even though the Succubi weren't supposed to be able to feed off of the same sex.

My fingernails bit into my palm thinking how stupid I'd been. When I'd been sleeping or off at work, she'd been slinking off to the local Succubi Den and making a snack of one of their

Incubi. If she'd only told me that she'd needed men to survive, maybe we could've worked something out. Or maybe not—I would have wanted her all to myself. But no matter what, I wouldn't have wanted her to die.

Numbly I found myself at a carousel that screeched as it carried luggage around the semi-circle of rusted equipment. Even though we were inside, the air smelled of salt and grains of sand glinted in the tiles' cracks. People waited about in groups and the air hummed with excitement as if Miami were a place of dreams.

Sonya had been my dream, and now I was trapped in a nightmare without her. But she'd sentenced David to die. His death was a horror permanently etched into my brain. If she'd only talked to me—I shook myself. There was no point in rehashing a relationship that I could never mend. Sonya needed sexual energy to survive, and she could only get that from men. Even if she was bi and could swing both ways, I couldn't. Being with Sonya would mean that she'd need to have a guy. And if I was going to allow that, I would want to participate. But just the mere thought of it sent chills up my spine.

Besides those issues, I was human now. Even if Sonya couldn't feed off of women, a succubus could still kill. It was too dangerous—even if it was just to say goodbye.

"Excuse me, Miss?" a man with kind eyes said.

I blinked at him. "Yes?"

He scratched the back of his head as if he were trying to remember something. "Have I seen you before?"

I gave him a raised brow. Instinctually, I pushed a thought at him to *go away*. He was being seriously creepy and annoying, but when he patiently waited for me to reply, I sighed. "No. I don't believe so. I haven't been in Miami since I was a kid."

He frowned, not seeming convinced. He looked like he could have been my mom's age, had she still been alive. She'd been killed in the fire that had also taken Sonya's mom. It's how we'd met and probably why we'd had such a close bond. No one else could have understood that kind of pain to not only lose a mother, but to lose the only other person in the world who knew what it was like to have your specific supernatural powers. Now that I was human, I missed her even more. She would have known what to do.

My bag appeared, a cheery red and pink striped suitcase that now held everything I owned. I wiggled past the man that was blocking me in between two pillars and waved him off. "See you around."

He called after me, but I grabbed my bag and got the hell out of there.

My small wad of cash secure in my pocket, I made the sweltering walk to the taxi service and frowned. There was no way I was going to blow everything I had on a ride.

The man appeared again, this time with a sheepish smile. "I remember you now," he said. "You're Amelia's girl."

I froze. My mom had never mentioned a friend in Miami. But as I slowly turned to take a better look at the man with attractively disheveled hair, he smiled and let a gleam of blue filter into his eyes.

He was a muse—and since there were only three male muses in existence, there was a good chance he was my father.

SHANGHAI

Sonya

"You're taking me to freaking Shanghai?" I shrieked. Not that a trip to Shanghai didn't sound cool as hell, but come on. The last thing I wanted to do was be kidnapped by the Incubus King to be a sex slave for his baby maker wife under threat of my soulmate being tortured if I didn't comply. Actually, if it weren't for the kidnapping and torture part, that sounded pretty good.

"You'll love it," Derek promised with a smile that made my thighs clench. After everything he'd done to me, my mind was still muck around him. Without the help of the resistant made of Silvia's blood, I was little better than one of his human thralls.

My fingers twitched, wanting to go for the single resistant that his wife had given me as a parting gift. The knobby pill had its own little case in my pocket and I wanted to rip it out and digest its disgusting contents, if anything just to spit in Derek's face.

I made a fist, reminding myself with what living brain cells I had left that there would be an opportunity to get away from him. I'd need the resistant to do it, but not now.

A gleaming silver airplane was proof that this was not the best time to plot an escape. A wide-open asphalt sea spread behind its slick tires. I turned to gaze over my shoulder at more of the man-made desert. But this time I saw that I wasn't alone. A string of women, eyes glazed as they watched Derek, stood in a neat row. They weren't bound, but they all stood with their hands clasped behind them.

"I require a few… snacks, before we get to Shanghai," Derek informed me.

I blinked at him, my surprise shaking me from my own lust for him. He was going to kill those girls. "Snacks?"

His thumb caressed my chin. "Yes. I had to go into an angel's den to retrieve you, my dear. That cost me dearly. I have needs to replenish." His gaze raked over the row of women and his lip curled with distaste. "There was short notice for so many, I'll admit. They're not all my type, but I didn't want the police looking for them until we were already well on our way out of the country. A king must sacrifice for his people, now and then."

My hand reached for him of its own accord. I hated myself when I wrapped my fingers around his collar and pulled myself closer to him. "I hope I was worth it, my *King*."

He smirked and his mouth made the most attractive of curves.

My tongue wet my lips and I wanted to lift on my toes and taste him. He smelled delicious and it was taking all of my willpower to keep my sanity.

My chest burned with the Blood Stone as I drew from it. My sexual need tripled around Derek, and the only thing that kept me from throwing myself at him was the nourishment I gleaned from my necklace, as well as the reminding itch of my runes telling me that I was not meant for him. He'd played his role, now it was time for me to find my four.

His eyes dipped to the pulsing red gem at my neck as I drew on the power of the Blond Stone. "Clever," he murmured as he pressed his fingers into the small of my back. I arched against my will at his touch. "Come," he commanded, "my wife is anxious to see you again."

Shifting in my seat, I glared at the two men who held me captive and tried to ignore the rising sounds of moans coming from the rear compartment of the plane.

One of my captors was an attractive black-haired dream and he leaned against the curved wall with graceful ease. He wasn't watching me, and instead crossed his arms as he gazed through a tiny window. The sun reflected specks of gold in his otherwise breathtakingly blue eyes.

The other, an Asian who boasted colorful tattoos that accented his refined biceps, didn't look outside, but fearlessly watched me as if daring me to attempt an escape.

Not that I had anywhere to go. My hearing was dulled by the air pressure trapped in my ear cannals that I couldn't relieve due to my bound hands. I opened and closed my jaw until the dull throb eased. My stomach rolled as the plane leveled off altitude.

At the very least, I had my wits. Derek had gone into his own compartment of the plane to feed and replenish his power. As the moans decreased, some of the women already gone silently to their deaths, I contemplated why he didn't feed on me.

The last time I'd lain with the Incubus King and his wife, I'd helped to create the first Demonspawn to walk the earth. My

Blood Stone had been empty at the time, which had likely saved my life.

Another sharp cry pierced the cabin as a woman endured a powerful orgasm, followed by utter silence.

"He's killing those women," I snapped to my closest captor.

When the Asian guard spoke, it was in a flurry of round words that were beautiful, but made absolutely no sense.

He paused when I blinked at him with incomprehension. "Really? A succubus who can't speak Shanghainese. Where did Derek dig you up?"

I frowned. "Did you just say 'Shanghai-nese?' Is that really a word?"

He glowered. "Yes, it's a word. It's the official language of Shanghai; a dialect similar to Wu."

I blinked again. "Wu. Like, deja wu?"

He pursed his lips. "I believe you meant *déjà vu.* Shanghai also has a large French quarter, so don't insult me with improper French."

My French sucked, but it still pissed me off that a dude who spoke something called "Shanghainese" would let me know it sucked. "Wu," I repeated the word. "The fuck is Wu?"

"It's a language spoken in China," he informed me coldly.

"Like Mandarin?"

He rolled his eyes. "Sure. Whatever. Let's just call it 'Chinese.' That work for you, blondie?"

I growled and strained against my restraints. My wrists throbbed against the iron chains that lovingly pressed my arms into the heavy armrests. Judging by the cold the chair leeched into me, it must have been made entirely of metal. Derek didn't take any chances.

"Father says only I can talk to her," one of the Incubus' sons reminded my Chinese-Wu-Shanghainese captor.

He rolled his eyes again, seemingly just as annoyed with the bastard prince as he was of me. "He's not *my* father, *piyan*."

"Did you just call me a 'peon?'"

Dream Asian-man rolled his shoulders. "No, I called you a *piyan*. Apparently, I'm surrounded by monolingual morons."

Instead of tossing a punch, like I expected, the human born of an Incubus waltzed to my side and gripped my arm, hard.

Tattoos bulged as the vein on the Asian's neck throbbed and his eyes blazed with anger. "Did he say that you could touch her, too?"

His smile sent a shiver of warning down my spine. "I don't need permission." His fingers slipped over my collarbone. "If my brother can touch her, I'd say she's free game."

The time I'd spent with Nate was nobody's fucking business. I was going to find him, Luke, and then get the fuck out of Shanghai. *Nobody* was allowed to touch me right now. Rage made the Blood Stone at my chest go red hot and he yelped, jerking his hand away as blisters formed across his palm. "The fuck!"

My tattooed captor laughed with genuine amusement. "Careful, she bites, *piyan*."

"Bitch," the Incubus King's son muttered before bursting through a curtain and out of sight.

"Sorry about him," my captor said, as if he was going to actually be cordial.

I narrowed my eyes. "Careful, or I might think you guys are playing 'Good Cop, Bad Cop.'"

He smirked. "Hmm, maybe you're not such a blondie after all."

I would have tried to think of a comeback, except I balked

when his full array of colorful tattoos swirled across his skin, only to disappear a moment later.

He grinned at my reaction. "I suspected that if you didn't know Shanghainese, then you probably hadn't ever met a Chen Lung Dragon."

My gaze snapped up to his, and for a fraction of a second, his irises slit into a reptilian stare, before blinking back to human. I shivered. "Holy crap. No, and I can't say I'm pleased to meet one."

Dragons. I'd known that they were real, as were many mythological creatures vaguely known by mankind, but I'd never expected to meet one. They were rare and not keen on leaving their den.

He hadn't looked once out the window, and now I realized why. If he was a dragon, he'd long to transform, to spread his wings and fly home and free himself of the metal encasement and stale air. Instead, he watched me with an unerring stare, keeping to his goal with cold precision.

"So," I said, my voice holding a tremor I couldn't hide, "I guess I should be glad I'm not a virgin."

He blinked, momentarily taken aback.

"Because," I added, "you know. Dragons always kill the sacrificial virgins."

He laughed, and it was the most genuine, beautiful sound. Dragons were charmers, often considered an offshoot of the incubi, at least, that's what my mother had always said about them. "I think I like you, blondie," he said with a wink.

"Stop calling me that."

While he grinned, I couldn't help but feel a dangerous magnetism around him. I was tired of being around supernaturals who had power over me. "Can you turn that off?" I snapped.

He blinked. "What?"

I jerked my chin at him. "The… dragon glamour, whatever you're doing. Stop it. I get enough of that shit with Derek."

He gave me the biggest grin I'd ever seen. "Oh, sweetheart, that's not one of my powers."

My cheeks flushed and I refused to speak to him for the next three hours of the flight.

Unperturbed, he grinned at me the entire time.

SUNSET

Sarah

I started walking. Never mind the heat and the unforgiving sun that beat down on me so hard I wanted to swelter into a little puddle and die. No way was I going to talk to a muse.

"Wait!" he called as I hurried away from him.

"Nu-uh," I said. "I didn't come all this way to Miami to get brainwashed by someone who thinks they're my long-lost-daddy who can just walk back into my life." Never mind the fact that he was exactly why I was here. Best not to let him think he had the upper hand.

He chuckled. "You sound just like her, you know. She liked to run from me too."

My shoulders shot up to my ears as I hurried my gait. My mom hadn't been bashful about letting me know exactly what she thought of my deadbeat dad. A male muse was a rare and powerful creature, one of three that kept my race in existence. A muse could only mate with one of their kind and since there were only three men, they made sure to travel the world and spread the 'love' to other female muses.

In my hurry I didn't notice that the sidewalk ended. My suitcase careened over the curb and a crack sounded as it landed hard on the steaming asphalt. When I tugged again, it didn't budge. I'd broken the wheel. "Damn it!"

He caught up to me and blew out a whistle. "Well that thing isn't going anywhere." He gave me a raised brow. "What I don't get is why you're out here alone dragging your luggage about like some sort of mortal. You didn't compel anyone to help you? Why don't you have a ride?"

I glowered. "You ask too many questions."

He got close to me and… sniffed.

I leaned back and grimaced. "The hell are you doing?"

He blinked a few times. "Your powers…" His words trailed off. He straightened and jerked his thumb over his shoulder. "Look. I've got a car. I'll take you wherever you want to go. I don't know what happened to you, but Amelia wouldn't want you wandering about Miami without someone watching your back, especially in your… condition." His eyes dropped to my belly.

Sweat gathered in places I didn't even know could sweat as I desperately wished I had another option. A muse lost her powers when she was pregnant, and it was as good an excuse as any to win a sympathy card from good ol' dad. It was also a lot easier to explain than trying to convince him that a human had manipulated a succubus' powers to suck out my own and now I was a husk… or human… or something else entirely.

I flayed out my palm and shrugged. "You got me. Knocked up by one of your buddies."

He immediately took my luggage and ushered me to his car.

"Let's get you out of this heat. Poor thing. Do you have any friends here? Did they ditch you? Tell me their names. I'll have them strung up and beaten!"

He continued on in a slew of questions and threats for anyone who would dare leave me helpless and alone, not stopping for breath to see if I would have any answers. Ironically he didn't berate his brothers, had I really been pregnant. Apparently ditching a muse they'd impregnated was standard practice.

It was just as well. I wasn't good at lying. I'd never had to be. So I just let him fuss over me and guide me into a comfortable SUV.

After we'd dodged through traffic and he got the hint that I wasn't in the mood for talking, he finally shut up. I took the blessed moment of silence to ask some questions of my own.

"So, what were you doing at the airport?" I asked as I crossed my arms. "I don't find it a coincidence that you were just wandering around the baggage pickup when I arrived. Plus, you don't have any bags of your own. How did you even get in there?"

He smirked. "I'm a muse, darling. And life as a male muse is entirely different than what you're used to. I need sirens to help me find mates. Procreating isn't just a necessity for our race, but a magical need I can't get away from. They're great at luring other muses here so I don't have to travel the world to find them. In exchange, I bring them victims." He glanced at me. "They told me there was a soul of great suffering coming today. They could smell you from miles away. And I've tuned my magic to find suffering as well. You reek of it."

I frowned. It didn't make me feel any better that my misery was so apparent to the supernatural community, nor did I like the idea that I was a siren's idea of a tasty meal.

As if I literally reeked of sorrow, he rolled down his window and let in the salty air. The blast of heat and rust made me wrinkle my nose.

"How can you stand it here?" I asked.

He chuckled as his muse magic sparkled like blue diamonds in his eyes. He could have used his powers on me to force out answers, but he didn't seem interested in compelling me to do his bidding. Instead he flashed me a charming smile. "Your mom hated it here too. She only fell for Helen's song once, and after that, she never came back. I had to go all the way to Seattle to see her again."

I snorted. "You act like you know her so well. You knew her, what, all of thirty hours of lust before you were out of Seattle and chasing sirens and muses again?" I wasn't naive enough to think his "alliance" with the sirens was entirely based on an exchange of victims and mates. He was a muse and as he'd so grossly admitted, driven by the need to have sex. Sirens were sexual in nature, and I grimaced at the thought of my father having a harem of them.

His smile dimmed as he eased onto another road lined with palm trees that seemed to grow like weeds in this place. "It wasn't like that. I cared about your mother." His gaze shifted to me as he hesitated. "Didn't Helen ever talk about me?"

I flinched at the name. My mother had one best friend in the whole world, and that was a siren named Helen. The fact that she'd lured my mother to Miami to mate with a male muse hadn't been mentioned, but those were my mom's skeletons. I wasn't one to judge.

"No," I snapped. "But mom told me everything I needed to know. You left us. She never cared about the 'future of our race' or how important it might be for you to impregnate others. Bottom-line was she fell for you, and you left her high and dry." My lips pinched together at the grating memory of pain when mother had talked about my father. What I didn't add was the festering hate I had for him that he'd left me, too.

He sighed and lifted his foot off the gas. We hadn't arrived at a neighborhood, but eased to a stop at the edge of a long row of shacks lined in front of a beach.

"What are we doing here?" I asked as I crossed my arms.

He pointed at the closest shack that had a cardboard cutout of a pinup girl holding a fishing rod. "I'm not trying to read your mind, but I still sense primal cravings. You've been screaming for lobster the whole ride." He flashed me a grin. "May not look like much on the outside, but they have the best."

Frowning, I tried to silence my thoughts lest he was secretly reading them. Of course, that only made me think all my secrets louder. I was going to scarf down the biggest lobster I could find and then go get myself trapped by a siren.

His lips twitched. "If you want to sample the sirens as well, do be careful."

I jerked the door open. "You said you wouldn't read my mind!"

When I turned to glare at him, he cheerily waved from the open car window.

I scoffed and stomped towards the shack. "I'll be here when you come to your senses!" he yelled. "If anyone gives you trouble, just let them know your daddy is Apollo, and he's right outside."

Apollo. My mother had never spoken his name, but now I knew why. What a ridiculous name.

When I gripped the splintered door to the shack that smelled of fish and beer, I took one last look at my father. He'd slumped down into the seat and had already closed his eyes. Didn't look like he'd follow, but he wasn't going anywhere, either. Whether I wanted it or not, I had someone watching my back.

Entering into the bustle of the popular bar that seemed to be more of a hut than a building, I immersed myself into the excitement and lazy chatter of a place where bathing suits were the evening wear and dogs obediently rested on their owners' bare feet.

I found myself a seat in a shaded corner where I could watch the crowd. I'd always enjoyed people-watching. As a muse, I'd been able to blend into the shadows and control the world around me without notice. Now, I settled for being a stranger in a strange town.

A couple nearest to me swirled ice in their glasses. The guy with a tattoo sleeve and spiked hair flirted with the waitress while his girlfriend frowned. If I'd still had my powers, I would have made the waitress dump the entire tray on him—but now all I could do was mournfully watch.

When the waitress had gone with a shy giggle, I'd expected the girlfriend with luscious blonde hair to complain. But her frown disappeared, apparently having been caused by her drink going empty rather than jealousy sprouting its green head. The boyfriend pushed his glass to her that wasn't quite finished and she beamed a smile. To my surprise, she eased closer to him and asked, "Did you see the size of her breasts? We should ask her out with us!"

I blinked a few times before returning to my menu that was garnished by a painted dancing lobster on the top. If I'd had my powers, I would have fixed something that hadn't been broken. I could have easily ruined a good time the couple had planned. It was eye-opening, to say the least.

When the same waitress returned to take my order, I desperately wanted to read her mind and find out the truth. But after paying attention to her body language, it became apparent that she was attracted to the couple at the nearby table. My suspicions were cemented when the blonde gave the waitress a flirtatious wink.

After my meal had been delivered, and held up on its promise to be the best lobster I'd ever had in my life, the total came to a modest thirty-eight dollars. My father most likely knew the trendy restaurants with imported crustaceans that charged a ton, and which ones had a team of guys that had regular traps of their own and reasonable prices to match. I pulled out the wad of cash that was the last bit of money I had to my name and put all fifty dollars on the table before I walked out.

I didn't head towards the door I'd come in, but made my way to the open balcony that descended onto the beach. The sun had set and now the sky bled brilliant reds and pinks as earth's star drowned into the gulf. Night was a more bearable time for Miami, and even I could appreciate a beautiful sunset.

Lanterns sprung to life across the beach and night-goers gathered around bonfires. I didn't need my muse powers to spot the sirens scattered among them, or to recognize the soft melody of their songs that drifted on the salty air. They were the women with perfect bodies, most who sported tattoos or piercings, and seemed to float along the beach as they wandered from group to group looking for their prey.

My mother and her best friend had taught me enough about sirens to know that I should keep my distance. Helen had been like an aunt to me, and if she ever found out that I'd come to Miami or what I planned to do, she'd yank me by the wrist and drag me right back to Seattle.

My mother had given up three years of her powers to give Helen what she needed to break her ties with the shore and roam the world without the incessant need to feed on sex and sorrow. I wasn't blind. I knew that Helen was my mother's lover, but she'd always respected me and accepted the title of "Aunt" when I'd slipped and called her Aunt Helen one day.

But those days were over. My mother was dead, and Helen and I had a fractured relationship that would never be mended. My mother had been the foundation of our family, and without her, it had all fallen apart. Only Sonya had understood what it was like to lose everything that kept you sane and solid.

I took my time picking out the sirens before I decided which one I would approach. I wasn't going to change my plans just because my father was out in his car waiting for me, nor would I get overconfident that his name would protect me should I get into trouble tonight. I was going to play this smart—or at least as smart as I could when it came to playing with undead predators of the deep.

"Hi there, gorgeous. You alone?" a siren said as she slipped out of the shadows and appeared in front of me. Mist clung to her legs like sea-foam and camouflaged the sparkle of scales along her calves. I was glad to see that even though I was technically human, I couldn't be fooled by her mirage. She pushed a wave of magic over me that was clumsy and new. To my luck, she'd been recently Made, and I shook off her magic with ease.

"No," I said, my voice shaky with the effect of her presence. I knew what she was and the smart part of me was terrified, but I was going to go through with my plan. Still, sensing the enticing song that she hummed under her breath, I was afraid that I was going to fall into her trap before I could get her to agree to a trade.

"Apollo's in the parking lot. I'm his daughter," I blurted. It was to buy myself time. I hated to panic and name-drop my deadbeat dad's name already, but if I'd learned anything about survival, you used the tools you had available.

Her ice blue eyes went wide and shimmered with the kiss of

salty oceans and mystery. "Oh?" she said, backing away. "Didn't realize one of his spawn was coming for a visit."

I frowned at the term. Sirens didn't have offspring and found the whole process of pregnancy and birth distasteful. Their existence revolved around pain, suffering, and death. New life didn't have a place in their world.

I crossed my arms and gave her a sweeping appraisal. A sea-green bikini stretched over her plump breasts and her bikini bottom curved tightly between her thighs in an attractive V-shape. She'd donned a sheer wrap around her waist that added a sparkle of glitter to her movements that was accentuated by a sprinkle of salt and scales permanently embedded into her skin like diamonds. "You haven't shed your skin yet," I remarked. Sirens were an off-breed of mermaids. Mermaids kept their tails and broke ties with humanity completely. It was a better existence than what the sirens endured. Those with unresolved ties in their life remained bound to the shore, and thus a siren was Made.

This one was young, and stupidly brave. She eased closer to me, having recovered from the threat of my father's name. Her hand slipped under my shirt and caressed my stomach. "You're not showing," she remarked. "And I don't sense life in you. Only emptiness." She didn't seem interested in learning why I was a muse without powers, but not pregnant. Instead she seemed more interested in why I'd sought her out. Her gaze found mine and she wet her tongue with anticipation. "Delicious sorrow. Have you come to feed it to me?"

My gaze dipped to her lips that sparkled with magic and sea salt. I wanted to taste her, and even though I'd pushed away her magic, I wasn't immune to a beautiful woman—especially one irrevocably flawed. I had terrible taste when it came to partners.

Steeling myself with resolve, I gripped her wrist and stopped her painfully delightful caresses that were inching higher towards my breasts. "I've come to trade."

Her eyes softened with delight as she curled her fingers through mine, still trapped underneath the thin layer of my shirt. "I'm listening."

ARRIVAL

Sonya

Our arrival in Shanghai filled me with a flutter of emotions: rage, fear, anxiety, and a dash of excitement. I loved to travel, but I wished it wouldn't have been as the Incubus King's captive—much less alongside a cargo of bodies.

The women were rolled out the back of the plane under the cover of night. A single lamp betrayed Derek's handiwork, and I spotted faces frozen in orgasmic pleasure, their cheeks gone hard as blood languished in their veins.

I'd killed my share of human lovers, but I wasn't proud of it. And I'd certainly never had so many victims at once. I forced myself to count them now, thirty-four women, all who would have families who would never know what had happened. Even if it was Derek who'd sucked the life-force from their willing bones, I was the one at fault.

"You'll pay for this," I hissed, the words coming out forced but true. My Blood Stone burned at my chest as I drew from it to spit the insult. But when Derek waltzed to my side, his features attractive with satisfaction and the blue glow of his power ablaze, I released my resistance. It would do me little good to drain my Blood Stone now, just to throw more insults at Derek's face.

"You will learn to accept what we are," he said, his fingers drawing a line down my neck.

I shivered at his touch, my eyelids fluttering closed as I leaned into his warmth and my lips parted.

His fingers ran down my collarbone and rested on the Blood Stone. "Careful with this gift, my succubus. If you drain it again, you'll force me to have it refilled. I need you, and your mother's gift, at full strength for what I have planned."

My fingers clenched at his threat. He'd forced Luke on me, a half-angel who was supposed to be my soulmate. We hadn't gotten off to the best start, but if we were ever going to have sex, I'd wanted it on my terms. Instead, it'd been rough, orchestrated, and awkward. The deed had only had the goal to fill my necklace with sexual power, and it had felt more like a duty than the gift it should have been.

I'd get Derek back for that, I promised myself.

"Where is Luke?" I asked. "Or Nate?" I'd bonded with both of them and I was incomplete as long as they were out of my reach. My insides hurt more than I cared to admit being separated from them.

The Incubus King stood before me in all his glory, ignoring my pain. He'd showered in the plane's suite, his damp hair slicked back, and now garbed a silken black shirt open down to his navel. His jeans hugged his hips and I teased my lip between my teeth, trying not to let my eyes dip any lower. Another trickle of power evaporated into my body, feeding the energy it took to form those words, and keep my sanity as I waited for him to answer my question.

Derek frowned, but chose to answer me honestly, likely

concerned I'd only use more of the Blood Stone to thwart him. "Your angel lover preceded us here. He's being held someplace close, just in case you are foolish enough to drain your Blood Stone again." He sighed. "And my son, he's been such a disappointment. I was so proud that he'd seduced you and survived it, but now he's grown far too attached. I forced him to procure half of the women I fed on tonight, and now he's serving penance by filling my other thrall houses." His jaw went hard. "You won't see him again."

My eyes went wide with the truths that hit me like a blow. Luke was so strong, yet tormented, and had spent most of his life trapped in a cage. I couldn't imagine what he was going through now. He was once again a prisoner, and even if I wasn't sure if we were even on the same team, I'd witnessed his memories. I'd seen what his life had been like and wished better for him. He didn't deserve to be a prisoner.

And Nate, the human who I'd grown too fond of and was undoubtedly a piece of my soul, also suffered because of me. I knew how he disapproved of how the incubi lived in order to survive, even though he was born because of one. He'd approved my Blood Stone and my goal to find a way to live my life without taking anyone else's. There was an understanding and connection between us that ignited a deep need within me. We'd had sex, which had been brave and stupid of him, and both of us had found comfort in each other's arms. It pained me to know that the Incubus King had forced Nate to help him take lives. I promised myself that once I got out of this, I'd find Nate and make sure the Incubus King had no power over him anymore.

"Jet will be escorting you to the tower," Derek announced, and his voice sucked me out of my thoughts and into a foggy world where he was the only thing that mattered.

"Will you be coming with us?" I asked, not able to look at the tattooed man who took my wrist.

Derek gave me a devilish smile. "No, dear. I've matters to attend to. But rest assured, you will be seeing me again very soon."

I cursed myself when I was out of Derek's influence and in a small black cab that barreled down a brilliant freeway nesting between buildings that pierced the sky.

"That piece of shit is too powerful," I growled.

Jet, my tattooed-dragon captor, chuckled with amusement. "I've never seen anyone resist him, but you tried, I'll give you that."

His gaze dipped to the Blood Stone at my chest. Its red brilliance had dulled when I stopped draining it and now it looked like a simple locket. I wrapped my fingers protectively around the warm metal. It was my lifeline. I could feed without killing. I could resist the Incubus King, even if it was only enough to annoy him and ask a few questions.

"Why are you helping him?" I asked.

He glanced at the driver before settling his gaze back onto me. "How about a drink?" he asked, ignoring my question. "You look thirsty."

It'd been a long flight, and I'd been bound to a chair the whole way. My back ached and there was a maddening itch on my left foot.

But now, I wasn't bound at all. I wasn't stupid enough to try and escape, not with a dragon beside me. He'd snatch me up before I blinked twice. Dragons were known for their speed, as well as their lack of mercy.

But as I agreed and watched him pop open a compartment for Derek's famed whiskey, I didn't find that he matched that description. Fine layers of muscles rippled on his otherwise lean frame, a trait that made Asians very attractive. The tattoos, they were magical, and I found myself wanting to run my fingers over them and uncover their meaning.

"Here you are," he said, offering me a glass that reflected the city's lights off of its golden liquid contents.

I downed it without hesitation. I'd had one hell of a couple of days, and if I were a betting woman, I'd say it was only going to get worse.

"Whoa there," he said with a laugh, "take it easy."

I thrust my glass back at him and glared until he gave me a refill. "Why?" I asked curtly. "Do I need to be lucid for whatever Derek has planned for me? He wants me to get his wife pregnant again. I'm in no mood. At least I can be drunk."

His laughter faded and he glanced at the driver again. I thought he'd say something, but he sat in silence while I sipped my drink.

A SIREN'S KISS

Sarah

The hairs on the back of my neck stood on end when I realized that we were being watched. The sirens filtering through the crowds had gone silent, even their melodies drifting away into memories, and now they were eyeing us with interest.

"Don't mind them," the young siren said. She gave me a smile and leaned in closer. "They're just interested to see how I handle my first time."

I knew that she was young, but to be her first victim meant she'd been recently Made, perhaps in the past few days. "Well, Apollo won't be pleased if you try to feed off me."

She shrugged. "They don't have to know that. Let's make it look good, okay? Then I'll listen to the terms of your trade."

I pinched my lips together before I agreed. She was going to feed off me, and even if an older siren could potentially feed without long-term effects, a newborn could easily kill. But she eyed me with such confidence. She knew that I needed something from her, and I needed it bad enough to risk my life.

"If I kiss you, then you are going to agree to the terms of my trade no matter what. Got it? Or I'll make sure Apollo wipes out every waterlogged brain cell in your pretty head until you're a sea slug."

She grinned, clearly delighted by my spunk. "You got it." Her gaze dipped to my lips, but she waited for me to make the first move. A siren didn't take, she received.

Every survival instinct in my body screamed to get away from her, but the heat building between my thighs only wanted her touch and my tongue wanted to taste her lips. I gave in, releasing her fingers so that she could run her icy fingers under my bra and squeeze. It was a delightful pain, as if I was burning with fever and she offered the cooling reprieve of the oceans.

I gasped as her leg pushed between my thighs. Her lips parted and she accepted my kiss.

Her tongue caressed mine and left a trail of magic and lust sparking through my senses. Her thigh pressed higher and eased a sensual pleasure through me. I leaned into the kiss and let her run her grip around to my ass and press me close as she prepared to feed.

Unlike a succubus, a siren could feed off of either gender. She didn't need sexual energy to survive like Sonya, but fed on sorrow and need. Lust broke down mental walls and opened my mind to her, making it easier for her to take her pick of what sorrow she wished to feed.

She curled her magic in me, making me want her more and more, and it was a siren's way to never fulfill. The building lust made me kiss her harder as I yearned for fulfillment, even knowing that it'd only get worse the more I tried. The compulsion was impossible to resist once in a siren's trap. A low hum reverberated in her throat, sending a powerful song vibrating through my bones. It was a melody I could get lost in, could forget who I was and why I'd promised myself I wouldn't completely give in.

No, I thought to myself. *Resist. Don't let her overpower you.*

As if she sensed my resistance, she grated me over her thigh, sending friction and icy heat through every nerve between my legs that awarded me a building pleasure, but only made me want more. I moaned into her kiss and pulled away to gasp for breath.

So many eyes were on us now. Guys nudged each other and dared to come closer to watch our exchange of lust and desire.

What the humans couldn't see was the fine mist of my sorrow filtering through trailing magic that wound around the siren's body. She gasped with pleasure as tastes of my misery bled into her like knives.

A siren thrived on the pleasure of pain. It was the same pleasure that came with melted wax sent dripping low on a navel, or a sensual pinch instead of a soft caress.

I had enough sorrow in me to feed an entire pod of sirens. But my captor was surprisingly careful as she licked the dark grief from my lips. She fed on the bleeding, old wounds of the loss of my mother, leaving the fresher misery of Sonya's betrayal to remain lingering in the air before it reluctantly ventured back into my heart.

"Heartbreak can mend," she promised me as she continued to massage my breast. "I'll leave that one to heal on its own."

Seeming satisfied with the exchange, the other sirens nodded in approval and their songs resumed as they filtered back into the crowd. They waved their hands and danced across the sands, sending the men who'd been watching us with mouths agape into a trance. They forgot why they'd been so interested in us, and instead followed the sirens to the bonfires as their captors prepared to feed.

"So," the siren said, her cheeks flushed from our exchange of pleasure and pain, "what's your name?"

I smirked as I eased away from her and shivered as I tried to extract her magic and scent from my skin. She was mesmerizing and beautiful. I'd never expected a newborn siren to be able to feed and leave me so… relaxed.

"Sarah," I said, wondering why it was that even if I didn't feel fulfilled, I wasn't consumed by the dangerous need that drove many siren victims into a pit of depression and madness. "What's yours?"

She beamed. "Vikki."

I smiled. "It fits you." For a siren, she was surprisingly perky and full of life. Vikki was the name I expected of a girl that had spunk, excitement, dark secrets, and would be someone great in bed. I had no doubt this siren met that criteria and then some.

She took my hand and drew me closer to the sea. It was away from the bonfires and away from the promise of protection of Apollo's presence. He would still be in his SUV with the window rolled down. If I yelled right now, he would hear me, but if I let Vikki take me much farther down to the shore, the crashing waves would drown me out. The pun made me shiver with fresh fear.

"So, what kind of deal did you have in mind?" she asked as her icy fingers played with mine, wiping away my spike of adrenaline with the soft touch.

She was so comfortable with me. In turn, I wanted to feel the same. It was as if we were a new couple and this was the first stage of an exciting relationship. There were new delights to explore and Vikki was going to take away all of my sorrow.

But then I recognized the soft melody beneath the soft exhale of her breath. She was still trying to control me.

I snatched my hand away and frowned. "Stop that. You promised."

She shrugged, but didn't try to reclaim my hand. "Sorry. Siren nature and all."

We stopped when we reached the shore. She settled on the sand and after waiting patiently, I sat down beside her.

I half-expected Vikki to drag me into the waters and drown me, but instead she drew circles in the sand. Drowning a victim would release ultimate suffering and be delicious to a siren. Drowning was also how they'd been Made and how they'd suffered. Their own pain eased when they drank in that familiar choking off of oxygen in another life and snuffed it out of existence. But of course, as was a siren's way, they'd never be completely fulfilled. The urge to feed and drown would never go away—not unless they found a friend in a muse willing to give up years of their power to break the supernatural bond to the sea. The sea was the source of their incapability to fulfill that need. The sea was endless and full of mystery and darkness. It was a depth that could never be filled and only a freed siren could find relief.

"I can break your bond with the shore," I began, making sure to lead with the most desirable of promises. Even though Vikki was newly Made, she would know the weight of an immortal life that awaited her without promise of reprieve. She wasn't yet broken like the older sirens who were already dragging men and women to the shore. This was a popular siren nesting ground and I shivered, realizing that my father had likely brought me here on purpose. If I wanted to get myself in trouble with the sirens, this was it. It showed that he trusted me, and I wasn't sure what to make of that.

The ease with which they took their victims to the water

should have surprised me, but it didn't. I knew that my father lingered in Miami for a reason. He kept their secrets secure. Any soul that was snuffed out would be wiped from the minds of anyone who knew them. Male muses were the most powerful of our kind. They could follow a thread of memory to anyone connected to it and break it. It only took a moment, and then it was if that person had never existed at all. No one would be missed. No one would mourn their losses. Only the sirens would know what they had done, and they would relish in the surge of suffering for days to come.

Vikki followed my gaze to watch the horror parade that was heading to the shore. Some sirens bedded their victims first. Naked skin flashed and pink nipples sparkled with magic making it look like an orgy that would be enticing to join, but they were playing with their food. First, they would suck away any sorrow or misery that laid in their victims' hearts, then delight in the suffering of their death.

"I haven't killed yet," she offered. Newly Made, she still had a shred of humanity in her soul. It would only take a few kills before she lost the capability of remorse. She turned her gaze to me, full of hope and hinting at the human soul that had drowned before she'd been Made. "If you could break my bond to the shore before I give in to the need to take a life, perhaps you could keep me sane. I don't want to be like my sisters."

Her fingers crawled across the sands until she found mine. The icy grip that she took me with was one of fear and need and a girl who was scared and alone. If I'd been a muse, I would have been able to read her thoughts, but the emotions were painted clearly on her face that I had no need of magic to read her. Her brows creased with worry and her icy blue eyes frosted with a mist of tears. I listened, but even her siren's song had ceased.

"What do you want in return for a muse's boon?" she asked. She broke her gaze from the couples writhing on the shore.

I drew in a deep breath before letting it out. "Well, as you've already noticed, I don't currently have my powers, and I'm not pregnant. My father thinks I'm with child and that's why I've reverted to mortality, but that's not the truth." My blood went cold at the memory of Detective Anderson shoving a dagger into my chest. "My powers were drained by a supernatural I don't fully understand. I'd thought he was mortal, but he'd twisted a succubus's powers to be able to take others. He has the power of a muse and left me dried up like a husk."

Her eyes went wide. "You met a chameleon?"

I shifted uncomfortably on the soft padding of sand. "You know what he is?"

She nodded. "When I was Made I gained the knowledge of my sisters. They've met all kinds of supernatural creatures. We ally ourselves with muses and the occasional succubi, but steer clear of chameleons." Her grip tightened around my fingers. "Those things are the worst. They're even emptier than a siren. They are an endless void that unlocks their true nature when they find a way to feed on other supernaturals. They can only copy and mimic. They have no powers of their own, they don't even have a soul."

I shivered, but found myself inching closer to Vikki in spite of the fact that she filled me with icy need. "Have any of your sisters ever been fed on by one?"

She hummed and leaned her head against my shoulder. Her melody started again underneath her words. "It's happened. A siren is empty and not meant to be fed on. The process is deadly." Her melody enticed me and drew me down to lay on the sands as she curled into my chest. "You're lucky to have survived, but that's because you're a muse and your heart is strong. I can help you regain what you've lost." Her lips pressed a light kiss against my throat and made me shiver. "You'll have to give me everything if you want your powers back."

Everything. The word meant something incredible and horrible.

My lips parted with refreshed excitement as Vikki's hand trailed over my breasts. I knew I was about to have the best sex of my life, and then I was going to die.

DEPTH OF SORROW AND SEA

Sarah

This time we didn't have an audience, nor did my father burst out into the open to save me. If he knew what was going on, he respected my choice enough not to interfere.

Vikki didn't pick and choose what suffering to feed on this time. I would be her first kill and before she drowned me, she needed to take every bit of sorrow I had in my heart if this was going to work. I needed to be empty to replicate the process of a Making of a siren. Born of a muse, I wouldn't turn, but there was magic in the process nonetheless, perhaps enough to win me back my powers, or perhaps it'd just kill me outright and I'd never come back to life.

It was hard to care about what was to come when Vikki's song sprang to life and her lips found mine. I wore a button-up shirt and she slowly peeled away the fabric until my skin was exposed to the cool breeze. Miami had been unbearably hot in the day, but now I shivered under Vikki's touch.

Taking her mouth with mine, I relished her taste, sea salt mixed with tears, and reached around the curve of her neck to tug at the string that held her bikini top intact. One slight pull and it unraveled, revealing her plump breasts that sparkled under the moonlight.

She rolled onto her back and let me lead. Her magic worked in me and made my sex swollen and dampness gather between my thighs, but it was more than that. I'd been celibate since my breakup with Sonya. To have someone again, someone lost like Vikki who needed my touch, filled me with desire. I gathered her breasts as I cupped my hands and licked over her nipples. She gasped as I did it again.

Her ice blue eyes fluttered closed as she moaned. I released one breast to run my thumb across her bottom lip. She lazily slit her eyes to watch me. "You're not what I expected," she breathed, the pounding melody of her magic a surging beat that matched my own heart.

She hooked her thumbs into the curve of my shorts and tugged. I undid the bottom and allowed her to pull the fabric over the curve of my ass. I stood and let the shorts fall, but my most private of areas were still covered by a thong. My shirt still wrapped tightly around my shoulders, but was open to expose my breasts. She smiled at the sight and eased onto her knees. She rubbed over the plump nub of my clit and rolled across the slick fabric. My knees wobbled when she ran her tongue over the same place she'd touched.

"No," I breathed and eased to the sand. The grains dug into my skin as I ran my fingers over her breasts. "I must give and you must receive. You have to take everything from me."

She pushed me onto my back and rolled my thong away until it strained against my thigh and exposed my flesh. "I can do both," she teased as she pushed her own bikini bottom aside and descended on me.

When her clit touched mine, both of us gasped with the shock of pleasure. She rolled across me, our skin sliding on each other's slickness.

She moved her hips to the melody of her song, going back and forth as she held my breasts tight. My own fingers followed her as she moved with the grace of a wave crashing into me.

That's when she began to feed. Ice gripped around my heart as she took the freshest of my sorrows. She rolled pleasure through me, only to take some more. It was a cascade of ecstasy and agony as she built my need to feel her. Her skin sent tight friction across mine, nearly sending me over the edge, but I couldn't orgasm, not yet. She eased away long enough for me to come down from the tall climb, only to slowly start again.

After my mind had gone numb and I was crazed with the need to have her, she took me to the sea. We eased into the crashing waters until they lapped about our waists. "I'll breathe for you," she promised.

This was how a siren was Made. She pressed her lips to mine and plunged me into the deep.

My lungs complained when I first refused her borrowed breath. I didn't know how to breathe that which wasn't of the air.

But as she wrapped herself around me and pressed her sex to mine, pleasure and pain mixed and I drew in a deep breath.

Dizziness swept over me as she exhaled her breath into my lungs. It wasn't quite oxygen, but it was a magical composition of nourishment that would keep me alive long enough for the deed to be done.

Each new breath I took she danced with me deeper into the dark, icy depths. Her magic kept us locked together and her sex pressed hard against mine. She rolled without stopping, bringing me close to climax, but she wouldn't let me, not yet.

Each time she moved she pulled that thread of sorrow out of my heart. Every time I nearly reached my peak, she kept the deliciously painful spasms at bay.

Please, I begged, shoving my thoughts at her. *Hurry.* I couldn't take this pain and pleasure much longer.

Her eyes were glowing now with the power of my sorrow. *There's so much,* her song whispered. *You have to let go. Give it all to me.*

When I realized what she meant, it was the love I was still holding on to for Sonya. It was a love so strong that it hurt, and if I were to fulfill the siren's curse, I had to give all my suffering to the feed.

I closed my eyes as tears pricked along my lashes and blended with the gulf. *Okay,* I promised, and let go of the final thing that was holding back.

She rolled across me again, and this time her magic tugged hard against the last sorrow stuck in my heart.

When my love for Sonya vanished into memory, a climax came, and Vikki arched her neck back as she came with me.

The next breath I drew in was of the sea, and my pleasure quickly transformed into pain that spread needles across my chest. I convulsed, but was too emptied to feel the fear. I stilled until Vikki's blazing blue eyes melted into darkness, and only death was left.

ELEVATOR

Sonya

My plan formulated as Jet took me into the glittering hotel. The whole place reeked of Incubi that served the King. I'd heard of his "courts," but I hadn't imagined that I'd ever visit one.

Where there weren't Incubi, there were dragons. This was the Shanghai Royal Court. Swirling tattoos and flashes of reptilian eyes made me queasy. I didn't like being around supernaturals I didn't know very well. Heck, I didn't even know if my powers worked on them.

Determined to learn the truth, I kept Jet in my sights. My first mission would be to seduce him and see how far I could push him with my powers. If it worked on him, I suspected I could win over any dragon. Derek would have put only the strongest and most capable as my caretaker.

I didn't imagine even my gifts would be enough to get him to let me go, but perhaps I could get something more valuable: information.

Women, succubi or not, all have a sexual gift for procuring information. Men called it pillow-talk, but as a succubus, I knew the truth of the phenomenon. Draining a man's sexual energy broke down the walls in his mind. It makes them more pliable and willing. As a succubus, I could do more with sexual energy than simply breaking down mental walls. I could dive in, bend a man's will. The sexual energy that I extracted wouldn't just evaporate into the air. It fed me and kept me alive for as long as my head remained on my body. The price, however, was that I couldn't live without it. I wasn't exactly immortal, but close to it by human terms.

Unfortunately, I was only twenty-two years old and I hadn't yet developed the virtue of patience that the older succubi were known for. It took time to lure powerful men. Jet, I figured, was one of the most powerful of all the Chen Lung Dragons if Derek had chosen him as my bodyguard. He wouldn't have put anyone in charge of the key to his goals, whatever those were. I just knew that my Blood Stone and I were an integral part of his plans, and if I had a say in it, I was going to screw them up big time, sexy Chen Lung Dragon or not.

I pushed my cloud of influence over Jet as we walked through golden halls filled with luxury and decadence. A few of the other dragons stopped talking and turned, as if they were hounds who'd just smelled prey. Jet's glares were enough to keep them at arm's length.

"You're to be held in the guest quarters in the penthouse suite," Jet informed me, pointedly not looking me in the eyes. "You'll have your own keycard once you can be trusted."

I balked at him as we walked into an elevator. "Trusted?" I shrieked when the doors closed. "I was kidnapped, chained to a chair and flown half-way across the world, and you expect me to cooperate?" My rage stirred the Blood Stone, inadvertently scenting the closed confines with a powerful dose of my power.

He turned to me, the force of his bulk pushing me into the cold metal of the elevator's wall. Both his fists slammed on either side, too close to my head for comfort. He hadn't touched me, but a familiar heat burned the air between us... fuck, no. He wasn't...

"You really need to turn that off," he hissed, his lips inches from mine.

I sensed the musky need that wafted from him now and flinched when one of my runes blazed to life. His arms trembled as he resisted me. I gave him a wicked grin. "So, my powers do work on you."

And little did he know, he was one of my four.

It delighted me to see how Jet suffered because there was no way he could resist the power of being one of my four. One of his fists opened, the fingers reaching for my abdomen. He spread his fingers, as if he were about to grope me and connect with the rune that blazed below my navel, then growled and shoved himself away. The elevator dinged, lighting the header with brilliant blue as the doors opened to reveal a room I'd never have been able to afford on my own.

"Get inside," he barked, his voice husky and raw, "before you make me transform."

I grinned with victory. Information was already mine.

"So, you're more powerful in your dragon form?" I asked nonchalantly as I waltzed inside, swaying my hips as I trailed my fingers down a marble bar. I'd been buzzed from my bout with the whiskey in the taxi, but my flare of power from the Blood Stone had already healed the effects of alcohol. I groped chocolate brown cabinets as I searched for more.

"Of course," he answered and stepped inside as the elevator

closed behind him, "but I promise you, it's not something you'd like to see."

I grinned at him over my shoulder as I stretched for a glass on the top shelf. "Oh, I disagree. Scales and fangs sound sexy."

He rolled his eyes, pushing me aside at my pitiful attempts to retrieve the glass and yanked it from the top shelf. He handed it to me with a complimentary scowl. "Whatever, blondie."

I frowned. I'd learned that I could, in fact, seduce him, but his threats were real. Flashes of slitted green in his eyes told me that if I pushed him much farther, he indeed would change into something that was likely terrifying. A dragon wasn't just a beast, but a killer, and I wasn't sure if our connection would hold when he shifted. My mother had dubbed the dragons the "Shanghai Killers." Even if Derek had charged Jet with my protection, he'd probably given the dragon authority to subdue me should his free will be in danger. I didn't want to test how much Derek really needed me for his plans to work. Perhaps all he needed was the Blood Stone, and I was just a convenience of someone who knew how to use it.

"If it's so difficult to be around me, then why are you still here?" I waved to the elevator that was the only exit to my luxurious prison. "Can't you scurry on down to the lobby and play with your friends?" I leaned over the bar and took a swig of my drink. "Or did daddy Derek say you weren't allowed recess?"

He brushed past me, his hips grazing my backside for a fraction of a second, as he opened another cabinet and procured a new bottle of golden delight. "No," he said, ignoring the zap of tension that our momentary contact had flung into the air. "Like I said, once you're trusted, you'll be allowed to do whatever you please. But for now, I will monitor you and let Derek know how you're cooperating."

I growled. "Seriously, I don't get it. Why the hell would I cooperate with that douchebag of a king, hmm?"

He tensed as my rage scented the air again. His tattoos seemed to harden, soft lines forming that could have easily been scales across his arms. "I told you," he warned, "you really need to turn that off."

"Sorry," I said honestly and coddled the drink before taking another sip. The warmth slipped down my throat and dulled the fresh surge of power from the Blood Stone. It had something to heal, something to focus on besides the powerful dragon in the room I wanted to bend to my will in inappropriate ways. "I can't really control it. I'm sort of new to this Blood Stone stuff."

He blinked at me with surprise and his tattoos inked to their normal shade. "But you're the wielder of the Blood Stone. You're immortal and powerful."

I smirked. "I'm twenty-two, dude."

He blinked again before taking a sip of his own glass. "Holy shit," he said after a moment. "Well, that changes things."

"How do you mean?"

He glanced at me, his eyes flaring with emotions I couldn't understand. "My brother is the leader of the Chen Lung Dragons, and the alliance he made with the Incubus King is based on the wielder of the Blood Stone becoming his consort." He ignored me as I snorted on my whiskey. "Unfortunately, we weren't told that you were just a child. My brother is going to flip."

JET

"She's *how old*?" Jin shrieked in our native tongue that Sonya had adorably thought wasn't a real language.

As leader of the Chen Lung Dragons, Jin had his fair share of wives and consorts, but he'd had his sights set on the wielder of the Blood Stone, one of the famed succubi lineages that promised ecstasy beyond a man's wildest dreams. I also suspected he wanted what Derek had also craved: a child that would inherit the Blood Stone's gifts. It was no secret that the Incubus King had a new daughter, one with irises rimmed in red and a power unlike anyone had ever seen.

I couldn't fathom why the Incubus King would give up the wielder of the Blood Stone, but no matter his reasons, my brother had standards. My brother was over a thousand years old, and he didn't take a consort a day younger than five-hundred. He took age very seriously, as most dragons would. A dragon's power stemmed from their material wealth. The more gold they had procured during their lifetime, the stronger they would be. It impacted every area of our lives, even our ability to reproduce.

Succubi wouldn't be held to this rule, their power coming directly from their lineage and the occasional artifact like the Blood Stone that could amplify their gifts. But I knew my brother. Jin curled his lip in disgust at the idea of taking Sonya as his consort. She was a child to him, and even if the rules didn't apply to her, it certainly didn't make her appealing—at least not to Jin.

She'd tried to use her magic on me, and even though I'd pushed it off as best I could, I could still feel its lingering tension wrap itself around my cock. I shifted, hoping my brother wouldn't notice the curve at the front of my pants.

"We must call the deal off," Jin snapped and, to my relief, turned to peer outside. His reflection in the two-story window glared with a fiery red, betraying his anger that I knew all too well. I was only a hundred and I'd been living in my brother's shadow my entire life. When he was angry, I was the first to feel his wrath.

"We can't," I said gently. I didn't approach my brother, but I knew that if we called off our deal now, the Incubus King would make sure that Shanghai would be the first to experience his new army, half of which was comprised of our own dragons. I didn't want to test their loyalties when it came to a war at the end of time. "You know what's coming, brother. We need to be on the right side of things."

Jin snorted and a soft tendril of smoke filtered from his nostrils. He was dangerously close to losing control, and I didn't have time for that. The leader of the Chen Lung Dragons did not morph inside headquarter walls.

I dared a step closer to my brother and rested a hand on his shoulder.

Jin relaxed, his gaze shifting into a simmering glower. "Do

you propose we maintain our deal, but take nothing in return?" he asked. "Where's our pride?"

"Of course not," I said, releasing his shoulder as I gazed at the tower that nestled in the heart of the city like a dragon's dream. The Incubus King was no fool. He'd had the entire tower cast in gold to attract the dragons of Shanghai. He kept his court happy, and lights flashed in hazy windows, assuring onlookers that any pleasure they could imagine would be met inside its golden walls.

The royal court of Shanghai had been a work in progress, and ever since Derek had stuck his finger into things, had gotten a whole lot wealthier. Now, our kind partied every day, losing our numbers to his plans without batting an eye anymore.

I frowned. "We're in too deep," I warned him. "We need Derek just as much as he needs us." Derek and his wealth had become a part of our infrastructure. If that fell apart now, the dragons would be pit against one another, bringing about a vicious civil war unlike the supernatural community had seen in millennia.

That tower represented our enslavement to the Incubus King, and at its pinnacle, Sonya, the most desirable pleasure of all, rested as his prize. I shoved my fingers into my pocket, fondling the keycard to her room that no one else had in their possession. Derek had entrusted me with her safety, and me alone.

"I could take Sonya as my consort," I offered, making sure to keep my voice flat lest I betray my interest in the idea. Something unlocked in me when I was around her, urging me to cement a bond that drew me to her with a craving I'd never had before. I cleared my throat, trying to think of the practical reasons I could have her as a consort. "She would still add to our family's lineage, and you would be seen as generous to give your younger brother such a prize."

Jin snorted as if the idea were ridiculous, filling me with rage. "While I appreciate that, *brother,* it would make me look like a fool." His eyes slit into dangerous reptilian slices. "Your children would be more powerful than mine, and I couldn't have that." He sighed, folding his hands behind his back and resumed his calm posture. "No. I will have to think of the best way to handle this." He glanced at me. "I'm curious. Do you wish to steal the throne, brother? Or has the creature bewitched you already."

I turned before my brother could read my face, or see the bulge pushing at my zipper at the thought of taking Sonya as my own. "Don't insult me," I said, already going for the door. "I'm just trying to help." Sonya had indeed sunk her claws into me, and I couldn't shake the scent of her from my scales that lay invisible under my skin. I wanted to transform just to get it out, fire the city until it writhed in flames, or give in to the unrelenting need to sink myself into her.

"Where are you going?" Jin snapped.

I snatched the door. "Derek said I'm to watch her at all times, and I've already been away too long to tell you this news in person. Let me know your decision, and I'll be ready."

"Fine," he said. His voice followed me as I stormed down the halls. "But don't touch what's mine, *brother*. She won't be young forever. I can wait. Until then, I don't want your stench on her."

He'd said the only thing that would have made me break my promise not to touch the wielder of the Blood Stone.

Don't touch what's mine, brother.

SEX BOMB

Sonya

I lounged as I waited for Jet to return. After he'd found out my age, he'd made it clear that he had to run and tattle to his brother. It delighted me that I could already cause waves in the alliance Derek had built with the dragons. If I could get Jet to convince his brother to turn on Derek, I'd really put a kink in his plans.

Just to make sure he'd had the right idea in mind, I'd dosed him with a powerful waft of sexual need before he'd gone. I'd made sure to command it to seep slowly into him. It was a talent I'd never tried, but with the Blood Stone, anything was possible. I'd planted a sexual time bomb that was due to light… any second now.

I knew that forcing Jet to pine for me was only going to make his brother inclined to change his mind about his rules on age limits. I didn't really want to be a consort, but I'd play along. I'd let them believe me a weak woman and trophy worth fighting over. Men loved their trophies and pissing contests, and just when they'd beaten themselves down fighting over me, I'd take my turn to strike them all down.

And so I would seed disconcert between brothers in the dragon's realm. Derek would already be displeased if his alliance dissolved, but I couldn't just leave it at that. I needed the dragons to be off-balance as well. That meant that if I was going to seduce anyone, it wouldn't be the leader of the Chen Lung Dragons, but his brother… who now walked through the door with my sex bomb in full effect in his eyes.

His chest heaved, his tie undone and his shirt ripped open as if he was impossibly overheated. Sweat glistened on his taut skin as he stood in the elevator's frame and stared at me. Flashes of green in his eyes no longer frightened me, but rather fascinated me with their promises of danger and excitement.

I glided to my feet and a smile fringed my lips. My power had seeped into him. The red hue of his aura told me I'd been patient and given my magic enough time to bend his mind to me. This was a new trick that I'd add to my arsenal.

"Been thinking of me, I hope?" I asked in my most seductive voice.

He crossed the room in seconds, gripping me by the hip and pulling me hard against his erection. He groaned as my abdomen met the taut strain at his pants.

"I told you to turn that off," he said, his words sending hot breath on my lips.

I smiled and wiggled against him, enjoying how he still resisted me. But he wasn't in danger of turning into a dragon. His need was too strong and his mind too focused on having me instead. "I'm not doing anything," I whispered. It was a lie, but I smiled as I wrapped myself around his neck. "I just like you, that's all."

"Are you sure about that?" he asked, his hand gripping my hip harder as he pressed me against him. "You wouldn't prefer my brother?"

Here it was, my moment to wedge a sword between a powerful dragon family.

I deliberately shifted, sending him into tremors as I sent pressure over his groin. "You're the one I want." It wasn't a lie. No matter if I was trying to manipulate him or not, he resonated with a deep need in me that I would never be able to let go.

It was enough to push him over the edge. He claimed my mouth and forced his tongue between my teeth. He tasted of raw power and magnetizing desire. I drank it in without hesitation, sighing at the sweetness of it.

Besides the Incubus King and his wife, the unnatural creature that she was, I'd never had another supernatural man. I didn't know if Luke counted, but if he did, I'd been too influenced by Derek's control to notice this intoxicating addiction of magic.

I'd also had a muse, of course, now my ex-girlfriend; but due to her gender, I hadn't been able to feed on her enough to taste what her magic was really like. She was one of my seven sins, and I decided that she was greed. Her greed for me had both helped me overcome my apprehensions about embracing being a succubus, as well as shown me that life with just one person would never work. I was not a monogamous sort of creature.

But Jet. I'd never experienced anything like him. I leaned myself into the kiss, feeling the tingle of his skin that pressed against new places on my body and jolted excitement up my limbs.

I peeled away the remains of his shirt, delighting as the blazing heat of his chest pressed against mine.

When I went for his pants, he gave me a wild grin. "Do you want to play with fire, little succubus?"

LUKE

That bastard of an Incubus King made me watch, thinking the jealousy would drive me mad. He'd littered Sonya's penthouse with cameras and I had five different angles to see just how hard Sonya was being ravaged… and fucking enjoying the shit out of it. Jealousy wasn't the first emotion that spread warm fingers across my chest. Possessiveness, perhaps, but this was Sonya. She wasn't meant to be claimed by just one person. I was one of four. I was just a piece of what she needed, and I cared for her enough to recognize that.

I watched with fascination as the dragon moved with impossible speed. Their union was a blur that the cameras couldn't keep up with. Knowing the truth was one thing, but seeing the evidence was definitely something else. It brought everything into clarity. Sonya was mine… and she was his, too.

"I'm impressed," Derek said. "Even for the youngest brother, he's testing the limits of the Blood Stone. The dragons are truly an incredible force." He grinned. "And they're all mine."

He was right about one thing. The dragon gave Sonya such pleasure that she was screaming, her Blood Stone a bright red orb that blazed with the spark of their passion. It terrified me to watch, wondering if the dragon meant to fuck her or devour her… but something in me knew that as long as he stayed in his human form, Sonya would be safe. In fact, I felt a kindred bond with him, as if his hands on her might as well be my own. The sensation of her silky skin swept across mine and I shivered. Was that my imagination… or had I actually felt it?

The dragon shifter's tattoos had turned to flames long ago, his eyes gone a reptilian stare and very real scales slithered across his skin. When he produced fangs, I sucked in a breath, and jolted for the screen when he went for her neck like a fucking vampire, but it wasn't a blood kiss of the damned. He simply was a predator and he wanted to lock onto his prey. He wasn't human, and every movement and unnatural feature reminded me of that. Even his cock was overly large by human standards, somehow completely disappearing beneath the curve of her thighs, not that Sonya seemed to mind.

Watching them together made a truth ring in me that felt right. *She belongs to four.*

It'd taken days to get her scent out of my pores. Even now I longed for her with an ache I couldn't explain. I couldn't know if my need for her was succubus magic, dumb lust, or something else.

"Isn't she a sight to behold?" Derek taunted and gave me a hearty slap on the back, forcing me to lean closer to the screen as Sonya took the deep thrusts of the youngest brother of the Chen Lung Dragon's royal family. Did she know who it was she was dealing with? She was meant to be a consort to their leader, Jin, and Derek had been sure to rub that fact in my face.

But when he'd seen how Jet had looked at her, he'd set them both up. Poor Sonya probably thought this would upset Derek's alliance with the dragons—not play right into his plans.

Derek had a plan for the dragons, and a civil war seemed to be just what he needed to complete it.

What better way to start a war than have the two royal brothers fight over a woman? Helen of Troy had been a similar ploy to divide two nations, even if the world still didn't know that had been a supernatural one.

And so Derek had ordered Jet to stay with Sonya at all times. Even I knew that no man could resist her for long, especially in such close proximity. Even when I'd been with her, surrounded by Angelstone that should have rendered lust nonexistent, I'd found myself wanting her.

Jet had left her briefly to meet with Jin in the dragon's den, an old skyscraper that was dwarfed by the golden tower that Derek boasted. It'd been to tell Jin of her age. Which, of course, Derek knew would have been a problem. He *wanted* the two brothers to get into a fight over her.

It'd worked, and Sonya was playing on that sibling rivalry. She'd successfully goaded Jet into a blind, lustful rage. Together they glowed with a mingle of reds and greens as the dragon pounded into her over and over again. Even through the pixilated blur of their bodies, I could see how the room bowed with heat and magic.

Sonya was hell'a powerful now, and Jet wasn't just any dragon. He was the bastard child of an outlawed order of dragons that the world didn't even know existed, the Hugh Modali.

Derek had told me all about them. My teeth grated together as he laid valuable information at my feet. Either he meant to boast this knowledge, or I wasn't going to live long enough to tell anyone else about it. I needed to be alive. I needed to protect Sonya from whatever havoc Derek had planned for her.

The Hugh Modali had once ravaged the land, claimed virgins and killed more often than they'd taken the humans for wives. Supernaturals preferred to keep under the radar for good reason. Even if the humans weren't individually powerful, there were billions of them. Before long, after eons of hunting their kind for trophies of valor, the Modali bordered on extinction, almost dying out before they learned their lesson not to parade themselves in front of the humans again.

They'd found their foothold in China where they were worshipped instead of slaughtered, but even that'd had its ups and downs.

It was a valuable lesson that if taken as a frontal assault, humans would win. I would have been proud to count myself among them, but I wasn't human. My mother had powers to see the future, and my father, well, I still didn't know who or what he was.

But Sonya knew, and instead of telling me what I'd waited my whole life to hear, she now pumped another man until they both cried out in pleasure. I wasn't sure how it made me feel that I wanted to run my hands over her and add to her pleasure and strengthen her magic.

"You mean nothing to her," Derek said, stabbing into my thoughts. "You gave her the power to recharge her Blood Stone and now she squanders it to blend with a dragon like Jet. Her judgment is poor and predictable, to say the least."

"If you're displeased," I snarled, "then why'd you set her up?"

Derek laughed. It was a deep, arrogant sound. "Oh, I'm quite pleased. I just want you to see the truth." His smile faded and his eyes went wide and dangerous. "Sonya is the key. She is a lioness that must be broken before I can expect her to bend to my will."

The red hue in his eyes passed as I waited in silence. If I'd learned anything from my time with Detective Anderson, it was that psychopaths loved to hear themselves speak. I didn't have to prod him for answers. If I simply waited, he'd give me all the information I'd need to crush him, when the time was right.

"Do you know why I wished you to see this?" he asked. When I didn't reply, he answered me anyway, as expected. "Sonya must learn to control her gifts. My magic is too familiar. She knows how an incubus' power works. But she must experience so much more before she can become what she is meant to be." He turned to the screen and caressed the portrayed pixels of her cheek as she cried out in pleasure. "She's had you, and now she has a dragon. This is only the beginning."

I refused to respond, but a growl rumbled in the back of my throat in spite of my vow to remain silent and let the sociopath spill his secrets. Derek chuckled at my rage. "Oh, do understand, you are supernatural. You're something that she'll learn to unlock, layer by layer, until she can rip your power from your very soul."

I blinked as I sucked in a breath. He spoke as if he knew what I was. Could I get him to tell me, without revealing that I didn't even know? "Aren't there others like me?" I asked.

Derek's eyes widened. "Of course not. You are one of a kind." He turned again to admire Sonya enthralled in pleasure. "Once you hate her, you'll be ready to learn what you are." I glowered at him as he smirked at me over his shoulder. The bastard was toying with me. "It's pointless to love someone who'll never love you in return," he said. "She may be infatuated with you, but she'll never belong to just one man. It's against her nature. You can't live an immortal life with such tragedy in your soul. It'll make you go mad."

He phrased that as if it was meant to be a punishment, but little did he know I didn't mind sharing Sonya. She needed others to complete an ancient bond I couldn't describe. She needed her four, and I wanted to be one of the pillars of the foundation she needed. To take away any of the others would mean to watch her tumble, and that wasn't an option.

There was something else in Derek's words that however did streak fear down my spine. I was… immortal? No matter how much I'd healed, I'd hoped that age, at least, could one day take me. To hear that I would be an immortal prisoner in my own body was my worst fear. No one was meant to conquer time. Only vampires and unnatural creatures held onto the physical plane for that long.

"I'm immortal?" I asked, giving up the charade that I knew shit about anything.

Derek nodded. "That you are, my boy."

Without meaning to, my gaze swept past his shoulder and found Sonya. The prophecy had dominated every motivation and now gave me the clarity I needed to have the resolve to stand against the Incubus King. My will strengthened to see her head arched back and her fingers clawing into the dragon's hair as she moved under him. I promised myself I would keep her safe… we all would.

After the peepshow between Sonya and Jet was over, I'd thought that Derek would have taken me to some dark and murky cell. That's how I'd always been treated, but instead, he shoved me into the elevator with him and two other men. One produced a key and next thing I knew, we were going down.

When we were twenty levels underground, I shivered and gave Derek a wary glance. "You got some creepy cell waiting for me?"

Derek crossed his arms as if he was bored. "I wouldn't call it a cell, but I suppose it depends on your definition."

I glowered. "Any place I can't leave when I want to."

He shrugged. "Then a cell it might be, if you want to leave after I show you a piece of your home."

Intrigued, I watched with wide eyes as the elevator doors opened and bathed us with blissful light. It was as if I'd broken down Angelstone and crushed it into a fine powder, then set it on fire to melt into the very air.

I sucked in a breath and stepped into the soft golden glow of the room. "What is this?" I gasped. He'd teased me that I'd finally see proof of what I was, but I was no stranger to Angelstone. My uncles procured it by the masses, digging out deposits of it that rested beneath ancient churches and other holy sites. My mother, a powerful Seer, knew it was the only refuge from the plight to come. "If you've hurt my family—"

"Relax," Derek said with a soothing voice. He had that kind of smug "I know I'm amazing" look, but this time he might have earned it. "America isn't the only place with Angelstone." He propped his hands on his hips and smiled at the Angelstone. "Welcome to one of my hidden treasures, the Shanghai Sanctuary."

We were no doubt in underground tunnels, but everywhere I looked the walls, floors, and ceiling were polished to a fine golden marble sheen that illuminated our surroundings as if sunlight poured in. Light came from everywhere, but it was a soft and comforting glow.

When my eyes adjusted, I spotted furniture that decorated the lengthy rooms that wound with the natural flow of the tunnels. We were far from alone. The emerald velvet chairs boasted couples lost in their individual bubbles of intimacy.

I squinted as I tried to judge the tunnel's inhabitants. The women were human, but the men most certainly were not. Their eyes were slitted with a familiar reptilian streak and tattoos blurred over their skin. I approached, but they didn't seem disturbed by my presence. The one closest to me ran his hand down his woman's bare thigh, his touch light and gentle. Her eyes rolled back in her head as she eased down onto the plush sofa.

"Can they hear me?" I asked in a whisper.

Derek hooked an arm around my neck with faux camaraderie. "No. They're immersed in bliss. Thanks to the Angelstone, it's not sex, not here. It's something more intimate than that." He pointed at another couple. The dragon's emerald scales blazed over his arms as his woman straddled him, but they were both fully clothed and seemingly uninterested in anything more primal than what they were doing. She ran her fingers down his arms, her fingertips barely grazing the edges of his scales. "See what I mean? See how they're lost in pleasure, but barely touching one another?"

Mesmerized, I crept closer to the couple and watched how they continued to scarcely caress one another, both lost as if in the throes of orgasm with mouths parted. I turned to the Incubus King. He was the king of sex, literally. I didn't know why he'd create a place like this, nor what he gained from it. "Have you done something to them?"

He smiled, and it was a wicked kind of smile that said that he most certainly had. "Think of them as thralls, but not to me." He waved out his arms. "They feed this place with life. It's one of many reserves that I will call upon when it's time." He leaned in and his tone took on a conspiratorial whisper. "What I need your help with is a few more levels down."

I frowned. "You want *my* help?"

He grinned and wrapped his fingers over my shoulder. "Yes. Like I said, this place is a part of your heritage. If you want to know who you are, if you want to survive what Sonya will do to your broken soul, then it's in your best interests that we work together."

Even before his fingers squeezed hard enough to bruise, I vowed not to do anything of the sort. The Incubus King was a charmer, but I wasn't easily charmed. "Go fuck yourself."

AN ALLIANCE

Sonya

Curled in a dragon's arms, I relished the experience of sex with someone new, and someone powerful. I didn't have to worry that I'd break him, or that a lingering moment of lust between us would suck out his insides until he was a cold carcass. Sex with humans like Nate had come with a price, and even if I'd cheated a bit with the Blood Stone, I'd never felt so relaxed as I felt now. Jet was so warm and strong. My insides curled with reminiscent pleasure at the sensation of such heat in the most erotic of places.

Biting my lip, even as I relished the hard warmth under my cheek that was Jet's chest, I forced myself to remember why I'd slept with him. He wasn't just exciting and alluring; he was one of my four, and my ticket out of Shanghai. I doubted he was ready to accept our ancient bond, especially when I couldn't even describe what it was, so I stuck to my initial plan. If he wouldn't leave for me, perhaps he'd leave for the sake of pride.

"So, what's he like?" I asked as I forced myself to stoke the flames of his jealousy. "Your brother, that is?"

Jet sneered. "He's a *jiàn.*"

I smirked at his instant scowl of distaste. "What's a *jiàn?*" I asked.

He pursed his lips and hummed thoughtfully. "It could be translated a few ways. Let's go with 'he's a dick.'"

I snorted. "I see." My hand lowered, finding the erotic part of him surprisingly rigid. I would have thought it worn out by now. "If his dick is anything like yours, maybe Derek's alliance won't be so bad."

He rolled his eyes and pushed me away. His rejection stung, but I could only blame myself. I was trying to make him jealous and it was working. "His women never complain," Jet admitted, "but their eyes are dead after a while. You wouldn't want to be his bride, even if he wanted you."

I straightened at that. "*If* he wanted me?"

He regarded me with a flat stare, but I spotted the smug grin hinting at his lips. "You're too young. He nearly called the whole thing off when he found out you're only twenty-two."

I bristled. "What's the problem? I'm a full-grown woman." I pushed my breasts together with my elbows. "Not woman enough?"

Jet's gaze lingered on my naked chest, clearly indulging in the view before replying. "I didn't say that *I* found you too young." He matched my gaze with marked effort. "I'm only a hundred, myself."

Blinking, I tried to process that number while I took in the ageless perfection of Jet's angular face. I'd never really considered age when it came to supernaturals. Derek was technically eons old, but to me, I only saw a man in his mid-thirties. The same could be said of Jet, but I hadn't been prepared for his real age. When I unfroze from my shock, I snickered and covered my laughter with delicate fingers. "Holy shit. You're an old fart."

He glowered at me, clearly not amused. "In the world of dragons, I'm a derelict teenager." He cupped my breast and squeezed. "No matter what I see when I look at you, my brother would only see an infant."

With pouted lips, I leaned into his touch. "Does that mean the alliance with Derek is off?"

He stiffened. "What do you know of the alliance?"

I snickered and leaned onto my elbow, sinking into the plush mattress. Jet's fingers automatically ran down my curves and slipped over the blazing rune he'd activated. He didn't know what he was doing, but his fingers circled around it anyway, recognizing our connection on some innate level.

"I may have been kidnapped and traded around like property, but I have eyes," I said. "Derek thinks he can get along with dragons by using me." I shrugged. "Not sure what he gets out of it. Was hoping you'd tell me what I'm being pawned off for." I grinned as his fingers ran under the sheets and caressed my ass. "It's the least you could do."

His gaze had dipped again, but his brows drew together as he frowned. "The dragons haven't formed an alliance in a long time. But they're getting restless." He matched my gaze and I felt the tension inside of him itching to get out. He had secrets and worries about his people, and he only needed a nudge to share it.

Leaning into his chest and tracing the bold lines of his tattoo, I tried to sound bored when I asked, "There's a good reason that I've never met a dragon before, I suppose? Must be hard, never getting to leave Shanghai."

It was a complete guess that dragons would be trapped in Shanghai by some ancient rule, but it was a guess that was rewarded by a growl of frustration. "You have no idea what it's like," he said as he melted into my trap. "I've been stuck in this city for a hundred years, and many others in my clan have been here far longer. Rules dictate we must stay safe in numbers, but that's only because we have so many enemies and few to no allies. My clan has been greedy with territory, women, and gold." He released a breath, the soft heat of his frustration a wet kiss against my skin. "Derek is offering a chance to change that. He's an ancient and powerful incubus. He's offering gold, numbers..." his fingers cupped my face, "and you."

I frowned. "What good am I if I'm so 'young' to a dragon?"

His gaze dipped to my necklace. "You hold power over an ancient relic." His eyes flashed to that eerie reptilian slit before returning to a golden-rimmed rounded stare. "The only thing dragons love more than gold is ancient power."

My fingers instinctively went to my necklace, cupping it for warmth and strength. I couldn't imagine living without it now. "All my necklace does is keep me from having to feed." I shrugged, hoping Jet would believe the Blood Stone an irrelevant relic to the dragons. "It's like a supernatural battery. I can draw power from it, instead of feeding off sexual energy." That was an understatement, but accurate. I would need an orgy of a hundred men to duplicate the kind of power that I'd used last night. My lips formed a thin line, realizing that before Jet, my Blood Stone had been empowered by Luke. Even if our sex had been awkward and forced, it meant that he was more powerful than I'd realized.

Not wanting to think of the half-blooded angel that I also happened to be soul-bound to, I leaned closer into Jet's embrace. "Even if your brother found a way to use the Blood Stone, it wouldn't be much use to him."

He tucked his face under mine, but continued to caress the skin around my necklace, delicately tracing until goosebumps spread across my chest. "I believe that you and the necklace to be a pair. The necklace alone may not provide strength, but with you to tap into it…" His fingers drifted across my lips which parted at his touch. "Derek knows you're special. I refuse to believe that he'd give you up, even for what my brother is offering." His lips pressed against my throat and I released a soft moan. "He couldn't be that stupid."

"Or your brother, if he refuses me," I forced myself to whisper.

Jet growled and tested my neck with his teeth.

As his fingers roamed across my skin, his touch hungry with fresh need, I closed my eyes and shivered. I didn't know how much longer I could maintain this portrayed interest in his brother, not when I was becoming addicted to Jet.

ELEVATOR DOWN…

Luke

When Derek asked for my help, I'd expected the request to have something to do with my healing ability. Detective Anderson had wanted to study me as a means to replicate my power, and I had no doubt that even an incubus as powerful as Derek had his limits. Infinite regeneration could come in handy, and if Derek was going to piss off a bunch of dragons, I had no doubt he sought a means to recover from dragonfire.

But the dragons I saw in this new layer of hell didn't even attempt to burn Derek with their ancient gifts. We hadn't taken the elevator, and I suspected that these tunnels weren't manmade—or incubus-made or dragon-made. These were natural spirals into the earth.

Derek took me deeper into the tunnels and left his henchmen behind to guard the only exit. I swallowed as I echoed Derek's footsteps past dragons and their women trapped in painful ecstasy. It was hard not to feel claustrophobic once we got past those that littered the furniture and delved into a new, tighter pit of the tunnels. New victims appeared as we rounded a corner and I sucked in a breath.

The golden glow took on a red hue and dragons, some half-transformed into hissing, dangerous reptiles, bled against its walls.

There were too many to count. My jaw hung open as I stared at the long row of men pierced upon jagged shards. They weren't fully transformed into dragon-form, but their tattoos swirled across their skin, tripping over half-formed scales and while they didn't scream, they hissed through fresh fangs as they endured their pain. The tunnel itself was their entrapment, the jagged teeth lined the walls and skewered the dragons who rested on it.

When Derek's hand clapped on my shoulder, I jerked with a yelp. "The fuck, Derek?" I hissed, whispering as if I'd rouse an unseen monster if I spoke too loudly.

Derek scowled. "It's 'Incubus King' to you." His disapproval turned to delight when he surveyed the dying dragons. "Isn't it incredible?"

I stared at him as he boldly stepped deeper into the constricting canal of blood and death. "Incredible?" I echoed as I caught up to him. "Are you insane? The dragons are going to kill us all once they discover this!"

Derek boomed laughter, clearly unaware that there was a sleeping monster unseen in the red haze of this dungeon. A hot breeze twirled around our legs in response. "I'd be quite surprised, given that Jin gave me these dragons as part of our alliance."

I frowned, unable to look away from one of the unblinking dragons who growled at us, his blood soaking into the red crystalline shards of the wall that strangled him. "What..." Words left me as I blinked. My face screwed up as disgust roiled in my stomach. I'd been tortured hundreds of times, but I could bounce back. To see this kind of suffering—permanent suffering—made my stomach turn. "What do you gain from this?" I managed to ask. Another, lingering question that I was too much of a coward to voice was, *Why are you showing this to me?*

Derek's laughter sent chills down my spine. "Oh, dear boy, you're as white as a sheet. You don't think that I plan on skewering you on these, do you? No, you're far too valuable for such a dismal end."

My gaze remained locked on the horrific scene before me. The dragon's chest rose and fell as a hushed wheeze filtered into his snarls. My eyes darted to the blotches of red that fed into the crystals where it pierced his lung. I squinted, realizing that I'd seen this color somewhere before. Then my eyes widened. "You're making more Blood Stones."

Derek's slow clap echoed sharply across the jagged crystals. The dragons skewered on its teeth groaned, but didn't move. "I knew you'd figure it out." His features went manic with delight, a disturbing change from his regular, smug demeanor. The Incubus King was excited about this, and that terrified me. "Can you also guess what this all has to do with you?"

I pressed my lips together as I dug for any reason why he'd bring me here, if it wasn't to feed my power into the stones. "I have no fucking idea."

Derek's amused smile was irritating the shit out of me. "So, you going to tell me or what?" I sneered, allowing my voice to raise a fraction even though the hairs on the back of my neck stood on end. Derek might be cool as ice, but I knew we weren't alone with dying dragons. I sensed another presence here, and it was unlike anyone or anything I'd ever met.

"It's time you know what you are," Derek said and ran his fingers through his lush hair.

He was the embodiment of sexual perfection and I glowered at the glimmering strands of black that he swept away from entrancing eyes. I was as straight as guys came, but even I could admire Derek's beauty. "And what am I?" I growled. I was tired of being the only one in the world who didn't know what kind of supernatural creature I was.

He grinned perfectly white teeth that still somehow made him look sinister. "You're like my daughter. It's why I've brought you here." He jerked his chin. "She's been waiting for you."

I narrowed my eyes, only spotting Lilith as she appeared from a dark mist. She'd been hiding in plain sight all this time.

She managed to appear as a girl around sixteen, but her eyes still gave her away. Rims of red irises gleamed around emerald eyes. She was Demonspawn. I glowered. "What do you mean I'm like her?"

Lilith offered me a shy smile. "Did your mother ever talk about your father?"

Beyond patience, I overcame my repulsion of the Demonspawn and stomped to her and gripped both her wrists. "No, and I always believed there was a good reason for that."

She didn't flinch at my touch, and instead tilted her head back and fluttered her eyes closed as if enduring a vision. "Your parents made you what you are. You're capable of incredible regeneration. You're immortal in a way none of us are. You can also see into futures and manipulate destiny itself." Her eyes slit open to regard me with wonder. "Your mother, a powerful Seer, and your father… an angel."

The world spun around us as I took her claim at face value. Derek might be a manipulative shrew, but this girl wanted my trust. I'd seen that when she'd told me all of Derek's plans back in Seattle. She wouldn't lie to me about this.

My grip tightened, but she still didn't flinch. "What do you mean, an angel?" I growled.

Derek's warning warmth ventured across my shoulder. I released his daughter. "The heavens know I'm manipulating things that they would rather be left to divine judgment." He twirled me around to face him. "They sent your father to spawn you, so that there could be one powerful enough to challenge a forged destiny of the Incubus King. Where there is great darkness, a great light must rise to face it." His face took on a feral grin. "How stupid, to believe you'd really side with ones who've only caused you pain. You're meant to be light, but look at the darkness that swirls within you! No, you'll help me achieve my goals. With the power of the Blood Stones we'll create, we'll bring an army of Demonspawn into this world, and destiny will be in our hands to mold as we see fit."

I froze and controlled my features lest I give anything away. This was what my mother had warned me of. Hell on earth was about to break loose and I was the only person in the world who could stop it. With the power of Angelstone, Derek was messing with destiny itself.

My mother's prophecy rang through my mind again and I struggled not to glance at Lilith. I was meant to save Sonya, the very creature who'd created the first Demonspawn in centuries, a creature who now stood by my side. Perhaps if Sonya had the power to create them, she knew how to destroy them as well.

"My only concern is Sonya," I snapped. "Whatever you want me to do, I won't do it if Sonya is given over to the dragons."

Derek gave me a wry smile. "Taken a fancy to her, have you?" He rolled his shoulders and sighed. "I can't say that I blame you. She is quite exquisite. But, alas, she has her role to play. The dragons will teach her things I cannot. She must taste other supernatural magic to empower her command over the Blood

Stone. I've set her new destiny into motion and it can't be stopped now."

I crossed my arms. Something in me warned that Derek meant her to become a slave to that rock. He might have seen the prophetic runes across her stomach, and he might even know what they meant. The fact that he had plans for her meant that he knew she had power… power that he was going to use for his own purposes. "Then no deal. Not like I was really going to help you bring demons into this world anyway. You're an insane bastard."

Derek's eyes flashed with anger. "Takes one to know one."

"Enough," Lilith hissed. "You said he was mine. Force him if he's not going to comply."

I whirled to face the traitorous Demonspawn. "You little—" my words cut off as pain jabbed through my temple. Lilith's raised hand and flashing red eyes were all I could see. "Do it," she said through gritted teeth.

Derek sighed. "Very well. I had hoped he'd come around. I have no idea what he sees in this world that he means to maintain it. Even a half-blooded angel would have been a useful ally." Both his hands rested on my shoulders. "I cannot enthrall you. But, with my help, my daughter can." Derek's magic, a blue mist, strangled around my neck and sifted pain and pleasure through my body. I cried out in rage as free will was ripped from my soul.

Suddenly, as a tingling settled into my limbs, I blinked up at Lilith and wondered why I'd only ever seen her as an enemy.

She was beautiful, and I'd do anything she asked of me.

RESOLVE, SORT OF

Jet

Watching Sonya sleep was therapeutic, but I knew I'd indulged in a fantasy long enough. This imaginary bond I had with her was just my own pathetic failure. I had to keep my head on straight.

With one last look at the way her hair unfurled over her naked shoulder, I reminded myself that my brother was not only a force to be reckoned with, but he was the dragon's last hope for a new way of life.

Sonya no doubt wished to be freed from her predicament. In spite of her jabs that she wanted to taste my brother, I sensed her ploy. She wished to seed dissension and undo the alliance my brother had built with the Incubus King.

As I entered the elevator and watched the doors close, I felt another door close in my heart. My own reflection looked back at me in the steely cold of the elevator. My hair was disheveled from her touch and my lips were red from her kisses. I made a mental note to clean up in my own place before I went to my brother, or else display my deed all over my face.

I'd made a huge mistake. I was a young, unruly dragon who lived in my brother's shadow. But as I stepped onto the wet streets and basked in the neon lights of Shanghai, I knew that he was a necessary evil. I had to think larger than myself. My dragons were a lost people, often angry and miserable. But when I spotted them now, their eyes for the first time had light and excitement. They gave me passing nods as I went, believing that we'd soon be strong enough to explore a world that shunned us long ago.

Filling myself with steely resolve, I ignored the cabs, and jogged all the way to the tower, sweating out any hopes I had for a future with a succubus that wasn't mine.

TIME FOR GAMES

Sonya

"It's time," Jet informed me. I would have thought our fantastical sex just an epic wet dream if it hadn't been for the bulge across his jaw as he clenched his teeth. But his eyes were cold and hard.

He'd gone somewhere while I'd been asleep. Shanghai's musk hung around him and he'd changed in the time we'd been apart.

I'd been asleep and near delirious from our lovemaking. To awake now was a grudging acceptance of lucidity, with the only motivator to taste him again. My body ached in that delicious way after a night of passion. Jet had seared me with his kisses and dragonfire. My insides complained as I shifted to the edge of the bed and let the sheet fall from my naked chest.

Jet flung a shirt over my head. He was in no mood to relive what spark of passion we'd had. "Get dressed," he snapped.

I snatched it away and glared at him. "What's wrong with you?"

He didn't flinch at my biting tone. I noticed the reptilian

gaze. He was using his dragon to resist our bond. "Your initiation party is tonight. Jin will expect you clean and fed. I've had breakfast sent up. After you've eaten, you can take a shower and get ready. There'll be a hairdresser and makeup artist coming in three hours."

I blinked at him. "What?"

He didn't repeat himself, but narrowed his eyes and waited for me to realize that he was serious. Not just that I was supposed to go to some party, but that whatever we'd had was over… for now.

Yanking the bedsheets off of me that still smelled of sex and lust, I growled at him. "So, you're just your brother's puppet? Derek's pet lizard? What happened to you?"

"My people—" Jet began, then sighed. "You couldn't understand. Just get ready."

The rest of the morning went on in silence as I digested how hard I'd just failed. Perhaps I shouldn't have slept with Jet. I wasn't very good at the manipulation part of sex. That just wasn't my style. I'd wanted to keep him possessive and jealous, but as my heart twitched when he looked at me, I knew that I wanted something more.

Jet kept up pretenses of bodyguard as I went through the morning routine. After a shower, I caught him looking at me in the mirror, a hint of what we'd had the night before in his eyes, but then it was gone in a flash as if I'd imagined it.

Jet believed that giving me to his brother would help his people, and when I tried to think outside my own shitty situation, I tried to sympathize with him. He was young, by dragon standards, but he'd been cooped up in this city that seemed more like a prison than a home. Dragons were meant to roam the world, not be stuck in one place.

So I decided to play along. With damp hair sticking to my face, I pointed a hairbrush at him. "So, these hairdressers of yours, they coming any time soon? You do not want to see my idea of formal hair. It involves hair gel and spikes."

He cleared his throat and yanked his phone out of his pocket to check his messages. "Yes, they just arrived. I'll get them."

All the primping and polishing was an unusual decadence I'd never tried. I'd lived my life as close to human as I could, but I had to remind myself that I was being sold as a consort to royalty. Life was going to be different, however long I believed I needed to play this game.

If I could just get Jet to cooperate, I wouldn't be playing it for very long.

"Tell me," I asked Jet while a woman curled my hair, "what does Derek get in return for this alliance?"

As I suspected, the hairdressers and the woman who dotted a beauty mark on my lip weren't privy to this kind of conversation. They gave Jet nervous glances as he ignored me.

"I thought Derek needed me to make more crazy-babies," I said, pitching my voice louder. "Giving me away to your brother means he's found another way." I braced myself as Jet stomped through the doorway. "What is your brother giving him that lets him make more—"

Jet's hand clamped around my mouth as he snarled. "Stop talking," he hissed. With a jerk of his chin, the women creased their lips and scuttled out of the room. He didn't release me until the elevator dinged and its doors clamped closed. "Are you trying to get yourself killed? Because if my brother's plans are spouted in front of the help, then I don't care who you are. He'll kill you himself."

I dabbed at my lips where Jet had smudged the makeup and gave him a triumphant smile. "So, Derek *is* getting something that replicates what I can do." My stomach turned at that realization that Derek no longer needed me to bring Demonspawn into the world, but I kept my fear off my face. "What's Jin giving him?"

He glowered. "I can't tell you that."

Jerking to my feet, I matched his unwavering gaze. "Do you want Demonspawn running the streets? Are you *trying* to create hell on Earth?" I gripped his wrist. "Jet, you have to tell me what Derek gets out of this."

His shoulders relaxed at my touch. "I don't know."

"You don't *know*?" I asked incredulously. "There's a historical alliance between the Incubus King and your loony brother, and you don't even know what the dragons are trading in return? You know what I did for him, right?"

He frowned. "I've met this 'Demonspawn' you're so afraid of, and she's not half-bad. She explained it all to me. Her people are locked away on the other side, just like mine are locked in Shanghai."

I sighed. My daughter had actually gotten a dragon to sympathize with demons. Time to stop underestimating her. "I don't know what she told you, but you don't want Demonspawn in this world, especially ones who owe Derek a debt."

He crossed his arms and backed away from my touch. "You wouldn't understand what it's like. Dragons have been trapped in Shanghai for centuries. With the Incubus King on our side, he'll enthrall anyone who gets in our way, and his sons will guide those of us who explore the world and teach us how to keep our presence hidden. This is our only way out."

I sighed. "Look, I get it. I'll even cooperate and play good consort, but you have to promise me something." His eyes narrowed, but he was listening. "Find out what your brother is giving up in return for Derek's protection. That's all. It's something you should know anyway, right?" His demeanor didn't change, but I took his silence for agreement. "Great!" I exclaimed and grabbed a curling iron. "Now, how do you use this thing?"

A PARTY TO DIE FOR

Sonya

The initiation party was way over-the-top, as I should have expected when it came to cooped up dragons who also happened to be wealthier than the King of Timbuktu. Dragons apparently loved their gold. Golden chandeliers glittered from cathedral ceilings. Golden champagne bubbled in perfectly fluted glasses toted on trays held aloft by scantily clad women, all who wore appropriate streaks of golden makeup.

Fountains overflowed with golden chocolate, and I certainly hadn't known there was such a thing. Jet dipped a metallic pastry into the flow before offering it to me. "Try one."

I frowned at the decedent pastry. This whole place was too much. "The hell," I said, lifting my lip in a sneer. "You expect me to eat that?"

"Suit yourself," he said as he popped the pastry in his mouth. He fluttered his eyes closed as he chewed.

Ignoring Jet, I tugged at the suffocating strap of gold that wound around my neck. A long, silk dress slipped over my body, making me feel naked in front of everyone here. The shape of the dress pushed my breasts high, allowing the pendant that held my Blood Stone a pedestal to rest on as if it were a cherry atop yet another golden pastry waiting to be savored.

The dragons in attendance kept their gazes on me, but they didn't linger. They freely sampled the girls wearing gold, but tension made the air taut as if they were waiting for something.

"Where's your brother?" I asked, tapping my foot. I didn't want to be handed over to the Dragon King like a pre-packaged prize, but I hated waiting even more.

"Oh, he's waiting for the fun to begin."

I teased my lower lip between my teeth. "What, all this eyesore of gold isn't your definition of fun?"

He jerked his chin to the doors as they eased open. "The only thing dragons love more than their gold is…"

I sucked in a breath when a row of girls caressed in white lace entered the room. Where the world around them was glittering and gold, they were pure. White powder covered their arms and faces as if they were porcelain dolls. Adding to the look were long white eyelashes that fluttered over their cheeks. A soft glitter gave them a luminous glow as they filtered into the room with shy smiles and graceful twirls.

"Virgins," I finished for Jet.

He didn't respond, but all the mirth left his eyes, and when I followed his gaze I found out why. I'd never met the Dragon King, but there was no mistaking him. His tattoos swirled with an angry red and fresh fangs curled over his lips. I marveled that they didn't make him look like a vampire. He rather looked like a Sabertooth Tiger, especially as he prowled through the crowd and looked hungrily at the virgins who danced away from him. His appearance seemed a natural state, as if he'd forgotten how to be human some time ago.

"He's not what I expected," I said.

Jet hummed, but kept a respectful distance between us. "Having second thoughts of going through this willingly, little succubus?"

There was a warning in his reptilian gaze. I shot another glance at his brother and tried to find what linked them together that Jet would give me up so easily. The Dragon King was only like his brother in the sharp angle of his jaw and the wavy midnight hair. But everything else about him was completely different, down to the cold golden sheen of his eyes and curled fangs. Jin had broader shoulders and didn't seem to share Jet's attractive leanness. And that's when I realized a dangerous truth. They were too different to be full-blooded brothers, which meant that Jet and Jin only shared one parent.

Jet was a bastard.

Jet had slept with me not just because we had a connection that he still hadn't recognized, but because I was a toy meant for his legitimate brother. My stomach lurched as I realized how wrong I'd been in seducing him, even if he was one of my four—he could resist our connection because of his dragon. In spite of that, I was in the wrong, too. I'd hoped to seed dissension and chaos, but that'd been a foolish mistake. The brothers already naturally hated each other. Any fuel I added to the existing fire wouldn't change anything. Jin had the world, and Jet was a pawn to be used. Being my bodyguard made sense now. Jin would want to flaunt his trophies in front of his illegitimate brother just to remind him who was boss.

As if he felt the change in the air, the Dragon King's eyes snapped to me and his nostrils flared. I shivered when his eyes took on reptilian slits, his irises framed by a sickly gold instead of Jet's metallic green. The Dragon King sniffed, then surveyed the crowd as his tongue lashed out to taste the air. He seemed ravenous and my muscles unclenched as his attention diverted away from me… until I realized what he was staring at.

"I thought you said that dragons didn't like young women," I hissed at Jet.

He sighed. "Oh, my brother won't fuck a virgin girl, but that isn't his only appetite."

I swallowed, but a dry, stubborn lump in my throat wouldn't go away. "And what kind of appetite are we talking about?"

He frowned. "Remember when you said you were glad you weren't a virgin?"

"Yeah?"

"You were right on the mark."

"Shit," I hissed. The Dragon King wasn't going to sleep with those girls.

He was going to eat them.

"We've got to do something!" I hissed under my breath.

Jet shushed me. "There's nothing you can do. Besides, he's not going to feed and end the fun early. He'll want to meet you first."

The Dragon King sifted through the crowd, stopping to exchange pleasantries with dragons who donned more gold than seemed physically possible to carry. When he finally crossed the room enough to be within earshot of me, Jet gripped my shoulder to keep me in place. "If you want those girls to live, then behave," he whispered. "My brother will only feed on flesh when he's angry."

I wondered if that was really true, or if Jet believed it a simple way to control me. Whether or not that was his goal, I stayed put as the Dragon King approached and took my hand into his scaled grasp. I struggled not to screech with disgust. Even though the Dragon King was handsome, even with his gruesome fangs, I could feel the wrongness of his magic. He wasn't like Jet, magnetizing and sweet as honey. Jin was ancient, malevolent, and still reeked with the faint scent of blood.

"So, young succubus," he purred as he lifted my hand to his lips, "we finally meet." He pressed his lips to my fingers. I shivered as my knuckles grazed his fangs.

"Dragon King," I acknowledged, having nothing better to say.

He released me and gave me a smile. His lips struggled to stretch over his fangs and his golden eyes glittered with a distinctively inhuman quality. "I hope you find yourself comfortable in my city, although thanks to your own ruler, we shall be free of its confines soon enough."

He turned to appraise his brother. "She seems docile, my brother. Did you tell her of our decision?"

"Docile?" I hissed through clenched teeth. "I'll show you—"

Jet nicked me in the ribs with two fingers. He moved so fast that I couldn't see the blur of his strike, but my breath was instantly taken from me as he responded to the Dragon King. "She's not been made aware. I was hoping that after you got a chance to know her, you'd change your mind."

"What… plans?" I gasped as I forced air into my burning lungs. It shouldn't have surprised me that Jet knew some dragon-arts-judo, but his lithe and speed didn't seem shared by his brother. I imagined that if I ever picked a fight with Jin, I'd be facing the full force of his brutish wrath.

"Come, dear," the Dragon King decided. "My brother believes you will intrigue me as you've intrigued him." He grinned at Jet's frown. "Let's see, shall we?"

The last thing I expected was for the brutish Dragon King to glide me across the velvet floors for a dance. The music changed with his movements, as if he controlled this little golden bubble in its entirety.

His grace flowed with a slithering, reptilian quality, but his slitted eyes allured me with magical magnetism. "So," I breathed through the compulsion as he twirled me, sending my golden dress fanning out, "dragons do have the power to enthrall."

He grinned. "Only the King of Dragons, my dear." He pulled me close and the sharp tip of his claws pricked at my spine. It seemed a fluid, easy threat that Jin made to remind me he could shred me apart right here.

Jet was alluring in his own right, but his brother Jin was different. His charm wasn't innate. My draw to him was forced by his magic. All it took was a trickle of red from my Blood Stone to break his power over me. His eyes widened as he realized what I'd done and I smirked.

"My," he breathed, "I'm no incubus, but that little trinket of yours is capable of impressive things if it can break my charm so easily." A claw ran up to my necklace and the warmth of his touch lingered on my breasts. "I am patient, young succubus. I look forward to when you come of age." His gaze lingered on my lips. "But, perhaps, just a taste, for now."

My whole body went rigid as he leaned in. I didn't know how to kiss this creature with Sabertooth fangs, and a flood of terrifying images of my face shredded flashed before my eyes, my own look of horror reflected in Jin's golden gaze.

"Don't shame yourself, brother," came Jet's voice. Jin leaned away, and I found myself grateful to my bodyguard who smiled at the Dragon King. "The dragons wouldn't respect you if you ravished her in front of everyone. She's barely two decades old. Think of our family name."

Jin frowned, but apparently his brother was right. The crowd was staring in open shock. "How old are these dragons?" I whispered.

Jet winked. "You don't want to know."

Before Jin could reply, the doors smashed open and Derek stepped through, a group of incubi and his handsome human sons on his heels. "Well look at this," Derek boomed with his charming smile plastered on his face. Unlike the Dragon King, the Incubus King held power over me in intimate ways. My Blood Stone was helpless as the sweet musk of his power swirled through me and made my knees go weak.

Jin frowned at my reaction, then released me and stormed over to the Incubus King. "You weren't invited," he boomed. "This is an initiation of my consort into the dragon community."

Derek frowned, pausing only to wink at the blushing virgins who held each other for support. Their white powder streaked over their arms as they clawed at one another to keep from falling. "Looks like you've invited some human playthings. Are these for me?"

Jin growled. "The dragons' hoard of virgins was not part of the agreement. You got what you asked for, which is more than you deserve."

"You speak of such loyalty when it comes to your dragons. Do you all share such sentiment?" Derek's gaze had found me and wasn't about to let me go. "Let's retire to somewhere private, my friend. I have something important to share with you."

Jin frowned, but seemed intrigued by Derek's request. "Fine," he snapped, and pointed to the end of the chamber. "We'll talk in the suite."

ET TU, MY BROTHER?

Sonya

Jin slammed the doors behind us and rested his palms against the polished oak rimmed with gold bands. His tattoos swirled over his muscular frame, powerful enough to shine through the fine layer of his silk shirt. He turned and stared Derek down, one king to another. "What is so important that you must take us away from our festivities?" he asked curtly. His gaze shifted to me and Jet. "Much less that it requires their presence."

I knew that the Dragon King saw me little more than a prize, and his brother was simply another toy he played with. But Derek was up to something, and every muscle in my body was taut with the readiness to drain my Blood Stone to fight him. For now, I sucked just enough of its power to keep my mind my own.

There was one last resort I had, should I need it, and it was the nubby white pill that I'd tucked into my locket along with the Blood Stone. It was the sole resistant I had to Derek's powers made by his wife's blood. She was the only woman on this planet who wasn't affected by his magical charms.

I secretly cursed my chosen hiding place as Derek's gaze flashed to my locket. This dress was horridly impractical, so there hadn't been a better place to hide it. I only relaxed when I realized he was looking at my breasts.

"It seems that I made a poor choice in Sonya's babysitter," Derek said with a forlorn look that couldn't have been less genuine. He sighed and produced his phone. "I believe it best that you see for yourself."

Jet went stiff beside me as his brother took the device. I was baffled at what Derek could have meant... until the video began to play.

The sounds of my own recorded moans filtered through the room and I gasped as I realized that Derek had rigged the penthouse suite with cameras.

"What is this?" Jin snarled and shoved the phone at his brother. A damning image shone of Jet thrusting into me as he pushed me against the wall. The filter of our arousal and magic made the image blur with red.

"I..." Jet began, but his words trailed off as his mouth hung ajar.

As Jet floundered, the Dragon King's eyes grew impossibly red, the magic in him brewing like a storm. His breaths came faster until soft smoke drifted from his flaring nostrils. "You, bastard brother, unworthy even of the pits of a lair, choose to defy me and claim that which is mine?" He tossed the phone to the ground and it splintered into pieces. Derek only smirked at the Dragon King's rage. This was exactly what he wanted.

Jet's jaw snapped shut, and even though there was fear in his reptilian eyes, scales erupted over his shoulders and a fine mist of his power flared. "What is yours? You've always claimed that which you do not deserve. Perhaps it is time that you earned your crown."

I was certain that Jin would transform into a terrifying dragon right then, but Derek exhaled just a moment before that rage snapped. The sifting blue of his magic forced us all to relax. "As one king to another, I have a proposal to solve this little indiscretion."

Jin regarded the Incubus King with a raised brow. "You test my patience."

Derek bowed. "Perhaps if you included your brother with the other dragon sacrifices, I would be persuaded to expedite your release from Shanghai. He would help us to make significant advances in our plight, I assure you."

"Sacrifices?" I screeched and latched onto Jet's arm. "Do you see? I was right. Your brother is doing terrible things to help this monster. You have to do something!"

Derek boomed with laughter as Jin ripped me away from Jet's arm. "Dear Sonya, the men are talking." He ran a finger down my cheek, making sure to infuse me with knee-buckling desire. "You be a good girl and speak when you're spoken to."

"Don't you dare touch her—" Jet snarled, but one wave of Derek's hand and he slammed into the wall. As powerful as Jet was, he was no match for the Incubus King. He groaned as blue wisps swirled around him. Desire was what kept Jet pinned to the ground, unable to transform.

My locket burned with heat as I drew from it to resist him. My rage blurred my vision, but I ripped open my locket and shoved the pill into my mouth. The moment it crunched under my teeth I was ripped from Derek's influence. My Blood Stone flared to life as I called upon it and my fingertips burned red. "I'm a modern woman, remember? I speak when I fucking feel like it."

Derek snarled and Jin came at me, all fangs and rage. I

pushed back with my power. Its intoxicating wealth that tasted of Luke and Jet gave me power, and lots of it. The marble under my heels singed black and both kings buckled to their knees as they clutched their heads. I wanted to make their blood boil. I wanted to end them, now.

But I was unfamiliar with a dragon's power. "Sonya, run!" Jet shouted, but it was too late.

The Dragon King grew three times his size until he filled the suite with a reptilian stench. Rusty scales scraped against the walls and his neck elongated until he wasn't human at all.

He opened a long snout, now lined with fangs, and my world filled with dragonfire.

My Blood Stone shielded me from the worst of the blast, but it was Derek who used his own body to protect me when my world cracked like a mirror. My fingertips went numb and spearing needles found their way through my chest. When I looked up, I expected to see Derek's rage, but I only saw his pain as he endured Jin's wrath as he protected me.

I was wrong to believe that I'd simply been tossed aside. The Incubus King had plans for me, and that required keeping me alive. I refused that he would protect me for any other reason.

"Foolish girl," Derek hissed, "you don't know what you've done."

Pain crashed through me after the blast was done, and when I reached for my locket I realized why.

My locket had turned to ash, and what was left of my Blood Stone fell from my collarbone in tiny shards.

"My wife made a special concoction, it seems. She didn't want you to lust after me." He smirked. "She may not lust for me, but she loves me, and she's certainly the jealous type." He traced his finger over the blister at my chest. His caress should have made my stomach clench with desire, but I swayed as I felt nothing but the nauseating wave of pain from my wound. "She didn't care if it cost you the Blood Stone." His gaze locked onto mine. "Now you're just like her."

I blinked. He was right. The resistant wasn't temporary; it was permanent. My Blood Stone had shattered and infused that power into my chest. My fingers trembled as I covered the gash. I'd never be influenced or aroused by the Incubus King again.

Jin growled, having returned to his human form. "My rage has been tempered," he announced, and that's when I found Jet unconscious on the floor. "Sacrifice them both, for all I care. Just make sure we're able to leave Shanghai soon." He glared at Derek. "And by soon, I mean at first light." He waltzed to the door and pushed it open. "I have some virgins to entertain me until you're ready." One last glare and he added, "I do hope you can keep good on your promises, or I'll show you the true force of my power." He smirked. "That was only a taste."

When he'd left, Derek hefted Jet over his shoulder. "You heard the dragon," he said, "time to go unleash some demons."

"What the hell is wrong with you?" I shrieked. I'd followed Derek to the streets not because he'd expected me to, but because I wasn't about to let him sacrifice Jet. Without my Blood Stone, I was powerless, but its loss had granted me a permanent resistance to his charm. Nothing was going to hold my tongue. "You're a bastard if you think I'm going to let you 'unleash demons.' Do enlighten me, oh mighty king, how such an act will allow the dragons to leave Shanghai? How that'll help anything?"

Derek chuckled. "When demons roam the earth, do you think

the humans are going to worry about missing virgins or lost hoards of gold? No. This is the kind of distraction that'll let the dragons roam free and unchecked." He grinned at my slacked jaw. "It's time that supernaturals walk free, my dear, all of us."

I blinked. "Are you mad?"

He shrugged and adjusted the unconscious Jet over his shoulder as he walked. His henchmen followed us from a respectful distance, but Derek didn't seem inclined to ask for help even though remaining embers burned in the torn shreds of cloth at his back. If he'd been seared by the dragonfire, his wounds had already healed.

"When you've been alive as long as I have, you learn that the humans are the enemy." He frowned. "On a one-to-one basis, they're weak and fragile, but they outnumber us by the billions. It's why supernaturals have been forced to hide in the shadows since the dawn of time." His gaze found mine, and even if I wasn't impacted by his magic anymore, I could appreciate the attractive lines of his jaw. They went hard before he spoke. "It's time to even the odds."

I scoffed. "Demonspawn? Seriously? That's your solution to humans hunting dragons down if they knew they existed?"

"The dragons aren't the only ones," he snapped. "I'm tired of hiding, we all are. Demonspawn are supernaturals, just misunderstood. We all have darkness. They deserve to be a part of this world just as much as you and I. We're no different, trapped behind a veil while the humans roam free." He turned and began his march anew. "If I have to unleash hell on Earth to change that, then so be it."

THE BLOOD CANALS

Sonya

"You're not going to sacrifice him, are you?" I asked with a hysterical lilt to my voice as I followed Derek into the confines of an elevator. Two of his men followed us inside, both leering at me with lustful gazes. Apparently losing my Blood Stone hadn't made me lose the force of my allure. I growled. "Tell your sons to stop looking at me like that."

He smirked and gave the impossibly handsome bodyguards a nod. Both immediately averted their gazes while one produced a key and inserted it into the elevator panel's slot.

Derek leaned against the cold bars as we descended to a secret level illuminated by red numbers, Jet still unconscious on his shoulder. "You may think me a monster, Sonya, but I assure you, I'm not the monster here. I'm trying to make right by the world." He gave me a mournful glance. "Had I known it would have cost your affections, I would have done things differently."

"Yeah, a girl loves to be used in political games."

He smirked. "I was always going to save you from the big bad dragon after he gave me what I needed." His gaze fell on Jet.

I gasped. "Holy shit, did you plan on me seducing Jet?" My mouth hung open as I realized that I'd done exactly as the Incubus King had expected. "You wanted it to play out like this all along."

He sighed. "Yes, albeit, I didn't know about my wife's little scheme. Clever minx."

When the doors opened, I shielded my eyes against the unexpected flair of light. "The hell?" I asked.

"Now, dear," Derek chided, "I wouldn't curse in the presence of Angelstone."

With a growl, I followed him into the brilliant halls. My vision fought to adjust, revealing limp bodies strewn across velvet sofas. "What happened to them?"

Derek frowned. "It seems things are escalating. We need to get Jet with the other dragons, fast."

In spite of my distrust of the Incubus King, he had Jet, and I'd lost the power of my Blood Stone. I followed him into the halls that burned with light as if the world had caught fire. Heat seared from all directions and my nose wrinkled when I smelled my own flesh starting to cook. "How far in do we need to go?" I asked.

Derek increased his pace. I'd never seen the Incubus King go anywhere in a hurry. "Luke must be nearly done with his part." He glanced back at me. "If you care for Jet or Luke, you'll stay right on my heels, got it?"

I swallowed and nodded. I'd play along, for now.

Just when I thought I was going to cook alive, the light took on an angry red hue. The tunnels grew tighter and I bit back whimpers from the building claustrophobia. I didn't like this place one bit. It felt wrong on so many levels.

"There," Derek said with an excited tinge to his voice.

I skipped around him only to find the source of his enthusiasm was Luke kneeling and pressing his palms against a translucent shard sticking from the ground. Smoke drifted from where his skin met the crystal as he chanted.

When I got close enough to touch him, I hovered over his shoulder, but instinct made me curl my fingers. He was oblivious to us and the jagged crystal he hovered over smelled of blood and death.

Derek unfurled the unconscious Jet from his shoulder. At the same time he produced a dagger and sliced a line down Jet's wrist.

"What are you doing?" I shrieked.

Luke's chants interrupted and his lips moved as he mumbled. Derek frowned at me. "Don't distract him if you know what's good for you." He held Jet's arm over the stone and let the blood run over its sharp edges. Instead of flowing onto the floor, the crystal sucked up every last drop.

I sucked in a breath when I realized what I was looking at.

This was the birth of a new Blood Stone.

"You're killing him!" I shrieked and launched for the Incubus King who was bleeding my newest lover over a magical stone. This was one of my four. I couldn't let anything happen to him.

Derek put up a hand to stop me, expecting his powers over lust and sex to infect me, but I was immune. I slammed into him and ripped Jet from his grasp.

Derek blinked at me before his eyes crinkled with amusement. "Don't get all out of sorts. I only needed the blood of the true Dragon King to complete the ritual."

Jet groaned in my grasp as I dragged him into my lap. I didn't have time to register what Derek had said that Jet was the "true" king.

I whirled to face Luke. His eyes had gone white and he still chanted over the jagged lump of crystal that now thrummed with a heartbeat of its own. My hairs stood on end as an unseen tension built.

A thousand voices filled the chambers and I whirled to find its source. My hair flung in my face as I panted with fresh panic.

"That's our cue," Derek said, and stood. "Time to get out of here."

"Like hell I'm going to let you leave!" I shrieked. He'd unleashed whatever hell was about to break loose in this place. I wasn't going to allow him to abandon his victims.

He shrugged. "You're welcome to try and stop me, little succubus, but I believe you have other souls to worry about." His gaze fell to Luke, then to Jet in my arms. "Your lovers are adding up, my dear, and it looks like they'll be first on the menu." He grinned. "I'll be back to collect our prize after it's fed from their death."

I gaped at him. "You'd leave me, too? I thought you said that you needed me alive."

He huffed a laugh. "Oh, little succubus. You're their mother. They'd never feed on you. You're quite safe, and if you wish to stay here to witness the consequences of your love, then so be it. It'll be good for you to realize that your place is with me once this is all over."

With that, Derek disappeared into the fog of red as the voices grew louder.

Panic threatened to make my vision go black, but I forced myself to focus. I leaned Jet's head back so that he could breathe easier. "Jet," I whispered as I stroked his cheek, "can you hear me?"

All I got was a groan in reply.

"Okay, then no rescue from the scorned Dragon King who'd had his throne taken. How about you, Luke?" I asked, carefully resting Jet onto the scorching ground.

Luke's eyes slowly closed as he swayed over the pulsing gem. The voices were growing louder, their shrieks and cries echoing down the tunnels. It felt like they were coming from all directions, and this stone was what was drawing them.

I had to silence it somehow. I wrapped my fingers around the jagged edges, wincing when it pierced my skin. "Thing is sharp as hell," I cursed.

Tingling swept through my body as the stone tasted my blood.

"I wouldn't recommend doing that," said Lilith. I snarled to find her standing over us, her arms crossed in front of her chest. She leaned into one hip like a bratty teenager. "Your blood is too powerful. My brothers and sisters are already going mad with the violence and rage that comes from the Shanghai dragons we've already sacrificed." She tilted her head. "Your lifetime of guilt and seduction is only going to make them more dangerous and difficult to control."

No matter if my daughter was speaking the truth, I wasn't about to do anything she wanted me to do. I gripped the stone harder, growling as pain grazed against my bones. "It won't matter if I stop them."

Her gaze flickered to the red fog billowing around us. "It's too late for that, Mother."

Silhouettes lingered in the shadows. The shrieks were real now, not just echoes from another world.

"Shit," I said under my breath and tried to lift the stone, but it was too heavy.

"Here, allow me." It was Jet's voice. I nearly fainted with relief as he wrapped his scaled fingers around mine. "It's going to hurt," he warned, then helped me to lift the stone.

I ground my teeth together as pain made me dizzy. "We have to destroy it!" I yelled over the growing cascade of voices. The Demonspawn were in our plane now, but I knew they were linked to this thing. The red fog all around us was evidence of their world merging with ours. Whatever ritual Luke was helping Lilith complete, it wasn't done yet. If we broke the connection, there might still be a chance.

Lilith rolled her eyes. "You think dropping it is going to break it? Please."

Jet's fingers tightened around mine. "Feed from me," he whispered.

I closed my eyes and focused on the sensation of his body pressing up against my back. I recalled how he'd thrust into me, how I'd tasted only the finest layer of his power. I'd thought Jet to be just like any other dragon, but now I realized that I'd recognized he was something special. He was an uncrowned king, and I was going to use his power to stop the end of the world.

Dragonfire swelled in my stomach as I drew from Jet's well. It could very well kill me, but there was a whole nest of Blood Stones to draw the power now. I would overwhelm it, make it shatter into a thousand pieces just like my necklace had done before.

"What are you doing?" Lilith asked, her voice going up in a concerned lilt.

"Don't you dare come any closer," I snapped as Lilith took one step towards us. "I'll make sure you die along with this wretched thing." Her gaze zipped to my fingertips which now dripped with molten red. I was controlling dragonfire.

The ruby shadows swept apart like a curtain as the Demonspawn broke through the mist. They snarled, their saliva dripping from long fangs. They'd all taken on the appearance of the Shanghai Dragons who'd been sacrificed to bring them into our world. Their eyes slit with reptilian irises rimmed with red.

"Focus," Jet instructed.

I drew in a deep breath and closed my eyes. It took effort to push down my bubbling fear. I told myself that I had all the time in the world. There weren't Demonspawn just feet away about to rip Luke and Jet's throats out. There wasn't my Demonspawn daughter just seconds away from snatching the crystal out of my grasp.

"You can do this," Jet said.

When his fingers tightened and his lips caressed my neck, I took down the last remaining wall that I'd held up to keep myself apart from Jet's true power.

I let it all in.

My world exploded in flames and I screamed both with ecstasy and agony of the fresh wave. The possibility of death didn't cross my mind. All that mattered was this intense feeling of magic that I'd denied myself when I'd slept with Jet before. I'd allowed my Blood Stone to absorb that gift, but now it was mine to savor in its entirety.

Demonspawn shrieks filled the tunnels and my own daughter's cries joined the fray. I reveled in their pain, until I heard Luke's voice raise with them.

My eyes flashed open and I found him free of the crystal's hold. "Luke!" I shouted and jerked one hand free to reach for him.

Jet tried to stop me, but my fingertips brushed Luke's until he found my grip and held on tight.

I soothed a cooling protection through him as the world around us burned.

THE TRUE DRAGON KING

Sonya

When the flames hissed into grey smoke and dissipated, I sucked in a breath and coughed in the dusty air.

"Sonya," Luke wheezed. His grip clenched around my fingers and his knuckles went white as he flexed. "What the hell was that?"

Unable to shake Luke, I turned to find Jet smiling. Fangs framed his teeth and his wild eyes were alight with excitement. "That was fun."

I smirked. Hand it to a dragon to think banishing hell from our plane of existence to be the definition of fun.

The ground trembled, breaking our momentary reprieve. I whirled, but couldn't find my daughter Lilith anywhere, or any hint of the Demonspawn that had threatened to invade our world.

"That's our cue," I said, and stood. Luke finally released me and needles tingled in my fingers as blood rushed back into them.

I half-expected Derek to be waiting for us at the elevator, or to have at least disabled it, but the keycard was waiting for me, perched neatly on the panel's shelf.

With a frown, I ushered Luke and Jet in behind me before inserting the card to go back up to the top level. Something inside of me warned that, once again, we'd played right into Derek's plans.

The sense of unease that made me want to run was validated the moment we stepped out onto the streets.

Jin and a hoard of dragons waited for us. Each with flexing scale-covered muscles and dangerous reptilian irises flashing their warning.

"So, you've finally discovered your true heritage," Jin boomed.

Jet shoved me behind him. "It seems you've been lying to me, brother."

Jin grinned, his Sabertooth fangs making his lips strain at the motion. "Your mother was queen of the Hugh Modali, the last of the clan before our father killed her." He snarled. "Your clan was the reason we've been trapped in Shanghai for thousands of years. Father was mad not to have killed you too the moment you were born." His eyes narrowed. "He never could give up the idea that he could suck the power of the Hugh Modali from your marrow."

I wasn't one to pin Jet with "daddy issues," but the air around him sizzled with hints of flame. I remained where I was, just a hair's breadth from touching his flexing frame. Jet and I had become one, and where he had dragonfire, I had an inferno inside of me. Even without the Blood Stone on my chest, I still felt its heat beating against my chest.

Luke's grip on my wrist brought me back from the edge. "Sonya. We shouldn't be here for this."

There wasn't fear in his voice, simply an acknowledgment that we didn't belong in the dragon's world.

"Then you go," I snapped. "I belong at Jet's side just as much as I belong at yours." He might not have dragonfire in him, but I did, and this was now my fight too.

He flinched as if I'd physically slapped him. "Very well," he said and stubbornly shoved a cell in my hands. "Call me when you're ready. I'll be at the airport making sure you can still leave." His gaze flashed to mine with unhidden hope. "Jet will protect you, but you can't stay here. I'll be waiting for you."

Before I could fathom how Luke got his hands on a cell phone, or what it was he wanted from me, he disappeared into the shadows of Shanghai's streets.

Stretching of skin and beast-like snarls brought me back to the problem at hand. Jin was growing into his true form and now there was a full-sized dragon snarling in the middle of the street. He spread leathery wings and human screams filled the air.

I cursed under my breath and brushed Jet's shoulder. "The Demonspawn were supposed to be a distraction. Jin thinks they're here." The only thing that's going to be on the news tonight is a Sabertooth dragon.

He grinned at me over his shoulder. "Then we have the advantage."

Scales and heat shifted under my touch and I snatched my hand away as Jet transformed. I staggered back as my jaw fell agape to see Jet become a dragon. His scales glimmered with pure emerald hues. Green fire licked around his elongated snout and even though he'd become a beast of nightmares, his reptilian eyes still held a soul I recognized.

He turned from me, the sweeping waves of his wings sending a warm blast that slapped my hair away from my face.

Out of instinct, I raised my hands to aid him and a familiar ruby red filtered through my fingertips.

"What is this?" I asked under my breath.

The answer came from within.

You've unleashed me.

I froze.

The Blood Stone might have shattered, but its power was now inside of me, and it was sentient.

Jin, a wretched beast with twisted horns, roared and sent the air steaming with his breath. Jet didn't hesitate and launched into the sky, his own emerald flames licking the air.

Once Jet was clear, I pushed my power to the dragon who snarled. A blast of ruby magic sent him sprawling into his scaled men. When bones cracked under his weight and cries of agony filled the air, I realized that only royalty could fully transform into the mythical beasts.

A grin overtook my face as Jet followed my power with a blast of his own. Jin snapped at him and sharp, serrated fangs found Jet's neck. He roared with agony as steaming blood fell to the streets.

"No!" I cried, and pushed my power again into the brawling dragons that filled the sky. My panic took form of a magical rope and wrapped around Jin's legs, yanking him hard.

The surprise of the attack made him unlatch his maw. Jet roared as a fresh splatter of steaming blood hit the ground. Terror swept through me when Jin redirected his attack. The vile dragon was coming straight for me.

I screamed and protected my face. I'd expected to be eaten, but the ground shook as Jin's dragon body hit a forcefield that I'd erected around myself. I lowered trembling fingers to find Jin's scales cracked and a wing bent at an odd angle. The Blood Stone, or whatever it had become now, just saved me.

You're welcome, it said with a smug tone. *Now, you're going to want to hold onto something.*

Jet roared and inhaled. I protected my face again, hoping my shield would hold as an emerald blast came crashing down.

My world exploded and I crashed to my knees. When the flames cleared, Jin was dead, and those who remained stared up at their new king.

MEMORIES OF A MUSE

Sonya

Well, that was fun, the Blood Stone echoed in my mind, its words reminiscent of Jet's attitude.

"Who are you?" I asked as I watched Jet softly land, his claws digging into his brother's corpse. His snout flared as he arched his neck and gave a triumphant roar.

Questions later. For now, I have a deal to propose. Get me to that Muse of yours, and I'll restore the powers that had been stripped from her. We're going to need her for what's coming next.

My eyes went wide. Because of me, Sarah had lost her powers as a Muse and was nothing more than a mere mortal. It'd been bad enough that I'd lied to her about my need to feed on men to survive. But now, with the Blood Stone burning a new power inside my chest, I wondered if I needed to feed at all.

"Do you think she'll take me back?"

A mocking laugh. *I doubt it, but you can certainly try. Even if she's not one of the four, she is still one of the seven.*

Jet's eyes found mine, and there was acceptance in that

reptilian stare. He knew I was leaving, and I didn't want to, but I had to help Sarah, and I needed to find my fourth.

"Jet," I whispered, "come for me when it's time."

The streets echoed with a building cry of men and their dragons. The world was about to turn upside down now that supernaturals were out in the open. If my ex-girlfriend ever needed her powers back, it was now.

"Hold on, Sarah," I said through clenched teeth, "I'm coming."

NEVER TRUST A SIREN

Sarah

Man, I wish I had never lost my powers so that I didn't have to go through this. A fleeting thought went through my mind wondering what Sonya was up to right now. Probably shacking up with all the guys she could find while completely forgetting about me.

That should have made me depressed, but everything had changed.

I should have known better than to trust a siren. When I awoke, I had a fucking fin.

I'm sorry, Vikki's song whispered. I blinked, and shivered when I realized it was a third eyelid that slid sideways across my eyes. My vision cleared into perfect clarity when I kept the third eyelid in place.

The depths of the ocean crushed around me, but my chest rose and fell as water filtered through fresh scales at my neck. *I'm a fucking mermaid!* I shrieked. My words careened through the ocean and bounced back at me after they'd hit rocks, making my head ache with the force of echolocation now drilled into my skull.

Vikki should have guided me through the process it took to become a siren, which would have given me the surge of magic to regain my powers as a muse. But instead of staying with me through the transition, she'd let go. It could have killed me had I not given up everything. I needed to eliminate all ties with the land to become a mermaid. If I'd been left alone with even a single shred of my connection to the land and anyone in it, I would have surely died.

It's only temporary, Vikki promised, finally appearing as a shifting shadow in the waters.

I flicked my tail, *my fucking tail,* and barreled towards her. She deftly slipped out of the way.

You'll get your powers back, she promised, *but first, you need to find something for me.*

I hissed as rage filled me. I had no desire to be a mermaid, nor to be ordered around. While I'd cut all ties to the land, I wasn't completely transformed. I had twenty-four hours before the fin was permanent, and my memory of my previous life was completely wiped clean.

Let me be your anchor.

The voice that came was my father's and I looked skyward to where I knew the surface would lie. I couldn't see the moonlight, but I could feel its silver kiss across waves and knew that my father was there, somewhere, and he was reaching for me.

I locked onto the memory he fed through magic that wound deep into the waters and into my heart. My mother, young and in love, and happy.

Vikki might have taken my sorrow from her loss, but my love for her remained. It didn't bring pain or dread, only happiness, to be reminded of the small seed of her that remained in my soul. Love for my mother was pure and unhindered, and my father reminded me of that as I solidified my connection to the land.

Do what she wants, he commanded. *She can release you from your fin, and you'll be returned to me restored. You should have told me you'd met a chameleon, but you are your mother's child. Stubborn as always.*

I ignored him and faced the blue flames that housed Vikki. *What do you need me to find?*

Vikki's desire was something that even a muse couldn't give. She wanted a sea pearl, and only a mermaid would have a chance in hell in finding one.

The ocean was a magical and mystical place. Water washed everything away and took it into deep, dark crevices of the sea unexplored by man or supernatural. Only the mermaids could go where forgotten magics gathered.

I dove. Power propelled me through the deep as my fin waved up and down. I kept my arms tight to my naked chest as I delved into the abyss.

Magic wound freely through me and even if I didn't want to be a mermaid, I relished the freedom that this life could offer. I didn't need to surface and I could go where no other supernatural had been.

When the gleaming blue of a mermaid city came to life, I couldn't help but smile.

They welcomed me as I slowed my descent. I was one of them and they were free of emotions that plagued humans or supernatural. They shushed me and brushed fingers through my floating hair, assuring me that in a day's time, I'd lose the last of my memories and I'd forever be free to swim and dance with them.

Mermaids were a peaceful race. They made love and stretched their long fins along cushions of magic and seaweed. There wasn't a need to procreate, so the lovemaking wasn't as I knew it to be. It was pleasure through magic and kisses and something deeper and sweeter than a siren's song that thrummed through the waters.

I swept past the orgy of mermaids. Their call was strong, but I knew if I gave in to the song of mermaids and mermen, I'd never see the light of day again.

When I declined, they reluctantly let me go as I went past the waves of magical aqua pleasures and entered into the crevices of the Earth's crust.

The caves sparkled with energy and magic. The bottom gleamed and glittered with the treasure I sought, the tears of the ocean.

The blue pearls illuminated my surroundings and thrummed with ancient magic. It was a mixture of all the magic in the world that was forgotten and had sunken deep into the sea.

Guilt stabbed at me as I snatched one up. This was magic so pure that no supernatural ever got their hands on it. Tears of the Sea were legend. The mermaids collected the magic and put them here for safekeeping. They weren't guardians, for no-one could ever find this place camouflaged by their magic. But they knew how to keep things hidden.

I considered taking more than one, but something in me knew that these pearls were impossibly precious. Taking even one was a crime against magic and my heart ached as I clutched the single pearl to my chest and swam towards the pull of my father's memories of my mother, the only connection I had to land and love.

A MUSE REBORN

Sarah

The closer I got to shore, the more I remembered who I was and what I had suffered. Vikki had taken my misery, but it hadn't erased the memories. I held onto any that drifted up from my subconscious as my father filled me with images of my mother, and then of me as a baby in her arms.

It was the last memory that started to change me back to a land-bound creature. I pushed myself harder to blast through the icy layers of the sea as scales melted from my enormous fin. Flakes of magic scathed off of me as my father showed me why he'd left. Helen had arrived shortly after I'd been born and had given my mother what my father never had. She'd smiled, full of love, and when my father saw them together, he knew the right thing to do would be to leave. Even if she hated him, even if she never forgave him, she didn't love him like she loved Helen.

And so my father had done the right thing and abandoned us so that my mother could live in happiness, and I could have a siren who I lovingly called Aunt Helen.

The realization shot pain through my lower body as my fin split into two and transformed into legs. The slices at my neck started to close and panic wound through me. I still hadn't reached the surface and if I turned back into a human body now, I'd be crushed by the sea or drowned.

Use the pearl! Vikki's voice encouraged me. *It has more than enough power to get you home. Use it!*

The blue bauble in my fist glowed profusely as if angered I'd taken it from its nest, but when I reached my mind into it, I found the swirling mix of magic that made up its heart.

Ice glowed blue through my veins as the pearl gifted me a sliver of its power. I was its wielder now, and I had rightfully laid claim to it as a mermaid. It couldn't let me die, not after all I'd gone through to retrieve it.

Black, sparkling dots cleared from my vision as my body filled with oxygen. Water was full of oxygen and the pearl extracted it with ease to lessen the strain across my chest.

I kicked, now having legs, and the last of my scales drifted into the darkened deep below. There was a sliver of light above me and I swam towards it as hard as I could, ignoring the tingle of needles along my limbs as I grew fatigued from the battle to reach the surface.

Vikki found me just when I was about to give up and drift back into the darkness. Her blue eyes glowed with delight. Her gaze twitched briefly to the ancient magic I clutched to my chest, but her grip wrapped around my arms and pulled me upwards through currents and schools of fish. She didn't have a fin, but a shadowed cloud of power clung to her like an underwater fog. She moved with power and grace, likely the boon of having fed on my suffering and my death. Scales lined her arms and her naked body gleamed with threads of blue magic.

When we burst through the surface, I gasped in my first

breath of air, reborn, and I lifted into the sky as the transformation took hold.

Where the ocean held mysteries of the deep, the powers of a muse were transcendent of time and space. A muse thrived off of passion and the wistful wonders that knit the world together. A smile lifted my lips as I was reborn, and the gift of a muse's boon transcended onto my mortal flesh.

I was back, baby.

MUSE AGAIN

Sarah

I was a muse again, but it had come at a price. I'd died and lost all my love for this world. Only the fresh memories of my mother that had been fed to me to restore a connection to the land had brought me back, but I still had nothing in me anymore. Vikki had taken it all, and although she glowed with the power it had given her, guilt painted her face. She rolled the glowing blue pearl across her palm. The mystical, ancient power known as a Tear of the Sea should have enthralled her. Instead, she seemed lost in thought as the toyed with it.

I eased back onto a sofa. My father had taken us both in, not wishing me near the sirens in my current state. I was renewed, but half of me felt missing. I struggled to remember why I cared about this world.

I sat closest to the window that overlooked the beach. The sea still called to me with promises of reprieve. I wouldn't have to worry. If I simply went back into the water, pulled the lofty sheets of waves over my head, I could sleep, and rest in her embrace.

"Stop that," Vikki chided. She scowled and shoved the Tear of the Sea at me. "You need this more than me. It'll help with the call of the sea. Take it."

Blinking with surprise, I took the pearl and coddled it to my chest. A tension I hadn't known had been there eased.

My father leaned in the doorway and gave Vikki a grin. "I knew I liked you." He jerked his chin at me. "I believe you owe Vikki a muse's boon."

I frowned. I was in no condition to give up my powers for three years. Already I felt splintered and lost. My powers as a muse swirled inside me, familiar, yet foreign at the same time. It was as if I had forgotten how to be what I'd been born to be.

Looking at Vikki, I eased my magic towards her. She grinned. "If you wanted me to sit with you, all you had to do was ask." She jumped from her seat and squished in beside me, wrapping her arms around my waist.

With an affectionate smile, my father nodded. "I'll leave you two lovebirds alone. Stay as long as you like." And then in a whisper of shadow, he was gone.

Vikki gave me a sweet kiss on my cheek. "I can wait. We can stay here until you're yourself again."

Looking into her ice blue eyes, I wondered if I'd ever be myself again. "You'll stay with me?"

She nodded and ran her thumb across my lower lip. "I'm not going anywhere."

I cupped her face and took her mouth with mine. Her kiss grounded me and gave me something to hold onto in this world.

When her magic mixed with mine and my muse's powers told me that this was something more than lust, that Vikki cared for me, I felt something I'd never expected from a siren.

I was fulfilled.

BABY GOT WINGS

Sonya

The voice of a sentient Blood Stone now a part of my body had promised me the impossible.

I could give Sarah her powers back.

Though it wouldn't much matter if I couldn't escape my current predicament. The world had gone to shit. There was no way we were going to get out of Shanghai alive.

Dragons had been cooped up for far too long. Jet was their rightful king, and even if he'd slain his own brother to take his place as their leader, too many had turned. Now more than ever I wanted to be by his side. I'd finally found the third piece of my heart. It was no coincidence that he'd been the one to escort me. Destiny was bringing us all together and I hoped I would find my fourth soon. But for now, Jet had to help his dragons. Without his guidance, they were nothing short of Derek's dogs.

Jet had his work cut out for him. Dragons streamed across the sky and I shielded my eyes against the flashes of dragonfire.

"Come on!" Luke shouted as he grabbed my wrist and jerked me along.

I had the power of a newly born Bloodstone, and it was damn chatty.

Why are we running? it complained.

I scoffed. "Because dragons are destroying this city and it's time to get out of here." Luke gave me a raised brow, but there wasn't time to explain it to him. There was a Blood Stone inside my chest mixing its voice with that of my runes and both forces wanted answers. "You got a plan?" I asked Luke instead.

He gave me a wicked smile. He had those eerie kind of blue eyes that made me want to stop and watch him, just to see the shape of his soul that lingered behind such a glassy exterior. "You bet your ass I've got a plan."

Luke led us to the airport. On foot, it took a while and I was sweating profusely by the time we got there. My clothes hung loose on my body and I was lucky that I still wore anything at all. I picked at the edges frayed from dragonfire that had leeched beyond the forcefield I'd erected around myself when Jet had killed his brother.

"There," Luke pointed at a private plane off in the shadows.

The plane was barely discernible under the moonlight. Only the occasional blast of dragonfire illuminated its rusted panels. It sure wasn't like Derek's with all the bells and whistles. I wasn't even sure that it had seats. I made a face.

Luke slapped me on the back. "Aw, come on. Think of it as an adventure."

"That piece of junk isn't going to get us all the way back to America."

His eyes went wild with delight. "No, but with a little magic, it might."

Fuck. That's the word that kept repeating itself over and over in my head as I strapped myself into the seat—at least the damn piece of junk had seatbelts.

"Okay. So I'm going to turn it on and then you're going to use that nifty power of yours to get us back home."

I scowled at the array of buttons and levers. There was no way I knew how to fly a plane, much less how to use magical powers to speed it up enough to get us home before it fell out of the sky.

"We're not going home," I informed him as I strapped the seatbelt tighter around my waist. "We're going to Miami."

He stabbed buttons until the plane eventually reacted like an old man and sputtered to life. "I can understand you've had it with the supernatural community, but you're sure you want to run away to a paradise island?"

"It's not an island," I snapped, "and it's certainly not paradise." He didn't know that Miami was home to the most dangerous race of supernaturals known to history.

Luke pulled a lever and we began to move—or more like we jolted in place. A horrible screeching of metal sounded and Luke cursed until he found the lever that unlatched the brakes.

Sarah hates Miami. What do you think she's doing there? the Blood Stone asked.

I frowned. There was no way I was going to speak to a voice inside my head like some kind of nut job.

Fine. Ignore me. Let's see how much good that does you when you try to fly this piece of junk.

I sighed. "Okay, fine."

Luke gave me another raised brow. "You going to tell me why you keep talking to yourself?"

I glowered. "It's the Blood Stone, all right? It's talking to me."

His eyes went wide. "Well, damn. What's it saying?"

Tell him he's annoying.

"It says it likes you," I said, betraying the lie with a twitch of my mouth.

He narrowed his eyes. "Sure."

Shouts sounded as we staggered down the runway. I was pretty sure the ride we'd picked had a flat tire. "This is a terrible idea."

Luke pushed on the lever and the plane sputtered, but we sped up. "If that talking Blood Stone of yours likes me so much, then why don't you ask it to give us a hand?"

Fine, a voice said inside my head, *but it's for you, darling. Not for him.*

Before I had a chance to snap a retort at my snotty Blood Stone, red light blasted from my fingertips and I screeched. Red hot electricity jolted through the panel and lit up every button with reds and oranges. Alarms blared, but the winds picked up as we moved faster down the runway and the voices retreated.

"You're doing it!" Luke shouted. He banged his fists against the panels. "Keep going!"

My stomach turned as the plane lurched upward, and then we were airborne. Luke hooted with excitement as if we weren't about to die.

"Quit shouting and steer this thing!" I gripped the sides of my armrests and clenched my teeth as heat flashed through me. My Blood Stone burned inside of my chest and blasted such power through my body that all I could do was endure.

Luke thankfully did as I asked and wrapped his fingers around the stick and yanked. We jolted left, but it was enough to right our unbalanced climb.

I closed my eyes when the Blood Stone gave me another flash of heat. I knew it was like the echo of thunder and another strike was going to come.

Pain speared through my temples and I released a scream as my world engulfed in red veins. Electricity crackled and wrapped us in power. A portal opened at the nose of the plane.

"Holy shit," Luke said.

I wholeheartedly agreed.

HELLO MIAMI

Sonya

So, as it turns out, traveling through magical portals hurts. A lot.

My mind knew that only an instant had passed. Electric zaps streaked through the tunnel that sped us across the world, but pain warps one's sense of time. I gritted my teeth together as I stifled a cry of agony. I could barely think straight as we catapulted out of a massive red ball that marked the end of our near-instantaneous journey between Shanghai and Miami. Pain unlatched claws from my chest and allowed me to breathe as Miami's salty air blasted into the cockpit.

We didn't have time to relax. A radio blared to life, its sound barely distinguishable above the lashing of rampaging winds. My fingers still numb, I stretched for the headset, but groaned as a pathetic sense of uselessness swept over me. My Blood Stone hummed a silent power in the background as the portal closed behind us, and I got the sense that such a massive display of power came with a cost. Whatever, or whoever, was the sentient voice of my Blood Stone likely wouldn't pipe up for a while.

Luke was the first to overcome the shock of our magical travel and jerked the headset on. He gripped the plastic hard against his head as he struggled to listen. His eyes went wide. "Don't shoot!" he yelled into the com.

My knuckles poked white against my skin as I gripped my armrests for dear life and attempted to keep what little food I had in my stomach in place. "Who's shooting?"

Luke leaned on the panel and looked skyward, but it was too dark to see anything. Then he looked down. "We've got to be close to the ocean. I can see a reflection." His wild blue eyes found mine. "We gotta jump."

A manic laugh came with a short hiccup. "Are you kidding me? I can't—"

Luke unlatched my buckle and ripped me out of my chair. "They're going to *shoot,* all right? The humans are freaked out about what's going on in Shanghai. And now an airplane appears out of a ball of red electric power? I don't blame them. I'd shoot too."

A screech of fighter jets barreling past us made me cringe.

"Those were warning passes," he shouted. "Trust me." He offered his hand, and I drew in a shaky breath before I took it.

The ocean looked very far from where we stood on the edge of the plane now dipping without a pilot to keep the rusted stick in place. "On three," Luke said.

I squeezed my eyes shut. "One," I began.

"Two," Luke said.

Three.

I screamed as we fell. My eyes hadn't deceived me. We'd been way too high to hope for a survivable fall to the waters below. A split second as I came to the realization that I was going to die.

Don't be so dramatic, came the chiding voice as icy wind whipped up the remains of my pants. I clung to Luke's hand as we continued to plummet.

A red aura surrounded us, slowing our descent a fraction. My Blood Stone shouldn't have been able to speak. I sensed its weakened state and how it wanted to rest. But power engulfed us to protect our fall.

A crash came, and I thought we might have hit the surface, only to find that we were still descending. I looked up to find our plane a ball of flames plummeting out of the sky.

Damn humans, said the Blood Stone.

I swallowed, but the red aura crept warmth up my legs until we were drifting instead of plummeting to the dark waters below.

Luke laughed and pulled me into his arms. The red haze of magic wound around our wrists. "Who needs wings when I've got you?"

Luke was part angel, and wings would have been useful right about now. But as I curled my fingers across the folds of his shirt I was glad that this time, I could be the savior.

We landed in the waters with a soft splash and our romantic moment was over. I spat out water and coughed at the sharp sting of salt as it went up my nose.

I blinked and splashed as the icy waters tore me from Luke's embrace. The next dilemma was apparent. We were nowhere near shore.

Luke sputtered and began swimming with long strokes across the waves.

"How do you know that's the right way?" I asked.

"Intuition," he said with a smile, and then continued swimming.

I growled. Damn intuition was going to get us killed.

I hated water, and it hated me. Salt spewed up my nose and every time I tried to cough it out, I seemed to swallow more of the wretched stuff. Just when it felt like my arms were about to freeze off, Luke slowed down and kept a wary eye on me. His movements were natural as if he belonged in the ocean, which wasn't what I'd expected of someone who was half-angel and built for the skies.

The final blast at slowing our descent seemed to have had a detrimental effect on my unseen ally. The Blood Stone went quiet and only supplied a steady hum of warmth in the center of my chest, enough to keep me alive, but my extremities quickly grew numb against the biting cold of the water. Luke swam on without a shiver, able to rely on his powers of regeneration to resist the cold.

I growled as I tried to keep up with him. It didn't matter that we were on the outskirts of Miami, a place supposed to be wretchedly hot. The breeze swept over the crashing waves and I was freezing in the midnight air that curled over my shoulders. The cold spray of moonlight only seemed to make things more frigid.

"We're almost there," Luke assured me.

I didn't have the energy to argue with him. My teeth chattered too hard to form a reply anyway. I continued to battle on with the crash of salt and waves with jerky slaps of my arms.

"Stop," he insisted and gripped my shoulder. "Let's rest."

He instructed me how to turn onto my back and let the salt keep me afloat. Water rushed into my ears as I stared at the stars, but I was too tired to kick myself upright again. Once I'd stopped moving, I felt like a shark that was ready to die. "This was a bad idea," I said, my voice reverberating over the water.

I wasn't sure if I was referring to stealing a rusted airplane, traveling to Miami through a magical portal, or jumping out of a plane, but I was pretty sure all of those things had been a terrible idea.

"Do you hear that?" Luke asked.

His voice had come to me as a dulled echo through the layers of water intruding my ears. "No."

He kicked himself upright and trod lightly. "Shh, listen."

I rolled my eyes. "If you're trying to scare me—"

He gripped my wrist, yanking me upright, and the fear in his blue eyes told me that this wasn't a joke.

Then I heard it. A song, faint and mysterious on the winds. It called to me and told me that if I followed, I'd be warm, safe, secure.

My eyes went wide. "Sirens."

QUEEN OF COLD

Sonya

I knew why Sarah was in Miami and it wasn't for the tourism. She hated the sun and the palm trees and all the pink Hawaiian shirts that had nothing to do with Miami. She'd always told me that muses were better suited for crappy weather. She could better capitalize on a human's potential for passion and creativity when they were all cooped up inside with nothing to do.

No, there was only one reason Sarah possibly had for coming to the most dangerous place in all the world for supernaturals. She believed that she could get her powers back.

The sirens might have helped a powerless muse like Sarah. I felt stupid for not thinking of it earlier. Of course she would seek them out, no matter how dangerous it might be. Sarah wasn't meant to be mortal. She wouldn't have lasted a single day being unable to bend people to her will. I wondered what it had taken to get her to change her mind that she had things under control. Maybe one rude customer at the bar where she tended, or just the fact that she couldn't get a quick ride home without paying a tab.

"They're everywhere," Luke said with an edge to his voice that I hadn't heard before. "What are they?"

"Sirens," I hissed. "Stay close to me. Men are more susceptible to them."

He *tsked*. "If you couldn't seduce me, then I'm not worried about a couple of sirens."

I rolled my eyes and yanked him close. "I *did* seduce you, even in the presence of angelstone," I reminded him.

He growled in reply.

The red heat of my Blood Stone zapped at our skin contact. I hoped for its power to come out, to keep us safe, but nothing happened. "Where are you?" I snapped to my Blood Stone. We couldn't just float around the ocean powerless as sirens closed in.

Still, the Blood Stone was dormant, as if waiting for something. Forms shifted underneath our feet deep in the water and I shivered as goosebumps spread across my skin. I'd had nightmares of this. Sharks and creepy things lingering in the deep as I drifted in the ocean where no one could hear me scream.

One of the forms grew closer until it was a black orb beneath us and I kicked wildly to get out of the way.

Luke gripped me hard. "No matter what, we stick together."

"Fine," I said through gritted teeth. "But that doesn't mean we have to get eaten together."

Blonde hair glinted against the moonlight when the form was close enough to distinguish. What I had thought to be a siren wasn't a siren at all. She looked up at me with brilliant amber eyes that only one person in the whole world boasted.

It was Sarah.

"The hell?" I screeched as Sarah surfaced and spit water in my face. I coughed and slapped her on the shoulder. "I thought you were a flesh-eating siren!"

She smiled, and I was surprised to see delight and mischief in her eyes. "Oh come on. You deserved to be a little scared." She glanced at Luke. "Oh. You've brought the mute."

He glowered, but didn't prove her wrong by trying to speak.

I narrowed my eyes at him. "Luke's not a mute."

She splashed water in my face again. "Who cares? You're back! Race you to the shore!"

Before I had a chance to tell Sarah that I had no idea which way the shore was, she sped off with a thrust that sent the waves reeling. I gawked at her as she left a trail behind her like a speedboat.

Once Sarah had disappeared into the haze of fog, Luke coughed. "Damn muses. I can't speak around them. They jumble my brains." He nodded. "Come on. Apparently the shore's this way."

Luke splashed through the foamy remnants of Sarah's departure and I trailed behind him trying not to sputter from the saltwater searing up my nose. Give me demons to fight, dragons to seduce, or humans to save, but toss me into the sea and it's not pretty.

Once we finally reached a sandy platform I stood and snagged my fingers through my sticky hair. Luke snickered at me when I made a face. "You look fine."

I glowered. Guys always said you looked fine when you totally didn't. "Just keep walking, angel-butt." Luke's blue eyes shimmered with silver moonlight and now that I knew what to look for, I could spot the supernatural elements in him. His black hair was perfect and slick against his neck. His muscles pleasantly flexed under the clinging t-shirt and his bare feet left deep sink marks as he marched towards a gathering of women who were waiting for us. His gait said he was fearless, but the tension in his shoulders said he knew that he was walking into a nest of dangerous supernaturals. I didn't care how new Luke was to the supernatural world. Everyone innately knew to stay away from a siren.

Going against my instincts, I followed Luke up to the group. The women didn't hide their nature. The younger sirens twisted into each other's arms and scales glimmered on their legs, proof that they hadn't quite finished their transition into a more humanoid creature.

The elder sirens could be recognized by the depths of madness in their eyes. I kept close to Luke's side as we approached the group and stared them down. My fingers instinctually went for the Blood Stone around my neck, but it was no longer a necklace and my fingers only met my wet skin. I made a fist. The power of the Blood Stone was within me now, but it felt strange not to have something physical to hold onto.

Most of the sirens staring us down were elders. I expected the depths of blankness and sorrow in their eyes, but what I didn't expect was to see the same bleakness in Sarah's. In the water, she'd been happy. But now that she was back on land she seemed lost. The glimmer of light in her eyes was gone and my heart clenched when she looked at me and there wasn't a reflection in her dead gaze.

"I've regained my powers," she stated flatly.

I blinked at her and gripped her fingers. Her frigid skin greedily leached my heat and I shivered. "What was the cost?" I wanted to strangle her. "Why didn't you wait for me? I'm stronger now. I could have helped you."

She tilted her head as if confused. Her brows scrunched. "Wait for you? Where have you been? I wandered alone and desperate in Seattle hoping you'd return like I was some kind of lovesick idiot."

I sighed. "I had to find Luke, remember? You told me to go for my soulmate so I could stop *killing* people, remember? So I found him. And then before I could figure out what to do next, I got kidnapped and taken to Shanghai and…" My words drifted off when I realized that Sarah actually looked bored. "Are you even listening?"

She sighed. "Sorry. It's just that you and I are over. It's just not that important." She straightened. "Did you say you were in Shanghai? Did you see what happened with the dragons?" She glowered. "Don't tell me you were involved."

My fingernails bit into my palms. "What's wrong with you? How can you act like everything between us means nothing to you anymore?"

She shrugged. "You and I were only bonded by sorrow. I'm glad you didn't come back. Anything you could have done for me would have been more of the same. I regained my powers as a muse by my own actions, my own strength. The only cost was the sorrow you had burdened me with, and now it's all gone."

I steadied myself on Luke's waiting arm. "You mean your feelings for me are gone." Tears stung my eyes and my stomach churned with dread. I snapped my gaze at the sirens and searched them for answers. I landed on one shifting behind Sarah, young, with ice blue eyes and guilt written all over her face. "You!" I said, flinging Luke away as I shoved past Sarah and stabbed a finger pointed in accusation.

"Leave Vikki alone," Sarah snapped, her words sharp as a dagger.

I blinked at her and let my hand fall to my side. My palm slapped hard against the wet sheet of my jeans. "Vikki?" I bounced my gaze between them. "You've already replaced me?"

Vikki, a short-haired siren that was breathtakingly beautiful, straightened under my disbelief and rage. "I can see why she wanted to leave you," she said with a satisfied smirk. "I've never seen so much sorrow in a person. Your grief is wrapped in red rage." She crinkled her nose. "Even I don't want to feed on it."

Luke pressed his fingers into my shoulder before I launched myself at her.

I growled, happily using Luke as an excuse to change the topic. "Sarah. Luke can't talk around you. It's a muse thing. It messes with his head."

She glanced at him, looking him up and down. "I almost didn't recognize you without all the blood and grime. You were that guy trapped in Detective Anderson's dungeon." Her eyes narrowed. "It seems Sonya has found her soulmate." His jaw flexed as if he wanted to retort that statement, but he stayed silent. Sarah sighed. "Okay, fine. I'll leave. If you've come here for me, then you've wasted your time. But my father will want to talk with you. The supernatural community is being ripped apart and he's going to have to be the one to wipe the memories of the world. He could use your help if you've been in Shanghai and can bring him up to speed."

I blinked at her. *"Father?"* I staggered. We'd come here for a male muse. They were the only ones that could fix what was going on in Shanghai. I supposed it was dimwitted of me not to realize that Apollo could be Sarah's father. There were only three possible candidates, after all.

Warily, I gazed at the sirens who watched us. "I assume your siren friends are cool with his daughter being among them?"

Sarah straightened and looked down at me along the perfect ridge of her nose that I used to kiss in the darkness of night. "My father has befriended the sirens and they work for him. They're not a race to turn your nose up at. I've gotten to know them as well and they may be lost souls, but they've helped me to find my way again." Her grip tightened on Vikki's and I bristled with jealousy. "If you've come to rekindle what we've once had, it's too late. I've found my people now."

Anger and pride roiled in my stomach. I didn't like that a male muse had somehow found a way to control the sirens, must less that Sarah seemed to be neck-deep in seaweed with them. "I didn't come here for you. Don't flatter yourself," I snapped. "I came because I need to talk to your father. I'd heard that there was a male muse in Miami. One of the dragons is my lover and I won't see him harmed. I'll trade information for his safety." I left out the bit where the entire supernatural community was in danger of being exposed. She'd find that out soon enough.

If Sarah was affected by the statement, she didn't even blink. "A dragon suits you better than I ever did."

I glowered. "Don't be so petty. What we had was special and you're the one who wanted to throw it all away."

She shrugged. "I'll leave you to the sirens to discuss your business. They confer with my father on such matters." She turned into Vikki's embrace and gave her a long, sensual kiss. Sarah glanced at me and a flicker of a triumphant smile twitched at the edge of her mouth before she sauntered away.

Luke kept his grip on my shoulder, even when I started to glow red with the power of my rage and fought the urge to chase after her and tackle her to the ground. The Blood Stone lived inside of me and reacted to my emotional whims and I hated how everyone could see how Sarah affected me. I'd been with her so long that even though she wasn't one of my four, her connection as one of the seven, one of my sins, left a lingering bond that wouldn't quite go away.

The sirens didn't seem perturbed by my magic, just fascinated. They pressed in and ran their fingers over the red hue across my skin and made soft, sensual sounds of appreciation.

With so many around us, their magical song slipped through the barrier I'd put around myself. I swayed under the power of the enticement they wafted over me like a net. A siren's magic worked on any creature, and I wasn't surprised to see Luke's eyes droop with interest.

"Well now that I can speak," he said, his voice low and husky as he cupped Vikki's cheek, "I can say this," he leaned in close, then pinched her chin hard, "back the fuck off."

Vikki squeaked with surprise and flailed out of his grip. The others pushed away with frowns of disapproval.

"All yours, Vikki," said an older siren with a song underneath her words that crashed like waves. "We're not looking for this kind of food." She crinkled her nose at me, and then gave Luke a steady glower before retreating.

Vikki sighed when we were left alone. "Finally. I thought they would never leave."

I gave Vikki a raised brow. "Really?"

She nodded. "I'm so glad you're here. I made a mistake with Sarah and now she's..." she turned to glance over her shoulder, "different."

Luke frowned. "How do you mean? Like she speeds around waves like a fish? Or she's a completely different person on land?" He grinned. "You mean she wasn't always like that?"

I slapped him on the shoulder. "Quit being annoying."

He shrugged.

Vikki grabbed my wrists as a frantic tone crept into her voice. "You don't understand. This is all my fault. I told her to find a Tear of the Ocean for me and now she's becoming worse. It's doing something to her."

My eyes widened. "You turned her into a fucking mermaid?"

Luke gave me a raised brow. "I think I missed this class in supernatural school. What's a Tear of the Ocean?" He glanced the way Sarah had gone. "And she's a mermaid? Looked like she had legs to me."

Vikki sighed. "Tears of the Ocean are coalesced supernatural magics that have drifted to the bottom of the sea. The mermaids make them and protect them. When I restored Sarah's powers, she was a mermaid for a few hours, and she got me one of the sea gems."

"What did you want it for?" I snapped. "She could have been lost to the sea forever. No one becomes a mermaid and comes back."

Vikki swallowed. "A muse can. Her father told me—"

My hand shot out before I could think and wrapped around her throat. "She said you worked for her father. Never trust a male muse. What did he want with a Tear of the Sea, hmm? It was all his idea to risk his own daughter's soul?"

Luke pried my fingers away from Vikki's throat. "Loosen up, Sonya," he chided. "She's just the messenger."

"No," I said, glowering at the siren who stumbled to the sands and rubbed the blossoming purple bruises at her neck. "She's the one who did this to Sarah." I nudged her with my foot. "What are her father's plans?"

Vikki frowned. "If I tell you, he'll kill me."

I kneeled and slammed my fists into the sand, sending grains splattering and the power of my rage rushing around us in a red wave. "You should be more worried about what I'll do to you if you don't tell me what's going on."

She trembled. "Apollo isn't like the other two male muses. He doesn't want to keep supernaturals hiding in secret forever. He told Sarah that he's gone to commune with them to deal with the dragon uprising in Shanghai, but actually he's gone looking for the chameleon."

Silence strung between us as I narrowed my eyes. "What's a chameleon?"

She glanced at Luke. "From the sound of it, it's the guy that imprisoned your boyfriend. Word was that the chameleon had a prisoner that could get Apollo something valuable. It's unfortunate that Sarah recognized you. Now that the other sirens know you're here, they'll tell Sarah's father that he's barking up the wrong tree." She shivered. "He might come back sooner than I'd anticipated."

Luke bristled and his skin flushed red, as if the mere mention of Detective Anderson made his blood boil. He cursed. "I knew that monster wasn't fucking human."

Vikki pouted, and I could have sworn the expression was one of pity. I growled. "Who are you to feel sorry for him? You're a fucking soul-sucking siren. You know only sorrow and death." I glowered. "And he's not my boyfriend." No, he wasn't... he was just a lover bound to me by destiny and I'd kill anyone who tried to take him away from me.

Vikki gave me an exasperated sigh. "Whatever. And who are you to judge me, huh, succubus? You kill anyone who gets near you, which I guess is why your not-boyfriend is alive."

I went for the Blood Stone again, but my fist only grabbed air. My fingers wound across my collarbone. The power of the Blood Stone pulsated in my veins, but it had lost its voice as if my rage had wiped out all its thoughts. "I'm working on that," I said honestly. "So," I began, "why does Apollo want Luke?"

Vikki shivered. "He needs the last power stone to complete the set. The other two are already in his control. There's the Tear of the Sea, which I already have, and the Incubus King promised him a Blood Stone."

My eyes went wide and I flashed Luke a worried look. "You only made the one, right?"

Vikki blanched. "You guys actually *made* a Blood Stone? I was hoping that was a bunch of crock. Holy shit."

Luke shook his head. "Derek wouldn't have let me go if he'd thought that the Blood Stone we were making was the only one. He's got to be up to something."

"And the third stone?" I asked.

Vikki shook her head. "I don't know. The Sky Stone is the last one and it's said to be the soul of an angel." She laughed. "Ridiculous, right?"

Luke and I gave each other a shared look of dread. "Shit."

Retreating indoors, we sat around a wooden table in the beach's siren bar. We'd ordered our food and my clothes had nearly dried, but I couldn't shake the feeling that everything was about to go to shit.

Sirens' magical songs drifted around us, but even the enticing melody wasn't enough to drain the tension from my bones.

"Derek didn't come into my bunker in New York just to kidnap me," Luke said. "The incubus bastard must have gotten the Sky Stone," Luke continued, his tone turning frantic. His blue eyes bore into mine full of haunting memories of the endless torture he'd suffered. "It's why I had no control around him. I thought it was because he was the Incubus King, but it's because he took my soul."

My stomach wound into knots as I pushed a shrimp around on my plate. "So let's say that Derek managed to make another Blood Stone, and he also has your soul. If he's working with Sarah's father, then that means that Apollo has two of the objects he needs to overthrow the other muses."

"He's not going to just overthrow them," Vikki said as she coddled a strawberry cocktail. I bristled that she chose Sarah's favorite drink to flaunt in my face. She took a long sip and ran a manicured nail across her lip. "He's going to kill them."

"But that would mean he'd be the only male muse left," I said. The idea sounded preposterous. "He'd be endangering the entire race." If anything happened to Apollo, then there wouldn't be muses anymore. There'd be nothing to control the chaos of supernaturals entering into the world. I thought of how Derek liked to run things, and I imagined that if supernaturals came out of the closet, he'd think himself our leader. He'd expect the humans to bow to him. I shivered. "I don't like where this is going. Demonspawn are only just the beginning. Derek is going to do a whole lot worse than releasing hell on earth. He's going to become a god."

Luke pinched his lips together. "The only thing stopping him is Sarah's Tear of the Ocean. That's the only stone of power that he or Derek doesn't have." He gripped Vikki's wrist. "You have to convince Sarah to give it back to the mermaids."

Vikki frowned. "I can't do that. It's the only thing keeping her alive. And even if she could part with it, mermaids don't come near anyone. They live in the deepest part of the unexplored ocean where no one can go. And even if she just threw the gem into the sea, it'd come back to her. She's its owner now."

I leaned back into my chair and it creaked with protest. "I'll talk to her. Maybe there's something I can do." My hand spread across my chest. "Or something this power can do. It has to be good for something."

Vikki gave me a raised brow. "What is that red magic? Did you overfeed or something? It seems so angry and strange."

I shrugged. "I'm just a powerful succubus." I gave her a smile. "I guess you better watch out."

ROMANCE ME

Sonya

It felt weird to make myself at home in Apollo's beach house, but my hair stuck out at all angles and my breath smelled like crustaceans. Sarah ignored me when I passed her in the living room and made my way to the guest room, but it was progress that she didn't kick me out. Vikki had invited us, after all. Even if it was just her hoping I didn't out her to Apollo, it was nice having someone be kind to me.

I paused in the bedroom, wishing I had my cell phone. A single tablet rested on the dresser and I considered if I could try and reach out to Jet. Not that I knew his social contact info. I supposed I could search the internet for "crazy dragon leader," but that probably wouldn't go too well.

I'd just have to meet up with him later. He had a whole civilization of hot-collared dragons to get under control and I had a whacked-out muse on my hands surrounded by Sirens. Not to mention Nate was still out there and my runes blistered over, punishing me for letting him down.

One thing at a time. I decided first I was going to get a good, long wash under hot, fresh water that didn't stick to my face, I felt a lot better after that and then rummaged through the guest supplies lined up on the marble counter. Apollo no doubt often had siren sleepovers and it seemed that he doted on them. There was everything I could possibly want; fancy toothbrushes, teeth whitener, waterproof mascara, and the expensive type of razors, not that I needed them. Sirens were originally human, so they kept mortal traits such as growing hair on their legs. As a succubus, I was built to be a sensual creature. The only hair that grew on me was eyelashes, eyebrows, and lush curls atop my head. Sarah had always teased me that one day my genetic makeup would get confused and I'd lose all my hair like a naked mole rat. I teased my fingers through the fresh comb of curls at my temples and sighed. Being so close to her, but not being able to touch her, was killing me.

Her scent lingered everywhere. Lilac and her favorite sweet perfume. I opened the closet, only to be greeted with a full array of outfits ready to pick from. I chose a red dress, perhaps a little formal, but I wanted to remind Sarah what she was missing. I liked to dress up when there was someone around to appreciate me.

"Wow," Luke breathed as he waltzed into my room, not having bothered to knock. He hung on the door and looked me up and down. "What are you wearing?"

I glowered. "What are you doing barging into my room? I was naked a few seconds ago."

He grinned and it was hard not to appreciate the masculine lines across his jaw. "I'm a few seconds too late," he said without missing a beat. He came to me and slipped his hand around my waist with such familiarity that I just stood there and blinked at him like an idiot. "You seem tense, and I don't think it's just the near-death experience from a magic portal and dragonfire." He stroked my face. "Are you worried about the others?"

He didn't have to specify. Even if he didn't know about Nate, his hand slipped to my stomach, pressing knowingly against my runes. I tried to keep a straight face. "What do you know about them?" I asked.

His lip quirked in a smile. "I know that Jet makes you orgasm literal fireballs, and I know there's someone else out there you can't live without. You worry about them. Tell me about them. Talk to me."

I swayed on my feet. "I... They're not the only ones I'm worried about." I wasn't ready to talk about my four, because that would be admitting a mystical bond that went deeper than I was ready to go. My gaze flew to the doorway. Even if Sarah wasn't one of my four, she was one of my outlier runes that still twinged, its soft pink skin remembering her love and her touch.

He followed my gaze. "I know you care for Sarah, but that's just because you have history." He eased the door closed and came back to me, taking me into his arms as he cupped my face. "Maybe you'll help her remember what you two had, but that won't change how I feel about you." I stiffened at the honest tenderness of his touch. "We're bound by destiny, remember? I know you're a succubus. I know I'll always have to share you. I can be okay with that, but only with those who deserve you."

I'd never been talked to that way. My relationships had always been intoxicating followed by the insanely jealous, whether the affections had been deserved or not. Sarah didn't want me with anyone and she'd looked at me with such betrayal in her eyes when she'd found me with a new victim, no matter how many times I'd nearly died because of the guilt. I couldn't help what I was. I couldn't change that I needed to feed. Even with the Blood Stone, my cravings were more powerful than ever. The only thing it changed was that I didn't have to kill my lovers. It was the only thing keeping me sane.

As Luke pressed a kiss to the top of my head, my eyelids fluttered closed. "I have to talk to Sarah," I protested, but was unable to slip away from the warmth of his embrace.

"Stay with me for a little while," he whispered.

My fingers curled around the soft shirt he'd found from his own secret closet. It seemed that Apollo had male guests as well. "Do you really want me?" I asked, forcing myself to pull away. "Or are you still under Derek's influence?"

The Incubus King had forced Luke to want me. Before that, even though Luke and I were bound by destiny, he'd seemed only mildly interested. I knew the dark truth of his feelings. Luke had only wanted to unravel the secrets of his own tormented life, and I was someone capable of helping him to do that. In the end, answers were more important to Luke than anything he felt for me... or so I'd believed.

I shivered as he pulled away and cupped my face; his touch seemed to protest my thoughts. "Sonya. I don't know why I feel what I feel. You might think it's Derek's power over me. I'll be honest with you. He wants me to empower your Blood Stone." He caressed his fingertips lightly down my neck and rested his touch against my heart. My breasts seemed to swell with his hand so close to my hardening nipples and I bit my lip. "It doesn't explain what I felt before," he insisted. His blue eyes found mine and it was hard not to miss the tempest of emotion in them. He had suffered so much, but what he feared most was to be left alone. I recognized it because it was a reflection of my own worst fear. "Just stay with me for a little while. I'm not asking anything of you. I'm not telling you not to be with anyone else. I just want to be near you right now."

It was so genuine that I wrapped my fingers around his wrist and pulled him to the bed. My thighs ached and my heart thundered in my ears, but I denied my basic impulses to take him. Luke was too sensitive and emotional. To use him for my own lust was wrong. I had always only fed when I had no other choice. With the power of the Blood Stone in my chest, I didn't have the crippling hunger that threatened to end my life if not sated. There was only the cravings that came with what I was and I suppressed them… to an extent.

We lay across from each other on the bed, our hands roaming across each other's bodies. It felt strange to be clothed, but to feel so much passion in a caress. His fingertips sent lightning and goosebumps across my skin and my senses swirled with delight as our breaths mingled. I closed my eyes and indulged in the sensation of being so close to him. It was only when his chest eased into a rhythmic rise and fall under my hand did I realize that he'd fallen asleep.

I didn't want to sleep. I drifted into a half-lucid state as I watched him and memorized the lines of his face illuminated by moonlight that trickled in through the open window. The crash of the distant waves combined with faraway sirens' songs and amplified my yearning for him, but I told myself to be happy with this moment. When he opened his eyes, having roused from a deep sleep, he smiled, and caressed my face. "Beautiful," he whispered before he drifted off again.

It was the most romantic night of my life.

FISH MEN AND... FISH PARTS

Sonya

Luke was still asleep when I got up in the morning. He'd been through so much. He'd finally escaped from Detective Anderson, unable to die even when his own heart had been ripped out of his chest. Because of me, he'd scarcely been free for a few months before Derek took him. I didn't know what Derek had made him do in Shanghai, but I couldn't imagine that it had been anything good. Guilt tugged at my heartstrings as I smoothed the wrinkles in my dress. I'd been hips-deep with the true Dragon King while Luke had been a prisoner. When I'd found him in Derek's tunnels, he'd been under a spell, compelled to feed his power to the creation of a Blood Stone. Not only that, but he'd been a part of something that ripped at the veil between this world and another. Wherever demonspawn were trapped, Luke had been the dagger to pierce it and I feared what he was capable of if he ever truly learned to master the powers in his blood. His father was an angel, which meant that Luke was the first of his kind in known history.

Angels weren't meant to walk the earth. If they ever did, they were known as demons, a reduced, dark form of the greatness they'd once been.

I closed the door softly behind me and wandered the halls in the quiet of morning, the estate framed by the crashing of waves from the open windows everywhere I went. I followed the scent of lilac until I found Sarah sipping morning tea surrounded by white and pink hibiscus blooms. She glanced at me as I approached.

She looked back to the tablet she was reading and continued to scroll. So, she wouldn't send me away. It was a start.

Then I noticed the tea set, a very British setup with the tiny cups my grandmother liked. I frowned at them as I eased onto the wicker chair. My grandmother had gone missing, along with Nate. According to Derek, Nate was serving penance by filling his many harem houses. I knew that my grandmother could take care of herself, but the fact that I still hadn't heard from her had me worried.

"You seem to have a lot on your mind," Sarah said with her familiar, melodic voice that made my thighs clench in reaction. An entire night of foreplay with Luke had gotten my blood pumping and it took every ounce of willpower I had not to straddle Sarah right there and devour her.

I gave her the sweetest smile I could manage and poured myself a cup of steaming tea. "You seem hospitable. I thought you hated me now."

She leaned back into her chair and coddled her drink. She gazed out the window at the sea with a whisper of longing in her eyes to plunge back into the depths. "I don't hate you. I don't feel anything at all. That was part of the process to bring me back. I lost all love I had for anyone in this world." She frowned. "It feels so strange. I was so angry with you." Her gaze found mine and my skin crawled with the emptiness that lived in her eyes. "But now I don't feel anything when I look at you. I would have thought to feel something. Even if it would just be an echo of what we once had and how you'd made me feel. But it's like that part of me has died. It's just gone."

I suppressed the urge to growl. "Your new girlfriend did a real number on you." I set my cup onto the glass table. It clinked harder than I'd intended it to and I grimaced at the fine glimmer of a crack that spidered across the porcelain.

Sarah sighed. "I know you're jealous. If I still had my feelings, I likely would be too, now that you've found your soulmate. I see that he's shared your room." She forced a smile. "I do hope you're happy."

"I'm not," I spat. It took no hesitation to admit that I wasn't happy. Everything about this was wrong. Whatever existed between Luke and me was a result of Derek or the cosmos or my own supernatural instincts. It wasn't a natural development, not like it had been with Sarah. I leaned in and took her hand, trying to ignore how cold she felt. "What we had was a real relationship. Luke and I are just—I don't know what we are. But it's not like what you and I had."

"No," she said and reclaimed her hand. "You think that our relationship was real, but it was just as manufactured as anything else. What we had was just the result of a shared sorrow. We both lost our mothers that night. We had a kindred pain. It made sense that we would find comfort in one another." She ran her touch around the edge of her cup. A layer of frost webbed across her tea, but she didn't seem to notice her blatant display of magic. "I don't know who I am anymore," she said absently. "The only place I feel happy again is the sea." Her empty gaze found mine, but this time it flickered with a single emotion: fear. "If I give in, if I dive deep into the ocean, I'll never come back."

I shifted uncomfortably in my seat. The source of this was the gem she'd gained as a mermaid. "Can I see it?" I asked. "The Tear of the Sea."

She closed her eyes briefly, then opened them again and a ring sparkled on her finger that hadn't been there a moment before. "I've learned how to cloak it with a siren's mirage," she said. "It seems I've picked up a few new tricks."

I frowned, but examined the ring as she presented it. "Does your father know you have this?" I asked.

She laughed. "Yes, of course. If it weren't for him, I wouldn't have survived at all. He helped me to retrieve it, as well as helped me to regain my legs and my powers as a muse."

"What if he wants the Tear for himself?"

She scoffed. "What could he do with it? It only reacts to sirens and other sea creatures. Since I was a mermaid, it seems to have bonded with me."

I smirked. "I still can't picture you as a mermaid." I cupped my chin in my hands. "Did you braid your hair and decorate your nipples with seashells?"

She snickered. "No." She waved her hand and the ring vanished. "Although life as a mermaid didn't seem so bad. Most of their pastimes seemed to consist of orgies."

My eyes grew wide. "What? How?" Horrifying images of fish men with penises unwinding from fins sprouted into my mind.

She smiled as her gaze grew distant and she leaned towards the window. "It wasn't sex as we know it," she said, easing my fears of fish penises. "It was something different. Like they were barely touching each other, and yet it was the most sensual, erotic thing I'd ever seen. It was hard to resist."

I hummed in response, unable to erase the images springing to my mind. "Interesting."

She pulled herself from the memories. "So, why do you ask about my father?"

I sighed. This was going to be difficult. "How well do you

really know the guy?" I considered outing the new girlfriend, but that would just make me look like the jealous ex. Vikki hadn't told Sarah that Apollo intended to overthrow the male muses for a reason. If I wanted Sarah to listen to me, I needed to find out why she trusted her deadbeat father. "You said Apollo helped to bring you back, but I don't get it. You wouldn't resist the call of such powerful magic just because your long lost daddy asked you to. Why did you come back, Sarah? If it wasn't for me, then what?"

Her eyes grew wide. "I just," she stammered, "it's what my mother would have wanted me to do."

I pressed my lips together. We both loved our mothers. They had been strong women who had guided and nurtured us, and just as their deaths had bonded us, their memory linked us together. "I miss my mother too." My fingers spread over my collarbone where my Blood Stone rested its power into my chest. "I suppose it's what's kept me going, too. She wouldn't want me to lose myself to grief or sorrow." Sensing the break in Sarah's defenses, I wafted my power around us like a fog. She scratched her nose but didn't react to the tug of my influence that spidered around her wrists.

After a few moments of silence, Sarah sighed and seemed to finally relax into the haze of my power. "Our mothers would have been great friends. It's so hard to accept that she's gone."

I leaned back with a sigh. "They're just memories now. And if all you came back for was a memory, you're going to need to find something new to build a foundation. You're empty, Sarah. I can see that." I continued to push my magic over her, tickling her nose with my intoxication. She licked her lips in response. "If you don't fill your soul with purpose, you'll lose yourself to the siren's curse. I don't care if you're a muse, you're not *just* a muse." I indicated the frost that had spread into her teacup. "You're something else now."

Sarah frowned. "I suppose you're right." She smoothed invisible wrinkles from her skirt, pushing away my magic without realizing it in blue layers of mist. "When my father returns, we'll discuss this with him. He'll know what to do."

I frowned as the last of my red haze disintegrated into dust. She was powerful and the Tear of the Sea protected her from my influence. Even a Blood Stone couldn't change what she'd become.

With a sigh, I left her alone. There was no way I was going to get through to her when she was like this. I needed to find something else to ground her to the mortal plane other than her parents. Apollo was a male muse and a lying cheat. Somehow, Sarah had forgotten that he'd left her and her mother when she'd been just an infant. When he came back to Miami, I'd make sure she saw who he really was.

When I returned to the bedroom, Luke was already awake and had showered. He leaned over the marble bathroom counter as he shaved, only a loose towel hanging around his waist. Heat fogged over the mirror, blocking my reflection from view and I silently slipped behind him. He tensed as I ran my fingers around his neck, pressed against his bare back and caressed the smooth ridge of his chin. "Angels grow stubble?" I asked.

He smiled. "It's a curse, it seems. Everything is on overdrive with me. My hair grows too fast. Regeneration has its downfalls."

I ran my fingers through his scalp and indulged in the silken luxury of his hair. He closed his eyes and made a rumble in the back of his throat. "I don't know. Seems nice to me," I said with a purr to my words.

"You shouldn't touch me like that," he said and gripped my wrist.

I frowned. "We're soulmates, or whatever, why shouldn't I flirt with you?"

He wiped the mirror and stared at our reflection. The hard

lines across his jaw had come back. "It's something Derek said to me. He told me you'd 'unlock' me once you'd had enough supernaturals. You'd already slept with him, and the dragon."

I dug my nails into his shoulder and spun him around hard. "What are you saying?"

He pressed his lips into a thin line before replying. "You really think Derek wouldn't put up cameras in the suite in Shanghai?"

The blood drained from my face. "Yeah, I found out he recorded it, but," I swallowed, "you saw it?"

He scoffed and his damp hair fell into his face. "I got a front row seat to the live show."

"Shit, Luke, I'm sorry."

He smirked and ran his fingers up my arm. "It's okay. I told you that I don't mind sharing you." His hand dropped. "You're a succubus. Sex is part of your world. I couldn't ask you to be something you're not." He glanced at the doorway. "You're probably hungry. Did Sarah seem open to rekindling old flames?"

I narrowed my eyes. "No, and I don't want to rekindle anything anyway."

He laughed and kissed my cheek before going into the bedroom. "You may be sexy as hell, but you're a terrible liar. Deceit is not one of your succubus skills."

I stared after him. "Does that mean you're offering?"

He grinned. "Only foreplay. The next time we have sex will be on my terms."

I bit my lip. "What defines foreplay?" I followed him inside and ran my finger over his bare chest, lingered my touch down the long scar until I hit the knot of the towel around his waist.

He gripped my wrist. "Foreplay means you can want me." His breath misted my lips and I leaned in to taste him. He pulled me hard against him so that the ridge of his erection pressed against my thigh, but evaded my lips. "Foreplay means you can't have me."

A red haze filtered around us as my desire bloomed to life. I'd never had anyone deny me, or tease me like this. My gaze fell to his lips. "But you saw how much power I used to get us here. My Blood Stone is weakened. It used the last of its strength to break our fall to the ocean." I peered into his eyes, hoping I didn't sound too desperate. "Apollo is coming back to Miami and he's going to be coming for Sarah's Tear of the Sea. I need to be strong enough to stop him."

He trailed his thumb over my lower lip. "Sex between us can't be about power or politics. When we sleep together, it'll be because you want me, and no other reason."

I frowned, because I did want him, but he was right. I had ulterior motives. "Then I suppose we're at a stalemate," I said with a touch of disdain before forcing myself to peel away from him. I swayed my hips as I walked out of the room.

His husky chuckle followed me down the hall and made my knees buckle.

Damn, was I hungry.

ON THE HUNT

Sonya

Luke denying me was an exciting and frustrating experience. But I was a powerful succubus and I wasn't about to go hungry. My Blood Stone resisted as I plucked at it looking for strength and sexual nourishment. *Go find a siren,* it teased. *Anything I have to give will be a snack. It's time for a meal, as well as some answers.*

I growled with frustration, but the sentient Blood Stone was right. The other sirens would know more about Apollo and his plans. I needed to know if he was really working with Derek and what the Incubus King had promised him before he came back to town.

Finding a siren to seduce was dangerous, but I had to admit that the idea excited me. I fed off of sexual energy and a siren fed off of sorrow unlatched in the thrall of sex. It would be possible to feed off of one another, but it was a risk. Should the siren get under my skin enough, she could lead me to the ocean. I couldn't breathe underwater.

I purposefully left the house and stomped across the sands towards the sirens nesting on the shore. Without Apollo around to cleanup after them, a few victims still lay on the sands. But their silhouettes hazed like a mirage in a desert. Humans walked by, enjoying a morning on the beach, unaware of the bodies strewn about them. I thought about what Sarah had said. *I've picked up a few siren tricks.*

The sirens could hide their victims from view. I marveled how remorseless they seemed for their crimes. Even if it was for survival, killing an innocent wrecked me with guilt. But the sirens didn't seem perturbed at all. Most of them seemed sated, lazily sleeping on the sands with towels and fancy drinks. They'd be in full heat come night, but now they rested and indulged in the short burst of peace that feeding on sorrow gave them.

Frowning, I decided against approaching the sirens. Plus, the sight of lifeless bodies did wonders for killing the mood.

I veered away from the shore and headed for the siren's bar. I wasn't going to find what I was looking for in the broad light of day, but even Apollo's bar thrummed with life and promised I'd learn a thing or two, if not be able to find a snack inside.

Grabbing a seat in a corner, I waved at a waitress making her rounds. "Anything to eat, sweetie?" she asked. The younger staff seemed to be exclusive to the evening shift and the older woman who smiled down at me held out a glass of orange juice.

I smiled and took the drink. "Just coffee, please. Thanks."

I tried to listen in on the conversations humming around me that hinted with sirens' songs, but I felt distracted. My thighs ached and my thoughts felt muddy.

You really need to get laid, my Blood Stone quipped.

I frowned and stirred the frothy orange juice with a straw. "Go away," I hissed. "I'm trying to listen."

This was a siren's bar, and I had a sinking suspicion that Apollo owned it. The sirens were too relaxed as they slumped into chairs, their breasts swollen under their tight bikinis and their cheeks flushed with arousal.

The waitress returned with my coffee and then left me alone with my thoughts. She seemed human, and I contemplated why a siren bar would keep such staff as the conversations thrummed on.

"Are you looking forward to the party?" a young siren asked her sister as the waitress gave them fresh orange juice.

I leaned over my coffee and inhaled its steam as I listened to the reply. "Of course! Didn't you hear? Apollo invited Derek."

A gasp. "The Incubus King? Are you serious? Holy mermaids. Imagine how delicious he'll be."

"Are you insane?" the other siren squealed. "I'm going to look, but I'm not going to touch. He's dangerous." She leaned in and glanced around the bar. I amplified my hearing with the power of my Blood Stone to catch her breathy words. "I heard he's even sucked a succubus dry. I don't want to test my luck with him."

The other girl laughed obnoxiously and I winced at the sharp ring of sound. "Your loss. I'm not afraid to take risks." Her eyes sparkled. "We're sirens. We dance with death every day. At least if I go down, I'll go down… on him."

The other girl chuckled. "Go for it. I'll live vicariously through you."

Taking a sip of my coffee, I shivered. The steaming liquid wasn't enough to quell the ice forming in my stomach. If Apollo planned for Derek to come to Miami, it meant they were definitely working together. Something was going to go down and I needed to know what.

The sirens continued to gossip, but news of Derek's impending visit was the hottest topic. It was as if they'd only just heard about it. I wasn't going to find the information I was looking for here.

Leaving a hefty tip and exiting the bar, I wandered Miami,

going through shops and looking for clues. It was only when I found myself in a dive shop did I find anything interesting.

Between snorkels and dive gear was a flyer that showed a fuzzy picture. I would have missed it had my Blood Stone not whispered to me. *Look,* it insisted, drawing me closer to the image. *Is that...?*

I plucked the flyer from the wall. Handwritten script etched the top stating "Mermaid Spotted. Reward if Found."

It seemed ridiculous, but the image itself was from deep underwater with a single ray of light illuminating a fish. Only when I looked closely did I see a topless woman with full breasts and striking amber eyes that reflected in the flash of light.

This was Sarah when she'd been a mermaid.

"Oh, I see you found the local hoax going on," said a man with beach-blonde shaggy hair.

Startled, I stared at him, helpless as my gaze fell to his open shirt that revealed a pack of abs that made my mouth water.

He laughed at my expression. "You must not be from around here." He pressed his hand against the wall and leaned in. "My name's Nick. I own this shop." He pointed at the image. "What do you think? Is that picture real?"

I blushed as I looked again at the image that was clearly of Sarah. "Who took this?" I asked, looking up into his face and ignoring how close he was getting. My powers as a succubus affected men even if I wasn't trying, and I didn't blame him for becoming aroused around me. I was hungry. I couldn't deny that. And when he leaned in even closer and smelled my hair, I tried my best to ignore him. I wasn't a killer, not anymore. I would take what I needed from a siren... or from Luke, if he'd have me.

"I took it," he said, his voice going low and husky. His fingers wrapped around mine as I clutched at the photo. "I put it up hoping someone would come around that had seen her too. I've told everyone it's a hoax, but you look like you've seen a ghost.

Maybe you're the person I've been looking for." His eyes fluttered closed as his lips brushed my cheek. "Why do you smell so good?"

I shook him off and he fluttered his eyes back open. He shook himself, his cheeks turning red as he rubbed the back of his neck. "Sorry, uh, I didn't mean..."

I ignored his blathering apology for getting hot and heavy around me. It wasn't his fault.

"It's fine," I said, then narrowed my eyes. "Why are you so convinced you saw a mermaid?"

His gaze went back to the photo wrinkled in my grip. "I know what I saw. I'm not going to let it go." He looked up at me and frowned. "Do you know anything about it? You seem like you know something."

I sighed. Even if he had seen Sarah, it didn't change anything. She was still entrapped by the Tear of the Sea and Derek was still planning on taking over the world. A human getting mixed up in this mess was only going to be a distraction. "If I were you, I'd keep this quiet and stay away from the beach." When he frowned I added, "Unless you want to get yourself killed."

I'd hoped that my warning would have been enough to scare the dive shop owner off, but he was a human. Humans were good at one thing, and that was running straight into danger head-on.

I lingered outside of the dive shop long after it had closed and night had fallen on the city. Streetlights loomed over glistening asphalt and a humid breeze cooled the layer of sweat at the back of my neck.

Just as I'd expected, when Nick came out and locked up shop, he didn't jump on his bike and head home. Instead, he walked towards the beach, and I fell into the shadows behind him.

He looked over his shoulder as if he sensed me on his tail.

My Blood Stone piped in with an exasperated tone. *If the human wants to get himself killed, just let him. In fact, you should just feed on him. He's your find. A siren doesn't deserve him.*

I frowned. "I'm not a murderer. Humans are curious. That's why muses wipe their memories. Once they catch a hint of a supernatural they just don't let go," I whispered under my breath.

Passing strangers glanced at me as I talked to myself, but I pushed them away with a red haze of power.

I followed Nick all the way to the grainy layer of weeds that opened up onto the beach, but I'd already lost him. "Damn it," I hissed.

Dousing the sudden surge of panic, I slipped out of my flip-flops and sifted through the sands littered with sirens. They squealed with delight as they chased one another. Some had already latched onto their victims and were doing only what I could call "playing with their food." They'd mute their songs just enough that their human toys began to gain awareness. Shaking their head, intelligence and fear sparked in their eyes. Just when I thought they were going to bolt, the sirens started up their songs again, lulling their prey back into a sense of false security.

I didn't like it. My fingernails bit into my palms as I shoved past them.

"Hey!" one complained when I bulldozed through the crowd.

I ignored her. A red haze burned across my skin with my rage and was enough to keep the sirens from turning their melodies on me.

I wanted to save the victims, but it would have been a pointless practice. Sirens fed. That's what they did, just like succubi. The only difference was that I had met one of the soon-to-be victims and if I could spare just one life, it would be his.

He reminds you of David, the Blood Stone acutely observed.

"Shut up," I snapped, and continued storming across the beach. "David had hair like midnight, and this beach bum looked like a wet dog."

A hot, wet dog, the Blood Stone countered.

I sighed.

Just when I was about to give up, I spotted my target with a lone siren near the shore. She wasn't taking her time to play with him like her sisters were doing with their victims. The short-haired siren seemed desperate as her song permeated the air and she dragged him to the sea as if she wanted to drown him as fast as she could to suck the sorrow from his bones.

"Wait!" I shouted and broke into the run. My eyes grew wide when I realized that the siren that had snagged Nick was Sarah's new girlfriend. "Vikki?" I shrieked.

Caught in the strong current of Vikki's melody, Nick staggered. His legs crumpled as he collapsed into the shallow waters and groaned.

I growled and yanked him by his shirt. "What do you think you're doing!" I shouted at Vikki. "You're supposed to be feeding off of Sarah. You don't need to kill innocent humans!"

The blood drained from Vikki's already pale face. Tears streamed down her cheeks, illuminating scales I hadn't noticed before around her eyes that glimmered with emerald greens. "You don't understand. I *have* to do this."

"You don't *have* to do anything!" I growled. "You don't need to kill. You feed off of sorrow, but now you have Sarah. You should be the happiest siren alive."

"I'm doing this for Sarah." She stabbed a finger at Apollo's villa that illuminated like a soft jewel in the distance. "She's not just a muse anymore. She's something new. She feeds off of sirens, and once she figures that out, she's going to insist that she return to the sea." She continued on, her words jerking over hiccuping sobs. "I have to keep up my strength to keep Sarah on dry land. If she doesn't feed on me then she won't be able to stay here anymore." Her eyes went wide as she pleaded. "You don't want that, right? You care about Sarah?"

With a yank, I tossed Nick towards the sands. He groaned. With a flick of my wrist I wrapped my powers around him and instructed him to *leave.*

He gave us a wild-eyed stare before he scrambled to his feet and got the hell out of dodge.

Turning back to Vikki, I crossed my arms and glowered. "Okay, spill. What do you mean you're doing this for Sarah? She's a muse. She doesn't need to feed. Is it the Tear of the Sea? You should just take it from her. That would solve all of our problems."

Vikki shook her head and her glittering tears flung from her face. "It's bonded to her. It's keeping her alive. I told you, she's not just a muse. She might have regained her powers, and her legs, but she's something new this world hasn't seen before." Her lower lip quivered as she hugged herself. "I shouldn't have listened to Apollo. I didn't know what Sarah was like. All I could think of was this terrible ache of being what I am. I didn't want to turn into a monster like them." She sniffled and jerked her chin at the lazy sirens who played with their food. One lured her victim to the shore and I stiffened. "But now I'm worse. Only a few of them drown them. Some just feed on the sorrow and let them go. But now I have to help Sarah, and I can't keep up anymore. I have to kill to give her what I need." She jerked me by the arm and squeezed. "I *have* to."

The icy magic wrapped around my skin and locked my lungs around a single breath. I wasn't sure if I should have believed her, but that was before her desperation permeated my chest. My Blood Stone instantly reacted, blasting my body with heat to counteract the invasion.

Vikki's eyes went wide as her grip languished down my arm. "Wow," she breathed, drawing closer to me as if by instinct. Her gaze fogged over with the intoxication of my power. "You're so warm."

I'd never been close enough to a siren to feel their power, but the impact of Vikki's touch was like ice lightning, and then there was another more familiar twinge of recognition.

Fuck, she's one of my seven linked destinies? A damned siren?

The rune on the outskirts of my abdomen throbbed with cool ice, a different sensation than I'd felt before. But it was the kind of cold that was a delicious pain and I found myself leaning into her caress. Before I knew what was happening, her melody surrounded me like a gentle purr and my eyelids fluttered closed.

This is dangerous, my Blood Stone warned. *Even if she is one of your seven.*

I'd learned that much already. Seven souls were bound to my destiny, four of them my protectors, which left the other three as wildcards. Sarah was my first, a rune I couldn't shake from my life. Then there'd been Derek, the key to charging my Blood Stone and a dangerous source of chaos that could be my downfall. Now I'd met the last one… a siren who only wanted to help Sarah.

I knew that Vikki was trying to feed off of me, but I didn't care. If she really needed to feed in order to keep Sarah on land, and alive, then I couldn't stop her. I'd already hurt Sarah in more ways that I could have possibly realized. She'd drowned, turned into a mermaid, and now she was a husk of herself and barely hanging on. I had to help figure all of this out and get her back to normal.

Vikki's lips brushed my neck and I shivered as goosebumps swelled across my arms. She was shorter than me, but when she leaned her head back, I couldn't deny the unspoken command to give her a kiss.

Frost ran across my tongue as I tasted the siren. Her magic was exquisite and powerful, but what amazed me the most was that the part of her power that lured me into her trap was sexual. Anything that was sexual was something I knew how to work, and I fed on her just as quickly as she began to feed on me.

The exchange made us both relax into the kiss. I drew in a deep breath through my nose as I gripped her arms and brought her closer to me. Her breasts crushed against mine and her soft whimper of need made my thighs clench.

When I pulled away, Vikki blinked up at me, her glistening eyes full of magic and wonder. "I can feed off of you," she said as if that hadn't occurred to her. Her gaze fell to my lips again and I knew they were the perfect, plump pink from my arousal. "Can you feed off of me?"

With a slow nod, I ran my fingers up her neck and gripped the roots of her hair until she leaned back. I tested her neck with my teeth. "It seems we can benefit one another."

She bit her lip with anticipation. "Then you'll let me feed off of you?"

"Yes," I promised. As waves splashed against my calves, bringing a cool reprieve to my burning skin, I tugged her to shore. "But I won't have you drown me."

She smiled, meeting the fresh wave of heat with an icy mixture of her own. Her lips found mine and her deft fingers tugged at my shirt. I allowed her to slip it over my head and peel away my bra, parting from her mouth just long enough to rid myself of the constrictive clothing.

As she guided me to the sands, I expected to endure sharp grains shoving into uncomfortable places. But I was happily surprised when her magic soothed the shore into a velvety sheet. She smiled as my eyes widened. "You're not the only one with gifts." Her finger twirled around my nipple until it hardened. "Are all succubi like this?"

I knew what she meant. Each kiss gave me long, delicious drags of sexual nourishment that would have killed most people on the spot. But this was a siren. Every taste I took from her, she took my own sorrow in turn. It wasn't painful, as I would have expected. The arousal and the cold numbed the slow spread of her magic as it ripped open my soul and found the freshest wounds for her to glean.

As her lips parted and some secret, dark part of me swirled in the air like smoke, only to disappear on her tongue, I gave a nervous chuckle. "I don't know, are all sirens like this?"

Her fingers ran down my thighs, making my muscles clench with anticipation. "You have so much sorrow, so much guilt. You'd make any siren happy." She smiled as she teased me, her fingers gliding around the seam of my jeans.

Growling, I took her hand and pressed her onto me. Hot need spiked through my body as she exhaled a long, delighted sigh. "Sex is painful for your heart," she observed. Instead of being turned off by my fucked up way of getting off, she undid my button and ran down the zipper. I obeyed her silent command to free my legs of my jeans. When the cloth disappeared past my ankles, she crawled over me and continued the tease of her fingers.

Feeling impossibly swollen, I let my head fall back to the soft cushion of sands. "I have a soulmate," I explained. "And an ex-girlfriend who I'm trying to help, even now, by fucking you."

She ran her tongue around my earlobe, making me shiver. "But you hate what you are." She bit, making me twitch with the sudden stab of pain. She licked over the small hurt. "Take some advice from a siren." Her touch ran beneath the soft layer of my underwear, making me gasp as her fingers ran over my wet clit. "Embrace what you are, or be consumed by sorrow."

"No," I countered, overcoming the paralysis of my need by peeling away Vikki's bikini and running my tongue around her nipple. When she gasped I fed on the long, delicious breath of her arousal, her sexual energy delving into my Blood Stone and making my chest glow with the embers of my power. I blew on her nipple now wet from my kiss, watching with delight as it hardened impossibly further. "My sorrow is what will keep Sarah alive. No matter how much guilt I feel, I still take what I need. I'll need this strength to be ready for when Apollo returns. We're going to get Sarah out of this mess, even if I have to fuck her girlfriend to do it."

Vikki groaned as I tugged her bikini bottom aside and slid my fingers into the folds of her flesh. She gasped when I flicked against her inner muscles.

Grappling against my underwear, she ripped it aside. I drew my fingers out of her so that she could descend, sending pain and pleasure rolling through me as she pressed her need against mine. "Stop talking," she complained, and claimed my mouth with a kiss.

She rolled on me and I gripped her hips to keep her in a rhythm that was slow, deliberate. With each new wave of pleasure I drank in the power. I wanted to nourish my body which felt so cold from her drain on my heart, but I resisted and pushed all of the power into the red gem within. Heat burned in my core, and even if my fingers grew numb, I knew that this would give me what I needed when it was time.

Vikki squeezed my breasts and rode me, sliding back and forth as the pleasure built into delightful pain. "Tell me about Luke," she commanded.

Guilt wrapped around my chest as her clit rubbed against mine. I knew that if Luke saw me now, this would hurt him. He might tell me that he knows what I am, that he can accept it, but

I'd seen the hurt and betrayal in his eyes. He wanted me to do something I couldn't. He wanted me to be loyal.

Vikki wrapped her fingers around my throat. "Tell me."

I closed my eyes and gave in to the sorrow that her pleasure gave me. Just as I rode the building wave of a powerful climax, I forced the words out. "I'll never deserve his love," I breathed. "I'll never be what he wants me to be."

Vikki came with me as the sorrow of that admission drenched the air. I allowed myself to be overcome as the climax hit, taking her long strides on me as my fingers curled into fists.

She rolled on me, sweat drenching her hair, and continued to slowly roll back and forth as the last quivering spasms wrecked our bodies. When she breathed out, frost tinged the air. "There," she said as she slumped over me. "It's done."

A SIREN'S SIN

Luke

Sonya thought that I wasn't watching. I expected to be jealous, but the only thing that bothered me was that this wasn't one of the four. I felt no connection. No hinting caress of her skin over mine. This time it was a siren, and Sarah's girlfriend of all the sirens she could have chosen.

I crossed my arms and leaned back against my makeshift hideout, a canopy of weeds against one of the beaches many outlets. The ground made me scratchy and I was pretty sure I was attracting ants by the dozen, but I didn't move. I kept my gaze locked on the writhing couple at the edge of the lapping waves.

The sirens ignored the spectacle, having victims of their own to enjoy. I couldn't understand how Sonya could fuck one of them, but I had an idea why. She'd saved one of Vikki's victims. Some guy who looked like he had fallen out of 'surfer dude' magazine had stumbled off shortly after Sonya had found him. At first I thought she'd been looking for a victim of her own and was angry with the siren for taking what was hers. She'd been staking out the dive shop for quite a while and had been far too focused on watching the doors to even notice that I was lingering in a coffee shop nearby.

Now I watched, mouth agape, as magic engulfed the pair. Sonya's deadly ember reds and Vikki's vibrant blues clashed as they fed on one another. I hadn't even known that such an exchange was possible. A siren fed on sorrow, and it didn't take a genius to figure out that Sonya was conflicted and miserable. She hated herself and what she was. I had tried to accept her, to show her that it was okay. I knew she couldn't control it, but to watch her now, fucking someone else just moments after she'd teased me with promises and sweet words made my fists clench and my dick hard.

I gained a sick sort of pleasure to know that Vikki was draining the very guilt that wrecked Sonya as she rolled under her, naked and exposed to my lingering gaze. That guilt was because of me, or so I hoped. Sonya wanted me. I had seen it in her eyes. It wasn't just a succubus' need to feed. She'd always wanted me.

But I wasn't going to give in, not when she wasn't ready for me. My dick strained against my jeans as I watched the siren bring Sonya to climax. She quivered and magic exploded around them in violent, furious waves. No one else would know what was really happening. This was already a unique pairing of succubus and siren, but I sensed another magic in the air. One of the runes on Sonya's stomach blazed and made a low throb react in me, making me shift uncomfortably. I was close enough to feel the union of one of the seven… one of the sins that tormented my succubus. The knowledge came to me as a distant vision my mother had left in me. I was one of the seven, too; I was pride. I was glad to be one of her four connected to her destiny and her heart, not just someone that would linger on the outskirts like this siren who was always looking for the easy way out. I recognized the sin of slothfulness as Vikki yawned, lazily drinking in power as it lingered around them.

Having finally noticed the spectacle, a few sirens stopped feeding and openly stared. Vikki slumped over her victim, and my breath caught when Sonya didn't move. A siren couldn't outright kill someone. They had to drown them, right?

Then Sonya groaned, rolled Vikki off, and snatched up her clothes.

I eased into the shadows of the weeds, gritting my teeth as ants feasted on my ankles, and didn't move a muscle as Sonya put on her clothes and stomped towards the villa.

I considered going after her, but curiosity got the best of me and I stayed to watch what Vikki would do. Embers still swirled in her veins and when her gaze focused across the shore to the other watching sirens, a red gleam flickered across her eyes. "What'cha looking at?" she snapped. She flicked her wrist. "Get back to your victims while you can. Apollo's going to be furious with this mess."

DADDY'S HOME

Sonya

Apollo towered over the community of sirens. Dead humans lay strewn behind them like a fleshy sheet of blankets. "I'm gone for two weeks and this is what you call 'behaving yourselves?'" he boomed.

The sirens closest to him shrank into themselves as he stormed up to them. "We're sorry," one murmured. "It won't happen again."

He gripped one of the girls hard, making her scales shimmer as her eyes widened with fright.

Heat burned in me and I dug my fingernails into my fists, reminding myself that the frightened siren I felt compelled to protect had just contributed to a massacre.

"Don't interfere," Luke murmured into my ear, his heat inches from my back as he leaned in to whisper the warning. "You'll need your strength when Derek comes to town."

Dammit. I knew he was right.

While Apollo continued to berate the sirens for their lack of control, I found Sarah with her hands clasped in front of her, a familiar pink skirt flirting with the wind as it whipped around her thighs. Except, there was no wind, and a vortex of her own icy power seemed to make her hair and clothes fling around her.

The sirens were afraid of Apollo, but they seemed to be even more terrified of Sarah's growing powers. "It's because of her," one managed to say as she lifted a shaking finger in accusation. "She keeps messing with our heads!"

Apollo narrowed his eyes at his daughter. "Is that true?"

Sarah didn't acknowledge the accusation. Instead, she blankly stared at the sea as if she hadn't heard anything at all.

Vikki wrapped her fingers gently around Sarah's arm and gave her a light shake. "Sarah, you feeling okay?"

Jealousy stabbed through me that Vikki's soft voice was what got through to Sarah. The invisible winds calmed as she looked down at her girlfriend with a genuine smile. "I'm fine."

Apollo glanced at me. "And who is the succubus and her friend?"

Ignoring the desire to cower as the male muse pummeled me with his attention, I straightened and drew on the power of my Blood Stone. His eyes widened just a fraction in surprise as I resisted his command to fear him. "I'm one of Derek's lovers," I said, my words coming fluidly with the truth. Apollo was a powerful muse and I knew better than to attempt a lie. While I wasn't about to tell him why I was really here, I could find enough truth to get through a conversation. "I heard there was a party. Is that true?" I pushed my lips out into a pout. "Derek didn't invite me." I grinned. "But I know he'll be delighted to see me there."

Apollo appraised me with burning amber power in his eyes. I hated that I could see Sarah in him that way, all mysterious and enticing. A muse was an incredible creature with their beauty hidden in the soft whispers of their power. Even Apollo, a fairly handsome man but otherwise normal, betrayed his true gifts when he captured me with those eyes.

He glanced at Sarah. "You're okay with your ex coming to the fete?"

She shrugged. "If she wants to go, I have no qualms." She patted Vikki's hand that was still on her arm. "As long as Vikki can be there. She wants to go too."

The other sirens bristled with jealousy. The party, or *fete,* as Apollo eloquently called it, seemed to be by invitation only. I was dying to know what the Incubus King and ambitious male muse were up to, but I'd just have to go to the party to find out. Whatever it was, it wasn't anything good.

Apollo stretched, the folds of his shirt lifting to expose sculpted abs that disappeared in a ridge down his jeans. "Very well," he said. "Can't resist the wishes of my beautiful daughter." He cupped her face as a smile cut through his handsome cheeks. "Derek will know how to help you," he whispered, hope a strange tone in his voice. "We'll make this right."

Alone with Luke in our bedroom, my cheeks burned with heat, both with the realization that Apollo was actually trying to help Sarah, and the fact that I hadn't faced Luke since I'd fucked Vikki.

I glanced at him as he sat on one of the long-armed sofas sharpening a knife. "Where did you get that thing?" I snapped.

He grinned. "Apollo gave it to me. Pretty cool, huh?" He lifted the blade for me to see. I frowned when I noticed a dragon spiraling around the small hilt.

"Aren't you supposed to hate dragons?" I asked as I leaned back onto the bed and interlocked my fingers behind my head. "Why would you want something like that?"

He shrugged and resumed the irritating grating of whetstone against steel that made my teeth itch. "I don't think Apollo is so bad," he said, not answering my question. Another sweep of his hand made my toes curl as the terrible sound riveted through my body. "Maybe we'll learn more at the party before we make any rash decisions."

"Rash decisions?" I said, jerking upright. "You remember who we're talking about, right? Derek, the Incubus King, who forced you to charge my Blood Stone. Derek, the bastard who kidnapped me and tried to sell me as consort to the dragons." I thumped my fist against my chest. "Derek, the lunatic who tried to unleash demons on Earth by using us, and forcing us to make the Blood Stone that now sits in my chest." I pointed at the closed door. "Apollo is in league with Derek. That means that Apollo is our enemy and we need to figure out what he's up to and stop him."

As if I hadn't just listed every logical reason we needed to take Apollo out, Luke screeched the stone against his blade again, making my shoulders curl with irritation. "We both heard him. Apollo is trying to help his daughter. Maybe he thinks this is the only way."

I yanked myself off the bed and snatched up the whetstone and threw it across the room. "It's because of Apollo that Sarah is in trouble!"

Luke frowned. "I think we both know whose fault it is that Sarah is here."

My eyes grew wide as rage wound around my chest. Sparks of red flickered across my arms. "What did you just say to me?"

He sighed and stood, his dagger hanging loose from his hand. "You misunderstand me, Sonya. I just mean that it's okay to feel guilty for it, for everything—"

I punched him, right in the stomach and as hard as I could. Tears sprang to my eyes when he crumpled over. He glared at me, recovering with impressive speed and straightened. "Punch me again."

It wasn't a taunt. He could regenerate from any wound, and we both knew that I was about to lose my shit.

"No, Luke, I didn't mean—"

He moved so fast that my powers reacted out of reflex. His dagger came at my throat and I blocked it with a red metallic haze. My fingers curled into a fist and slammed into his face.

He went down and a bruise blossomed across his cheek. The dagger still in his hand, he came at me again.

I retaliated.

Before I knew it, we were caught in a dance of blinding speed as the bedroom swirled. I unleashed my anger and my rage. I punched him as hard as I could. I screamed, not giving him time to recover as I slammed my fists into him over and over again. I lost myself to the guilt and hatred that tore through me. I hated what I was. I hated everything that I'd done. I hated myself, because Luke was right. If it hadn't been for me, Sarah wouldn't have even been here.

The room glowed with the ruby wisps of my power as tears sizzled down my face. I'd lost the energy to keep going after him. He tossed the dagger to the ground and wrapped his hands around my waist. He pulled me close, and I stared at his busted lip as it healed before my eyes. He took his thumb, ran it across the glistening blood, and then glided his finger over my lips. "Accept what you are," he commanded, his voice husky and dangerous "because I've decided to accept you, whether you like it or not."

I stared at him, ready to make a retort that he didn't know what I'd done, that I'd fucked Vikki and I hated myself for it. Before the words could come out, he drew me in and kissed me hard.

My body went rigid as the electric power of his passion

swept through me. It was more than just the typical lust I tasted on a man's tongue. This was something deeper, something far more powerful. When I managed to pull away, I gasped for breath.

He waited as he watched me, his hand still in a possessive grip around my waist. It was only when I realized what he was waiting for did I let the words fall from my lips. "Prove it to me that you accept me. Prove that I mean something to you, no matter what I've done."

With a grin, he took on the challenge and claimed my mouth again. Warmth spread across my chest as my powers kicked in, but I couldn't hurt him. Sexual energy wafted from him in exuberant waves. His power was a delicious honey that could fuel me for lifetimes to come.

"Luke," I whispered, "please."

It was a simple word, but for a succubus to plead for sex showed him more than I could ever put into words. I needed to know that he forgave me for all the terrible things I'd done. If he could forgive me, then perhaps I could forgive myself.

He sat onto the bed and drew me on top of him until my thighs straddled his waist. His hands roamed up my back, under my shirt and explored my skin before running across the rune that lit up under his touch. "Tell me everything you regret."

Fresh tears stung at my eyes as images of past victims sprang to mind. "I can't."

He pulled me close and pressed his cheek to my breasts. "Your heart beats so fast, but it's strong. I feel the heat of your magic, but I also feel the passion that lives within you." He turned and kissed my left breast. "Your heart is beautiful. Don't let it be broken. Let it mend."

Looking into the depths of his impossibly blue eyes, I reminded myself what Luke was. His father had been an angel and his mother was a powerful Seer. There was so much ancient power and magic in him that if I looked closely, I could see the storm of it behind the glassy mystery of his eyes. "Do you intend to fix me, my sweet angel?"

Luke smiled, the gesture absolutely charming. "I intend to show you that you don't need fixing."

I hated his persistence, so I decided to go along and prove to him that this was a foolish errand. "I've killed six men. Not all of them were innocent, but I still snuffed out life. But the innocent ones—" I broke off as my voice cracked. Trying again, I whispered, "David."

Luke frowned. "Anderson killed that guy. He sucked him dry."

I shook my head and squeezed my eyes shut. The only thing that kept me from reeling back into the horror of memories was Luke's hard grip on my body. "Detective Anderson is a chameleon. I gave him the powers to steal life, and he used my own gifts on David." My throat strained with grief. "And before that, I'd fed on him when I was supposed to die."

Luke jerked me closer to him and his hot breath puffed against my face. "What do you mean 'supposed to die?'"

I shivered under his touch. "I was trying to starve myself. It's because of what I am. I couldn't be loyal to Sarah. I couldn't live a normal life. All I know is how to feed and steal life-force which isn't mine to take." My fingernails dug into his arms. "Luke. Please stop this. I can't."

Shushing me, he rolled me onto the bed. He flicked off the lights and then a rustle of cloth told me that he'd disrobed.

"Luke?" I asked, my voice a scratchy sound in the darkness.

"I want you to feel safe. It's easier for me to resist you if I can't see you. Just know that your powers won't work on me, not when I'm in control."

I shivered as he removed my bra. He lifted my hips until I

reluctantly allowed him to pull down my jeans, and then I sighed as humid air kissed my naked skin.

"Relax," he commanded, and then crawled on top of me.

I expected him to take me, whether he thought he was in control or not. Even though my heart was crumbling into a thousand, tiny pieces, I couldn't deny the instinct to fix all my problems with sex. Luke was a part of my destiny, and sex with him would dose me with so much power that I could drown in the intoxication. I could forget, even if just for a few moments, why I didn't deserve to be alive.

The hard ridge of his erection rolled across my leg as he moved, but he didn't go to penetrate my swollen flesh. Instead he leaned, popped open the nightstand drawer and pulled out a bottle. A burst of lilacs and herbs filled the bedroom as he untwisted the cap and I realized that he'd found massage oils. "What is—"

He shushed me and rubbed his hands together. "I know you're a succubus and you need sex, but I have an idea. Just let me try it."

Pinching my lips together, I tried not to squirm as his hands found my arms and he began to massage. He ran his warm, graceful touch down to my fingertips, rolling across my knuckles and coming back up again. Goosebumps spread across my skin as he leaned in and ghosted a kiss on my lips.

I couldn't feed on him, not when it was just teasing. But my powers couldn't tell the difference and wound around him and coaxed his cock. He couldn't resist the demand of my pull and rolled against my hip. "No cheating," he said with a smile against my teeth.

He pulled away, continuing to explore my body as the warm musk of his need mixed with the oils. "Don't you want me?" I asked, my words going breathless as his fingers ran up my ribcage and cupped my breasts.

"Of course I want you," he said.

He slowly kneaded my flesh, forcing a soft moan from my throat. "Then why are you teasing me?" I complained.

He brushed a kiss against one nipple, then copied the insufferable pleasure on the other. "I want to see if you can gain control of your powers if you're forced to have sex without having sex, which means feeding without feeding."

I frowned. "I don't follow."

His erection pressed between my sex and my thigh, fitting into my groin and pressing heat and need against me. I squirmed, but his weight kept me pinned in place. "You hate what you are because you link sex with your gifts. I want to give you a chance to experience passion without feeding. I think it'll help you."

I groaned with frustration. No matter how much I wound my powers around his cock and made him impossibly hard, he still found the will to resist me. "I think you're just going to make me angry."

He pressed a kiss against my neck and grinned. "Just roll over. Trust me."

With a sigh, I obeyed and allowed him to run his hands up my arms until his fingers interlaced with mine under the pillows. His cock rested between the curve of my butt cheeks and made my wetness soak the bed. "You're too close," I complained. "I can't think of anything else."

His fingers roamed down my back. "On your knees."

Blushing, I wanted to ask if he'd changed his mind, but I found myself obeying just to find out. My breath hitched when his fingers ran down my slickness. "Luke?" I asked with a tremor.

He didn't respond. Instead, he rolled onto his back and fitted his head between my thighs. Then he grabbed me, and pulled me into his mouth.

A cry escaped me as the shock of pleasure ran through me as

his tongue thrust into the folds of my flesh. My whole body clenched as an orgasm hit without warning, and to my shock, the pleasure was so sudden that my magic hadn't been able to keep up with it.

I rolled my hips as I pressed my convulsing sex to his mouth. My fingers curled into the sheets as I rode the wave of pleasure with long, delicious shocks.

When I rolled off of him, he lazily crawled on top of me and licked his fingers. "You're so beautiful."

I laughed, and it was a free kind of laugh as a knot in my stomach melted away. "You can't even see me. It's too dark." A soft blue spark told me otherwise and I gasped. "Holy shit. Do your eyes fucking glow?" A hot blush crawled up my neck as I realized that Luke had been able to see every inch of me this whole time. "You said no cheating!"

He laughed, and the low delighted sound made my insides curl. "But it worked."

My face burned as I realized that he was still on top of me, and his dick was still inches away from where I wanted it to be. "You gave me pleasure without me feeding," I marveled. "That's never happened before."

He positioned himself at my entrance and I held my breath. "What was it like? Having sexual pleasure without your powers dominating you?"

I shivered as his dick nudged at my swollen flesh. Tension began to build again and my powers continued to pluck at him, but he didn't fuck me, not yet. With a slow exhale, I pulled my powers away until it was just us, just Luke and I together in a bed about to have sex.

"There it is," he said as his fingers curled behind my neck. He eased inside me, the thrust painfully slow. "Now I can have you."

Every inch made me crazed and by the time he'd fully sheathed himself in me, I cried out and contracted around him.

He moved, fucking me like I'd never been fucked before. His cock thrusted into me slowly at first, then his pace quickened until my eyes rolled back in my head. I held onto him for dear life as he gave me exactly what I wanted, again and again, not stopping to give me a reprieve from the agonizing pleasure.

When his breath came in long, deliberate gasps, I readied myself for the power of his climax. Together, we came, and not once did I feed as the wave of Luke's ecstasy overtook me.

TIME TO PARTY

Sonya

Such a waste, my Blood Stone complained.

Curling my fingers through Luke's hair as the morning sun kissed his face, I ignored the irritating growl in the back of my head. I just wanted to enjoy this small moment before it inevitably shattered. Luke had never given me a chance to tell him about Vikki. Once he found out, I was sure he'd be disgusted with me. I'd never get to touch him like this again. It would all be over, just like it had ended with Sarah.

So much sexual energy, and you pushed it all away, the Blood Stone continued, ignoring my inner turmoil.

With a sigh, I got out of bed and left Luke sleeping. He seemed so relaxed and at peace. Once I washed up in the bathroom and got dressed, I eased the door closed and made my way down the hall. "You're such a pain," I complained in a whisper. "Can't you just let me feel normal for once? I've never had sex without feeding. I've never known what it felt like just to be enveloped in passion and not have to worry about draining my lover's life away. Luke gave me something precious, and all you can think about is yourself."

The Blood Stone made a guttural sound, and I startled when I realized the vibrations were coming from my own throat. *I could take over your body, if I wanted to, but I'm nice. I know that your body is not mine to take, but if you starve me again, you'll test my patience.*

Swallowing as a cold sweat broke out down my back, I entered into the sunroom and found Apollo waiting.

His face glittered with a grin as he sipped a porcelain cup of steaming coffee. He waved at a tray with a silver pot and sugar cubes piled into a small mountain in a bowl. "I heard that you prefer tea," he said, his voice a low and mesmerizing purr.

With a polite nod, I made myself a cup. "Yes, thank you."

I hadn't intended to approach the muse, in fact, I wasn't sure why I'd gotten out of bed with Luke at all.

That's when I realized that Apollo was watching me with a smirk cutting into his face. "Sorry to lure you out of bed, but I needed to talk to you."

Glowering, I studied the air around me until I discovered the faint blue lines of enticing power that had lured me there. "Seriously?" I hissed.

If you'd fed like you were supposed to, I could have resisted him, the Blood Stone snapped.

Apollo shrugged. "I care about my daughter, and when her ex comes to town with the dangerous supernatural that I've been hunting, a father's bound to be concerned."

The blood drained from my face. He not only knew about Luke, but he knew what Luke was. "Dangerous?" I asked, my voice a squeak.

He waved away my fear with a puff of his magic. Reluctantly, I eased into a chair and coddled my tea. "I don't know what you've heard about me," he said, "but I'm not the one you should fear. My brothers, Hades and Ares, have stifled the supernatural community for centuries. They're the monsters that should behold your wide eyes."

I clamped my jaw shut, my fear turning to sultry anger. "You mean they've kept order," I snapped. My mother had always been a staunch supporter of keeping supernaturals secret from the world. The succubi who were revealed were often burned as witches or worse. No good came from the world knowing what we were. "If you're trying to overthrow your brothers, then you're siding with chaos."

He smirked, seeming amused rather than irritated by my bluntness. "I can see what Derek likes about you."

My chair creaked as I eased up, fighting Apollo's powerful magic that insisted I stay calm and docile. "When's he arriving?" I asked. "The party is tonight, right?"

"Yes," he said, still sounding amused. "It's going to be a grand affair. I think you'll quite enjoy it." He took a sip of his coffee. "It's more than just a party, I'll admit. I have a surprise, and I have invited all my allies in the supernatural community to witness it."

Apprehension clenched a cold fist around my chest as blood thundered in my ears. "What other supernaturals are going to be there?"

He got up and stretched, his loose shirt straining against taut muscles. "I've invited my favorite sirens, of course. They'll be kept in check by the incubi and succubi I've invited in equal numbers." He winked at me. "As you've discovered, a sexual exchange between succubus and siren can be quite beneficial to both parties."

A blush broke out over my face. I chose to ignore his comment. He was a muse and had the power to rummage around in my brain. It was a threat, no doubt, that he could tell Sarah and Luke what Vikki and I had done. "I don't react well to blackmail."

"Oh but I've invited other supernaturals," he continued, ignoring my protest. "There will be a few witches, werewolves and vampires—"

My eyes bulged. "What?"

He openly laughed. "See? My brothers stifle the supernatural community so badly that even our own don't know about one another. How many species have you believed were myth, I wonder?"

I shivered. I'd always joked about vampires, but to hear they were real made my head spin. Werewolves just sounded too impossible to be true. "Who else will be there?" I managed to ask.

He grinned. "A special guest, but you'll have to come and see to meet her."

Apollo was up to something and I didn't like the feeling that he had me right where he wanted me.

"It's going to be okay," Luke said in his softest voice as we walked down the boulevard towards the Apollo Hotel. It irritated me that the muse's party was in a place he'd named after himself. But I'd still gotten dressed in the finest sequin black slip that Luke had offered me from one of Apollo's many closets. I'd dolled up, played the part, but my mood was even worse that we couldn't go in powers blazing. I hated playing along.

"Hey, slow down. You're going to break an ankle in those heels," Luke said as he caught up to me.

I continued to click my way down the sidewalk. "I'm just tired of feeling like I'm constantly being manipulated," I complained. "First Derek uses my powers to get his wife pregnant with a freaking demonspawn, then he tricks me into helping him make a Blood Stone, and now he's teamed up with a rogue muse to take over the world." I growled and sped up my pace. "I know Derek's bad, but Apollo is probably worse. This guy is such a douchebag. He abandoned Sarah when she was a baby and left her mom to raise her by herself. Then when she lost her powers and came to the sirens for help, he took advantage of her. He made sure she got him the last stone of power he needed to overthrow his brothers."

Luke gripped my wrist and forced me to stop. I hadn't realized that I'd nearly broken into a run and tiny red flames had erupted over my skin. He glowered as I won us some curious stares. "Listen. I've lived my whole life with some stupid prophecy hanging over my head. I hated the idea that fate had it in for me. I was supposed to rescue you, and if I didn't, the world would come to an end." He gave me a light shake. "You know what I think? I don't think that prophecy isn't literal. It's not my job to keep you out of danger, even though I'll die to protect you. I think it's my job to save you from yourself, because if you lose your grip, the world is going to go tumbling with you, as well as those of us bound to your fate."

I swayed as I digested his words. I wasn't sure what surprised me more, the fact that Luke just admitted that he'd die for me, or that he thought I was so important. "I know your mom showed you some screwed up prophecy, but I don't believe in that stuff, okay. Our future is what we make it, and I'm not afraid to admit that I'm losing my grip. There are some powerful supernaturals in this world and I'm only twenty-two. I can't keep up."

He shook his head, his brilliant blue eyes sparking with very real power and excitement. It was hard to miss the change in him. I wasn't the only one evolving. "You don't have to believe. I know that you're the key to whatever is coming." He pointed down the street to the towering hotel that glittered with lights winding up its walls. "We're going to go in there, and we're going to figure out what Apollo has planned. It doesn't matter if we're doing exactly what he wants. As long as we stick together, we're the ones who are going to come out on top."

I hated how confident Luke sounded, as if we were some kind of team. He jerked me towards the hotel but I resisted. "Luke, there's something I have to tell you."

The glitter in his eyes faded when he saw my face. "What is it?"

I swallowed. There was no way I could have Luke looking at me like I was some kind of savior. He had to know that he couldn't count on me. "I fucked Vikki. It was before we had sex. I—"

Before I could ramble on, he squeezed my hand. "I know."

Entering into the hotel without guilt weighing me down, I finally felt like I might be ready to take on whatever craziness Apollo had in store for us tonight.

No one took notice as we passed by the guards, a couple of Derek's incubus sons who I'd recognize from a mile away. Their harsh jaw lines and slick black hair, as well as striking eyes, reminded me of Nate. But their amused, arrogant stares as they waved us inside made me want to punch somebody.

"Easy," Luke murmured as he took my hand and wound it through his arm. "Don't get all tense on me yet. We need to sum up our enemy first."

Glowering, I leaned onto him for support and tried my best to look bored. It was hard to do in the grandeur of the Apollo hotel. After a short entry hallway decorated with jewels and gold, we were ushered into a marble canopy filled to the brim with supernaturals. A long dance floor spanned out with a covered object in the center blocked off by velvet ropes. "Is he going to give away a car or something?" I asked with a smirk.

Luke shrugged. "Who knows, but I doubt there's anything good inside that thing."

I tried not to stare at the box guarded on all sides by strange supernaturals. Men dressed up in suits and eyes that glinted red against the light made a shiver run up my spine. "Are those what I think they are?"

Luke tugged me to the bar. "I don't even want to know."

I swallowed and tried to match the vampires' stares. I relaxed when I realized that they weren't looking at me, but rather at the group of rowdy men parading around the alcohol, each with girls perched on their hips.

I smirked when I guessed we'd come upon the werewolves. "These supernaturals look more my type," I said, and nodded at the bartender. "Whiskey, neat."

Taking my drink, I sidled up to one of the empty chairs and pointed to the other side of the room. "There's Sarah."

Luke took a sip as he peered through the crowd. Sarah and Vikki danced to the delicate jazz thrumming through the air. A band swayed behind them as if the music was all for them. Knowing that Sarah was Apollo's daughter, it likely was.

"I hate Jazz," I complained.

Luke smirked. "Don't get your panties all in a bunch." He jerked his chin. "Look, there's Apollo, and he's arrived in style."

I followed his gaze up to the banister to find Apollo descending on a fucking floating throne. "The hell?" I hissed. I looked for wires or something to explain how he was floating down, but all I could see was an annoyingly arrogant smirk plastered on his face. I looked down, only to find a circle of women dressed in sleek, tight dresses with their hands outstretched and palms upturned. They chanted as Apollo descended into the circle. "Are those actual witches?" I asked.

Luke nodded. "That or there's some strong hallucinogens in this whiskey."

Apollo raised his hands as the witches parted, and the crowd roared with excitement. "Welcome, fine members of the supernatural community," he began. A hush descended over the groups of vampires, werewolves, incubi and succubi alike as Apollo gathered the folds of fabric that covered the mysterious box in the center of the room. "Today, I bring you a spectacle not seen in the entirety of our existence."

He jerked the sheet away and a gasp shocked through the crowd.

"Holy shit," I muttered as I gripped Luke's arm.

It was impossible, but somehow, right there in the middle of the room was an aquarium that housed a very real, and very terrified mermaid.

"What is this?" Sarah shrieked as she ran to the aquarium and pressed her palms against it.

As if she already knew who Sarah was, the mermaid flicked her tail and turned, pressing her own fingers against the glass.

Apollo crossed his arms and marched his way around his prize. "This, my daughter, is what must be done." His amber eyes, so much like Sarah's, went wide with determination. "I require the power of three elements to save supernaturals from endless imprisonment. You have a Tear of the Sea, but it keeps you alive. So when a mermaid came looking for you, I made sure that she was captured."

Vikki eased to Sarah's side and moved to pull her away, but Sarah shook her off. "Did you know about this?" she snapped.

Vikki shook her head. "No, of course not." She found me across the expanse of the room and I shrank into Luke's shadow. She pointed at me, making my attempts to hide pointless. "It's her fault!"

It felt as if the entire room turned to stare at me. "Get me out of here," I hissed through clenched teeth.

"Nu-uh," Luke insisted as he tugged me towards the spectacle in the middle of the room. "You wanted to save the world, you gotta get your hands dirty."

Growling with frustration, I jerked out of his grip, but kept walking. The line of witches glared at me with eerie stares that made the hairs on the back of my neck stand on end. I didn't know much about covens, but something about this one reeked of Apollo's influence.

Blocking me, the tallest witch glowered and matched my gaze with magic swirling in her eyes. The purple onyx touches were more mesmerizing than they were terrifying. "Who said you could approach the King?"

I rolled my eyes. "There's no King here. Just a prick."

The crowd gasped, and just as the witches raised their fingers to entrap me with a spell, Derek's laughter boomed against the marble walls. "Making friends everywhere you go, I see."

I glowered past the aquarium to find Derek with a slew of sirens hanging off his arms. He shrugged them off as he approached. "Sorry I'm late," he said to Apollo with a handsome grin. "I was enjoying your… gifts." The sirens gave a collective sigh. "Let the succubus in," Derek said, turning serious. "She's one of mine."

With a growl, I shoved past the row of witches who glowered and hissed. One glance over my shoulder showed me a very worried looking Luke. Because of him, I was going to be okay. I was in control.

"Not one of yours," I corrected as I crossed my arms and gave Derek a glare. "Not now, not ever."

"*Au contraire,*" Derek said with a smug smile. "You were born and raised in Seattle, the capital of my domain. As a succubus of the d'Ange family, you're under my protection."

"And good thing," Apollo said. "I'd have made her cut off her own tongue by now if you didn't fancy her. She's broken my poor girl's heart, and now she waltzes around with that boy on a leash. It's disgusting."

Derek chuckled. "Ah, Luke. Almost didn't recognize you with that tan. Why don't you come and join us?"

Luke narrowed his eyes. Low blow. The poor guy had been locked up in a dungeon for heavens knew how long and had always been unnaturally pale, but he pulled it off. I don't think it mattered how much sun he got; a tan wasn't going to happen.

The witches parted to allow Luke through. He backed up a step, only to find himself blocked in by a row of growling werewolves. He straightened and made his way to my side. "Derek," he said with a nod, "can't say it's nice to see you again."

"Always a pleasure," Derek said with a toothy grin.

Apollo clapped his hands. "Great. I'm so glad we're all here to enjoy this wonderful moment." Apollo grinned and caressed the glass. The mermaid shrank away as if he could reach straight through and strangle her. "It's time."

Sarah stomped her foot. "What's going on? Why have you taken a mermaid? Just look at her. She's terrified!"

The mermaid's gills on her neck flared as her chest fluttered like a caged bird. Her wide, turquoise eyes that observed with eerie otherness watched Apollo with an unerring stare. She knew that he was her captor, and that he was dangerous.

Apollo glanced at me as he held out a hand. A witch appeared at his side with a ceremonial dagger. The blood drained from my face. I didn't like where this was going.

"Since I require power from the three sources of magic to do what must be done, your little fish friend is going to give us a small sacrifice." He ran the blade over the glass, sending a grating screech cascading through the room. "I'll be taking her heart."

Sarah gasped with horror. "You'll do no such thing!"

Apollo swirled on her with rage flaring in his eyes. "You are my daughter, but do not test my patience. Changing the world requires sacrifice. It's already begun and we can't stop it now. All we can do is embrace it and prepare for a new era."

What was he talking about? I was afraid I didn't want to find out.

Sarah straightened. "Taking the life of an innocent mermaid isn't sacrifice." She presented her hand and a blue gem appeared on her finger. "Sacrifice means giving something up that you care about. If you truly care about me, then you'll take my ring, and spare this poor creature's life. That, *Father,* is sacrifice."

He scoffed. "Don't be ridiculous. Why do you care about a fish? If the mermaids had their way, you'd be swimming among them with seaweed wrapped through your hair." He thrust his knife into the glass, sending it cracking and water spurting through the leak. "You'll see. Once the water drains, she'll suffocate because she's a *fish.* She can't breathe air."

The entire room went silent, waiting and watching for what Sarah might do. The fires of my Blood Stone burned within me, and had I not learned control, I would have snapped and gone for Apollo myself. But I exercised the new strength that Luke had given me. This was Sarah's battle, and if she needed me, I'd be there for her, but I wouldn't take that which wasn't mine to take.

A moment later, the room bathed in a brilliant blue as Sarah's ring came to life. Her hair flung about her face and she lifted from the ground. Wide-eyed, I watched as she transformed, scales erupting over her skin and the air growing thick and dark as if we'd been submerged under water.

Apollo extended his hands and pressed his power over her, but if he was trying to control Sarah, it wasn't working. "Daughter!" he cried. "Stop this!"

Sarah wasn't listening. A song began, and I realized that the sirens had begun a melody I'd never heard before. It was one of secret lamentation and sorrow, but also of a faraway homeland that they'd longed for and lost.

The mermaid flicked her massive tail and broke the glass, sending water and shards of glass into the air that instantly hung free instead of crashing to the ground. Sarah encased the water around the mermaid, keeping her safe in the ball of life-giving liquid.

The song intensified and Apollo's enraged cries muffled as the air began to transform into water. Out of instinct I wrapped the Blood Stone's power around myself and Luke. I wasn't the only one with gifts to keep ourselves alive. The witches chanted until they blocked out the melody of the sea, wrapping their coven and Apollo in safety. The werewolves had scrambled to the exits, some now swimming in the air. But the vampires, I watched them through the red haze of my power as they enveloped into the witches aura. I made a mental note that vampires and witches seemed to be on the same side. Perhaps that'd be useful knowledge in this "new era."

The witches raised their hands, parting the waters long enough for Sarah to stumble. Apollo launched through the opening and ripped the ring off her finger. He said something to her, but the words wouldn't carry through the wall of water between us.

A blazing portal deep with purples and ancient magic opened up behind Apollo. He sneered at his daughter before launching himself through it. If he wasn't going to find his sacrifice here, then he was going to find it somewhere else.

I grabbed Luke's hand. "Come on!" I urged him. Apollo couldn't get away with the Tear of the Sea. If Sarah didn't have it to keep her grounded, she'd turn into a mermaid herself, or die.

With a single look at her face as the mermaid wrapped her

fingers around her arms, I saw a rainbow of emotions erupt to the surface. Sarah was afraid.

I expected Vikki to separate Sarah from the creature that clung to her now, but instead she bound hands with her sisters and raised her voice in song, keeping the waters encased around them as the power of the witches ripped violently through the air.

"They're stable," Luke said.

That's all I needed to hear. Sarah would survive this, thanks to Vikki. She could survive without the Tear of the Sea, at least long enough until we got it back.

With a blast of controlled power, I gouged out a tunnel through the water, sending the witches choking as their bubbles began to collapse. Together with Luke, we ran through the portal, and in a blast of energy, found ourselves someplace new.

"The hell?" I snapped.

I looked up, my nostrils flaring at scent of water, but not of Miami. The soft lilt of a language I didn't recognize hummed around me, the intonations softer than a siren's song.

"Are we in… Venice?" Luke asked.

I looked around for where Apollo and his team of witches and vampires could have gone, but was met only by the cool, languid air. Moonlight trickled over mossy walls and slow moving crowds parted around us as if we hadn't just appeared from a magical portal. I whirled, but any hint of magic and danger was gone. The hairs stood on the back of my neck when I couldn't shake the sense that we were being watched.

My gaze shot up, finding a man standing on a roof with eyes that glowed red. He smirked, gave me a salute, and disappeared into the night as if I'd imagined him.

Wherever we were, it was vampire territory, and we had a whole new set of problems on our hands.

SUCCUBI DON'T WRINKLE

In lieu of freaking the fuck out, Luke opted for winding through the lopsided streets until we found a corner café to settle in. Forcing me into a seat, Luke ordered a coffee in fluent Venetian, he told me it was called, and made my heartbeat rise a good fifty percent.

"You speak fucking European?" I breathed as I accepted the minuscule coffee cup.

He laughed. "European isn't a language, sweetheart."

I frowned.

"Don't make that face," he chided as he eased into his seat. He took a sip of his own drink and his eyelids drooped until he gave me a sexy half-lidded stare. "You're going to get wrinkles."

"Succubi don't wrinkle," I assured him. "But seriously. How do you speak their language?"

He shrugged. "It must be an angel thing."

"Great," I thought out loud, not sure if it was good or bad that Luke was coming into his powers. With another glance at our impossible surroundings, I blew out a breath. "I don't get it. How are we here?" My gaze flitted to the rooftops. I couldn't see them, but I knew that we were still being watched.

Luke followed my gaze. "If I had to guess, your Blood Stone brought us here." He nodded at my chest. "Maybe you should ask it."

Sweat broke out when I realized that my Blood Stone had been quiet for quite some time now. "Hey, Blood Stone voice thingy, you in there?" I hissed.

Luke smirked. "Really? That's how you commune with some ancient power inside your soul? You whisper at it and call it 'Blood Stone voice thingy?'"

I shushed him, which only made him bark out with open laughter.

While I was enjoying the smooth sounds of Luke's joy, I looked up again, and this time spotted the vampire.

Tall. Dark. Handsome.

Definitely dangerous, and looking right at me in a way that made my fingers clench around my drink.

If my Blood Stone wasn't talking, then it had used the last of its power to bring me here, and I had a feeling that reason was in the sensual, red hooded gaze that looked down on me now. I needed answers, and there was only one way to get them.

I knew this vampire, and he knew me. A single rune I'd never felt before came to life, filling me with a burning need that completed the circle around my navel.

"Luke," I whispered, not taking my gaze from the rooftops. "Stay here. I'll be right back."

It seemed that I'd found my fourth.

A TODAY BESTSELLING AUTHOR

J. R. THORN

SEVEN SINS

VAMPIRE SINS

USA TODAY BESTSELLING AUTHOR

J.R. THORN

XAVIER

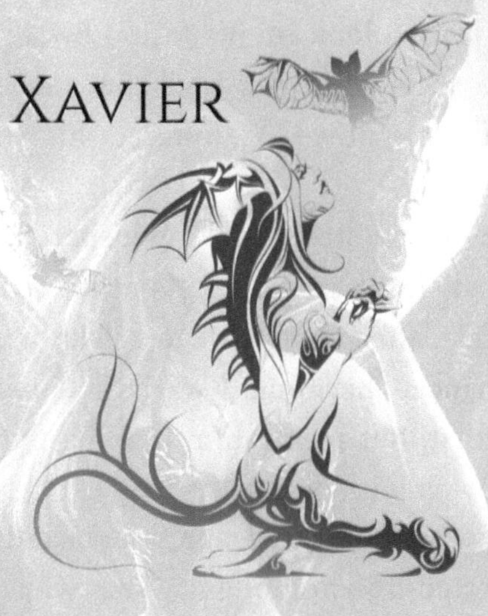

I have found my fourth... and he's going to bring out the worst in me

Sonya

Venice. Of all the places that I'd wind up when shit hit the fan, the romantic city of gondolas and gelatos was definitely not what I'd pictured. It was also the last place on Earth I'd imagine I'd find my fourth.

The runes surrounding my navel pulsated with the need to complete the circle. Four souls. Four pieces of my destiny. Four men who could control my heart and my future and stop my nightmares from coming true.

My fingers curled into fists as I fought the idea for the first time. I'd been so enraptured by Luke, by Jet and Nate, that I hadn't realized I'd been falling into a trap. The last piece of my soul stared down at me from atop a roof—a vampire, no less. He exuded confidence, arrogance, and danger in ways that made my skin crawl and my heart quicken. What kind of destiny paired me with such dangerous men?

The vampire with glowing red eyes watched and waited with

an annoyingly pleased look on his face. I broke eye contact as I stared up at the sheet of jagged rock that made up the ancient building. "I can come down," he offered, his voice carrying on the humid breeze.

Glancing down the street, Luke whispered in the shadows, blending amongst sleepy strangers. As promised, he was waiting for me by a quiet coffee shop instead of running to my aid like some kind of Prince Charming. I wasn't a damsel. I didn't need help. He knew that, but seeing him looking out for me anyway made my heart twist with delight.

He ventured a bit closer, revealing the beautiful, sharp angles of his face crested by moonlight. The way his brows knit together said he wasn't too happy about allowing me to face danger alone, though. If he saw what had gotten my attention, I'd never hear the end of it—no matter if the man looking down at me was one of my four or not.

Ignoring the vampire's offer, I grabbed one of the stones jutting out of the uneven wall and hauled myself up. There was no way I'd agree to meet this guy on the street. Anyone who saw him would know he wasn't human and our conversation would be cut short, so I dug my fingers into a crevice in the gritty rock and climbed.

He offered a sleek, pale hand when I reached the top and I glared at him, choosing to skid my knees against the unforgiving stone instead of accepting his help.

He huffed a laugh. "Stubborn one, aren't you?"

Growling and wiping away the stinging pebbles, I snapped my teeth. I figured a vampire might take that as an insult. "You're the one parading around in the open with those eyes of yours like you're not a creature of the night. The hell you trying to do?" I eased closer and tried to ignore the intoxicating musk of maleness that wafted from him. "Supernaturals are supposed to keep their presence hidden from humans."

He grinned, flashing very real fangs that made my insides curl. "Says a succubus who just scaled a wall."

Rolling my eyes, I glanced down the way I'd come. I'd thought it a short distance with some jutting rocks to give me purchase, but now I saw that we were three stories up and the side of the building glistened slick in the moonlight.

Okay, so maybe that had been showing off a bit.

I flinched as he ran a finger across my collarbone without warning. "I sensed the Blood Stone when you arrived, but I don't see it on you." His fingers dipped lower towards the curve of my cleavage and I slapped his hand away. He gave me a husky chuckle. "The magic is *inside* of you; how intriguing."

"I'm so glad I amuse you," I drawled. "How about you tell me who the fuck you are?"

He grinned, his fangs catching the moonlight and making me suck in a breath. "I can tell you're not accustomed to vampires." He cocked his head. "Am I the first one you've met?"

Snarling, I snapped a finger in his face and red electricity zapped around my skin. His eyes widened at my magic. "I'm the one asking questions here. Tell me who you are and what you want or this is going to get ugly." I knew why I had been brought here. My magic wanted me to complete the magic that pulsated in my runes, but I wasn't going to make it easy on him. If he wanted to be my fourth, he was going to have to earn it.

A dangerous glint flashed in his gaze, giving me just enough warning that he was up to something before he up and vanished into thin air. I gasped when his hot breath puffed on the back of my neck. I whirled to find him leering down at me, his red eyes glowing with excitement. "My name is Xavier," he whispered, his voice caressing me in ways that felt like a violation. "And whether you want to accept it or not, you're most certainly my mate."

Before I could reply at his audacity, a rock beamed him right in the temple. Velvet red blood splotched across his forehead and he snarled, facing the ground where the projectile had come from.

"Get away from her, fang-face," Luke growled.

Sigh. My angel knight in shining armor… or rather, tattered bits of a shirt that had survived the portal. The silver moonlight illuminated the cut lines of his chest that seemed to serve no other purpose than to reveal how ripped he was.

"Luke? The fuck you doing?" I whisper-yelled, trying to ignore how turned on I was by his protectiveness.

Xavier ran his finger down the trail of blood and drew it into his mouth, making sure to look at me as he licked. "Who's your charming friend?"

"My boyfriend," I answered without thinking, then my neck went hot with a flush as Luke laughed.

The most handsome smile I'd ever seen spread slowly across his face. "Yeah," he said. "I'm her boyfriend, and even if I share her, it's not with the likes of you."

I recognized the challenge in his statement. If he could feel Xavier exuding with the power of my fourth like I could, then he was going to challenge Xavier into earning me. The vampire couldn't just walk into my life and win a place in my bed… unless he kept licking his finger like that. He really needed to stop it.

Raising an eyebrow at me, Xavier finally lowered his hand. "Well, it seems I've gotten off on the wrong foot. Why don't we go to my place and have some wine?"

Glaring, I said, "I don't do wine."

He smiled. "Oh, darling, you're in Venice. We all 'do' wine."

He inched closer and my rune burned at his proximity. He was definitely one of my four, but the raw arrogance in his gaze pissed me off. Just because destiny had bound him to me didn't mean that I was going to just bend over.

"Why are you looking at me like that?" I snapped.

He grinned and his eyes swept over me, taking in the curves poorly hidden by my tight Miami-suitable clothes. "We don't get many succubi in Venice, especially not any that could handle me." His grin grew. "You can handle me, can't you?"

My nails bit crescents into my palms. If I said yes, that would just egg him on. If I said no, I was admitting I'd never slept with a vampire and I had no idea what to expect.

When I hesitated, he slowly licked his lower lip, riding his tongue up his fang.

Getting tired of this prick, I teetered on the edge of the roof, preparing myself to break my legs trying to jump off rather than spend one more second with the likes of this vampire.

He brushed my shoulder with a light touch and pointed to the stairwell. "If I may."

Sighing, I opted for the stairs.

It turned out that I *was* a wine kind of girl, I'd just never had the right wine before, apparently.

"What's in this?" I marveled, turning the glass to catch the light of Xavier's chandelier as the low golden glow splattered rainbows and sequins off my glass.

He didn't answer, and instead refilled my drink.

I sighed and took another sip, fluttering my eyes closed in bliss. When I opened them again, I wondered how I'd found myself from Miami's beaches to this place, the best Venice had to offer. His "humble abode," as he'd called it, was apparently a vampire hideout of the luxurious sort.

"So, a muse runs this city?" I asked, slipping into the comfort of an expensive leather couch. I shouldn't have been indulging in the poorly hidden attempts of my fourth trying to woo me, but I couldn't help it. I was exhausted. I could be wooed and refuel my energy stores at the same time, right?

Luke ignored his glass and instead peered out of the two-story window gazing at the stillness of the canals below. "It's nothing like New York, or Shanghai," he said. "It's too… peaceful."

Xavier poured himself a glass of wine—which was definitely *not* wine—and settled himself across from me. It didn't matter that he was out of arm's reach. The way his gaze raked over me made me feel invaded. I hated that I liked it.

"We work hard to keep things that way," Xavier said, his tone edged with accusation as he glared at Luke. "Hades runs things differently than Apollo, Ares, or Derek," Xavier continued. "He's only half a muse, after all. He's capable of some common sense."

Raising an eyebrow, I set my glass down. "Half-muse?"

He nodded. "My master is half-vampire, half-muse. He sleeps for decades at a time and awards the vampire community the magic of compulsion. It keeps the humans blind to our ongoings, keeps the vampires happy, and until recently, has kept Apollo and Ares out of vampire business."

"So, what's changed?" Luke asked, leaning against the window and crossing his arms.

Xavier frowned, not hiding his distaste for Luke. "Your arrival comes as part of provenance of a new world foreseen by my witches." I shivered as he said that with such confidence… *his* witches. "They've predicted chaos to engulf this city and the resulting flames will devour the world." His gaze fell on me, coating me with a wave of his desire mixed with aggravation, as if he wasn't sure if he wanted to rip out my jugular or plunge himself into me. My rune pulsed low on my stomach in response and I clenched my thighs, cursing low under my breath. Xavier grinned at my discomfort. "My witches have also seen the few key players who can derail fate. You, my dear, are one of them."

He shifted closer, making my spine go rigid as his grin widened, revealing lengthening fangs. "If I take you as my mate, the vampire community would gain the edge we need to withstand the Incubus King and a rogue muse."

I rolled my eyes. Sure, he was hot and the rune pulsing low on my belly was begging me to explore his body, but I was a succubus. I didn't do "mates." I had other men in my life. "Again with the mate thing." I motioned for Luke to sit with me. With a sly grin, he obeyed. I ran my thumb across his lower lip and gazed into the perfect blue of his eyes that held so much pain, mystery, and longing. "I am not made for just one man." I loved Luke. Just like I loved Jet and Nate. They all soothed a deep wound inside of me that had plagued me all my life. It was hard to believe that my magic believed Xavier comparable to the souls who'd won me over.

"He's no man," Xavier observed, ignoring the point I was trying to make entirely. "My witches never miss anything—or anyone. The only reason they wouldn't be able to foresee Luke's arrival is if he were a powerful supernatural." He set his glass on the table and the liquid inside sloshed in a way that made my stomach roll with nausea. "So, my friend, what exactly are you? Why does this succubus resist me when she has been destined as my mate? Why does she cling to you, when she should be draping herself over me?"

Luke ignored the provocation and kept looking into my eyes, his hand slipping up the back of my neck as he pulled me in for a deep, sensual kiss. Warmth flooded through my body and my world spun when he pulled away. "You're so much better than wine," I said with my smile against his teeth.

Xavier huffed a laugh. Instead of getting the point—again—he was amused.

Sneaking Xavier a glance, I glared. "So, your witches," I said, purposefully pushing him off topic, "what else did they see?"

His ruby gaze darkened for the first time as he leaned back into the embrace of the sofa. "Death," he said, the word an ominous growl. "This city will be the first to fall to Derek's madness. With the three stones of power, as well as the alliance of the other two muses, he will undo all the hard work that Hades has put in place." His gaze grew dark. "I fear the harsher possibility. They come to kill my master while he sleeps and I won't be able to stop them, not without inducing Hades into a premature awakening."

I shrugged. "Okay, so, go wake him, then."

He watched me with an intensity that displayed every facet of his inhumanity. He didn't blink, didn't breathe. Every muscle in his body was taut and ready to spring. "No one can wake a sleeping vampire, especially Hades. Only the power which gave all vampires life could rouse him from his current state." His gaze dipped to my breast where a faint red glow had begun to throb, and for the first time I dumbly realized that Xavier's eyes were the same kind of red as the power exuded by my Blood Stone. "I'm afraid you're the only one with that gift," his gaze snapped to mine, "but you won't be able to wake my master with the power of your Blood Stone alone. You must be able to speak to him, mind-to-mind." He leaned his elbows on his knees. "You must become a *vampire.*"

Shivering, I peeled myself away from Luke who'd begun to grip me a bit too hard.

"There's no way Sonya is going to become a bloodsucking vampire," Luke snarled.

I winced at the insult. "Am I so different?" I asked, my voice a weak whisper. "I drain life just as a vampire does."

Luke took my hand and the power of his blue gaze drew me in with such desperation that I couldn't look away. "No, Sonya. You're so much more than that." His touch threaded my fingers. "You're mine."

Xavier appeared beside us without warning, his vampire speed taking us both off guard. His red eyes glowed with wisps of power that bounced off the harsh arches of his cheekbones. "Do you hate what you are?" he asked me, seeming to be able to read my mind.

My first reaction was to slap him for getting all up in my face, but there was a deeper emotion in the backs of his eyes that made me go still. "Yes," I admitted. Only Nate had been able to get me to open up, to feel understood. But where Nate had given me solace, Xavier whispered of a kindred pain that shared my own.

He placed his hand on my shoulder and I couldn't help but feel a strange sense of comfort being between these two strong men that made my runes awaken with heat and hunger. Luke, my tormented angel, found ways to bring out my humanity and suppress my succubus impulses. But this vampire, there was another promise he offered in the cool strength of his grip. There was an understanding there that no one else could offer. "Perhaps," he whispered, "if you became a hybrid, like my master, you wouldn't be a slave to your impulses. It's why he became what he is."

My eyes went wide. "Let's say, just for kicks, I was up for this. How does one become a vampire?"

"Sonya," Luke began, but I held up a hand.

"It's okay," I said. "I'm not doing anything rash. I just want to hear what he has to say."

Xavier grinned, his tongue flashing seductive promises across his lips. "The secret of how to turn a female is one of the best kept mysteries of the supernatural community."

I raised an eyebrow. "Males are easy to turn?"

He grinned. "Wouldn't call it easy, but it's no secret. It's long, painful, and good luck getting the kind of blood necessary for the turn." His grin turned wicked. "Females, however, are not often turned, and for good reason."

"But you're going to tell me?" I asked.

He stood and crossed his arms. "Perhaps, but I'm afraid the angel can't be here for this conversation." We both startled at how seamlessly he guessed what Luke was—and how *not* surprised he was that Luke was a celestial being. Xavier pointed to the hall. "Your room is three corridors down. There's enough insulation in the walls to keep our conversation private and out of earshot, even for a supernatural. Should Sonya wish, she'll join you after we've had our little chat." His eyes blazed with power. "If she chooses to accept my proposal, however, you're not to interfere."

Luke eyed me warily. I couldn't miss the pain in his eyes. He'd watched me choose other men so many times before, and once again, he feared he was going to lose me to another. It wasn't monogamy he desired, it was the assurance that I'd always come back. I wanted to tell him that he had a piece of my heart. He always would.

He took my hand. "Don't look at me like that," he said and gave me a weak smile. "Don't look so guilty. I've told you before and I'll tell you again, I understand what you are. I understand to be with you means to share you. I love you enough to do that." He gave Xavier a dubious glance. "Not that I could comprehend anything this fang-face has to propose could be remotely enticing."

Laughing, I pushed him away. "Go on. I'll see you soon."

Xavier looked far too pleased with himself as Luke sauntered down the hall.

"Great," he said when Luke had disappeared from sight. "Let's talk secrets."

VAMPIRE SECRETS

Sonya

My body induced uncontrollable shivers with the conflicting urge to run after Luke… and to stay and see what this pulsing, undeniable connection with Xavier meant. That is, assuming I wasn't on the dinner menu. The way he leered at me as he ran his tongue over his fangs wasn't at all encouraging. I wasn't afraid of the powerful supernatural. Xavier might be a vampire, but I didn't doubt my own strength. Should he try to eat me, I could fend him off—probably.

Xavier circled me like a lion stalking his prey. He took each step with deliberate focus, not once taking his red gaze off of me. "Do you feel it?" he asked after I'd been watching him with fascination. The way he moved betrayed he wasn't human at all.

I wrapped my fingers around my elbows and straightened. My breasts spilled over the curve of my arms and Xavier's gaze dipped, his eyes unashamed as they filled with hunger. The way he looked at me was the desperate need of a man who hadn't had a woman in a long time—which seemed impossible. He exuded sex and desire. No woman would be able to resist him for five seconds.

"Feel what?" I asked, even though my body was already betraying me and my rune had turned hot with an aching need. His tongue flashed across his lips as he took a step closer, making my heart skip.

It didn't matter that I was a succubus. This creature was one of lust and allure just as much as any incubus. If I let my guard down, he'd wind me right around his little finger.

He came close enough to touch me and deliberately ran a cool finger over my arm, sending the tiny hairs to stand on end. "Your body responds to me," he said with a pleased grin.

I tried not to dip my gaze to the opening of his sleek shirt that revealed a curve of abs that disappeared into a tight waistband. "You're supposed to be telling me vampire secrets," I reminded him.

He grinned. "Such secrets are not given for free."

I glowered. "And the price?"

He leaned in and grazed his lips against my ear. I flinched when his fangs pressed their cool danger against my skin. "A taste of your exquisite blood."

I shivered. No way had I ever imagined a vampire lingering at my neck to be a turn on. My blood ran hot and excitement thundered in my ears. All it took was the soft whisper of his breath on my neck to make me arch—and then I recognized his magic winding over me like the invasion it was.

Red hot desire that wasn't my own whispered in my ear and made my blood rush to my core. My body begged me to give in to the promise of pleasure, but I recognized this drug far too well. Desire masked the truth: that a vampire was deadly and I would be his next victim if I let my guard down.

Shaking myself free of his compulsion, I groaned and collapsed to the floor. I dug my fingers into the plush carpet and inhaled, soaking in the pungent lilac potpourri of the clean room, the scent overlying the faint musk of dried blood. My nostrils flared. This was a vampire's den, no matter the wine and the luxury. Grounding myself in my other senses, I fought the vampire's compulsion as I flooded my body with the scalding heat of the Blood Stone, evaporating the worst of the binds his magic had clawed into me.

"You really want to play this game?" I warned him through gritted teeth. If he wanted to test me with magical lust, I'd show him how a succubus could make him fall to his knees—once I got off mine, of course.

His gaze flashed with challenge as I stood and straightened. "We're kindred creatures, you and I," he all but purred, pissing me off with his complete confidence that I'd be bending over for him any second now. I squeezed my hands on my hips to keep from doing just that. "I have no doubt of your power, but I am second-born of Hades himself and very much your senior. I doubt you—"

I flicked my fingers and sent a red wave of raw lust wrapping around his cock. That should shut him up. His eyes went wide and his pants bulged. He gasped as the pure power of my Blood Stone hit him hard and I grinned. "You were saying?"

He peeled off his shirt as a fine layer of sweat glistened across his skin. Even though I was winning, just the sight of him shirtless made me stagger. Magic had forged him into the perfect male specimen, hard and dangerous and completely in my league. His muscles pleasantly flexed as he clawed away the sticky layers of my magic. Once he'd shredded the last of my power, he bared his teeth at me. His fangs seemed larger than before and the red haze in his eyes burned with excitement. He seemed glad that I wouldn't be an easy target. "You took me off guard. It won't happen again."

Before I had a chance to send another wave of magical lust

and bring him under control, he disappeared, just like he had on the rooftop. I whirled just in time to find him materializing in a flicker of black shadows, his fangs so close to my neck that I froze with both anticipation and horror. "I won't bite," he promised, "not unless you agree to be my mate."

Growling, I planted my hands on his hard chest and pushed. I might as well have tried to move a brick wall for all the good that did me. I drew power from my Blood Stone and my energy sizzled along his skin, but he still didn't give me an inch.

He towered over me and wrapped his fingers around my arms, but not in a way that made me feel threatened. His touch was light and gentle, as if he was afraid to hurt me. He lowered, parting his lips and breathing in my magic, testing me, provoking me.

Pride surged in my chest, making me lift on my tiptoes and allow his fangs to press their cool danger against my lips. That was all the encouragement he needed before his tongue grazed across my lower lip, tasting me as he growled with need.

I found myself just as curious about how he tasted and I copied his motion, flicking my tongue across the soft crest of his lip between the sharp danger of his fangs. I regretted it the moment I did it as his grip tightened. If I'd thought his magic powerful before… tasting him made me buckle and fall against the unforgiving wall of his chest.

He tasted of bliss, roses, and blood, and all I could think about was indulging myself in the delicacy that was Xavier.

I opened my eyes to find him watching me as his entire body quivered with the naked need that gleamed in his ruby eyes. He was just as intoxicated by me as I was by him, and he was holding himself back. I was an idiot to be alone with this predator, but as my hands wound up his neck and pulled him in for another kiss, I knew he would never hurt me. The rune burning hot on my stomach didn't lie. He was one of my four.

His tongue danced across mine as he pulled me in close, his hands pressing at the small of my back. The hard bulge of him strained against his pants and throbbed against my abdomen.

To feel him so close to the rune that claimed him as mine made me shiver and I pulled away for breath.

"This… is very enjoyable," he said in a low, husky whisper, "however I still require your blood if you wish to know how to become a vampire. That is my price."

"Why do you want my blood?" I asked breathlessly as I played my fingers over the back of his neck.

He growled in warning at the teasing motion and pulled me even closer. "Because there is magic in blood. You hold secrets I desire to know."

Secrets. What secrets could I possibly have that this ancient vampire wanted so badly?

"Don't you want to become a vampire?" He ran a finger around the edge of my ear and tucked a strand of hair away from my face.

Wrapping a curled strand of his midnight hair around my finger, I bit down on my lip to prevent myself from kissing him again. I couldn't deny the attraction of becoming a vampire. As a succubus, I could live for hundreds of years, but as a vampire, I'd have eternity at my fingertips.

It wasn't true immortality that attracted me, although that was a plus. Some supernaturals hunted the vampires, torturing them in hopes of uncovering the secret to permanent life. The vampires never succumbed to coercion, not because they were a proud race, but because they were magically superior in every way. Vampires could turn off their emotions and pain like a switch. That was exactly what I craved. Ultimate strength. Ultimate confidence. The power over my emotions with precise control at my fingertips. Everything I'd need to abolish the guilt and depression that consumed me on a daily basis.

What made me hesitate was the shadow of grief in this vampire's eyes. How was that even possible? How could a creature so perfectly in control over his own emotions grieve anything at all? Why did he look at me as if I, a broken succubus, could fix all of his problems?

I motioned to pull away, but the iron prison of his arms kept me in place. He didn't force himself on me, but he wasn't letting me go, either. "Why do you wait for permission?" I asked, my words slurring with the drug of his magic that wafted over me in merciless waves. "You could take me, if you wanted to."

He growled and bared his teeth, the fleeting emotions I'd seen swept away by the predator's claim. "I am not a monster," he insisted. "I will never take a woman, not her body, not even her blood, without her permission."

My pride couldn't give him permission, but my magic could. The heat of my Blood Stone unfurled with frustration and spoke to my need, encouraging him to cup my breast. I arched against his touch and my lips parted with a silent moan.

"Don't toy with me, Sonya," he insisted. "I've waited for you for a very long time and I will savor every moment of making you understand what you mean to me." His fangs grazed my neck again and I knew that he fought the urge to bite down, making my thighs clench as I wondered what that might feel like. Instead of enlightening me, he licked a long line up to my ear. "You may not know me longer than a few hours, but I have known you every waking moment since I started having the visions a hundred years ago."

My eyes widened. "Visions?"

He reluctantly pulled away. "I could show you, if you like." His lip tugged in a grin that said nothing good could come from me seeing his visions, which I had a feeling were more appropriately named "fantasies."

I should have said no. Instead, I found my head bobbing up and down. Fucking treacherous body of mine.

He drew his wrist to his mouth with deathly silence. His fangs pricked his skin and dollops of blood pooled. He offered me his arm. "Drink, before I change my mind."

I grimaced. "If you think—"

He blurred, rushing closer until the erotic scent of his blood made my nostrils flare. The velvety blood glittered with immortal magic, nothing like human blood at all, and my stomach rolled that I actually found it *enticing*.

"Fine. What the hell," I muttered before taking his arm with both hands. I carefully brought his wrist to my mouth and covered the wound with my tongue.

Sensuality unfurled through me unlike anything I'd ever felt. This creature, this man, he was more than my equal, he was a refined object of desire down to his very genetic makeup. Visions exploded into view, a red haze of lust making the tension in the air seem like pathetic foreplay. I blinked as a bed materialized and Xavier, as well as another version of *myself,* fell onto a massive bed that could fit a mass of bodies. They fell on the sheets, the pure silk looking like cream against them as dream-Sonya straddled the vampire and wrapped the sheets around their waist, hiding the best of the view.

I watched from the edge of the dream-bed to see this woman that was me, but not me. She writhed atop him and looked so happy. A Sonya with pearlescent skin and eyes that hinted with a ruby gleam. Fangs garnished her plump lips and she parted them with a moan when Xavier slid his hand under the sheets. She opened to him like a flower, so full of trust and delight. He moved and fit his mouth to the curve of her neck and sank his fangs into her. It looked like it should have hurt, but the musk of pleasure that filled the room betrayed what agonizing lust his bite could give. There was magic in it, just as a succubus numbed the pain of her soul-sucking abilities, a vampire enticed his prey with orgasmic pleasure.

A hand pressed against the small of my back and a hot breath kissed my neck as the real Xavier interrupted the vision. I couldn't see him through the haze of this world where I was a vampire and I was his mate enthralled by him. His hands slid lower and caressed my hips, drawing ever closer to the heat gathering between my thighs. "You see?" he whispered. "In this future, you are mine. We feed on each other and your succubus instincts are diluted into the purest form of sensuality. No death. No suffering. Only pleasure."

Dream-Sonya bucked against Xavier as he unlatched from her neck, a stream of her life-force dripping onto the pristine pillow. He bent down and licked the wounds while rolling her onto her back as he eased on top of her. He yanked the bedsheets aside and settled himself between her thighs, rocking and teasing. She grappled at him to bring him closer, wrapped her legs around him and bowed her back, but he didn't take her, not yet.

Pressure radiated across my sex as Xavier's touch ran lower and offered a breath of reprieve. My lips parted as he circled his fingers over my jeans.

His other hand popped off the button of my pants, slowly moved down my zipper, and I leaned into him, resigning to the need crashing over me.

"Is it too much?" he asked, the vision still in full force. Dream-Xavier growled before thrusting into his lover with a single motion, bringing her to orgasm as her eyes fluttered closed and she cried out. Jealousy wafted over me, because I knew Xavier wouldn't pleasure me like that, not until I was fully his.

"I've never felt such… need," I admitted, my breath coming in short pants as his fingers slid down the gap of my jeans and pressed into the wet heat of me. He moved so agonizingly slow that my body yearned to take his fingers and shove him into me, but he anticipated the twitch of my body and took both wrists in a firm grip as he continued to tease.

His fangs brushed against my neck, pricking ever so slightly without breaking the skin. "I told you, this vision has compelled me for a hundred years. Now you understand why I wish to share the vampire's most sacred secret with you." His fingers went low, parting the folds of my flesh and I sucked in a breath. "I must have you for eternity." He thrust a single finger inside of me and I cried out. "You will be mine, but I will not take you by force. I want you to feel what I feel. I want you to know my agony." The cruelty in his words told me that he blamed me for his suffering. He both wanted me and despised me for making him wait a hundred years.

Then he did something I hadn't anticipated. His magic ripped at the connection between us until it was wide open and everything that consumed him spilled into me. All his torment, all his grief, every second of suffering and yearning funneled into me until black spots glittered across my vision. The raw desire he held for me made me marvel he hadn't taken me right there on the roof.

I bucked against him and gasped as another surge swept straight through to my core, making my jeans insufferably soaked with my desire. "Don't," I begged, but he continued to unfurl the yearning of a hundred years into me as he pushed his fingers deeper inside, the pressure more agony than relief until my wet heat closed around him in a hard spasm.

I couldn't take it anymore. I turned and pressed my mouth against his and shoved my fingers down the tight band of his pants. The swollen velvety hardness of him pulsated against my touch, but it was my runes that reminded me Xavier was not my only fated mate in this house.

"Luke," I whispered, guilty to speak his name as I stroked

another man, but I had to think of him now, *especially* now. I couldn't bind myself to a vampire. I couldn't let Xavier's magic overwhelm me to allow him to make me his mate, right here on this ruined carpet that now glittered with his blood I'd tasted and the evidence of my desire that still ran down my thighs.

Xavier's whole body went tense. He bared his fangs at me and I knew that he was barely under control. "My visions showed me this, too," he whispered. "You are not alone in our future."

I knew how much Xavier craved me, how much he needed me. I had been his sole purpose in the last hundred years. He'd been searching for me, this woman who would become his mate, not knowing who she was or if he'd ever find her.

I continued to stroke him. "I want this," I admitted, my gaze flicking up to take in the blazing red heat of his eyes. "I—" my words cut off when Xavier's gaze turned dangerous as he looked over my shoulder, a warning hiss escaping through his fangs.

I turned, one hand still down Xavier's pants and my own unzipped jeans soaked with my desire, only to find Luke watching us. "You said my name," he explained.

It had only been a whisper, but angels had damn good hearing. A blush crawled up my neck. I didn't want to cause Luke pain. He claimed to be all cool with sharing me, but to be faced with it... "Luke, I—"

He waved a hand. "I only came to make sure he wasn't hurting you." His gaze went to my grip still in Xavier's pants.

Xavier relaxed and softly took my wrist in a gentle hold, encouraging me to continue to stroke him. "She's bonded to you," Xavier observed, his fangs dangerously flashing as he grew harder under the stimulation of my touch. "Yet you would allow her to touch me?"

It was a taunt. I should have stopped him, but the knee-buckling lust of his vision still ran hot through my veins. Xavier continued to pour his feelings into me, his magic potent and his desire real. My eyelids fluttered. It felt so good to give him pleasure. The supple skin under my fingers beckoned me to stroke him, care for him, give him what he'd craved for so long.

"I have always shared Sonya," Luke said, a stubborn hard line ticking at his jaw. "I know what she is and I refuse to suffocate her with claims of monogamy. That's such a human restriction." His blue eyes glowed with supernatural power. "We are not human, are we?"

Xavier grinned. "Such a novel concept." His fangs grazed my neck. "Perhaps she'd enjoy it if you joined us since you are so… refined in your manners of supernaturals' sexuality."

I went still at Xavier's proposal. With wide eyes, I looked up at the vampire who grinned with mischief, but that shadow of pain had returned. "I can't have her, not until she's my mate." He stroked my face. "I'm aware that your bond with the others is not so… permanent. You wish to consult with them, do you not?"

In spite of his crippling desire for me, there was no room for debate. He would not take me until I agreed to become his mate and became a vampire. A decision like that could not be made without consulting my four. "Yes," I whispered. Nate. Jet. I missed them. They had to know that I hadn't forgotten about them, that I would never make a permanent decision without their consult.

Xavier slipped his fingers over my shoulder and slipped off my sleeve, revealing supple skin slick with sweat. His touch made my vision waver, lust sweeping over me renewed and vigilant.

Xavier chuckled. "I'm afraid I've overwhelmed her with a hundred years of my unsated desires, Luke. A cruel punishment for a succubus." His gaze flashed with challenge. "If you join us, you can give her what I cannot." In spite of all his claims to make me suffer as he had, he wanted me to have pleasure, even if he couldn't be the one to provide it. That made my thighs clench and a soft whimper escape my throat.

Luke frowned. "And why can't you fuck her?" He asked the question as if irritated, but with Xavier's magic thick in the air, I scented Luke's interest. To have me, even while Xavier was here, would be to remind me that he was my mate just as much as Jet or Nate—or even this vampire. It would be the ultimate possession to show that even if another dick was in my hand, I still belonged to the angel.

Xavier grinned with such devilish pleasure that I instantly knew the reason he couldn't give me what I wanted.

If Xavier fucked me, he would lose control, and he would make me his, turning me into a vampire whether I consented or not.

It wasn't just sex that turned someone into a vampire. It was the possession of lust and bite and the sharing of blood, as well as a hell of a lot of magic.

Lust, check.

Hell of a lot of magic? Fuck yes.

Sex and the sharing of blood… I'd never wanted something so badly in all my life.

I had a feeling that there was a bit more required to becoming a vampire, but the fated bond that marked me with runes suggested I shouldn't be testing that theory. If I let Xavier fuck me, if I let him feed on me, I would become his, damn the consequences. Those consequences probably involved me sprouting fangs and cementing an ancient, magical bond I didn't yet understand. What would happen to Nate, or Jet? Would they be yanked out of their lives and forced to be shackled to my side? They deserved more from me.

No matter the logic I told myself, Xavier's magic hit me with powerful waves. His desire and memories continued to flood into me as I allowed the lust to take over. It fogged the room like a drug and Luke's hands swept over my curves, peeling away my clothes that had suddenly become too restricting. I still had my hand around Xavier's cock. I refused to let go as if my life depended on it.

My breath caught when Luke came up from behind me and settled his erection between my butt cheeks. He began sweet, teasing caresses down my arms.

With my free hand, I moved to tug at the vampire's pants, freeing the rest of him. The lines of his sweat-glistened muscular abdomen gleamed in the moonlight that trickled in through the foggy windows, having gone hazy with the smoldering heat of vampiric magic dancing with my succubus powers.

I settled my knees onto a velvet ottoman and curled my fingers over the edge. With my free hand I wrapped my fingers around Xavier's supple length and admired him before indulging in a long, deliberate lick.

He groaned, and before I could enjoy his pleasure, Luke's need nudged against my entrance. I paused and turned to watch him, my eyes wide and my body shivering. The angel didn't seem the least bit perturbed that I was about to take Xavier into my mouth. Instead, his blue eyes sparkled with desire and excitement. There wasn't jealousy, and I realized that it was because I had called for him. I'd said his name when I could have lost myself in the powerful magic of a vampire and left him forgotten and alone. I would never do that to him.

"I want you," I encouraged Luke and leaned back, forcing him an inch inside of me. I gasped at Luke's pleasure as it swept through me. My fingers compulsively tightened on Xavier's cock. It felt so amazing to be between two men who both wanted me so much, who were my destined bonds.

"You shouldn't feed," Luke warned me, his gaze flicking to Xavier. "Remember what I taught you."

Before I could remind him that I was in control, he pushed inside, sheathing himself into me, making a cry escape my throat and any control I had over my senses shattered.

Luke was right. If I fed now, I'd drink the life-force from an angel and a vampire. I'd lose myself in a spiral of lust that I could never get out from. I wasn't ready for it, but Luke had taught me how to enjoy sex without feeding. My Blood Stone unfurled fresh power through me, helping me to ease the gnawing hunger in my chest.

"I can learn a thing or two from you," Xavier growled with admiration as he watched my magic that should have been invisible, but noted the raw heat in me. He curled a finger around my chin and brought my attention back to the pulsating flesh in my hand. "I can feel your pleasure," he told me. "Take me in your mouth now, or I will rip the angel away from you and take you for myself."

I glanced up at him for a moment to see the blazing fire in his eyes. A fire that reminded me of the Blood Stone and spoke to his magic that was dangerously close to overtaking him. If he lost that last fragile thread of control, he'd take me and the bond of four would be complete—I wasn't ready for that.

I couldn't complete the bond, not without discussing it with all of those involved beforehand—but I also couldn't resist the temptation to ease Xavier's hunger, as well as my own. I wasn't going to make him suffer a moment longer. He'd waited a hundred years and each second that went by filled me with more of that agonizing sense of longing. He hadn't taken a woman since the visions had started. He feared that if he did, he'd lose control and feed her with vampiric magic, forcing a blood-bond when one was not supposed to be made.

I took him deep until he pressed to the back of my throat. He bucked against the sudden release of pleasure my mouth gave him. "Yes," he breathed. "More."

I tried to focus and make my tongue dance across his sensitive flesh, but it was difficult to concentrate. Luke continued his slow thrusts. The pleasure he gave me curbed the dangerous bite of need that clawed through me. Wetness slid down my leg and gathered at my knee, hopelessly damaging the furniture that no doubt cost more than my monthly rent. My arms shook as pleasure threatened to make me crumble.

"I—I can't," I breathed, for the first time overwhelmed. Black dots sprinkled across my vision.

Xavier gave a husky laugh and his form flickered, his once rock-hard flesh in my fingers vanishing as he moved faster than my eyes could follow. My world spun and I found myself on my back, the wetness that had pooled on the ottoman sticking a cold patch against my spine. Luke staggered, growling at the shove, but he was between my legs and I instinctually wrapped around him and pulled him close, his dick nudging against my swollen flesh.

Xavier appeared behind me, and I let my head fall back. He took my offer and put himself in my mouth. I groaned as his pleasure hit me hard and I reached up until I found his muscular forearms. He held me as I rocked and took him deeper into my mouth.

He was right. This was better. Luke eased inside of me and began his thrusts again while his fingers played with the nub of my need. "Sonya," he breathed my name through the waves of pleasure mounting between us, "if you want me to stop, just push me away."

Even now, Luke feared I wanted someone else more than I wanted him. I curled my legs around him and nudged him closer as my response. He took the encouragement and moved faster, bringing tears to my eyes as the pleasure made me squeeze around his cock.

"We must release," Xavier warned. I knew he could have sex forever, as stamina was no issue for his kind, but the longer we teased each other, the more dangerous the need became. Xavier was meant to make me his. That had been his only thought for the past hundred years and to feel my touch now made him crazy. His fangs had gotten even longer, looking sharp and deadly from my exposed position. Sex, blood-sharing, and lust was the only way he could share with me all of his emotions, memories, and visions. The moment this ended, the moment that cord was cut, I'd lose access to everything that tied me to him.

I didn't want it to end. Every second that passed by I learned something new. As his cock slid across my tongue, a memory unfurled from the sweet musk of his magic and lust. He'd once been cruel, a dark vampire that had disappointed his father who knew that there was more to the world than sex and power. That's why he'd found a witch to curse Xavier with visions of a blood-mate he couldn't have for a hundred years. That's when he'd changed. It was all because of me, and the knowledge that he was going to have to wait for a hundred years had crushed him. Now, to realize that I was already bonded with three others, the threat to him relapsing into his dark ways was real. I couldn't let him believe that there wasn't a chance. I didn't know if I wanted to become a vampire, but Xavier had become a good man. He'd learned how to live off of the tasteless, metallic blood from refrigerated donations and had abstained from pleasure all for the sake of hoping it would draw me to him. There was magic in need, and so he'd starved himself, all so that one day I might find him and release him from his suffering.

I reached out and grabbed the hard thighs that bulged against the pleasure of my mouth. Even though he wanted so much more, I could give him this.

Fuck me as hard as you can, I commanded Luke in a mental wave.

With my hold strong against Xavier's thighs, I took Luke's long, growing thrusts and let the pleasure unfurl in me. I rejected the power that wanted to settle in my succubus heart, and gave it to Xavier.

He gasped when the power hit him. Luke's lust, as well as my own, fed a strong dose that stroked him until he exploded in my mouth. He moved, the length of him rolling and throbbing across my tongue, as he came hard.

Luke's cry as he came to climax echoed my new lover's and I lost myself in the bliss that threatened to take me under.

DADDY'S HOME

Sonya

After a long, needed shower, I rubbed my hair with a towel and exited the bathroom to find Luke sound asleep in a bed that could have fit ten people. It seemed most vampire bedrooms accommodated the possibility of an orgy. I would have admired Luke's ability to sleep so peacefully in a vampire's den, had said vampire not been lingering at the door with a satisfied smirk on his face.

"Do you plan on sleeping here?" I asked, not sure if my question was hopeful or concerned. The threesome had been amazing, but the tugging need to cement our bond had been too close. I needed to bring the others here, but in the light of day, my proposal seemed preposterous.

"Hey, Nate, Luke, Jet, I know all of you are powerful, strong men. But how about binding yourself permanently to me? I'll become a vampire and live forever, which God knows how that'll impact you, but hey, what do you think? Want to bring Xavier into our team of freaks and find out what'll happen?"

I bit my lip. There was no way they'd agree to that, right?

Xavier cleared his throat, dragging me from my thoughts. "No," he said, pushing away from the door frame, "I don't sleep." His eyes glittered with danger. "And if I stayed the night in bed with you, you wouldn't sleep, either."

I wasn't going to let him control this conversation. I let the towel fall and his gaze raked over my naked body. The lust and need was still there, but the power of his blood had burned out of my veins by the heat of the Blood Stone, or perhaps it had been Luke's healing magic. Angel's cum did strange things.

"Are you vexed with me?" he asked, his gaze not moving from my body. "You shouldn't tease me with your skin. You know how much I desire you." He stiffened as I stepped closer. "Perhaps I shouldn't have pushed you," he lamented. "My power has a will of its own. I only wanted to you to understand..."

I moved to him and pressed my hand against his chest as an unbidden smile stretched across my lips. "I'm not angry. I'm glad you showed me." I leaned in, nipping his neck with my teeth. He allowed it, remaining completely motionless as I toyed with him. "I have a lot to think about."

When he refused to move, probably restraining himself from taking me even while Luke slept, I released a deflated sigh. My hand fell and I walked back to the towel that had piled onto the floor. My point had been made. I wasn't afraid of him, and damn it, I could control myself.

A whisper of magic tickled across my ass as I bent over and picked up the towel, extracting a fucking whimper. I jerked up and glared at him, wrapping the thin protection around myself as he laughed.

"Don't do that," I snapped.

He grinned, his fangs flashing. He moved to leave, but then paused at the doorway again, looking pensive. "Can I ask you something, Sonya?"

I straightened. "I suppose."

He frowned, his gaze unfocused as he stared into a distant memory. "Bringing you here, it wasn't something that I did, was it?"

Silence stretched out between us. I averted my gaze, not wishing to see the open pain in his eyes. He'd shown me that he'd attempted to call to me by starving himself. I knew what that was like. Starvation was an empty exercise in self-harm and pain. I didn't know if that's what my Blood Stone had picked up on, but my runes seemed to have a mind of their own. I was drawn to my sins and to my four. Whatever ancient magic wove through my veins, it wanted to be complete. However, I didn't believe that there was anything Xavier could have done to bring me to his side before it was time. I came to him when I was ready, when I needed him. It felt terribly selfish, because he'd needed me for a hundred years and I hadn't been here.

"I don't know why my Blood Stone brought me here," I admitted, my fingers going to my collarbone. "Perhaps it's my duty to protect Hades, and the only way to do that is to complete this bond that I don't fully understand."

Xavier watched me with those dangerous eyes that gleamed with familiar energy. "I've seen such marks, once before." His gaze fell to my stomach hidden by the thin towel. My runes burned in recognition. He was permitted to touch me there. He was meant to seep ancient magic into me and wind it through my veins.

I shivered, the effect he had on me far too much like a drug. "Really?" I asked. No one had ever been able to tell me what the runes meant. When I'd tried to ask my mother about them, she would always change the subject. If she'd known anything, those secrets had died with her.

He flashed a grin, the seriousness evaporating into his arrogant charm. "Once you become my mate, I'll share everything I know with you."

I frowned. "You know what our bond means, but you won't tell me until I'm so far into it that I can't get out?"

He chuckled, the low rumble awakening heat low in my belly. "Talk to the others. They know more about our bond than they realize."

Before I had a chance to protest, he slipped out of the room in a flurry of shadows, leaving my hand hanging in the air hopelessly trying to stop him.

Damn it.

I hadn't expected to sleep, but the moment my head hit the pillow I'd gone out like a light. Luke's reassuring warmth as he curled his arm protectively around me made me feel safe. I woke up, tucked close to his chest, but it wasn't his steady heartbeat that made me stir. My brows scrunched together when a grating, foreign sound found its way into the peaceful bedroom, echoing through the night and sending the hairs on the back of my neck to stand on end.

Screams.

I jerked awake and untangled myself from Luke's arms. "What was that?" I asked, my voice still groggy with the need to fall under and not wake up until the weariness had left my bones. I hadn't fed, and my body was starting to feel the strain. I withdrew a sliver of power from my Blood Stone to compensate, but winced as an ache permeated my chest. My body was starting to retaliate from my avoidance to naturally feed. The Blood Stone's power could sustain me, but not forever.

Running a finger over my chest, Luke missed my discomfort and sat up and cocked his head, danger taking precedence.

He had much better hearing than me. He should have been the first awake. When I saw the red haze in his eyes, I swallowed hard. I hadn't fed on him, but there was no telling what kind of effect having sex with a succubus and a vampire had on his powers.

Another scream pierced the stillness, and then the city came alive as if it had awoken all at once.

"The bloody hell is going on?" I asked and swung my legs over the bed. Marching to the windows, I yanked one open and shivered at the onslaught of fear and panic that permeated the chilled air.

The city glowed with a golden predawn allure that glimmered against the staggered buildings that littered Venice, but it was the ruby motes that caught my interest. It wasn't just the spark of sunlight that promised to peek over the horizon, but the evidence of magic that came from vampires—or a Blood Stone.

A fine mist of magic wound through the streets in a wandering ball of hazy power. It went door to door and each home it touched left fresh screams in its wake. People stumbled out onto the streets clutching any weapons they could get their hands on. Kitchen knives, bats, and car keys wedged between knuckles seemed to be the weapons of choice.

"Something bad is happening," I told Luke.

He joined me and frowned at the growing panic that was taking hold of the city. "Do you think it's the vampires?"

I pointed at the winding ball of red that meandered through the streets. "Is that vampiric power?"

Luke wrapped an arm protectively around my shoulders and drew me in close. "I'd say that's proof that Derek got his hands on another Blood Stone. Although, I don't know how he externalized the power like that. It must be Apollo's doing."

Cursing, I shrugged off Luke's touch. As much as I wanted to indulge in the comfort he offered, I wasn't a damsel in distress. If

Derek was coming after this city, then it was because he knew I was here. My mess, my problem. I had to fix this.

"Do you think he's trying to flush me out?" I asked.

Luke smirked. "Don't get so full of yourself. One of the male muses lives in this city, remember? If Derek is trying to flush anyone out, it'll be Hades."

It didn't make sense. Surely Derek knew that the ancient vampire slept and couldn't be woken up. Then I remembered something Xavier had said. It would take two things to wake Hades. The power of a Blood Stone and a vampire who commanded it.

Shouts in another language broke my concentration as a mob chased down one of the vampires. He was impossible to miss with the red haze of panic in his eyes and flashing fangs. Vampires weren't supernaturals that did well out in the open. They innately lurked in the shadows, employed misdirection and seduction… and they never ran.

But this one did. He stumbled and crashed to his knees, scrambling to get away from the mob coming after him with weapons poised to strike.

"They're going to kill him," I hissed. I couldn't say I knew if this was a vampire worthy of being saved, but the raw panic in his eyes made me cringe. What if that was me? What if humans knew what I'd done and what I was capable of? There'd be a witch hunt for sure.

Luke gripped my wrist when I went for the door. "We need to figure out what's going on first. We can't just go—"

His words were cut off by a bloodcurdling scream. I shoved Luke aside and peered out the window again just in time to see the vampire clutching at the splintered end of a broken bat skewered into his chest. Blood gurgled at his lips as his eyes glazed over and he fell to the ground.

He didn't puff into ash like I half-expected. The corpse

remained there, motionless and holding me with a blank stare as it bled out onto the street. No one deserved to die like that. The mob shouted and cheered their victory, shifting when the lingering red haze overwhelmed them, sending them scattering with murder in their eyes.

Grabbing Luke's hand, I dragged him out of the room. "Come on. We can't just sit here and do nothing."

Luke followed me under protest. "We can't stop a city full of people who just realized that vampires exist."

I dragged him down the hall and only stilled when I heard the soft murmur of voices, then realized it was a news station. I swept into the living room to find Xavier glaring at a TV screen.

A surprising sense of relief hit me when I saw the vampire. Xavier should have instilled fear with the long, dangerous fangs at his lips and the curl of red power that wrapped around his wrists, but I'd seen a part of him that was vulnerable and beautifully flawed. When his gaze met mine, a shiver ran down my spine.

"I can't understand how this is possible," he said, his voice a low, dangerous growl. He pointed at the screen as a panicked camera zoomed in on the red ball of power that curled through the streets of Venice, bringing with it screams and people brandishing weapons. "That's the power of a Blood Stone."

Luke stepped in front of me, no doubt taking Xavier's aggression as a threat. "It's not Sonya's doing, if that's what you're getting at."

Xavier frowned. "No, I would have sensed such intentions last night. I know she's not at fault."

A blush crawled up my neck at the memory of Xavier ejaculating into my mouth while Luke… "So," I blurted as heat slammed between my thighs in response to the mental images sweeping across my mind, "we've established I'm not the one sending a sentient ball of magic parading around the streets.

That leaves only one other person we know of with a Blood Stone."

Xavier glowered. "Derek is just an incubus. He doesn't have this kind of power."

"And a king," Luke pointed out.

Xavier shrugged. "Still just an incubus. Just a bit older and more vicious than the rest."

"What if Apollo is working with him?" Luke offered. "Is a male muse capable of manipulating a Blood Stone?"

Xavier snarled. "They're capable of anything." He slammed his fist against the table and the thin-walled television wavered on its silver stand, threatening to topple over. "Damn it. This is why we need Hades awake. He's the only one strong enough to stand up to this kind of attack."

"Really?" I asked with a smirk. "You're an ancient vampire and there's no Plan B if daddy is asleep?"

Xavier scowled, the motion making him look adorably delicious. But then his eyes widened as a new idea struck him. "You're right. Hades wouldn't leave us defenseless in the event one of his brothers ran amok. There is something..." He sighed as his words drifted off. "You're not going to like it."

HECK OF A FAILSAFE

Sonya

Xavier wasn't kidding. "*That's* your idea of a failsafe?" I shrieked.

Luke scoffed. "What a terrible idea. There has to be another way."

The only way to stop supernaturals from overtaking Venice and getting to Hades would be to reverse the magic that made him sleep. Instead of restoring his sanity… we had to wake him prematurely and send the magic all over Venice.

"Vampires don't need to rest," he said, his fangs flashing as excitement lit his eyes. "But if we do, we become stronger and more stable. Hades knew that as a male muse going into hundreds of years of existence he was reaching the end of his mind's capacity. Perhaps his brothers have already gone mad, but he found a way around insanity. Vampiric slumber was what saved him."

"And now you want us to wake him up?" I all but squeaked.

Xavier looked out the window as chaos continued to envelop

the city. The red haze of magic poured in, as well as enemy supernaturals. Where the humans had mobbed against the vampires, now Incubi and sirens subdued them and herded them away. "It won't be safe here for much longer. We need to get to the bunker."

"Bunker," I repeated. "Vampires have bunkers?"

Xavier nodded and snatched up a bag. He went to the refrigerator and began stuffing it with packaged blood. "Hades isn't to be disturbed during his years of slumber, so he's secreted away in the tunnels of Venice where no one would think to look for him. Vampires will have gone there for sanctuary during this attack. We need to get to them and prepare for the failsafe."

"We?" Luke said and grabbed me by the wrist.

I didn't mind when Luke was being overprotective. I kind of liked it, but right now I didn't have the patience nor the time for his masculine tendencies. "We'll figure it out when we get there," I promised him.

His icy blue irises locked onto mine. "Did you not hear what he just said? The failsafe casts the entire city of supernaturals into slumber. Only the vampires will remain awake, which means either you and I need to leave Venice, or—"

"Or I become a vampire and end this," I finished for him.

There was no way we were going to leave Venice. Derek and Apollo prowled the streets looking for us. No matter where we ran, there wouldn't be anywhere to hide. I had to fight them. "This is our best chance," I said. I pressed a hand against his chest, my fingers slipping under his collar. His heart thundered under my touch. "I know it sounds dramatic and I should really take more time to think about something that'll change me for the rest of my life, but what's the downside if I become a vampire? I'll be able to survive without feeding on sexual life-force."

Luke leaned in close, his voice lowering. "What about the others?"

My fingers curled, leaving soft red lines across his skin. "There isn't time. They'll just have to understand." I blinked up at him, my eyes wide. "Do *you* understand?"

I was going to bind myself to Xavier. I was going to complete the circle of ancient power that wound around my navel without fully understanding it, without fully knowing what it would do to me or my four.

His hand wound to the back of my neck and he pulled me in, pressing a kiss against my forehead. "You know I support you no matter what you choose to do. I just don't want you to have any regrets."

"I can't keep living like this," I said, an admission extracting from my lips. "I can't keep feeding." *I can't keep killing.*

His fingers stroked through my hair. "You can feed on me and I won't die."

I pressed my lips into a thin line. He knew just as well as I did that my powers would eventually get the better of me. I craved sex and not just with him, but with poor victims that didn't deserve to die. "My powers control me," I whispered. "For once, I want to be the one in control."

Darkness passed over his gaze, but he understood why I wanted this.

"I won't ever let you go," I promised when I glanced at Xavier. "You've always said that you were willing to share me."

His grip ran around my waist and he pulled me close with a sigh. "That's because I know you don't have a choice as a succubus. If you're a vampire, then how am I to know that what feelings you have for me will remain? What if you are trading one dominating power for another?"

I knew what he was asking.

What if Xavier takes you away from me? What if they all take you away from me?

An explosion interrupted our conversation and the walls shook.

"Time to go," Xavier said. The stiffness of his body as he slung his bag over his shoulder wasn't just the cold stillness of being a vampire. He was just as conflicted as Luke about where my loyalties might lie. He'd dreamed of me for so long, but even he didn't know what turning me into a vampire might do. That frightened me.

I followed the vampire as he sped out of the room, his form blurring to his accustomed vampire speed. Fleetingly, I wondered if I'd be able to move like that when I changed.

Xavier paused in the doorway as he waited for Luke and me to follow, looking impatient beneath his tentatively calm visage. I took Luke's hand and gave it a squeeze. Fear gripped me, not just because I didn't know what was waiting for us outside, but for the first time, there was a future I wanted, and I desperately hoped that I was going to get it. I wanted my four more than anything. I was tired of being apart. Once we did this, we would be a family.

As if my Blood Stone sensed my desperate need, a warmth spread through my chest. It'd lost the ability to speak to me, but that sentient mind was still there. It spoke to my desires with hopes of its own. When I became a vampire, I'd truly understand the power from which it was born. I'd master a magic I'd been born into, and whether I knew it or not, I'd understand what I was destined for.

Shivering with that distant omen, I walked side by side with Luke, my angel, and followed my vampire out into the streets of supernaturals gone to war.

If I'd thought that Venice had looked intimidating from Xavier's luxurious apartment, then seeing the mayhem up close and personal gave me the chills. It wasn't just crazed humans, I realized, but sirens, incubi, and all of Apollo's army come to kill us.

"Watch out!" Luke shouted and shoved me out of the way just as an incubus bleeding red power blurred behind me. The ground thundered with the force of his body slamming to the ground and he spun on me, snarling and his eyes wild and crazed with lightning red jolts careening across his cheeks.

I'd recognize that power anywhere. My Blood Stone fueled me and gave me a red aura that infused me with strength and resolve, but in the wrong hands, a Blood Stone had a very different effect. Mind control marked the incubus before me, his features distinctive with their beautiful lines and the deadly song of his movements. The seductive allure that wafted from him was a scent I'd recognize in any incubus, yet there was something innately wrong with him. Streaks of red marred his face like poisoned veins.

"Succubus!" he shouted and shoved a finger at me. "For the King!"

"Shit," I said under my breath and grabbed Luke's arm. Xavier hadn't bothered to fight the unfurling army of supernaturals that overwhelmed the city. He blurred through the streets, pausing and waiting for us to follow as impatience made the soft lines go taut at his face.

"This way!" I shouted and yanked Luke towards the vampire.

The incubus wasn't alone. A siren careened around the corner. When a blade flashed from her hand, the blood drained from my face before Luke yanked me away just in time. He took the blow straight in the gut and groaned as fresh blood pooled around the steel embedded into his stomach. He yanked it out and threw it on the ground, sending it clattering down the cobbled streets before it splashed into a canal. The siren who'd stabbed him opened her mouth to sing, but Luke hauled off and slammed a fist in her face. She crumpled to the ground like a ball of paper.

My fingers shaking, I grabbed Luke and pulled him towards the vampire again. "I hope this bunker is close," I snapped.

Luke limped and I wanted to stop and make sure he was all right, but I reminded myself that this was the angel that had survived his own heart being ripped out. A stab wound wasn't going to do him in.

The haze of red continued to swarm the city and blocked off our path. Xavier, two steps ahead of us now, peered up a sheer wall face. "We'll have to scale it," he said. "If we touch the fog, I have the feeling that we'll be put under its spell."

I considered the three-story building that seemed to tilt to one side as if the ground beneath it had begun to corrode. "I don't know..."

Before I had a chance to protest, Xavier wrapped an arm around my waist and hoisted me up. "Hold on," he said, and then he began to climb.

I watched as Luke and the bloodied street retreated as Xavier took me up the wall.

"I'll get him next," Xavier promised.

My heart clenched when an incubus flashed another blade and went from Luke's back. "Look out!" I screeched and shot out a hand. Red power burst from my fingers and shot the incubus down before he had a chance to land the blow.

Luke whirled around and gawked at the supernatural I'd taken out while being carried up a freaking wall.

"It's the vampire power, darling." He grinned against my neck and the cool deadliness of his fangs kissed my skin. "Imagine your power when you're my mate."

I swallowed hard and realized that his erection was pressing against my abdomen. Xavier wanted me more than anything, and to be in his arms and feel a taste of the power he promised made my insides crave to give in.

If I became a vampire... *when* I became a vampire, I hoped that I could survive it.

THE BUNKER

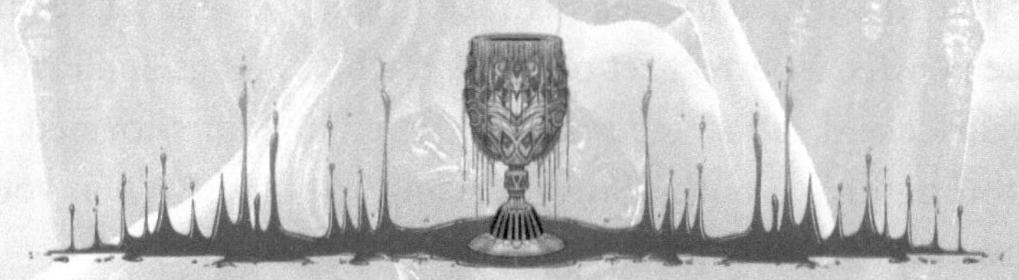

Sonya

Scaling the rooftops had been far more tedious than I'd have imagined. Xavier could have gotten to the bunker without us in a matter of minutes, but he went back for Luke and then patiently waited as we followed at a snail's pace compared to the vampire. Even though we'd made it to the rooftops, the enemies kept coming. When we passed the worst of the red fog, we climbed back down to the streets, only to run into a mindless horde of incubi. We lost them on the final round to the secreted entrance underneath one of the many bridges that linked streets.

I squeezed through the tiny door and the scent of musk and dampness hit me in the face, making my nose wrinkle. We spiraled down into pure darkness with only the light from Xavier's eyes to guide us. Vampires had perfect night vision, which was one of the reasons they'd gotten the reputation that they couldn't survive in the sun. Darkness gave them an advantage and they liked to use it.

"We're almost there," Xavier said as we crept through ankle-deep sludge. He'd been explaining vampire physiology as we walked, assuring me that there wasn't a downside to vampirism. "We like sunlight just as much as anyone else, but our eyes tend to give us away, as well as the fangs, if you're not good at hiding them." He grinned at me when we came into a section with dim lights that finally let me see his face. I startled when I realized that he boasted a perfect set of white teeth, no fangs at all. When I got closer and ran a finger across his chin, points formed and shot through his mouth. "Sorry, darling," he said. "When you're around, my control slips."

A blush crept up my neck and Luke wrapped an arm around my waist. It wasn't a jealous or overprotective move, rather an unconscious motion of familiarity. "Looks like we're almost there," he said, and jerked his chin at a red door streaked with peeling paint.

Xavier knocked on it, the sound ringing against hollow metal. "It's me."

A slider revealed a peephole and red eyes appraised Xavier, then us. I expected some questions, but if Xavier really was Hades' right-hand man, then any friends of Xavier's were friends to the vampires.

The peephole shut, then we stood there in silence. I shifted uncomfortably, wondering if they were going to second-guess letting us in. Then the door creaked open a moment later and Xavier motioned us to go inside. "Come. I'll introduce you to Nimra and Liam."

I'd expected more dank and dismal surroundings, but the moment the metal door closed behind us, I found the scenery much more upscale. A long hall wound downward into the depths of marbled walls and runes lined the floors. My spine went rigid when I recognized the writing.

It looked just like the runes across my stomach... but there were more. So many symbols I didn't recognize, and seven that I did.

"They're prayers," Xavier explained, mistaking my interest, and glanced at Luke when I didn't respond. "Vampires might have gotten the reputation as being a bunch of demonspawn, but vampires have always been closely involved with civilization and history. We are fond of religion and the powers which sustain us." He took in a deep breath. "Blood is life, and life is the evidence of a soul. We respect the creation of that soul, no matter where it comes from or where it goes."

I hummed and finally let Luke's hand go as I walked between the angel and the vampire.

Whatever the power in my runes meant, I was in the right place to discover what ancient destiny had claimed me at birth.

Chandeliers illuminated the downward slope of the floor with shadows and rainbow sequins. "I was basically raised by a nun," I told him, hoping to immerse myself in the past and ground myself in reality. "I suppose there's a soft spot for religion for me as well."

He grinned. "It's nice to get to know you. I look forward to more of these conversations." He paused when the hall split into three ways. "Come," he said, and guided us down the center path. "The others will want to meet you."

Red eyes glittered like diamonds as a hush settled over an uneasy gathering of vampires. Their chests did a collective sigh when they saw Xavier, then tensed up again when they saw me.

Luke gripped my arm. "Your chest is glowing."

I looked down to see that an unmistakable red glow pulsated in my chest and throbbed like a foreign heartbeat that didn't match my own. Dizziness swept over me. "Luke," I whispered, his name a plea. Terror gripped me.

What if Derek's power was affecting me? What if I was a walking time bomb and I'd lose my mind and become the slave he'd always wanted me to be?

"You're fine," Xavier said with a coaxing tone. He took my hand and drew me into the crowd, peeling me away from Luke's warmth and reassurance.

The vampires eased when they saw that Xavier trusted me, but I wasn't so sure that he should. Usually it was rage or high doses of sexual energy that made my Blood Stone's power active enough that it became visible. The sex I'd had with Xavier and Luke the night before had been for enjoyment and to understand Xavier's visions. I hadn't fed, so it didn't make sense for my Blood Stone to respond. Something was wrong.

"Vampiric power works differently than yours," Xavier said, speaking to my unspoken questions. "You'll come to understand it. Vampires are not something to be feared, nor is our gift."

"Our curse," corrected a woman.

Xavier grinned. "Nimra," he said, purring her name. "I'd like to introduce you to Sonya."

When he nudged me forward, I couldn't help but be intimidated by the female vampire. Lengthy legs bound by tight, black leather and a snug blouse made her more intoxicating to look at than most succubi. Plump cleavage boasted a red jewel that rested along the curve of her breast. It reminded me of a Blood Stone, but I recognized it as a ruby. "Not everyone can find the rare gem that gave us life," Nimra explained as she cupped the necklace, taking notice of my scrutiny, "but we aim to show respect, nonetheless."

I bowed my head. Nimra exuded sexual energy, but also control. I sensed that she was much older than she looked. "It's a pleasure to meet you," I said.

She smiled, her small, delicate fangs flashing. It made her appear oddly charming. "You're not like most succubi I've met." She glanced at the man who came to her side. He snaked an arm around her waist. "What do you think, Liam? Do you approve of Xavier adding this one to our family?"

The vampire named Liam appraised me with gleaming, red eyes that sliced with a noticeable streak of gold. "There's only one way to find out." He grinned as his gaze raked over me. "Perhaps I could have a taste before she turns, just to see what her nature is really like."

Xavier smiled even though my skin crawled with what sounded to be a very real proposal. "Liam was once a dragon," he explained. "Don't let him get to you. He's retained some of his rudeness from that species."

Luke scoffed. "I've endured my fair share of dragons. I don't think even vampirism could cure their arrogance."

Liam's eyes went wide as if he'd noticed Luke for the first time. "You didn't mention you'd be bringing another stray. Who's this?"

It was Nimra who slunk around us, her boots creaking, jarring against her otherwise deathly silence. "I sense... something new." She drew closer and sniffed, her fangs extending. "What is he?"

"If you behave," Xavier said, "perhaps I'll tell you."

Luke scoffed. "I'm right here. You can all stop looking at me like I'm a shiny new toy."

Nimra grinned, her eyes lighting up at the challenge. "Looks like a toy, sounds like a toy..."

Another explosion rocked the compound and the vampires locked their gazes on the ceiling. Nimra crossed her arms and frowned. "We should be up there," she complained. "This is our city. We can't just let them destroy it."

Liam growled and smoke exuded from his nostrils. My eyes

went wide at the realization that this vampire had kept more of his dragon traits than I would have expected after a turn. "I agree with Nimra. We came down here to make a battle plan per protocol. You're our leader." He bowed his head to Xavier. "It's your call, but my vote is we go en mass and take out our enemies before they get too comfortable."

Xavier shook his head. "This isn't a fight we can win without Hades. He needs to be woken."

Nimra rolled her eyes. "Well good luck with that. The master isn't supposed to wake up for another fifty years at least. A bomb could go off in this very compound and he wouldn't even flinch."

Xavier glanced at me and a shiver ran up my spine. "The power of the Blood Stone is what fuels our vampirism. It's a sister source to the power of souls and magic. It'll be enough."

Liam sniffed the air. "She wouldn't be able to reach Hades without becoming a vampire first. We don't have time to indulge a conversion." He glowered at Xavier. "You're thinking with your dick instead of your head."

A hot blush rolled over my collarbone, but I ignored it. Everyone knew that Xavier had the full intention of turning me into a vampire, and to do that, I had the feeling that he had to fuck my brains out. "Enough," I snapped. "I get a say in this."

Liam growled at my interruption. "And what have you to say, succubus?"

I glanced at Luke, because we'd both already established our plan was fucking nuts. "We need to amplify the sleep spell that Hades is under and cast it over all supernaturals in Venice. It'll give us the time we need to turn me into a vampire and wake up Hades."

Nimra ran a finger over the hilt of a dagger at her hip. She seemed the type that enjoyed playing with sharp objects. "Interesting," she purred. "But we need a witch for that."

Xavier grinned at Luke. "We've got something even better."

Luke's outrage completely warranted that we hole ourselves up in one of the luxurious vampire rooms. The place was built for sex with rows of chains and restraints, as well as a bowl of strawberries and a bucket of wine suitable for human guests, but as Luke paced on a velvet rug, I knew that sex was the last thing on his mind.

"How do they know about my mother?" he hissed and slammed a fist against the wall, sending yet another crack streaking through the stone. "If they know who she is, *what* she is, then they could have done something. She sacrificed her freedom to prepare me for my fate, but she'd never warned me about vampires trying to take over my life."

I rested a gentle touch on his shoulder and he stiffened, but didn't shrug me away. "They're a little bossy, but they've lived for a long time. They've learned secrets and have access to powers we don't fully understand. I'm sure they had their reasons not to get involved."

Rage burned in his eyes. "What if they could have prevented her from being taken to prison? I'm the one who told the humans about what she'd done to me, but if I'd seen supernaturals were real, if a single vampire had shown themselves to me, I would have believed in my mother's visions. She didn't have powers that I could understand, not at the time." He thrust a finger at the closed door. "But those *things,* no one can deny they're not human. Even my stubborn ass would have believed it."

Only wanting to console him, I shushed him and pulled him into an embrace. He bent to accommodate my stature and buried his nose into my neck. His fingers laced through my hair that curled at my back. "You're still going through with it, aren't you?" he asked, his words muffled.

I sighed and held onto him as tight as I could. I didn't know how else to assure him that even if I bonded with Xavier, I'd always belong to my four, *all* of them. We were meant for each other in ways that completed me and made me feel safe. "Why does everything always have to be so complicated?" I complained. "None of us asked for this life. It's just the way it is."

He pulled away and a hard line throbbed at his jaw. His fingers cupped my elbows as he looked into my eyes with such ferocity and devotion that I was glad he steadied my weight. "Xavier isn't the only one who's had visions about you," he whispered, his voice low and demanding. "My mother centered our lives around a future where you held me like you are holding me now. You and I are meant to save the world."

I smiled. Each of my four was a powerful piece of the puzzle of my heart. Luke was passion, capable of anything. I ran my touch up his arms and took his face in my hands, bringing his lips to mine. The soft kiss was gentle, one that cultivated a more familiar connection between us that grew every day. "And that's exactly what we're doing," I reminded him when I pulled away. I ran a thumb across his lower lip still plump from my kiss. "Your father was an angel, which makes you powerful in magic that this world needs. And your mother, she was a Seer, which makes you the only one capable of spreading the vampiric sleeping curse to supernaturals across Venice."

He growled and took me in another kiss, biting my lip, making me flinch. He growled again before running his tongue over the small hurt. "It'll mean that I'll go into slumber too. What if I never wake?" Darkness crossed his gaze. "Perhaps that's what you want so that you have an excuse to be with Xavier and the others without the inconvenience."

I'd had just about enough of his insecurity. Without warning I ripped off his shirt and lashed a hazy red power around his waist, tugging at his jeans until they unfurled and his erection was free for my fingers to explore. "If I have to prove to you that you matter to me, that I want *you,* then let's do it, right here, right now."

Luke began to protest, but groaned when my fingers wrapped around the girth of him and squeezed. "Perhaps," he managed to say, "just a little time together won't hurt."

I didn't take time to explore his body or tease him. That's not what Luke needed, nor I, for that matter. Luke's strong hands peeled off my shirt as I pushed him to the bed, straddling him as a growl rumbled in my throat. I was already wet for him, but I wasn't strong enough to resist the urge to feed on his lust. He tasted so delicious and when I lowered onto him and he entered my body, my mouth parted in a gasp and magic filled my Blood Stone with needed nourishment.

Luke fluttered his eyes closed as I lowered and inhaled a long magical strand of his endless life force. I wondered if he was immortal, or if this was the kind of magic that had no end that I could feed on forever. He shuddered under the intoxicating compulsion of my power that covered the pain with pleasure that sank into his bones. My powers wrapped around him, just like my muscles contracted around him, as I began long, deliberate movements to bring us both the comfort and ecstasy we desired.

I just wanted to forget that the end of the world was upon us for a few moments. I wanted to indulge in this feeling of what it was like to be a succubus, to feed on a man who only wanted to please me, and who fully knew who and what I was. I hated being a succubus, but I took the effort to enjoy one of the rare acts of sex where I fed, and didn't hate myself for it. I let myself feed on him because I knew that's what he wanted from me. He wanted to be punished, to be used… to be loved.

Luke would be weakened by this, but his hands groped and pushed up my bra to take my breasts in a firm squeeze. He encouraged me to keep going, to go faster and faster until I gulped for air.

"Come with me," he said, his words breathless on his tongue as pleasure rippled through him and fed me more power than I could handle. Red wisps of passion bled into the air and glowed across our skin.

I wasn't holding back. I wanted to show him how much he meant to me. What Luke wanted was for me to be myself with him, and that meant being a succubus who fed on sex. I never let myself go full-force, but this time I recklessly tossed the gates of my powers open and Luke cried out as raw pleasure wrapped around his cock and twisted through his body.

That explosion fed me with more sexual energy than I'd ever fed on before. I let the tidal wave come and didn't care when I was swept away by it. The room burst into flashes of red as I cried out with him and pleasure overtook me, turning my vision dark around the edges.

The orgasm lasted for a full thirty, glorious seconds, and then it was over. I slumped over him, my breathing ragged and sweat kissing a cold film across my skin.

He massaged my ass as we silently ground our hips together, inking out the last, lusting bit of our pleasure.

"I understand," he said at last when his racing heart had finally slowed to a dull thunder. "This is what it's like to be a succubus, to feed and become overwhelmed by sexual power."

My vision still rippled with red and even though I'd given in to my most sinful of indulgences, the sickly-sweet aftershock came with a rampage of guilt. I didn't hide it from Luke as I pulled away and took in the pale, sunken-in cheeks of the cost of my power. "Yes," I said, my voice hoarse. "I want to lose myself with you without hurting you." If I was a vampire, there wouldn't be a price when I threw caution to the wind. I traced the small cuts that lined his pale face. "You might survive, but this is what it's like when I truly let go."

He curled his arms around me and pulled me into his chest. Tears stung my eyes and he gripped me tight when I began to tremble with unspent sobs. He shushed me and rubbed my back. "It's okay," he promised. "I understand why you want to become a vampire."

He's the only one I could ever do this with, and even now, guilt tore at me to have hurt him.

Jet, Nate, perhaps even Xavier. They wouldn't be able to survive my passion.

Closing my eyes with resignation, I was glad that Luke had accepted my choice, but it didn't change my fears of the process.

Would I still be *me*? Would I still have these feelings for Luke and the others when I bonded to Xavier on such a fundamental level as blood?

There was only one way to find out.

A SPELL

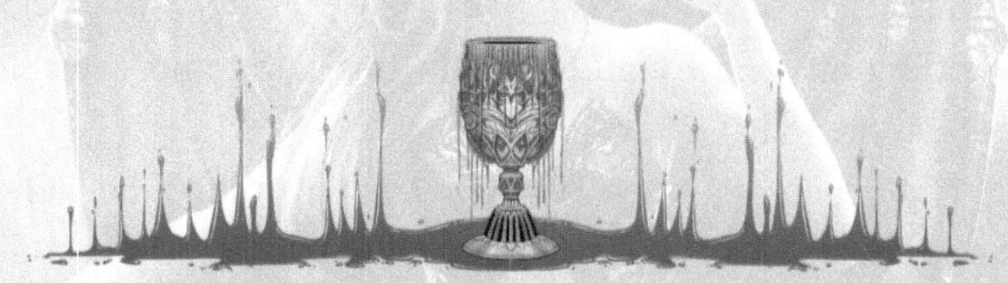

Sonya

I tried calling Jet first. It didn't matter what Xavier said about this super secret vampire bunker, my four needed to be here for this.

"How did you get a phone?" I asked Luke as he handed me the device.

His mischievous grin was all the answer I received.

Our guest quarters hadn't come with a phone, but it was stocked with a mini-fridge and a computer with extremely limited internet. Luke fought with it for a while, somehow getting around the firewalls enough to look up the hotel where I'd stayed—stayed being a loose term, more like where I'd been imprisoned.

When I dialed the number and a girl with the rounded sounds of Shanghainese answered the phone, my eyes went wide. I glanced at him. "Uh, do you speak English?"

The rounded sounds turned agitated and I winced.

Luke chuckled and held out his hand. "Allow me."

Giving him a raised brow, I handed him the phone. He grinned at me before launching into a fluent conversation with the operator.

Damn, that was hot.

Hearing Jet's native language made my gut twist. I missed him and the nausea only strengthened when I thought about Nate. I'd been so busy escaping Derek that I hadn't stopped to think if Nate was okay. He was the kind of human who could take care of himself… but he was still human.

Luke nodded, saying his final goodbyes and tapped the phone, ending the call. He smirked. "Will you stop worrying? You're going get frown lines."

I glowered. "Succubi don't wrinkle," I reminded him. I could frown all I damned wanted.

Slipping his arm around my waist, he tucked me against his hard chest and I naturally rested my cheek against his warmth. My fingers slipped under the loose edge of his shirt, automatically exploring to see if the damage I'd caused him was still there. The knots in my shoulders unwound to find his skin tightening under my fingertips, already recovering from the deterioration.

"It seems that Jet and a small faction of dragons have revolted," Luke said, his voice a low rumble against my cheek. "I don't think we'll be able to reach him."

My fingers continued to stroke across his collarbone, needing the assurance of his body right now as my insides twisted again. "There has to be something we can do." I squeezed my eyes shut. "At least we could get some sort of information about Jet. It sounds like he's okay, for now, but I don't even know how to begin to look for Nate." I bit my lip before admitting, "What if Derek hurt him?" I let the unsaid words drift between us. What if I failed to protect him?

Luke held me tight as if his mere embrace could protect me from all the evils of the world. "I know you want your four to approve your transition to become a vampire and to make sure they're okay, but look at where we are. We're in a bunker at the end of the world and Derek is raining down mind-control fog all over the city. You won't be much good to anyone if you fall under Derek's influence."

I knew he was right, but none of this was going how I wanted it to go. I slipped away from him, the cool air rushing in to replace his warmth. His soft blue eyes watched me as I moved, the force of his love apparent behind his gaze. He'd always put me first, just like all of my four would. "You think I should take Xavier's offer?" I asked. That's exactly what I needed to do, but I needed my four to tell me that it was okay. I wanted to complete this bond that had plagued me all my life, but I was afraid that made me selfish. Darkness still raked the backs of my dreams and this was my chance to finally banish it.

He didn't respond right away. Instead, he crossed his arms and leaned against the wall, carefully considering the question. "Let's go over the facts," he began. He held up one finger. "If Nate *is* in trouble, it's going to be something Derek has done. The best way to help him would be to neutralize the Incubus King." He lifted a second finger. "The division among the dragons is Jet's current issue. The dragons have assembled under Derek, so without the Incubus King in power, they'll be forced into line." He lifted a third finger. "Xavier is a powerful vampire, but he's been driven underground with the rest of his race all because the Incubus King has turned the male muses against him. If we can awaken Hades, then the threat will be neutralized and Venice can be reclaimed and order restored."

I sighed and wrapped my arms around myself. "So, the only way to help everyone I care about is to do this; that's what you're saying?"

He closed his fingers into a fist. Reaching out, he took my hand and placed it over his. I felt so small in comparison. The tips of my fingers barely managed to wrap around the ball of his fist. "We are all bound to you for a reason, Sonya. Each of us holds a power that can make this world a better place, but you are the one who must wield it. I am nothing without you. I think I speak for the others when I say they would feel the same. Whatever you choose to do, we support you. All of us."

I squeezed his hand before letting go. It was a lot of responsibility, but I knew that he was right. Nate, in his snarky way, would tell me to do what I needed to do. Jet, well, he'd probably chastise me for needing his permission to do anything. Luke and Xavier clearly approved of me taking the next step to cement this ancient bond, to become a vampire—to save the world.

"Okay," I said, my voice so soft that only Luke's angelic hearing would be able to pick it up. "Let's do this."

"First step," Xavier said as he instructed Luke on how to cast the spell, "is to make sure you pronounce the words correctly." He dropped a dusty tome into Luke's lap with a soft *thud* and stabbed a finger into his face. "Never, *ever,* mispronounce a spell."

Luke glowered at the vampire before Xavier finally backed off.

Yep. Luke was a cell-phone thief, multi-lingual immortal, and apparently half warlock. Sure, just another day in my crazy life.

Vampires didn't practice magic themselves, but they were the source of all witches. Their blood sang with magic, even if they couldn't directly use it other than for their own biological skills.

The vampires never let witches into the bunker where Hades slept. His resting place was a well-kept secret, and it spoke to Xavier's trust in me that he'd let non-vampires in such a sacred space.

Or, he realized no witches around to protect his master had been a really dumb decision, and he was going to settle for an angel with subdued magical powers.

Luke frowned at the dusty tome as he opened it and thumbed the pages. "How am I supposed to pronounce anything correctly. What is this shit?"

I peered over his shoulder only to find that the "words" were runic scratches that scattered like scars across the withered page.

"Angels can read any language," Xavier said. "Don't tell me you can't read witch writing."

"It's not a language," Nimra corrected. "It's magic in verbal and written form, but it's not a method of communication. It's a gathering of power, which means even an angel can't read it."

The remark was surprisingly informative as Nimra eased closer into our small circle. She paused, then slowly grinned as her nostrils knowingly flared, her gaze shifting between Luke and me. I shifted uncomfortably, wondering how good a vampire's sense of smell really was. I knew I should have showered.

Xavier politely ignored the light deterioration that marked Luke's face, but the angel was already starting to heal. I wished that we could have waited before returning to the vampires, but the explosions rocking the city were only getting worse. Derek was trying to draw me out and get to Hades. He'd demolish every beautiful building in Venice until he got what he wanted.

"Well, can anyone here pronounce it for me? I can't read it."

Xavier sighed. "That's dangerous."

"I thought that you said only Luke could perform the spell?" I asked.

Xavier tilted his head to the side thoughtfully. "True, however witch writings come with power. One does not utter them lightly." He sighed. "But there's little choice. I'll—"

Before Xavier could offer, Liam pushed him aside. "I'll do it."

His ruby gaze sliced with gold found mine. "It won't do much good to risk the spell before you've had a chance to turn our alarm clock into a vampire. At least if reading the spell goes wrong with me, I'm expendable."

Nimra slipped her arm through his. "You're not expendable, darling. You're just more resilient."

My mouth lifted on the side. "Did he really just call me an alarm clock?"

Nimra shushed me. "Quiet, you're not supposed to be going off yet." She poked me in the forehead. "Snooze button!"

Rolling my eyes, I wasn't sure if I loved or hated Nimra. Probably a little bit of both.

Liam seemed used to Nimra's antics and cleared his throat as he squinted at the text. He pronounced each word slowly, allowing Luke to listen.

When he was done, we all fell into silence and peered around the room. Aside from the slight rumble of bombs, no additional calamity descended on the city.

"Do you think you can remember that?" Xavier asked Luke. "You'll have to recite it perfectly."

Luke frowned and rubbed his chin. He did that when he was being self-conscious. "Yeah. I can do it."

"Good," Xavier said and clapped Luke on the back. My angel stiffened, but didn't retaliate. "You'll be on your own," Xavier warned him. "When the sun rises, Nimra will take you to the highest point in the city where you can begin the spell."

Luke glanced at me. He knew where I'd be... busy getting it on with a vampire. "You going to be okay?" he asked.

I blushed. "Yeah," I said. Xavier was all-business right now, but I noticed how he leaned towards me, his body betraying that he was more than ready to get to the next stage of our plan. When his red eyes found mine, I swallowed hard. "I'll be fine."

TO THE TOWER

Luke

Leaving Sonya with the coven of vampires was just about as easy as ripping out my own eyeballs, but this was what she wanted—what she needed.

I knew that she suffered from a darkness I couldn't explain. I could rationalize her nightmares just as much as I could explain the bond that connected her to me. I was one of her weapons, one of her strengths, a piece of her soul she'd somehow lost along the way. She needed me and I'd do anything to make sure she was whole again.

My insides still ached with the unforgiving power she'd lashed through me when we'd had sex. I knew that she was a succubus and what that meant, but to feel her merciless power was an entirely different story. She didn't realize that going full-force on me had nearly killed me. The noxious poison of her kiss had lulled me into a sense of security, but the overpowering pleasure eventually waned, leaving the knee-buckling agony that was left behind. Had I been human, I'd have been dead long before I'd given her the pleasure she needed to survive what was coming next.

It gave me a small sense of security to know that it was our lovemaking that would help her survive Xavier and the transition into becoming a vampire. She'd change from the Sonya I knew, and a little voice in the back of my head constantly worried about what ways she might change. Perhaps she'd lose what feelings she'd garnered for me. Perhaps she'd fall under Xavier's spell and become his thrall, breaking the fragile bond I didn't yet understand.

Or perhaps I was a giant douche thinking about myself and she'd finally be happy.

It didn't matter. I emerged onto the streets of a battle-torn Venice and followed the female vampire down smoky streets. Derek was ripping this place apart looking for Hades and Sonya. What few vampires had managed to trickle down into the bunker brought news of those who had been interrogated. Derek's incubi had killed any humans who resisted, but vampires they kept alive for questioning. They wanted to know where Hades slept, as well as where Sonya was hiding. Derek knew she was here, and it was my job to make sure he didn't find her until she was ready.

"Keep up," Nimra chided and I upped my pace.

Everything in me hurt and the last thing I felt like doing was prowling the streets with a vampire on my way to perform a spell. Sonya had fed on me before, but nothing like this. I didn't have time to sit down and allow my body to heal. There was a city to save.

When Nimra climbed cobbled steps of a tower covered in moss, I groaned. "Can't we just do the spell down here?"

Nimra paused and sniffed the air, her ruby gaze scanning the empty streets. The bombing momentarily paused while Derek's men worked their way through the rubble. We were in the heart of the city and there wasn't a soul in sight, but it didn't mean we were safe. Derek's men could come around one of the cobblestone corners any minute.

"Clearly you don't know how spells work," Nimra said as she glowered. She pointed up at the ancient structure. "Vampires built Campanile di San Marco under the guise as a lighthouse, but we've used it for years for witch spells. You need its height to reach that many people."

I raised an eyebrow. "Magic needs altitude?"

Nimra rolled her eyes. "It's just as much about altitude as it is about *attitude,* and yours stinks right now." She waved me on and stomped her boot on the first step. "Power's down, so we can't use the elevator the fat tourists prefer. We're taking the stairs."

With a grumble, I followed Nimra inside and the scent of old dirt hit me... as well as something else.

I was part angel, which was a heritage I was still trying to come to grips with, but I'd never considered that my mother's magic could have been hereditary. She was a Seer and could see the future, which meant she was some sort of witch. If that made me a warlock, then so be it. I didn't care what I was as long as it meant I could help Sonya.

When we reached the top of the tower, my legs burned and my head swam with exhaustion. I still hadn't recovered from Sonya sapping my strength. There was one thing I needed to heal, and it was one thing I didn't have right now: time.

"I hope I don't need energy for this spell," I said when Nimra pulled the grimoire from her pack. She'd said that I didn't need to read from it, but the spell wouldn't work without the original witch's runes. It was written power, which meant I needed to touch it as I spoke the words.

She opened to the dusty page and gave me a hearty slap on the back. "No need to be energized," she assured me. "You just need to be awake long enough to say the words." She took my hand and shoved it onto the book. A connection to *something* ran up my fingers and I shivered as she continued to bark instructions. "Once you start the spell, you'll get tired. Very tired. All supernaturals that aren't vampires are going to be affected, and even though you're a special breed, it'll hit you too."

I glanced at her, wondering if she cared at all about the rest of us. "And Sonya?" I asked.

Nimra held up her phone. "We'll get a text once she's started her turn. We don't have time to waste. You'll need to start the spell the moment I tell you we're ready."

Fire bloomed with smoke on the opposite end of the city and the tower gave an ominous shudder under my feet. "Come on, Sonya," I whispered. "You can do this."

A BOND TO DIE FOR

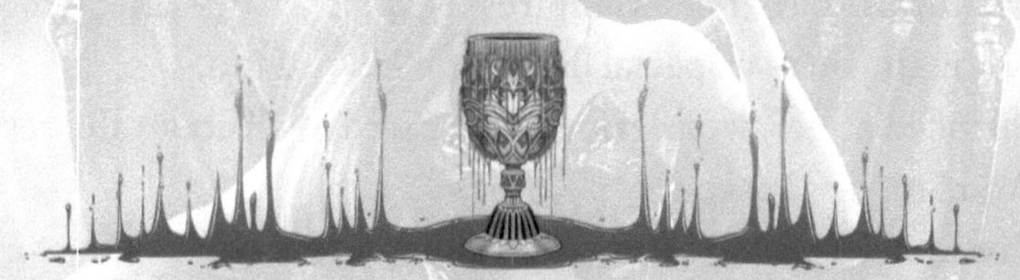

Sonya

A vampire mating ceremony wasn't at all what I'd expected. No flowers. No cake. No *booze*. Think ancient Norse mythology where men wore antlers and painted themselves with blood. That seemed fairly accurate to whatever the hell was going on right now.

A vampire whose red eyes gleamed in the shadow of her hood presented a glistening silver knife. Xavier offered his wrist and didn't even flinch as she sliced a long line up his arm.

He held his wrist over a silver bowl engraved with runes that glowed with power the instant his blood fell into it. The female dipped her fingers into it, smearing it over Xavier's face in a barbaric streak.

Xavier grinned at me, his gleaming red eyes peering through the smear of blood. "Your turn," he said as he offered a bowl that sloshed with the offending liquid, enjoying my squeamish reactions far too much.

He dipped his fingers into the blood that he'd just taken from his own wrist and traced a line down my face. My skin heated under the power that threatened to seep into me and take over. I resisted the terrible urge to lick at a droplet that tickled past my nose. The intoxicating scent of his blood hit me and I closed my eyes, gathering my strength before opening them again.

The dagger still gleamed with the slick nourishment of his power and hissed smoke into the air. The ritual had begun and it was one of the most powerful magics I'd ever sensed.

My Blood Stone hummed against the onslaught of foreign invasion. Vampires danced and sang and enjoyed themselves in the bunker's courtyard. Xavier would have loved to have had this ritual up on the surface, but they'd gotten used to doing it here, close to the sleeping vampire master where their power was at its strongest. Turning someone new wasn't a mild act and it took everyone's efforts to bring fresh blood into the fold.

As a succubus, my turning would be easier than most. I already understood the need to feed in order to survive. My body would accept the transition to feed on blood rather than sexual energy, and even if the bowl that Xavier presented me with made me want to gag, it was still better than killing.

I dipped my fingers into the liquid that was still warm and my stomach churned, but I made myself ignore it as I traced another line down the opposite side of Xavier's face. Dipping my fingers again, I continued the pattern down his muscular chest until I hit the place where his heart should be. Pressing my palm against him, there was only stillness. No beat. Nothing.

I hated that we were up on a pedestal, the raised platform garnished with blankets, pillows, and a single table where Xavier had set the knife. The female was gone, only a whisper of shadows betraying she'd been there at all. Vampires danced beneath us, music loud enough that they couldn't hear us, but it didn't change the fact that they could look up. I know I would.

"Can we turn the lights down?" I asked. It wasn't bright, but the warm light from the chandeliers did more than enough to illuminate Xavier's naked torso until it seemed like it glowed. He came to me and tucked his fingers in the waistband of my jeans, shoving his hands underneath to cup my ass and press me against his growing erection. "This only works if I'm indulged by every part of you," he whispered and he lowered his head to my neck and drew in a long breath as he scented me. He licked a line across my pulsating vein and goosebumps exploded across my body. "You're intoxicating."

My eyes fluttered closed at the hard presence of him as my breasts crushed into his chest. "Will it hurt?" I asked, fighting against the lust starting to bloom inside of me. I couldn't set aside the monumental change I was accepting. I was changing my freaking species.

"Only the first bite," he answered honestly as he pulled away and unlatched one hand from the confines of my jeans. He ran a finger across my lower lip. "Then there will be only pleasure—if you truly accept me." I couldn't deny the unexplainable feelings he brought out in me. Even if I couldn't feel the beat of his heart, the beat of the music replaced the rhythm I was missing and I tugged at the back of his head to bring his lips down to mine. I curled my fingers through his hair as I danced my tongue against his, the scent and taste of him sending heat unfurling between my legs. His fangs were dangerously sharp, but he expertly kissed me without pricking me.

When he eased me down onto the blankets, I allowed him to indulge in the pleasure of unclothing me. He tugged my jeans down each leg and left my underwear alone. My shirt went next, but my bra he tugged the straps over my shoulders until my nipples peeked over the cloth. He sucked one into his mouth and I drew in a shocked gasp. I hadn't expected a vampire to be so good with his tongue.

When he let go, he parted his lips and his fangs poised

dangerously over the curve of my breast. I watched him with anticipation, shocked that I actually *wanted* him to bite me. Not because I got off on pain, but because I knew how much he wanted to. I wanted to give Xavier relief from the years of waiting and abstinence, both from sex, and from feeding.

"You can bite me," I said breathlessly when he hesitated.

He grinned up at me, pleased with my permission. "Not yet," he said. "When I bite you, it's because I'm in you, and you'll be begging for it."

Desire slammed into me and my powers kicked in out of reflex, making his gaze go hazy. "You can try to feed on me," Xavier warned, "but it'll delay your pleasure. I need to be in full control when I take you and make you bonded to me by blood." He lowered his pants until his erection slipped free and I drew in a gasp. Was he even bigger than the night before?

When I moved to him and went to curl my fingers around the delicious ridge of flesh, he grabbed my wrist and grinned. "This is your turning," he explained. "I'm the one in control."

Magic hummed through the air and pricked at me like tiny bites across my flesh. The vampires that continued to dance beneath us donated a portion of their hazy energy. They'd been affected by our foreplay and when I glanced down, I took in an eyeful of the beginnings of an orgy. The dancing had turned to grinding and a woman threw her head back as a male tugged her breasts free from her tight corset.

Xavier took a finger to my chin and drew my attention back to him. "They're linked to us for the duration of the ritual," he explained. He lowered himself over me, his cock nestling against my clit and making me gasp. I wanted to rip my underwear out of the way, but he grabbed my wrists and pulled them over my head as he moved in slow circles. "What you feel, the females will feel." He took my mouth and his fangs grazed my tongue, but didn't cut me. He was distracted enough that I wriggled one hand free, shoving it down between us and grabbed him. I stroked hard and he jerked against me. Male voices echoed his own moan. "And what I feel," he breathed through his pleasure, "so will the males."

It was oddly intoxicating to know that this wasn't a sex show, but a *sharing*.

When Xavier bit his wrist and offered me the small wound, I didn't feel so squeamish anymore. This was a man offering his own life-force to me. He was in full awareness of his choice and he wanted me to share his blood. I wrapped my lips around his skin where his fangs had pierced him and ran my tongue across his warmth. His blood had been intoxicating before, but there had always been a telltale metallic tang that came with it. As I drank, the sour trait ebbed, leaving only a sweetness that reminded me of roses.

When I pulled away and sighed, he smiled. "What was that?" I asked.

"You're accepting the change."

As if that first vital test had been paramount, every muscle in Xavier's body eased a fraction of tension I hadn't realized had been there before. He peeled away my underwear so that his skin touched mine. I expected him to feel cool like the rest of him as was the way of vampires, but now he'd gone hot against me. No matter if he had a heart that beat or not, he was alive, and the friction of the magic that blended with him grated against mine.

His cock nudged at my entrance and I parted for him. "I accept you," I said, my vision dancing with the red glow in his eyes. "Take me and make me yours."

My runes blared to life, echoing my need to complete a bond that was so taut I wanted to scream.

His jaw clenched as he fought the urge to take me, but even Xavier's control had its limits. He wanted to take his time with me. He wanted to make sure that the ritual blossomed at its own pace, but when he entered me, all patience went out of the window. A carnal pleasure wrapped through me as he sheathed himself until our skin slapped together. "Sonya," he said my name with a moan. "You feel..."

It was incredible. My back arched to take him even deeper and I gripped his biceps to keep him in place. The pure pleasure of him made my vision blur. The fulfillment in his eyes made this feel so right. "Don't stop," I told him and rocked myself against him. The beat of the music had transformed into a rhythm that matched Xavier's thrusts. Slickness ran down the curve of my thigh as he pulled out, only to slam himself back in again and growl at me with fangs flashing, the largest I'd ever seen them extended. An echoing cry filtered over the crowd as they joined us in our pleasure.

He curled over me, his eyes on my neck and I knew what he craved. I rolled my head and presented myself to him. "Take me," I said. "Take all of me."

His breath hot on mine made me shiver with anticipation. The room stilled, anticipation making the very air taut with need. Xavier shoved himself a fraction deeper into me, making a moan escape my throat, and then he tenderly pricked his fangs against my neck. Pain sparked white lights behind my eyes, and as he growled with a primal instinct I almost expected him to rip my throat out, but he let me adjust to the swimming of pain before he sank his bite deeper. He moved, gently taking me in slow, caring thrusts until his fangs completely embedded into my neck and I went rigid.

He'd been right. It hurt. *A lot.*

Then his magic kicked in. When he took the first long suck of my neck and drank my blood, the tension snapped and rained embers of raw power onto my face and sprinkled onto the sheets. Hisses of pleasure swarmed around us in echo of the blood-sharing.

I fluttered my eyes open to see the swirling vortex of our blood mixing in the air as Xavier took me into him, and I took him into me. I had his blood in me, his body in me, and as he moved and gave a light gasp, I felt the heat of his seed come into me. The pain eased away as quickly as it had come, and then there was only pleasure, elation, and the sense of breaking into a thousand pieces under his touch.

Long after I shattered from our passion, he licked at my wound. I moaned when he bit me again, tenderly this time, and lazily drank my blood.

Arousal built when he hardened once again in me, and then an itch tingled at my gumline.

I ran my fingers up to my lips and startled when my touch pricked against sharp fangs. The moment of shock was overcome by the enticement I felt towards something else Xavier had to offer me. I'd thought he'd had no heartbeat, but I'd been wrong. There was a thrumming in his body that communed with mine, one of ancient power that I now understood on a fundamental level. I parted my lips and he lowered himself over me, pausing his revived thrusts to give me full access of his neck.

"Take your fill," he growled, as if he needed me to bite him more than he needed anything else. "Take all you want of me."

I sank my new fangs into his luscious skin. Liquid roses and magic melted into my mouth. I groaned, and Xavier began his movements again, softly fucking me as I clung to him and felt the last craving bit of my succubus life slip away, only to be replaced by the satisfaction of a vampire's power. Pleasure that could be sated. Lust that could be fulfilled. This was what Xavier offered me, and I took it with both hands as I wrapped my legs around his waist.

The satisfied gasps that sounded below us signaled that the rest of the vampire enclave had felt the explosion of pleasure, and now indulged in the slow rocking of flesh against flesh.

When Xavier flipped me over and sank himself into me, grabbing my breasts and crushing my body to his, I'd never felt more fulfilled in all my life.

In my ecstasy, I almost didn't notice my runes light up on my stomach, burning with warning before the air shredded with ancient, foreign power; something that was even older than vampiric magic.

My bond was complete.

EXPENDABLE

Luke

"It's done," Nimra announced as she peered at the glow of her phone.

I glowered and snatched the device before she could have a chance to whisk it away. "No, you don't want to see—" she began, but I knew what I was going to see. I had to see it. Nimra couldn't understand that there was nothing to be ashamed of. I just had to know that Sonya was all right.

The camera picked up the powerful aura that had overtaken the chamber. The raised platform showed two mingling bodies, but I could see Sonya's pleasure. My body shivered with chills when I spotted the glimmer of her fangs and the pleasure it gave her when she sank them into her lover.

I'd expected vampire sex to be fast, rough, and something like the video I had seen between Sonya and the dragon, Jet, but this was so tender and mystical. The writhing bodies on the floor beneath the platform showed the vampires that added their own power to the rite. Sonya was too lost in ecstasy to see their eyes lower and their bodies slump. Their faces showed pleasure, but the thinning of their bodies showed the cost of their life-force to supply the magic it took to change Sonya into one of them.

She also didn't notice how the air literally tore around her, as if the room itself was about to wither into pieces. Was that normal?

"Will they be all right?" I asked. I only cared about Sonya, but to see the vampires and what it cost them to change her had me worried. When I cast the sleep-spell, all of the supernaturals in this city would go under. If the vampires didn't make sure to clean up the mess, Derek's forces would only send in new reserves and there'd be no one to stop them.

"The cost isn't a light one, but they'll survive," Nimra assured me. "Come," she patted the dusty space next to her as a breeze caught the pages of the grimoire. I expected it to go flying, but it behaved as if it was a boulder and didn't budge. When I moved to lift it in my lap, I was surprised to find the book as light as a feather.

"Now," she said, "recall Liam reading the words. Think them in your mind until you're sure you have them right. Then place your hand on the page and repeat it."

I frowned as I stared at the runes that didn't mean anything to me. "Why couldn't Liam be here to refresh my memory?" I asked. "What happens if I recite it incorrectly?"

"You don't want to recite it incorrectly." At my scowl, she sighed. "Liam is one of our most powerful reserves of supernatural energy. He was once a dragon, which makes him a hell of a lot more useful than me." She glared, the fiery nature of her contrasting her statement. "I was a human before I turned. I don't have nearly as much power to offer. What I have in my blood is all thanks to the vampires of Venice." Nimra's gaze went distant and fierce when she said that, as if she were grateful to the vampires, but hated that she had nothing else to offer them.

Her ruby gaze locked onto mine with determination and I knew that this was her moment. If I couldn't do this, she was going to blame herself.

"You can help me," I said and Nimra straightened. "I can amplify my memory if you allow me to use your brainpower." I offered my hand. "It shouldn't hurt."

She took my grip without hesitation. "Whatever you need. I'll give my life to save this city if I must."

I chuckled. "That won't be necessary."

And then I closed my eyes and concentrated.

I'd never been trained in magic, but I'd been around it all my life. Every time my mother had whispered words to herself, they'd been spells. I knew that now. The familiar tingling that swept across my skin when I entered her room was one of her power. I'd never thought much of it before, but how else would a mere mortal have seduced a full-blooded angel who'd become my father?

Reaching into Nimra's immortal mind, I found the capacity I needed to think back to the words Liam had recited.

"A tape recorder would have been so much easier," I muttered.

"One does not record spells," she hissed back without opening her eyes.

Her grip squeezed over my fingers and her teeth grit together when I ripped open the veil that separated her mind from mine. Her power filled me with unexpected warmth. Vampires weren't all ice and stillness. There was a hot life force that swirled in them if one knew how to access it.

Liam's voice came into my mind and my mouth opened to repeat each word. Carefully, slowly, I traced my fingers across each rune as I repeated the sounds.

It was working. Magic pulsated and swept out in a wide arc. I opened my eyes to see the retreating blue ring of it gliding across the city landscape. The houses beneath us lost their burgundy hue, all color slowly draining from the sky as the magic took hold.

The power of the spell was supposed to be red.

I wasn't born a warlock, but that power lived in me. I continued the spell, enunciating each syllable with careful scrutiny.

Just when I was about to reach the end of the spell, a bomb exploded at the base of the tower and the force launched me away from Nimra. She screeched as the link between us shattered and the spell unfurled like a giant spring let loose onto the world.

The blue wave transformed from its languished glide into a crashing tumult of power that dove and crashed through the streets. Fresh cries filtered into the air as my power hit.

"Shit," I muttered as I clung to one of the overturned stones along the roof. I arched my neck to see Nimra heaving, but alive and still on the roof with me.

She glanced at me, her ruby gaze full of panic and fear, both of which were emotions I imagined she rarely put on display. "I need to get back to the bunker," she shouted. "Meet you there."

And then she was gone in a blur, a trail of smoke cascading down the tower. I sighed and stumbled towards the stairs.

Damn woman was going to make me fight my way back to Sonya. I'd officially become expendable.

MINE

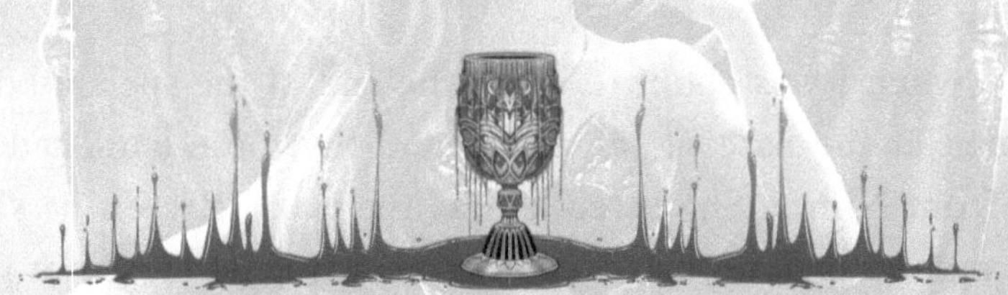

Xavier

The visions of Sonya naked before me had plagued me for a hundred years. They'd become a punishment to torture me until I remembered why I suffered. Hades had once been a muse and instead of succumbing to cruelty, he became a vampire. He was the father of vampires, of witches, and of supernaturals that believed in sanity and harmony.

Somewhere along the way the vampires took on the rebellious nature of the Blood Stone that had created them. I was one of them, and as one of Hades' sons, I'd greatly disappointed him.

I stared at him now, the calm and perfect visage resting its curves along the stone. Only his red eyes glowed to convince me that this was no statue. This was my father, and he was in the core of his slumber that should be impossible to disturb.

Sonya stood beside me with kindred magic running in her veins. She didn't understand the process of turning into a vampire, none of us did, but the old Sonya had died and this one was what remained. She was so beautiful. Her skin had paled just a shade lighter than before and a ruby gleam sparkled in her eyes. When I ran my thumb over her cheek, she smiled at me, her baby fangs pricking at her lower lip, and I knew that I'd never have to wonder if my visions were real.

She was mine.

ALARM CLOCK

Sonya

I wondered what Xavier was thinking when he looked at me like that, but now was not the time to explore my new bond with him. Luke had done his part. The city sang with his magic and now it was my turn. It was time to wake Hades.

"Are you sure you're up for this?" Xavier asked, his thumb still stroking my cheek.

I covered his hand with mine and leaned into his touch. "I will be," I promised. I met his gaze, determined not to feel weird about my next demand. "But I won't begin until I know that Luke's okay."

Xavier didn't flinch, but a shadow passed across his gaze. I'd banished his secret hope that turning into a vampire would make me forget about Luke. There was no way that was going to happen. If anything, binding myself to Xavier only cemented the certainty of who I was. The succubus part of me had diminished, but that ancient magic I'd been born with was still there. I didn't think that the vampiric transformation had fully worked, but I couldn't deny the fangs poking out of my teeth.

"Nimra should bring word," Xavier said, then fished through his pockets for his phone. He brought it out and frowned at the screen. "Something's wrong."

I peered around his shoulder. "What do you mean?"

He showed me a picture of the sky with an arc of blue light unfurling like a tidal wave across the city. My eyes went wide. "I have to get up there."

Xavier gripped my arm. "Luke is an immortal in every sense of the word. Even Derek can't kill an angel. You'll do him more good staying here and awakening Hades." His gaze flashed with warning. "If you don't, then we all will perish along with my father."

I growled and ripped free of him. Xavier startled, clearly not expecting me to be strong enough to overcome him. I grinned. Being a vampire was going to be fun. "Fine," I said, "but don't think I'm doing this because of you. Luke is just as important to me as you are and I know he can take care of himself, but I've seen what Derek is capable of." I clenched my jaw. "Luke might have survived his heart being ripped from his chest, but he almost didn't survive it being broken. Derek knows which buttons to press."

Xavier took a step away from me, giving me the space I needed. I hadn't rejected him, but he knew that if he pushed me, I would, bond or not. "I leave my fate in your hands, Sonya," he said, his foreign lilt stronger as emotion raged against him. He wasn't used to letting someone else be in control. "My only desire is to protect you."

I whirled from him and approached the ancient vampire trapped in stone. Hades' arms crossed over his chest and glittering red emanated from his eyes. "If you want to help," I said, "then be quiet while I concentrate."

I reached out and lightly pressed my fingers against Hades. I expected the stone to be cool under my touch, but heat speared through me the moment I made contact. Hades was alive and well—and aware.

The self-inflicted curse trapped him in this state for years at a time. But he wasn't aware of me or Xavier or anyone else in this room. He was inside his own mind. When I closed my eyes, I sensed him and reached for him.

"Hades?" I asked, the words echoing in an eerie ghost-like chamber as my spirit moved into Hades' consciousness.

An attractive man who could have passed for late thirties turned and frowned. He'd been buying a gelato from his favorite cafe—the very same one where I'd visited before meeting Xavier. Perhaps there was something to be said for vampiric magic. Hades kept an eye on his sons, even while he slept.

"Who's there?" Hades snapped and a sudden wind ripped the gelato from his hand. It crashed to the ground, the treat melting on the cobblestone street.

My presence was a terrible disturbance in this peaceful place where Hades let his mind rest, but there wasn't a choice. Derek had brought an army to take him down, and I didn't know what the Incubus King planned to do with me. Whatever it was though, I didn't want to find out.

"You have to wake up," I urged and punctured my nails through the veil.

In the real world, his statue fractured under my touch, sending sharp cracks digging across the stone under my fingers. Xavier's emotions raged with concern and fear that plucked at me, distracting me. He was just going to have to deal. This was exactly what needed to happen.

Hades finally sensed me, his gaze locking onto mine before a familiar red hot power shot through my chest. My back arched and my eyes went wide, my vision momentarily overwhelmed by brilliant red flames. Had I been a succubus, the power would have been too pure for me to handle, but Xavier had changed me. I knew what these fires were. Vampires seemed just as cold as the stone beneath my feet, but there was a fire so hot inside their veins that it could burn the world to ash if set free. This was the raw power of blood, of life and sacrifice. When blood spilled, magic itself was set loose.

The Blood Stone I'd worn as a necklace, and eventually absorbed into my chest, was just a construct to contain it. As a vampire, I more than held the power within me, I communed with it. When red-hot flames scorched through my veins, I should have turned to ash. Instead, I endured and become stronger for it.

Being able to survive the invasion of Hades' power didn't save me from the agony. A scream ripped from my throat and Xavier's hands extended to grab me, his movements and thoughts just as much a part of my awareness as all of my four who bled into my vision.

Luke, shaken, panicked, but running towards me right now, and otherwise healthy and alive.

Jet, silently contemplated a murmuring group of dragon shifters who whispered their concerns deep beneath China's soil. His eyes searched the cave's ceiling, sensing me. The air in his chamber echoed with familiar sounds I couldn't explain and he frowned.

My magic decided that Jet wasn't in immediate danger and searched for Nate. He was the only one I couldn't find and my blood ran cold wondering if he was alive or dead.

Xavier. He was the one in immediate danger. The world froze as I surveyed the situation from a place outside of myself. His arms outstretched, his jaw bulging and his eyes wild with panic. When I saw what he was looking at, I empathized with his uncharacteristic outburst. My body had twisted into an unnatural position, my head leaning back and lines of red power streaking across my skin. I knew if he touched me he'd die. I snapped out a hand and sent a blast of lightning, sending him flying to the other side of the room. The other vampires didn't dare touch me and huddled against the walls with wide eyes and fully-extended fangs.

The dream-world enveloped me and Hades snarled. His slicked-back hair and clean-shaven face transformed into a beast with red eyes that howled with rage. "Who are you?" he demanded. His words hissed through his fangs and it took every ounce of willpower to remind myself that this was just inside his mind. He couldn't hurt me… right?

When he blurred, moving too fast for even my vampire senses to keep up, he appeared in front of my face and grabbed both of my wrists. I resisted him when he tugged. If he managed to drag me any further into his world, I might fall into the cursed sleep with him.

"Xavier is in danger," I blurted. "The Incubus King is attacking the city and Apollo is helping him."

Hades scoffed, but his vice grip eased. "Why would Apollo attack my city, one full of vampires?" His eyes flashed with warning. "Even if he was foolish enough, Xavier wouldn't let anyone into this city."

I rolled my eyes. "Who do you think sent me here? Do you really believe that I found the super secret vampire bunker, converted myself with vampirism, and found you all by myself?"

Hades glowered, but drew in deeper to inhale my scent. "You have Xavier's blood in you. Your turning was recent."

"Yeah," I said with a grin. "Very."

He looked down at his hold on me with a grimace. "No, I don't believe it. My son wouldn't have turned you. He's plagued by visions of the girl he can never have. He won't turn anyone else except for her. He can't. He's tried before and they always died because he couldn't accept them, not fully. His heart belongs to a woman he's never even met." He squeezed his eyes shut and the ruby glow of his power illuminated his eyelids. "I regret cursing him with such a terrible fate. I'd only intended to teach him how to feel. He'd become so cold and cruel, but the witches didn't tell me the visions would never go away, never be fulfilled."

I shivered as Hades revealed the truth. Xavier had tried to turn women before? I couldn't imagine the guilt he carried with him for those failures, but it was a guilt only I could understand.

"The witches were wrong," I whispered and Hades' eyes flung open. "I'm the one from his visions."

Hades leaned in and furrowed his brows. His lips parted as he inhaled my scent again, this time his tongue flicking as he tasted the air. "It's impossible," he whispered, but the shock on his face said he knew that I spoke the truth. "The witches didn't learn that the visions were a future so utterly unlikely until it was too late. There's a better chance of..."

I grinned. "Of a succubus being seduced by a vampire?" I wiggled out of his grip that had finally loosened. "Yeah. It happened, believe it or not." Turning serious, I ripped the veil between us a fraction more. "You have to wake up, Hades. If you don't, Venice will fall to the Incubus King's mind control, and so will every vampire in it."

That got his attention. He growled and my footing wavered. I couldn't tell if it was from a bomb in the real world, or Hades unfurling his dreams into reality. "I'll need a fraction of the power you've brought with you," he said. "It's going to hurt."

Closing my eyes, I readied myself. "Do it. Rip the band-aid."

He hesitated, and depending on how long he'd been asleep, maybe he had no idea what a band-aid was, but then a low growl rumbled in his throat. Heat spread across my chest and electricity zapped through my hair. I grimaced when lightning hot flashes seared through me, but I fisted my hands and endured.

I filled my mind with visions of Luke lying in bed with me, smiling, content and happy. I don't think he'd been able to smile very much in his life. To be able to bring him joy gave me indescribable pleasure and I wasn't about to leave him to fend for himself on the war-torn streets of Venice.

Hades roared and the pain of his awakening cracked through my ears as his statue shattered.

Unconsciousness threatened to take me, and stubbornly I fought it.

"Luke," I whispered. "Xavier. Help me find the others."

The four men in my life. I knew I'd never be able to let any of them go.

"What are you doing?" Nimra shrieked as she entered the sacred chamber where Hades slept.

I was too far gone to fully understand her words or what she wanted. All I recalled was that it had been her duty to protect Luke, yet now she was here, and he was not.

Hades shifted under my touch and came close to his awakening. When I glanced at Nimra through the haze of my agony as Hades drew the power of my Blood Stone for his premature awakening, I noticed that her eyes dusted with a faint red mist that didn't match her vampiric nature.

"She's come into contact with Derek's mind-control fog," I said through clenched teeth.

Xavier moved to stop her, but it was too late. She snarled and dangerous fangs flashed before she sank her bite into his neck. Xavier groaned as the power of her jaw worked at his tendons and blood spilled down his chest.

"Nimra!" I tried to wiggle free of Hades, but the magic between us kept me locked in place.

As Xavier's gaze flickered and he crumpled to the floor, she grinned at me with his blood smeared across her face. "You don't deserve each other," she growled, then bared her teeth in a hiss before going for me.

I knew what would happen when she touched me. Too far linked with the father of all vampires, only the wielder of a Blood Stone could survive the power coursing between us. Red-hot magic seared through my body and I was barely keeping it together as it was.

When Nimra wrapped her fingers around my throat, her body jolted and her eyes went wide.

I knew it was Derek's mind-control that was making her do this, but I had a feeling she'd left Luke to fend for himself before she'd become infected.

"Have a nice afterlife, bitch," I said as Nimra turned to ash.

ALLIES

Luke

Hades was awake, but something was wrong. My spell should have cast all supernaturals into slumber so that the vampires could pick them off while Hades went after his brother, but something went wrong. The blue aura that overtook the sky rained down fine dust that tasted sweet on my lips.

I watched the horizon, sensing that I had called something to aid us instead. My magic wasn't a witch's power, but there were other supernaturals in this world that I'd yet to discover.

A howl sounded and I crouched as my teeth grated at the impossible sound.

Wolves.

In spite of my better judgment, I ran towards the sound, only to stop when screams followed. A beast burst through the red fog of mind-control, but he shook his fur and the dust drifted to the ground as dead ash of his latest kill.

Glorious blue eyes met mine, a kindred to angelic power in

that of a wolf. I reached out, barely brushing his snout, before he ran off in a blur and was gone again, sending more screams in his wake.

Perhaps I hadn't followed the plan, but I grinned, because I'd called freaking werewolves to help us fight Derek's men.

IT'S OVER

Sonya

"Vampires fly?" I asked as Hades soared through the air, leading us down the streets of Venice.

Xavier smirked as he paused at my side, then winced and adjusted the bandage at his neck. It amazed me that a vampire needed a bandage, but wounds from a vampire's bite took longer to heal. Something about kindred magic. "Just Hades," Xavier said as he cast his father an envious look.

Breaking into a run, I felt like I could fly myself, the vampiric power compelling my legs making me blur through the streets of Venice. "This is awesome!" I called to Xavier who managed to follow.

I lost sight of Hades as he blurred into a nest of buildings, but we were still bonded by the ties of blood. Focusing, I sensed which way he'd gone and followed.

I reached a very shocked Derek and male muse who faced the seething vampire.

"Betrayal!" Hades hissed at Apollo, his brother.

Derek was the first to break free of his shock. He glanced at me, his eyes going wide when I revealed my fangs. "Sonya," he whispered as if heartbroken. "What have you done?"

Glowering, I stormed up to him. "What have *I* done?" I hissed at him, not caring that my fangs probably made me look like a monster. "I did what it took in order to stop you."

Apollo rested a hand on Derek's shoulder. "He was only acting in my interests. If anyone is to take the blame, it is I."

Hades snarled. "I care not about the incubi. Why, brother? Why, after all these years, do you seek to destroy me?"

Apollo's face fell. "I intended to allow you to sleep. When the city would have succumbed to my control, then I would have made sure you were never to wake again. This world doesn't deserve you, brother, and you deserve eternal peace."

Claws extended from Hades' fingers. "I think you have that backwards, *brother*. This world deserves to be free of you."

Stunned, I locked my knees as Hades moved so fast that no one could have stopped him. He gripped Apollo's hair and twisted until the muse's neck arched in an unnatural direction.

Apollo's eyes went wide. "Brother, wait," he rasped. "I'm powerless against you. You know this. Have mercy!"

Hades growled, his vampiric nature swarming red streaks of power over his body and transforming him into a taller, bulkier version of himself. His fangs extended and he growled with pure rage. "You are no longer my brother."

Apollo cried out as Hades twisted further. He lashed out with an invisible wave of power, the compulsion of a muse knocking me to the ground and sending stabs of pain cascading through my body. The way that Hades flinched, I knew he felt it too, but he continued to *twist*.

A sickening crunch sounded, followed by an agonized groan

as the skin around Apollo's neck split, and then his head was no longer attached to his body anymore. Blood spilled onto the streets as the rest of him collapsed into a heap.

Derek's blood drained from his face and for the first time, fear crossed his features. He looked at me with desperate hope in his eyes, but I clenched my jaw shut as the echoes of Apollo's retaliation faded into nothingness.

Hades considered the incubus, but snarled his revulsion. "Be gone from my sight, incubus. You will repay your failures by serving me now. Clean up your mess, or you will join my brother."

Derek swallowed and bowed his head. "Yes, Hades. Thank you for your mercy."

Xavier slipped a hand around my waist as we walked through the streets of Venice. Blood painted the walls red and horror scented the air, but when I came to the wolves gnawing on Derek's men, I swallowed. We eased around the beasts that snapped and snarled, but otherwise ignored us. I straightened when I heard something I'd recognize anywhere.

Luke's laughter.

I ran. Rounding the bend I jerked to a halt when I found Luke wrestling with two wolves. Their fur glistened with a supernatural white that would have been beautiful, had they not all been covered in blood.

"It seems that your angel has found some new friends," Xavier remarked with a tilt of his head.

Luke laughed as a pair of wolves tussled with him. Their gleaming blue eyes set them apart from regular beasts, as well as their majestic coats.

When Luke caught my gaze, his laughter faded, but his smile remained. "Wolf shifters," he explained. He stood and brushed dirt from his pants. "They tell me that it's time they lived up to their end of some old bargain." When I gave him a confused look, he said, "I'm going back to Seattle. It's time I freed my mother."

My stomach dropped. I'd just reunited two of my four, and now Luke wanted to leave me?

"Then I'm going with you," I said without dropping a beat. I grabbed Xavier's hand. "Right? We're going with him."

Xavier gave me a raised brow. "How are a couple of mutts going to free a Seer from the confines of Seattle prison? If she wanted to get out, she would have done it by now. Seers are witches from powerful covens. They don't do anything they don't want to do."

Luke gaped at him as if the vampire had said something profound. "And if a witch is excommunicated from her coven? What then?"

Xavier tilted his head. "Then, I suppose, she'd have considerably less power to draw upon."

Luke clenched his fists. "Then she needs us. She's been rotting in prison all this time for a crime she didn't commit. She was training me, not torturing me. She doesn't deserve to be there anymore."

I gave Xavier a pleading look. "I must go with him. He's right. Everything is settled here, isn't it? The threat has passed?"

Xavier gave a raised brow to the toppled ruins and line of bodies. "Not sure I would call this 'settled,' but we're not in imminent danger anymore, if that's what you mean."

When Xavier gave me a smile that showed me his resolve was weakening, I grinned and wrapped my arms around his neck. "I'd do anything for any one of you. You know that, right?"

"Yes," Xavier whispered in my ear before unlatching me and pushing me towards Luke. "That's why we're going to help the Seer. Let's get on with it."

With a sigh I curled myself into the angel and fitted my nose to his neck. My love for him was no different than my love for Xavier, but everything about him made sure that I knew it was Luke who held me tight. Instead of Xavier's cool passion and deadly grace, Luke's brute force and deep mystery shifted under my touch. I moved to kiss him, but when I smelled the sweetness of his blood, my fangs extended.

Luke felt the cool danger of my fangs pressed against his skin and flinched away from me. "So," he said, running a thumb over my chin, "you're his now."

He misunderstood me. Just because his blood made me want to… bite, didn't mean I was a mindless vampire. My eyes searched his and I hated that my eyes glowed red. All he could see is a vampire, but I'd prove him that I was still the Sonya he remembered. "I still remember us," I persisted and gripped his forearms. I brought his hands to my stomach, slipping his fingers under my shirt so that he could feel the magic of my blazing runes for himself. "The bond is complete, but I need all of us together." My gaze flicked to the sky as my stomach churned with renewed dread. I'd cemented my bond just in time for what was coming next. Derek and Apollo hadn't been the real threat. The shadows of my nightmares were coming, and now I knew they weren't dreams at all.

They'd been visions of the future.

"I have to reunite all of us," I whispered, and didn't speak the rest of my thoughts aloud. Destiny had kept my men apart and spread across the planet for good reason, reuniting them with me one by one. A dragon, an angel, a vampire, and a mortal who was too smart for his own good would be a deadly combination. I couldn't simply just shove all of them into a room together and expect everything to work out. No, they would awaken a frightening force that rested in my soul, and there was only one person who would know how to handle that.

The Seer who had prepared her son to save me. Luke's mother was the key to saving us all.

COMING HOME

Sonya

Xavier's idea of travel was a lot faster than mine… and involved a heavy dose of magic.

"No way am I using that thing," I said stubbornly as I crossed my arms and glowered at the rusted archway that separated us from Seattle.

The low tunnels beneath Venice ran deep, with smaller branches leading out to portals the witches had activated to each supernatural stronghold. Because of Derek, being the Incubus King and all, meant there was a portal directly to the Seattle Mansion. Looking into the living room which held that alluring painting of Silvia made my skin crawl. It was a lifetime ago since I'd been there last, but that's not what had me on edge. We hadn't seen Derek ever since Apollo had been killed. He'd gathered as much of his makeshift army as he could and retreated. Apollo never should have let him go.

"It's the fastest way," Xavier insisted, slipping an arm around my waist. He glanced at Luke who glowered at the rippling portal, clearly just as reluctant as I was about stepping into the Incubus King's living room.

"Let's just get this over with," Luke declared before stepping into the portal without warning.

My heart lurched as soon as Luke was gone. The rune to the left of my navel flared to life without warning, punishing me for letting Luke out of my sight. I doubled over, but managed to keep an eye on the angel through the hazy shimmer of the portal.

Two incubi immediately accosted him, one punching him in the face, lashing the angel's head to the side. His hair slapped over his forehead and he brushed it away with a growl.

"Are you all right?" Xavier asked, seemingly oblivious that Luke was under attack.

I growled at the vampire. "Just get in there and help him, and drag me through with you!" I wasn't interested in being punished by Xavier's rune as well.

By the tight-lipped frown Xavier gave me I expected him to argue. Perhaps this had been part of his plan to get me all to himself, but my doubts were relieved when he wrapped his fingers around my wrist and pulled me through the portal.

Electricity and magic filtered through my veins, making sure I was fully aware that I'd just violated a whole bunch of rules of physics by bending time and space to get to Seattle.

However, unlike the time I'd made a portal with the power of my Blood Stone, this one wasn't nearly as bad. The pain sputtered out as quickly as it'd come. Perhaps witches would be a little bit better than me at making portals.

The incubi who'd been giving Luke a beating—which he'd been allowing with a manic grin plastered on his face—stopped in their tracks when Xavier and I stepped out of thin air.

I whirled around, wondering if I'd see the portal, but there was nothing there.

"Princess?" one of them breathed.

"Get the Queen!" another shouted.

I turned back around and blinked. Did they just call me a princess? Who the fuck was this Queen?

We all froze when Silvia stepped into view. There was no doubt about what she was anymore. Brilliant, beautiful wings spread out from behind her and she flared them, sending light from the chandeliers rippling over the dark, metallic feathers.

"Ah, my darling. I was hoping you'd come home." She spread her arms. "You've finally come home."

I was too dumbfounded to react, and was only brought out of my stunned silence by the sound of a fist smacking into Luke's face again. His face lashed to the side from the force, but he righted himself again, blood running over his lips and chin as he grinned. He was a master of pain and he was just toying with the incubus guard. "That all you got?" he asked.

"Silvia!" I shouted, rushing to put myself between Luke and his attackers. "Tell them to lay off!" We weren't here for her, or them. We just needed a quick ride to Seattle and it happened to land us in her living room.

The guards gave her a glance, and she nodded their dismissal. "I'm terribly sorry," she said as she swept to our side. She paused when she spotted Xavier, still as death, lingering at my back. I hadn't noticed him either. He was good at not being seen when he didn't want to be. "Oh," she breathed with a small smile lighting her face. "I didn't know you brought another one."

Xavier bared his fangs, but she didn't seem much bothered by it. "I've heard of you," he hissed with much more venom than I felt was warranted. We were the ones who'd intruded on her property, after all, and I hadn't forgotten that Silvia was the one who'd given me the resistant. Derek didn't hold power over me anymore because of her.

She bowed her head, elegance in every inch of her movements. "I should hope so, son of Hades. All good things, I would like to think. There aren't too many of us on Earth. I wouldn't want our notoriety to be diminished by rumor." She glanced at Luke when she said that.

"I'm very sorry that we've intruded," I explained, hoping my men wouldn't escalate the situation. Even though I was grateful to Silvia, I didn't know much about her, why she'd helped me, much less if she'd do it again. "If you don't mind, we'll just be on our way and—"

She straightened. "Oh, but dear, I've been waiting for you." She raised her hand and magic hummed, making my breath catch. She didn't imprison us, even though I had a feeling that she could have. She slowly lowered her fingers to her side, curling them into a fist. I should have run then and there, but what kept me in place was the look of desperation that crossed her features. "You see. I was hoping you could help me with something, before you go."

MY GUYS

Sonya

"There is no way I am helping that woman!" I shouted at the top of my lungs, not caring who was listening. I would say it right to her face. No. I would not help her free my—our, demonspawn daughter into the world.

Apparently Derek had trapped her in one of the lower levels of the house. Only the oldest homes in Seattle had basements, and naturally Derek's mansion was one of them.

"I'm not talking about helping Silvia," Luke insisted, standing aside Xavier, because for the first time, they both agreed on something that I very much didn't.

I growled with frustration. "This is no fair! Two against one!"

Xavier smirked and crossed his arms. "I'd say it's very fair. We're powerless against you, my dear. Strength in numbers is the only way to go when it's time to talk some sense into you."

Glowering, I stormed in a small circle, which was all the bedroom allowed. Silvia had insisted we stay the night, since the prison facility would be closed and we couldn't very well go rescue the Seer without a plan. I hated to agree with her, but I hated it even more now that Luke and Xavier had spilled our whole story.

"She did some sort of truth spell on you two," I insisted. That was the only explanation of why Luke had gone from toying with the guards to telling the half-naked woman in her white nightgown with brilliant wings all about our plans. "Now she's convinced you that you have to turn on me and protect *her*!" I felt so betrayed. I thought our bond was stronger than that. Hot tears formed and threatened to roll down my cheeks.

I could have used the power of my Blood Stone, or my new vampiric speed, but Silvia had one thing right: I didn't have much of a plan. When she offered us to stay in one of the bedrooms, I was grateful at the chance to get my guys away from her.

"She has witches," Xavier explained. "Venice is in a state of devastation and Hades has no witches to spare. I came with you to protect you, but Silvia is offering a coven, which is something I don't have. We need her."

Luke nodded his agreement, taking my hands in his and stopping me from my mindless pacing. I glanced up at him, hating how those crystal blue eyes trapped me with his sheer adoration. "Sonya, I know you think Silvia cast a spell on us, but she didn't. When I saw—"

"Her wings," I bit out. "You saw wings and suddenly you thought she was someone you could trust. Well, she is the mother of a demonspawn, isn't she?"

Luke leaned in closer. "And so are you. Should I not trust you?"

Growling, I yanked my hands free of him and barreled past Xavier to flop on the bed. The vampire eased himself down beside me and pushed my hair away from my face. His red eyes beamed with excitement. "What's got you in such a good mood?" I grumbled.

That only made him grin wider, revealing his glistening fangs. "I can't be in a good mood when I'm in bed with my mate?"

I rolled onto my back and stared up at the bronze ceiling. The intricate pattern was too luxurious, making me miss my old, stinky apartment I'd had with Sarah. "No, you cannot," I said.

Luke sat down on my other side, easing onto his back and gazing up at the ceiling with me. "I thought I was alone," he whispered. "That there were none others out there like me."

I hadn't considered what this might be like for Luke. His loneliness was so tangible, so painful that it drew me to him with a need to ease it any way I could. Now, his pain had been lifted, all by someone I didn't know and someone I wasn't keen to trust. Who would willingly bring a demonspawn into the world? And why would she want us to save her from the prison Derek put her in?

"Perhaps we should sleep on it," Xavier offered, running his fingers over my hip and pulling up my shirt to reveal my runes that blazed to life being in such close proximity with two of my bond.

Luke instinctually reached over and touched his rune, the blazing spiral to the left of my navel, and Xavier moved to his, the one painfully low that made heat build between my legs, wondering if his fingers might go even lower to relieve me of a new itch.

I sighed. "You can't distract me with sex." *They could totally distract me with sex.*

Luke laughed and pressed his lips to the curve of my neck. "Is that so?" he challenged.

Just as I'd feared, Xavier's hand inched lower and I set my jaw, determined not to egg them on any further. If I protested, they'd just—I gasped when Luke bit, and Xavier's fingers slipped over my zipper, putting pressure on my delicate folds.

"Not fair," I said again, this time my voice dropping low and husky as my eyelids fluttered closed. I snapped them open again, trying to keep myself from losing control. I was a succubus, dammit, I should be the one doing the seducing. "Did you just bite me?" I asked Luke and a smile played on my lips.

"Don't you like that sort of kink now?" His fingers slipped under my shirt, taking a firm hold of my breast as he squeezed with his merciless claim on me.

Xavier didn't stop his movements, sliding his fingers over my clothes, keeping the pressure on me and lighting up my nerves. "I think she liked it very much. Perhaps you should do it again," Xavier offered helpfully.

When I widened my eyes at him, realizing that he was serious about this, he gave me a wicked grin. "Xavier?" I asked, the question coming out helpless now that I knew they were going to play on my weakness. I wanted them—both of them—and if they were going to take me together, there was nothing I could do to stop them.

"You don't understand our bond, do you?" he asked, his fangs lengthening as he tugged my zipper down. He tugged my pants over my hips and yanked them off my legs, leaving me bare except for my thin underwear that was already soaked. Luke likewise tugged my shirt over my head, but left my bra in place, my nipples painfully hard against the fabric.

"I know we're bonded," I said, my runes lighting up in response. "But…" I trailed off, because it was more than a magical bond that drew me to them.

Each of my men gave me something I never knew that I

needed. Luke, with his loneliness and mystery, gave me someone to comfort, someone who I could help when I'd always been helpless, and someone who understood me on a level that no one else could. He was tormented, even more fucked up than I was, and challenged me to be better every day.

Xavier had opened up a whole new world to me. He was immortality, failure, and forgiveness all in one package. As he resumed his languished strokes over my underwear, a small moan escaped me.

Luke's skin heated at my sounds and he pressed himself to me. Even through the thick layer of his jeans I could feel the hardness of him begging for me. I reached to undo his zipper, but he took my wrist, stopping me. "It's our turn," he whispered, and ran his tongue up my neck before testing my skin with his teeth again.

Impossible pleasure and need spiraled in me and I squirmed, wanting to be rid of the building tension that threatened to break me in two.

Sensing my discomfort, Xavier surprised me by shifting between my legs and poised his fangs over my thigh. The threat made me freeze in place and Luke laughed. "Scared? It's just a deadly vampire when you're at your most vulnerable."

I could have laughed, but instead I swallowed hard with my gaze locked on Xavier's movements. He stretched my underwear, adding to the pressure of my sex, before running his tongue over me and making a cry escape my throat.

Luke slipped his hand under my bra and pinched my nipple, forcing an orgasm I couldn't keep any longer. Xavier growled and devoured me, shredding the thin fabric with his teeth and somehow sparing me a vicious cut from his teeth as he sent waves of pleasure through every nerve ending. His tongue worked magic, making me buck and stars crossed my vision as I lost all sense of myself for a few blissful moments before collapsing to the bed gasping for air.

I let myself come down from that high, my vision clearing and the red haze of my own magic making the room swelter with heat.

"You're getting stronger," Luke praised me, remarking that I was able to receive pleasure without feeding. That I could enjoy my own arousal with those of my bond. The sensation was so utterly freeing that hot tears gathered again, this time ones of joy as emotions bubbled within me.

When he gripped my chin and made me look at him, he gave me a long, deep kiss. My mouth parted for him, enthralled as his tongue danced across mine and the sweet taste of him filled my senses. When I opened my eyes again, I noticed his soft, angelic glow.

"So are you," I said and stroked the arch of his cheekbone just beneath his glowing eyes. I didn't know what it meant, what Luke would become, but I wanted the world for him. I wanted him to feel powerful, to feel needed and in control. It was something he'd never had before.

We shared a smile, and then a new surge of bravery swept through me. Xavier was still watching me, his eyes hungry and his fangs larger than I'd ever seen them. I wasn't sure if he wanted my sex or if he wanted my blood, but I was determined to give him one of those options. I jumped up and turned, yanking Luke in front of me and peeling his pants over his hips, his deliciously swollen cock jumping free just inches from my face.

I wanted nothing more than to take him, but I glanced over my shoulder to see Xavier whose attention had finally diverted to what I presented in front of *his* face. I shook my booty at him, making him blink, and then grin.

He didn't need more encouragement than that. He unzipped

his pants and teased his cock over my swollen heat, making me groan. I turned back to Luke and put his cock in my mouth before I forgot how to breathe. Ecstasy and elation filled me as Luke's moans mixed with Xavier's. Music to my ears.

I worked my magic, carefully and precisely. I was a succubus, and I was a powerful one. I had the ancient magic of the Blood Stone in my chest and a mysterious bond that allowed me to know my guys better than anyone else.

I sent the red waves of heat through my body, down my hips and across my tongue, giving both men a heavy dose of intoxicating pleasure. They both froze when it hit before moving again with renewed vigor.

Xavier impossibly hardened inside of me, taking me with long, deep thrusts.

Luke closed his eyes and leaned his head back, allowing me to taste and suckle at him. He was the most beautiful, exquisite creature and he tasted so delicious. I lapped at him before stroking him hard and sending another pulse of magic through both their bodies.

It took concentration to pleasure both of them at the same time, but the bond helped me do it. The bond wanted us to unite, together, and become one. Xavier's pleasure built to a peak, threatening to tip over the edge. He resisted me, wanting to prolong the pleasure, but I wouldn't allow him. He would come when I wanted him to.

One more wave of power and his release spilled into me, just as Luke's sweetness filled my mouth and masculine moans caressed me as I pleasured my men to their climax.

"That was..." Luke began as he rested his head against the wall, his fingers draping over my naked thigh.

"Divine," Xavier finished for him, his eyes still closed as he rested on my other side, sated, hands behind his head, his hair still wet from the shower.

We'd all taken a shower, one at a time under my explicit instructions. I didn't think I could handle two naked men in a steamy shower with me, not two of my bond. I needed to unscramble my brains and decide how I felt about Silvia's proposal to help her free our demonspawn daughter from Derek's imprisonment.

I ran my fingers over my glowing runes, only two of them alight to recognize Luke and Xavier in my presence. The soft heat glowed and ebbed like a heartbeat, seeming just as sated as my men with what we had done. I never thought it would feel so natural to have a threesome, but it wasn't for the thrill of it, like most people do. I'd had sex with both of them at the same time because it'd felt right. They both need me, just as I need them.

"If you were trying to get me to calm down and consider what Silvia told us, then it worked," I managed to say, my own eyelids too heavy to keep them open. My damp hair made me cold, but I didn't have the energy to dry it.

Xavier stroked his fingers through my hair, his red magic warming me, but not drying me. "Sorry, love," he admitted, his red eyes alight with mischief, "we need a dragon to dry you off properly."

I narrowed my eyes at him. I hadn't told him about Jet, not yet, but he seemed to know so much more about my bond than I did. "And where would we find this dragon, hmm?"

He continued to untangle my hair, working carefully as his fingers gracefully swept through my strands so deftly that I hardly felt the pull. “You do know that I have a coven, even if they’ve abandoned me now that my father is awake.”

I hummed thoughtfully and rested on my elbow. Luke lazily draped an arm over me and slumped into the pillow, spooning me. He didn’t seem interested in partaking in the conversation and soon was asleep, his soft breaths puffing at my back.

Xavier smiled. “You wore the angel out.”

I thumped him on the chest and he eased lower, brushing a kiss against my lips. “What aren’t you telling me?” I pressed.

His ruby eyes searched mine, his fingers ran over my lips and brushed my fangs I’d managed to keep mostly retracted. Luke was right. I was getting stronger. Even my vampire side wasn’t dominating me. “My witches told me a lot of things that I will share with you, and when all the members of your bond are in one place, I think that will be a good time to share what I know.” He grinned. “Wouldn’t want to repeat myself, now would I?”

I rolled my eyes. “Of course. We wouldn’t want that.”

Luke gripped me tighter around the waist at my sharp tone, forcing me to relax.

Xavier lowered his voice, as if he didn’t want to disturb the angel. “I can tell you this, Sonya; the runes are an ancient magic so powerful that it can derail fate itself.” His fingers ran down the curves of my breasts and circled my runes. The one lowest on my stomach flared to life at his touch and I suppressed the fresh heat it swept through me. “This is what Luke’s mother saw. It’s why there is a demonspawn in the world, and it’s why we’re here. This is all connected.”

I furrowed my brows. “I don’t understand. What’s connected?”

“You helped to bring a frightful creature into this world. Why do you think that is?”

My hand went to my chest, my fingers draping over the

heated skin where my power thrummed with a life of its own. "Because of the Blood Stone."

He chuckled, low and short as if I was an idiot. "No, Sonya, that's not why." His brilliant ruby gaze latched onto mine. "It's because you have power over Hell itself. You are its Queen, and you will be the one to save it."

What. The. Fuck.

Queen of Hell

Sonya

Of course I was the Queen of the Damned. I was a succubus turned into a vampire. I had survived Derek's blood canals and prevented Hell from ripping into our world, not just because of my power over the Blood Stone, but because of who I was.

Because of the runes that marked me for *what* I was.

I clutched at my head, which was starting to throb.

"I'm sorry," Xavier crooned. "You weren't ready to know."

I snatched my fingers away and stared at him, wide-eyed. "Is this why you turned me into a vampire?"

His features softened and he lowered his voice, "Of course not," he hissed before glancing over my shoulder to check on Luke who was still fast asleep with silken sheets draped over his lower half. He was really out of it.

"Why are you so worried if Luke wakes up?"

Xavier's gaze flicked back to me, danger flashing in his expression. "Because his power is a delicate one. He's not ready to learn the details of your destiny. It's why his mother hid so much from him. He will take time to process this. He's finally accepted you. Don't destroy that without giving him enough time to digest another shock."

I pressed my lips into a thin line, but Xavier had a point. Luke had looked at me as if I had grown two heads when he figured out I was a succubus. It'd taken a long time for us to strengthen our bond, and no matter how ancient or magical it was, Luke wasn't going to do anything he didn't want to do. If he learned that I was Hell's savior, I wasn't sure what he might do. I needed to prepare him for it.

Except, I still wasn't sure what *I* was going to do about it.

"So, what now?" I asked, feeling defeated. Xavier believed that Silvia was the answer to all our problems, and by now, I hoped he was right. I wasn't much interested in attempting to free Luke's mother with the power of hellfire.

"We get some rest," he said, running his hands up my arms. "After that, we'll help Silvia, and then she'll give us access to the coven that has allied with her. They'll help us free Luke's mother and we can go from there. She's from a long line of witches called Keymasters and if anyone knows what it means to prevent the destruction of worlds, it'll be her.

I let my forehead thump against Xavier's chest and he wrapped his arms around me. "Fine," I relented. "I'll listen to what Silvia has to say."

Once morning came, my hair naturally dried and smoothed to its perfect metallic sheen. I'd seen Sarah go to bed with wet hair once and I realized it was a superpower on its own what my body managed to do with unkempt strands. A woman simply did not wake up with perfect hair, but I always did. There were some perks to being a succubus, and I was glad to see I'd retained the majority of my powers after my turn and rebirth as a vampire. In fact, if anything, my powers felt stronger, more in control. My nature as a succubus would never again threaten my life, or the lives of others, and would serve me as long as I asked them to.

Silvia watched me from the end of the dining hall, sipping her coffee with a look in her eye that said she not only knew of my mystical powers, but her mischievous smirk after she'd surveyed my guys said she also knew what I'd done with them.

Luke devoured entire plates of hash browns, eggs, and strips of bacon. Meanwhile, Xavier gulped down three glasses of blood. I nursed my own glass of blood, finding myself missing regular food, but still enjoying watching Luke eat.

"So, you've made your decision?" Silvia asked after we'd gotten through the worst of our hunger. Her smug expression said she knew I'd already been convinced, but that didn't mean I wasn't going to try and strike a favorable bargain and get some information out of her while I was at it.

"First, tell me why, exactly, Derek locked our daughter down there." He'd been desperate for a child with Silvia, and once Lilith had been born, he'd put himself on a mission to bring more demons into this world. He wanted an army.

Silvia sighed and set her empty mug down. A handsome incubus servant immediately took it away. "Derek wasn't expecting our offspring to be so..." Her words drifted and her brows bunched together as she searched for the word. It was hard to pay attention to her as broad, beautiful wings swayed at her back. Had she used a normal chair, she would have been crowded, but she had opted for a stool and sat perfectly proper and straight.

"Human?" Xavier offered.

She blinked at him, then slowly nodded. "Yes, I suppose that is the word. Lilith is so wrapped up in emotion and empathy. I think it surprised him." She glanced at her wings. "I think he also was not pleased in the changes the birth brought out in me, either."

"But you weren't surprised by Lilith's nature," Luke said, dabbing away crumbs from his chin.

Silvia nodded again. "Given what I am, I expected a child of mine to have empathy, as well as compassion and all the things that come with our kind. Angels and humans share these traits, you see. There are differences, but how we feel is not one of them."

Luke listened to her more intently than I'd ever seen him listen to anyone. He was so desperate for more information about what he was, perhaps validation for why he felt the things he felt. "So, why lock her up?" he asked. "Has she become dangerous?"

Silvia shook her head. "No, quite the opposite, I'm afraid. Her emotions are eating her up from the inside and making her sick. Derek thought it an illness, so he put her into quarantine." She leaned onto the table and inched her stool back. Both Luke and Xavier stood along with her. Silvia clasped her hands at her chest as she pleaded. "It's not an illness to feel, but it will kill her if I don't teach her how to manage it. Please, help me release her."

I glanced at three women who'd entered, witches, I expected. Each of them bore a necklace with iconic rubies hanging on silver chains. Silvia walked to them and waved her hand. "May I introduce the elders of the Blood Coven."

I narrowed my eyes. "You mean, they worship the Blood Stone?"

The tallest of the three stepped forward. She had her metallic blonde hair pinned back, making her look much younger than I expected she was. She lifted her chin in defiance. "I would rather say that the Blood Stone serves us."

Silvia laughed, breaking the tension, and the other two girls standing behind the eldest lowered their hunched shoulders. "Freya. You are always so rebellious. Let's not make a bad impression with—" Silvia stopped whatever she was about to say at Xavier's threatening glare, clearing her throat before she amended, "with my new ally, Sonya."

I extended my hand, ignoring Luke's attempts to get my attention and ask me what that was all about. Silvia had nearly revealed that I was the Queen of the Damned. "Hello," I said, "it's nice to meet you, Freya."

My mother had always taught me that it was best to be polite to new supernaturals, no matter how much they terrified you, annoyed you, or made you want to punch them in the face. Freya was scoring in the latter two categories.

The witch considered my hand and narrowed her eyes, but finally took my fingers in an awkward shake as if she wasn't accustomed to the gesture. "I wish I could say the same," she offered.

Ignoring the comment, I smiled and leaned around her shoulder. "And your companions?"

She waved to the girl with impossibly red hair, either dyed or the result of a magical experiment gone wrong. "This is Olivia." She waved to the other girl, one with brilliant green eyes and a mischievous look about her, framed by her midnight hair. "And this is Iris."

"Great," Silvia announced and swept to the doorway. "Now that you're all acquainted, let's get this done."

Silvia guided us through a maze of halls and descending stairways until I was hopelessly lost. I would have felt nervous, except after the night I'd had with Xavier and Luke, my power was at its peak, rejuvenated by cementing two members of my bond and keeping them close to my side. They easily walked on either side of me, their smooth movements a deception to the lethal protectiveness they harbored for me.

Silvia explained that the witches of the Blood Coven were specialized in the magic that governed the Blood Stone. It was also the magic that governed a vampire's powers, but Xavier didn't seem concerned. I decided that the witches merely knew how to tap into it, that source that bled into our world. I was starting to piece it together now.

That source was Hell itself, and with my help, the Blood Coven could tap into it and free the demonspawn.

As we descended, polished walls gave way to crumbling rock. We kept going, our path lit only by the few flashlights we'd brought, until we reached our destination.

Two wide iron doors glowed red with power and bathed the tunnels in a supernatural glow. Heat bled into the tunnel and made sweat gather at my neckline.

"How did Derek lock her in here?" I asked, my voice echoing against the stones.

"He has a Blood Stone, as well," Silvia lamented. "I'm afraid he's managed to find a witch who can use it."

Freya's face scrunched, augmented by the shadows cast by the flashlight I pointed at her feet. "Our Coven has split. Only Olivia, Iris, and myself, are still loyal to Lady Silvia. The rest have sided with Derek, seduced by his claims for a world where supernaturals can live out in the open." She curled her lip with distaste.

"And you don't want that?" I ventured.

Freya glared at me. "Humans wouldn't know what to do with you, but they have plenty of experience in dealing with witches. We'd be the first to feel their wrath."

Shame tugged at my shoulders. I hadn't thought of that. Witches had been plagued by humans for thousands of years. Even the male muses were unable to fully protect them from the vicious nature of humanity against their kind.

"So, how is this going to work?" I asked.

Silvia flared her wings and backed away, giving the witches space as they surrounded me. Luke and Xavier glowered at them, not budging from my side.

"We are witches of the Blood Coven. We can draw your magic to break the seal that has been placed on this door, but it'll hurt," Freya said, and I believed her.

Luke inched closer to me. "You don't have to do this," he whispered. "We don't need their help to save my mother. I'm sure we can get her out on our own."

I rolled my eyes. "Just last night you were all about helping Silvia. Now you've changed your mind?"

He shook his head and his hair brushed over his face. "Maybe you were right. Maybe I'm blinded by my desire to understand that there are others like me." He took my hand in his. "You've shown me I'm not alone. I don't need anyone else like me. I have you."

I broke his gaze to get Xavier's opinion. "And you? Have you changed your mind?"

His red eyes glowed, battling the magic the door spewed out at us with his own aura. "I believe you should do what you feel is right, Sonya. That demonspawn in there is your daughter. Do you wish to help her?"

I hadn't really thought about it. The demonspawn didn't feel like my daughter. I'd barely met her only a couple of times, and none of them had gone very well. I didn't know her at all, but was that really her fault?

With a long sigh, I grabbed Xavier's hand on my left and squeezed Luke's hand on my right. With them, I could face anything.

The witches fidgeted. The red-head spoke first. "Are you sure you want to be holding hands with Sonya while we access her magic? You'll feel what she feels."

Both my men held my hands tighter and gave immediate nods. They weren't going anywhere.

"Then we begin," Freya announced, and pressed her hand to my chest where the power of my Blood Stone rested.

Instant heat spread through my body, and when Olivia and Iris pressed their hands over Freya's, it intensified until it felt like my insides were melting.

I grit my teeth together and growled as the magic ruthlessly tore through me, building until it wrenched free and spilled into the witches. I couldn't contain my fangs anymore and they extended as I unlatched my jaw with a hiss of pain. Only Olivia flinched away, but at a curt word from Freya, pressed her hand back again.

Once they had extracted enough power from me, their hands glowed red and dripped with molten energy. They chanted in low, monotone voices as they turned and pressed their hands against the door. Light flared at their touch and their chanting escalated until a low rumble swept through the tunnels.

"It's working," Silvia whispered, excitement making her wings flutter.

I shivered, suddenly feeling cold, and released my guys to wrap my arms around myself. They were shaking too, and Xavier drew me into his chest. Even though Luke was the one with healing powers, Xavier seemed to recover first, his skin growing hot as he tucked me closer to him.

"Luke," I managed to say, my jaw trying to chatter, but failing with my fangs in the way, "are you okay?"

He nodded, but his lips were blue. "I'll be fine. Just let Xavier warm you up. I need to heal on my own."

I nodded, then turned my attention back to the door that reverberated with power. The witches threw their heads back, shouting their incantation now, and one final shockwave burst through and the entire tunnel went dark.

The door unlatched, and I felt it more than I heard it as the displacement of air pressure hit my chest. A musty scent burst out into the tunnel as if the room beyond had been sealed off for a hundred years. Two red eyes glowed in the distance and blinked at us, and I knew we'd been too late.

My daughter had given in to her demon side. She'd gone insane.

DEMONSPAWN DAUGHTER

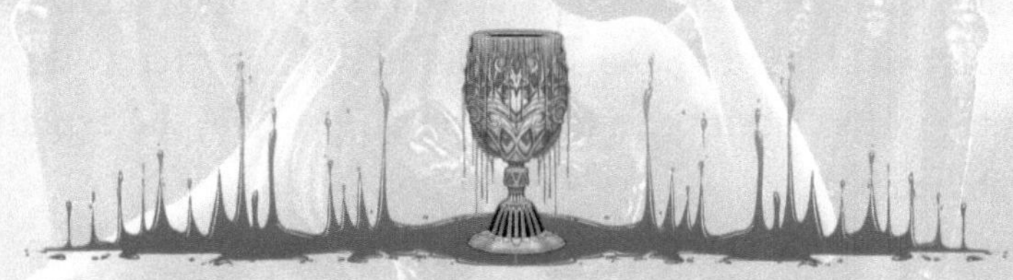

Sonya

Subduing the demonspawn proved difficult, mostly because my go-to response for dealing with enemies would be one: seduce them to death, or two: seduce someone else to kill my enemy for me.

When it came to my misguided daughter, I didn't know what to do. She launched at us, her demonic side having taken over and her red eyes wild as her teeth extended like a row of shark teeth. I turned on a flashlight just in time to see her deadly bite coming straight for me.

Luke launched in front of me and held out his arm. Lilith chomped down and blood sprayed everywhere.

"Silvia!" he shouted. "Do something!"

The angel just stared at the crazed demonspawn, stunned. Finally, she flared her wings and silver power I'd never seen before swept through her. Had we not been in a dark tunnel, maybe I wouldn't have noticed it. She pushed power into her voice as she commanded the demonspawn. "Stop!"

As if she'd been punched, the demonspawn unlatched her vicious bite and doubled over. She gripped her stomach and the most pitiful sound came from her throat as she crumpled to the floor. Blisters spread over her skin and she whimpered, suddenly much more helpless than she'd been before.

The nasty bite on Luke's arm stopped bleeding, but it would take a few days for it to heal. He winced as he ripped off his shirt and wrapped it around the wound. "It'll heal better if it's not trying to protect itself from the bacteria in the air," he explained as I watched him.

Xavier was the first to take action. He scooped up the demonspawn, whose welts were only getting worse, and gave Silvia a stern glare. "So, we've freed the monster," he declared, obviously none too happy about it. "What do you want to do with her now where she won't be of harm to herself, or others?"

Silvia sighed. "We'll create another prison for her, but this time, she's not going to be alone." She waved at the witches who pressed themselves against the stone walls. I imagined they'd expended all of their power breaking the seal on the door and weren't equipped to take on a demonspawn.

"Come, girls. You have one more spell to cast."

Silvia spun on her heel and marched through the tunnels, but her wings flared and her once light steps pounded against the stone. I didn't think this was what she'd been hoping for when we freed her daughter.

Our daughter.

I glanced at the girl now unconscious in Xavier's arms. The lesions were already healing, but she'd taken on more of a human appearance after whatever Silvia had done to her. Long, midnight waves of hair swept over Xavier's arms and her pink, plump lips most certainly marked her as a daughter of mine. The fangs were gone and her cheeks struggled to take on a rosy hue. Her slight frame was attractive for her proportions and if she hadn't been in a fit of bloodlust just a moment before, I would have thought her a beautiful, innocent girl.

"The poor thing," Xavier whispered as he shifted her slight weight in his arms. "I hope there's something Silvia can do for her."

My heart pinched to hear that Xavier cared. If a ruthless, ancient vampire could care about a demonspawn girl, perhaps there was room in my heart to care for her too.

Once we exited the tunnels, a group of anxious servants awaited us. Silvia snapped orders at them to get her chamber ready and they sprang into action. By the time we climbed the stairs and reached Silvia's bedroom, the servants had already brought a multitude of jars filled with glowing, silver water. I'd never seen anything like it.

"What is that?" I whispered to Luke.

His eyes went wide as he watched the first of the servants dump the water over the walls. "I believe that's holy water infused with Angelstone."

I gulped. Where was Silvia getting all this stuff?

"Xavier, if you would be so kind, please give the child to me," Silvia said and held out her arms.

"Wait," I protested, then leaned in closer to the girl. She still slept and looked so innocent. My heart twisted again and something inside of me compelled me to press a kiss to her forehead. She moaned and stirred, but didn't open her eyes.

"Quickly now," Silvia insisted.

Reluctantly, I eased away and Luke took my hand. I watched as Silvia took our daughter and backed into the room. I gasped when she shifted through an invisible veil and her wings transformed to the purest of white. Her skin paled and her eyes lost all their color.

The girl in her arms likewise changed, bucking and crying out as if in pain, but then slumped and her arms hung limply.

Silvia gave the witches a nod. "Now, please seal this door. This room has been enchanted with holy water and Angelstone. With my presence, Lilith won't be able to lose herself to her demonic side. I'll find a way to help her through it, but we need time." She straightened. "Seal the door so that she can't get out. She's going to try once she wakes up."

Freya didn't budge. "But, My Lady, that means—"

"You will not question me," Silvia snapped and hugged the demonspawn girl closer to her chest. "I brought her into this world and she is my responsibility. I will see to it that she is not lost to us forever." Silver flashed in her eyes. "I can't keep her under for much longer. Do it now!"

Freya flinched and I had the feeling that Silvia didn't often raise her voice. Moving to me, Freya gave me a grimace. "I'm sorry, Sonya, but I'll need one more boost to create the seal. If you don't mind."

I nodded and tugged away the edges of my shirt, exposing my chest. A bruise spread out where they'd extracted power from me once already, but if Silvia was going to lock herself in a room with our daughter, the least I could do was give her the power she needed to see this through. "Take what you need. Don't hold back."

Freya nodded and glanced at my guys. They grabbed my hands before I could protest.

Xavier bared his teeth. "You're going to need us for this," he insisted.

I didn't have time to struggle. The witches placed their hands over my chest again and began a new chant, this time one that made the previous encounter seem like it'd just been practice. Red hot waves swept through me and sweat broke out at my neckline. My veins illuminated with the red, molten power, and then it burst through my chest and into the witches.

All of it.

My vision blurred as a cold so final filled me that I was sure I was going to black out. I swayed on my feet, glad for the grips of my men holding onto me to keep me upright. What little heat they could offer bled through their fingers and into my body, only for it to be swept away in an instant as the spell sucked all power out of me.

"Don't take too much!" Luke cried. "You're going to kill her!"

"Almost there," Freya said through gritted teeth. "And… done."

The witches unlatched from me, their skin detaching with a soft *pop*. I fell to my knees and my guys came tumbling down with me. None of us were able to keep our heads up.

I watched through blurred vision as the witches raised molten hands to the room, sealing it with streaks of red power. They didn't need a doorway to enchant. The opening shimmered and solidified, perfectly translucent but thick like glass.

Lilith finally stirred, as if sensing her entrapment, and snarled. She shook her head, seeming dazed, but everything about her was human. Green eyes. Black hair. Normal teeth which she bared at us like an animal. She clawed her short, pink nails against the barrier and screamed.

I'd never seen Silvia look so forlorn as she sank to her knees. Her wings crumpled into ash and her skin went impossibly pale and I realized she'd reached the extent of her magic to imprison her daughter. "Please, sweet child. Do not blame yourself for what's to come. This was the only way."

Lilith blinked at her angelic mother, opening her mouth to say something, but then Silvia closed her eyes and slumped onto her side. I had a feeling that she would not be getting up again.

I succumbed to unconsciousness shortly after watching Silvia's sacrifice. I think she always knew that she'd have to give her life to save her demonspawn daughter, but it still wasn't fair.

"I was wrong about her," I said mournfully into my hands. I'd recovered, finding myself in our bedroom again. The first thing I did was crawl into one of the chairs at the edge of the room and cry my eyes out. I'd never felt like more of a failure in my life.

Luke squeezed my knee. Xavier was down in the sitting room discussing our terms with the loyal members of the Blood Coven. Now that Silvia was dead, it would be up to Xavier to make sure they kept their end of the bargain. If anyone could negotiate on my behalf, it would be the ancient vampire who shared the Blood Coven's source of power.

"You were right to be skeptical," Luke said, his words low and soft. "After everything you've been through, it's smart to question someone you don't know." He drew my face out of my hands and gave me a sweet kiss. "I'm glad you were wrong about her, though. We were able to help your daughter."

"But did we, really?" I asked, my cheeks still hot from tears. "She's trapped in that room with her dead mother and she probably blames me for it." I clenched my fingers into fists. "She *should* blame me. I'm the reason she's in there."

"That's right," Luke said, sinking to his knees and running his hands up my waist. I teetered on the edge of the chair, wanting to be close to him, but feeling as if I didn't deserve any source of comfort just now. "You are the reason she's there," he confirmed, "and the reason she's not trapped in a dark dungeon where she would have gone mad."

Tears brimmed again and I brushed them away.

That's when pain stabbed through my lowest rune that

connected me to Xavier and I jolted upright. "Xavier," I whispered, and then rushed out of the room.

Luke followed hot on my heels, shouting at me to stop, but blind panic took over. Something was wrong. Xavier was about to be taken from me and I couldn't let that happen. I scurried down the stairs, my feet fumbling over themselves and I gripped on the rail to keep from falling. Once I reached the ground floor, I saw what had made me panic.

Fucking portals.

The red swirling portal bore a gaping hole in this reality and my stomach dropped because I knew what was on the other side. Xavier's form blurred, having already been sucked into it and he staggered to his knees on the dusty, red hot sands from where he'd been thrown. A lake of molten lava rushed far too close to him, threatening to set him on fire and his skin was already smoking from the heat.

From the power of Hell.

The witches surrounded the portal and chanted, slowly closing it in on him. This was why they'd taken so much power from me. They aimed to break my bond with the vampire. I didn't understand their motives, but I didn't have time to give them the beating they deserved. I set my jaw and launched myself at the portal.

I hit the ground hard and heat blasted me from all directions. Instead of sweltering, it made me feel rejuvenated. Any pain or weakness I'd had was now gone and I jumped to my feet just in time to be slammed by Luke's body as he jumped through the portal just before it snapped closed.

The portal was gone and the roar of the lake of fire drowned out anything my guys were trying to say to me. I surveyed the landscape, but it was barren. Red sands that went on forever, a lake of fire that separated us from a darkness on the other side, and then I looked up and sucked in a breath.

A rolling black cloud with fingers that stretched over the sky. It's exactly what I'd seen in my nightmares hundreds of times. This was it. This was the destroyer of worlds, and everything Xavier had said about me was true.

I was supposed to save Hell.

THE SEVEN CIRCLES OF HELL

Sonya

"Okay, new plan," Luke announced as he scratched at a rune that glowed on his chest. The magic had activated, allowing us to hear one another over the fury of the river. "We'll save my mother after we save ourselves." He squinted at the landscape and I was so relieved to see that our bond protected him. His hair fussed around his face, but he wasn't burning. "Where the hell are we?"

Xavier chuckled, having recovered from his near incineration. He pulled aside his shirt to reveal a swirling rune that glowed just above his heart. "The first ring of fire, I'd imagine," he said.

Luke snapped his gaze to the vampire. "What?"

Xavier grinned. His fangs extended, but I sensed that he was excited. It was as if he'd wanted this to happen. He looked down and carved a line in the sands. Red liquid bubbled up. He bent and ran his finger through it, drawing it to his mouth and fluttering his eyes closed. "Blood. That confirms where we are. This is the layer of gluttony." When I balked at him, he shrugged. "It should come as no surprise that my sin is gluttony, my dear. I am a vampire, after all. We are known for our indulgence." He stood and wiped the blood onto his pants, leaving a deep crimson streak. "We'll find what we're looking for on the third layer. Come on. This way."

Luke and I stared after him as he approached the lake of fire. I shouted when he stuck his foot into the molten waves, but then he waded into it and turned to us, his red eyes alight with mischief.

"You bastard!" I shouted and ran after him.

He grabbed me the moment I was within reach and dunked me into the flames. I screeched in panic, but the lapping molten waves didn't hurt. In fact… they felt good.

I hit his chest in retaliation. "You scared me half to death! What were you thinking?"

He ignored me and waved at Luke to join us. "Come, angel. This is your one chance to experience hell for yourself and not get burned." Xavier's gaze dipped. "It's also where you'll get to face your darkest sin and finally come out the victor. It's about time, wouldn't you say?"

Luke blinked and his gaze bounced between the two of us. The fires had disintegrated our clothes and Xavier's rune bled with light. Luke looked down at his own rune and realization dawned on his face.

"Sonya has seven runes on her body," he said, the words full of accusation and horror.

I glanced at Xavier. He's the one that had told me Luke wasn't ready to hear what I was yet, but here we were, in Hell itself, and clearly it was my bonded magic that was keeping them both alive.

"Yes," Xavier confirmed, the mischief leaving his face. He released me and waded further into the river downstream. "I'll explain it later. For now, you need to come with us, or you can sit there and wait until we're far enough away that the bond loses its strength and you burn. Your choice, angel."

"Wait, Xavier!" I shrieked, but he kept walking. He was making me choose. The further he got from me, the weaker our bond became. He paused when I imagined the bond was weak enough that the flames would start to threaten him and he turned, narrowing his eyes at me to make my choice.

My breath started to come in ragged gasps. "Luke," I called, but he wasn't listening to me. He collapsed to his knees and pawed at the rune on his chest. I tried again, pushing my desperation into his name. "Luke!"

Finally, his blue eyes snapped up. I'd never seen him look so betrayed and my heart twisted. "Why didn't you tell me?" he asked.

"Luke. I didn't know until just last night. Xavier told me not to—"

Luke growled. To my surprise he struggled to his feet and waded into the lake of fire. He wrapped an arm around my waist and dragged me with him as I squeaked in protest. "Come on. The bastard just wants you all to himself. He wanted me to reject you and go kill myself. Well that's not going to happen. We're following him deeper into hell and we're going to work this out." His gaze snapped to me, full of danger and determination. "One way, or another."

I blinked at him. I didn't think Xavier would want me all to himself like that. Sure, maybe he was holding back information, but he wanted this bond just as much as I did. The ancient magic connected us all together and made us stronger. "Luke, you'll see that you're wrong about him," I whispered before bringing myself out of his embrace. I took him by the arm and dragged him deeper into the river. Xavier glowered at us and then turned once we were close enough that the bond kept him safe and we could keep moving. "Xavier," I pleaded. "Tell him. You want us to go to the third layer of hell. Why the third? Why not the second?"

He answered without missing a beat. "Because the first layer of hell is attuned to me. The second will be attuned to Luke. We have no need for either of those two, since we're already here. The third layer is where we'll find the sin of envy." He flashed me a toothy grin, fangs and all. "Your human no doubt fits that role and we can't very well resolve your curse without him."

Getting through the first circle of hell was easy, sort of, although a bit humiliating. At the end of the lake of fire was a drop off where the waterfall ended in a pool of blood. Don't ask me how that worked. Hell didn't make a lot of sense. Oh and the kicker, how was I to get out of the first ring of Hell? All I had to do was jump into this particular pool of blood… and drink a little bit of it.

Okay, a lot.

After an awkward scramble down the waterfall that transformed mid-way from molten flames to sticky blood, I landed and frowned as I slid across a smooth surface, as if this pool were encased by a marble floor. I stared down at the soft ripples sent out by the constant pouring from the waterfall. I gave Xavier a raised brow. "You want me… to drink?"

"We're in Hell," Xavier reminded me. "Not everything here works as it should. The realm you're in is dictated by the sin or spell that created it." He flashed me a smile and ran his tongue up one of his fangs. "I've had a lot of blood in my life, darling. You'll have to take that blood from me if you want to get us out of here." He pointed. "Start drinking and don't stop until it's gone."

When I glowered at him, he sighed. "Just, try it. I promise it'll work and it won't hurt you."

Grumbling that I thought this was a ridiculous idea, I gathered the blood with my cupped hands and gulped it down.

The waterfall continued to fill the pool with blood and no matter how much of the liquid I splashed into my mouth, I couldn't get the levels any lower than my ankles. I looked up at him again as panic filled me.

"Keep going!" Xavier encouraged.

I held my stomach which was starting to roll with nausea.

"This is ridiculous!" Luke roared and surprised me by getting out of the river. He wrapped his fingers around one of the larger rocks that he could barely wrap his arms around. His knuckles turned white and his muscles bulged until he growled and ripped the stone out. With a grunt he tossed it in front of the river, stemming the flow of fire. He narrowed his eyes at Xavier until the vampire sighed and helped him.

Soon the waterfall was dammed and the steady stream of blood eased off. I started again, drinking my fill. This time I wasn't getting sick. It was as if I could drink all of the blood in the world and it'd only make me stronger. Even if we were in Hell and the laws of physics—or stomachs—didn't apply, it seemed that a little help from members in my bond could get me out of sticky situations.

Once the levels had lowered far enough for me to see my feet, the bottom opened up and swallowed me whole. Luke and Xavier jumped in and came tumbling after me and then we were in the second circle of Hell—Luke's domain.

We landed on more sand. I tried dragging my foot through the grains, but it was all just dry, caked dirt. A cheer roared and lights flared, and I snapped my gaze up to see that we were in an arena—and we were the sport.

The cheers that came from the stands shrieked at us with

demonic cries and hoots. Claws and glistening daggers waved in the air, which I guessed was a demon's mimicry of those silly inflatable tubes people liked to bring to crowded events.

"Xavier?" I asked, my lilt going up with panic.

Xavier struggled to his feet, his ruby eyes blazing in the dim light as he took in our surroundings. He scooped Luke up, but that's when I realized they weren't naked, and neither was I.

I ran my fingers over a sleek, but revealing, getup of silver and velvety red armor that covered my vital organs. My fingers caught at the abdomen which was notched out to allow my runes to be displayed. Only Luke and Xavier's runes on my skin gleamed with life, leaving the rest of my runes fluttering with dull hunger after I'd been separated from the others for so long.

Both the vampire and the angel boasted gleaming armor with translucent red hues, as if they were covered in a sleek layer of gemstones. Luke's taut muscles moved underneath the armor, vaguely visible through the translucent layer. "What bullshit is this?" he growled at the vampire. "You want to battle us to the death?"

Xavier huffed a laugh. "I don't think we're supposed to battle one another." He pointed at a gate that cracked open and a row of men stepped out into the dim light. "We have to defeat them."

One by one, each man took off his helmet, making me throw my hand in front of my face to stifle a gasp.

Luke's face.

All of them had Luke's face.

My Luke staggered as a sword appeared in his hand in a flash of supernatural light. He gave me a wild glance which dipped down to my runes. "Sonya, I'm so sorry."

I followed his gaze and touched the rune on the left of my stomach. It burned red. I knew what Luke's symbol meant now. It was the demonic symbol for anger.

This was Luke's Hell, and we were living in it. The row of

armed men roared and unsheathed their weapons, then came running straight at us.

My eyes went wide. I didn't know how to fight a bunch of Luke-lookalikes. I didn't know how to fight at all. There was only one thing I was good at and without thinking I stretched my fingers out and released my power. The red fog of seduction rolled over the sands, lazy and languid compared to the men who stormed towards us, but the moment they barreled into the fog, their cries died in their throats and they choked, falling to their knees.

"Good work," Xavier whispered. "You can save Luke from his worst sin, Sonya. Keep it up."

My stomach burned with all the blood I'd devoured to save Xavier from his sin. Hell wasn't the same as the natural world. Here, it was about parody and rules. In order to save him from gluttony, I had to be a glutton myself.

Now, in the circle of Hell where the sin of anger burned hot, the crowds wanted bloodshed and violence. There was only one thing that I knew worked better than violence at releasing anger…

Sex.

I gasped when the lust hit me. All of the men who resembled Luke snapped their gazes onto me and began peeling away their armor. It was working.

Luke—my Luke—gave me a nervous glance. "Sonya? Are you sure you know what you're doing?"

Did I know what I was doing? I wanted to let out the hysterical laugh I was holding in. I was about to have a mad orgy with a bunch of Lukes. I couldn't imagine anything I'd want more.

With a grin I offered him my hand. "This is how we'll solve your anger, angel. This is what angelstone and your kind need most of all."

Angels needed to get fucking laid.

The first hand of a Luke-lookalike ran up my naked leg and I shivered. So many dirty images filtered through my mind about the pleasure I was going to endure, as well as the pleasure I was going to give all the versions of Luke that lusted after me.

Then, just as the hand reached the apex of my thigh, I realized one slight problem.

My armor worked as a chastity belt.

The first Hell-Luke ran his fingers over the smooth armor, growling with frustration and then trying for my breasts, but those were secure as well.

I gave Xavier a panicked glance. Luke had helped us in the first circle of Hell. I hoped there was something Xavier had in mind that could help. Maybe he could smash my armor?

By the grin that spread across his face, he had a wicked idea—one I wasn't going to like.

"What is it? What do I do?" I asked, panic rising in my voice as yet another Luke pawed at me, only to growl at me with frustration when I couldn't be touched. I tried to see if I could offer pleasure by reaching for his cock, but the armor was even more secure around his waist than my own.

"My dear, you're a vampire now," Xavier said as if that solved everything.

Real-Luke wasn't getting it either. He raised his sword. "Well if Sonya can't seduce them, then—"

Xavier snatched the weapon out of Luke's hand, taking advantage of him with his vampiric speed. "No," he stated flatly. "No violence. That'll just trap us here forever. Your sin isn't like mine. Gluttony can be filled. Anger, however, must be diffused."

Luke gave him a raised brow. "But the way we got out of gluttony was to be… gluttonous. Why would anger be different?"

Xavier shook his head. "Each circle of Hell works differently." He bared his fangs. "My sin has been my burden to bear for thousands of years. I caused death and drained the world dry. I hated what I was." He glanced at me. "Sonya shares my burden now. I'm no longer alone, and it has freed me from my Hell."

Luke frowned. "So I'm trapped by anger? I need her to share my rage?" He slapped his hands against his armor. "I don't want this rage! I don't want it anymore! I'm so angry all the time. At my mother, at Detective Anderson—"

"At yourself," I whispered and Luke went somber.

I gazed at each of his lookalikes and I spotted small differences between them. Each had a scar in different places. A jagged hole where an eye should have been. A raking scar down one of his legs. Perhaps this was his anger for every wound he'd healed from, emotional and physical. I glanced up, spotting more men pouring out of the gaping hole of the arena and the crowd cheered, having gone deathly silent when I'd first spilled my seducing fog.

"Your bite," Xavier whispered. "You can give pleasure with your bite."

My eyes went wide and memories flooded back of when Xavier had shared that most intimate moment with me. A blood-kiss filled with passion, rage, and love. That was how I was going to save Luke, whether Hell wanted me to or not.

The first fake-Luke that was growing the most frustrated gritted his teeth and his hand slipped around my throat and began to squeeze. I opened my mouth and bared my fangs at him. "Come closer," I whispered, pushing all of my seduction and power into the command.

He lurched, no doubt his cock standing salute in his pants, but he obeyed me, coming in close enough that his lips brushed mine.

I ran my fingers down the hard edge of his neck, following

my touch with soft kisses, and then I pricked him with my teeth. The instinct to flood his veins with my vampiric poison kicked in and I latched on harder. I was like a snake, venom in me ready to be injected into my prey.

Fake-Luke slumped at my side, his eyelids fluttering closed in bliss as he moaned with relief and his rage ebbed out of him as if it'd never existed at all.

I scrambled to my feet and took the next one, biting down without reservation with the slick poison still wet on my fangs

Working my way through the entire army, I put down Luke's pain, his anger and his rage that he couldn't let go, not just with the powers of a succubus, but with the vampiric power of the Queen of the Damned.

When I finished, the long row of fake-Luke's writhed in sated pleasure, their moans filling the arena, and then the bottom dropped out and the crowd booed us as we dropped into the third circle of Hell.

It was time to get Nate to join in on the fun.

DESTRUCTION IN DETROIT

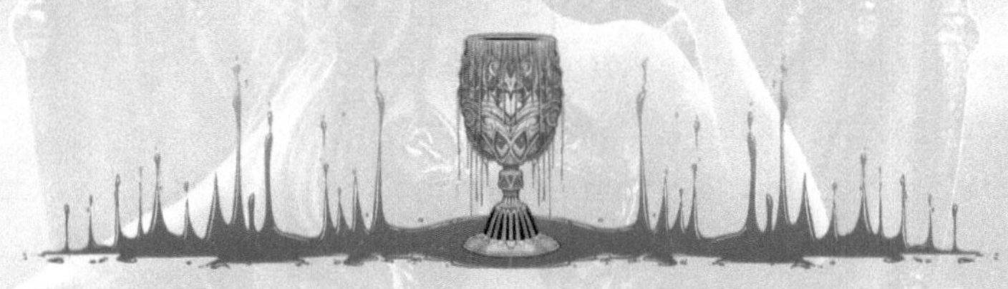

Nate

I was so fucking sick and tired of hiding. The only thing that kept me from going outside was the snow. I fucking hated snow. And Detroit. And the world.

"Will you stop brooding?" came a familiar British lilt.

I glowered at Sonya's grandmother as she sipped tea. Fucking tea. How cliché.

Instead of responding to her, I squeezed myself into a dark corner—my favorite brooding corner—and stared outside as clumps of snow fell to the ground. My stomach twisted wondering if Sonya was all right, if our plan had worked, if the world was really going to shit or if we'd somehow make it through this.

If I'd see her again.

Sonya's grandmother, who I had come to call Grans—she wouldn't give me a normal name to call her by other than Miss D'Ange—had helped me hatch a crazy plan to stop my father from taking over the world. A single television blubbered on about a riot in Shanghai that was finally dying down, as well as an unexplained massive earthquake in Venice, all of which I knew were lies. Male muses have been very good at keeping the supernatural community on the down low, and even I was impressed at how a single male muse was able to cover up such catastrophic events. There was no way Apollo would cover any of this up. Quite the opposite. He was trying to expose the community and working with my father to do it.

Dragons revolting in Shanghai.

Derek and Apollo declaring war on the vampires of Venice.

I knew the truth, not because I was supernatural—I'm too damn mortal for my own good—but I had connections.

A rapid knocking sounded at the door and I launched from my brooding spot to answer it. One of those connections was here. Fucking finally.

Grans rolled her eyes at me and took another dainty sip of her tea. "You really didn't have to call another one. I insist that I'm fine and—"

"It's not all about you, Grans," I barked, although I was more worried about the ancient succubus than I'd admit out loud. I turned from her so she couldn't see my expression. I was never very good at hiding my feelings from women. Opening the door, relief flooded me to see that not one, but two witches had answered my summons.

The first one, a tall pink-haired woman lifted her chin at me, looking every bit the same as I remembered her. Silver earrings dangled all the way down to the elegant curves of her neck. "Nathanial," she said, playing my name across her tongue with affection.

I smiled and yanked her into a hug. "Hey, Pink." She was like a sister to me. We'd grown up together and Pink was the main reason I had so many great contacts. She always saved my butt when I was in trouble, and I was never more grateful for her than I was just now.

Another witch stepped out from behind her shadow, a younger girl with flat, chocolate waves that folded her hands in front of her dress. I would have thought her completely harmless, had I not spotted the glimmer of magic sparking across her skin.

Most humans would never notice it, or play it off as their imagination. The effect was faint and gone before I had a chance to really focus on it. Perhaps it was because I was the son of the Incubus King, or maybe it was just because I knew what to look for, but I could spot a fledgling witch, especially when she had as much power as this one.

Pink squeezed my arm and beamed down at the girl, who I guessed was her latest protégé. "Nate, this is Emily. Emily, meet Nate."

I offered my hand, but the girl stared at it until I let it fall. "Well, it's nice to meet you Emily," I said, trying to keep my tone friendly. I gave Pink a sideways glance, and she gave me a slight nod, confirming my suspicions. This girl had just inherited her magic recently and was still in shock. A witch's initiation was pretty brutal.

I tried not to cringe as I guided the witches into the tiny studio apartment. Grans could have gotten us something nicer, but the outskirts of Detroit looked like a war zone and it kept our low profile to stay in a shack rather than anything remotely nice. We couldn't go too far into the surrounding cities, or else we might get noticed. People tended to stay out of Detroit, for the most part. I'd never seen a place with streets so empty, with the division of economy quite clear. Tesla and Audis sped by, on their way to downtown high-rises for work, and they'd be sure to leave before nightfall. Trying to keep up beside them were rusted and beat-up sedans better suited for a junkyard than anything else. Those were the residents, and the people that would help us blend in.

Pink nestled into one of the couches, not seeming to mind the small strings that frayed from it, and gladly accepted a teacup from Grans. "Thank you, Miss D'Ange, how nice it is to see you again."

Grans gave the witch a nod, but I could tell how weak she was. Dark circles shadowed under her once bright eyes and deepening wrinkles stretched across her cheeks. It must be so strange, to cause human deterioration for so many years, and one day succumb to it yourself.

"Thank you, dear. How are the preparations going?" Grans gave me a glance, her brows furrowing. "Nathanial hasn't been too demanding, I hope."

I glared. "You act like this was my idea."

Emily stepped to Pink's side, continuing to keep her hands clasped in front of her, even when Grans offered her a cup of tea. The girl just stared at it until she took it away. Finally, she spoke, her words soft and fragile. "Pain," she remarked.

Pink squeezed the girl's arm. "Yes, Emily. There's a lot of pain in this room."

The slightest of smiles lighted on the girl's face at Pink's praise.

I nestled into my brooding corner, but I wasn't watching the snow this time. I kept my gaze pinned on the girl whose skin glittered with magic. I realized she wasn't talking because she was concentrating. Even now, she was performing a spell to help extract the toxins from the suffering succubus. Her magic searched the room with silver fingers, tickling through Grans' hair and slipping over her sunken-in cheeks. No one seemed to notice it, so I flicked my gaze back to Pink and narrowed my eyes. "It was Grans' idea to extract the toxin." The succubus could have survived for some time longer, but now the illness was spreading through her body at an alarming rate. We'd opened a wound, and the only thing we could do for her was take some of the toxin out.

Emily shot her head up at me like I'd set off a gun and I winced. "The girls are dead," she whispered, but she might as well have shouted it the way the accusation thundered in my skull.

Grans cleared her throat and loudly set her teacup into its saucer. "Yes, we infected human females with my toxins. The same girls which the Incubus King fed upon. They would have died, with or without our help."

Emily shifted her gaze to the succubus. "But you chose them."

Grans pressed her lips into a thin line. It was true, but I understood her logic. It's why I'd helped her, but it didn't change how wrong it all felt. We were the ones who'd sent those girls to their deaths, and even though someone else would have taken their place had I failed to meet my father's demands to find him new thralls, we'd still been the ones to do it.

A sweeping shot of the destruction in Venice came on the TV and I snapped up the remote, turning up the volume. "This is why Grans poisoned those girls," I explained. The prompter was going on about the phenomenon, but the witches knew exactly what had happened. The supernatural community was at war and my father was leading the charge. "We can't let him get away with this."

Pink frowned and crossed her legs, taking another sip of her tea before she spoke. She made a face, the tea likely too bitter for her taste. She always did have a sweet tooth. "And that's why I helped you, Nathanial, but it's time I bring more of the coven in on this now that it's done." She glanced at Grans. "Miss D'Ange is only going to deteriorate faster. She needs a witch with her at all times." She nodded. "And that's what Emily will do for her as long as it's required.

Grans began to protest, but Pink held up a hand.

"I'm not questioning why you've brought Emily here," I explained, "I just don't know if someone so... if she's ready to hear about all of this." The girl was already giving me a horrified look with those wide, glittering eyes of hers. Magic slipped from her freely, out of control and in a frenzy. A ringing bounced around in my head from the magical overdose and I stuck a finger in my ear. "I am mortal, you know. If she freaks out, there's not much I can do about it."

Pink slipped her hand over Emily's shoulder and gave the girl a squeeze, calming her magic with effortless ease. "It's okay, darling. Now, remember why I brought you here?"

Emily bit her lip and nodded, slinking over to Grans and offered her hand.

The succubus considered it for a moment before taking Emily's tiny fingers into her grasp, then she went rigid as light flared between them.

I moved to stop her, but Pink held out a hand and gave me a stern look.

Curling my fingers into fists, I watched as it happened all over again. A succubus was meant to draw in sexual energy, their main source of drawing the life-giving force that lives in mortals. The soul is an endless source of power, but it is more like a battery, slowly going empty and returning to the source to be recharged. A succubus draws on that power, eventually killing a mortal victim where their soul is forced to leave the body it had chosen for this lifetime. However, what I was witnessing now was the direct opposite of that. A reverse sharing of power. This succubus, Miss D'Ange, she'd fed on so many lives and outlived too many mortals. The power in her had become toxic, slowly devouring her from the inside, although she didn't want anyone to know. It was a rare condition, one that only happened to the most ancient of supernaturals that fed to survive.

Vampires could purge themselves by sleeping and naturally rebuilding their stores, but one of the succubi, they didn't have such an option. They protected themselves by building a shield around the toxins that built up inside. A succubus could stave off the toxin for hundreds of years, but even Grans was reaching her limit.

Instead of allowing that toxic energy to destroy her from the inside, she decided to make some use of it, even if it sped up the process of her own death. Pink had already helped us put the toxic energy into the mortal girls my father had devoured on his trip to Shanghai, and now we were going to do it again.

It hadn't been enough. Derek was still alive and he had to be stopped.

Black ooze dripped from Grans' nose and I grimaced. She buckled over and gagged as the toxin fell in gobbled droplets. Instead of hitting the ground, it lingered in the air as Emily chanted, transforming the sickness into tiny shards.

When she was done, the shards fell into her palm, and she offered them to me. Her innocent eyes gazed up at me, as if that had been the most normal thing in the world.

I cursed and took out a handkerchief, opening it for her to drop them in. No way I was going to touch one of those things.

Death shards. Just as much fun as they sounded.

"There," Pink said with approval, "Emily is a natural, wouldn't you say?"

I glowered at her as I folded the shards safely into the cloth and tucked them into my back pocket. "You okay, Emily?" I asked, ignoring Pink. The witch forgot what it was like to be young.

The girl put on a brave face for me, but I was really good at reading people. She was standing a little bit too straight, and her fingers curled into fists briefly before she opened her hands again. She nodded, but I'd seen enough.

Glancing at Pink again, I narrowed my eyes. "Outside, now."

I put on four layers before venturing onto Detroit's frozen streets. The only nice thing about the cold was that it kept most of the undesirables indoors. I shuffled my way through the snow as Pink walked by my side, wearing only a light coat. Magic hummed around her, creating a shield that would be invisible to most mortals and would keep her warm. She glanced at me, glowering just long enough for me to know that she had more than enough power to keep me warm, if she so chose, but she let me freeze.

"You know what I'm going to say," I began.

She sighed. "We have so many new recruits, Nathanial, and you have no idea what it's like for them. The echoes of Death have been building for years and it's about to come crashing down on our heads." She looked up, her brows knotting with concern as if she feared the sky would fall on us just as she'd said. "We need them up to the challenge and to be ready as soon as possible. Making death shards is child's play, but it's one of the many skills that'll help witches like Emily learn their magic."

"Learn how to be cold and heartless, you mean," I countered and wrapped my coat a bit tighter around my shoulders. "She's helping an old woman die faster by extracting the toxins of her thousands of victims. You really think she's ready for something like that?" I scowled when Pink didn't respond. I huffed, my breath puffing in the air and I tried to suppress the endless shivers that swept through me. I'd grown up in Seattle, but it hadn't been this bad. An icy wind somehow found its way down my neck and mercilessly cut through my layers.

Pink rolled her eyes. "Can we go inside now? You're going to get frostbite."

I kept going and she tottered after me. "Tell me what's really going on. Shanghai? Venice?" I had to know that Sonya was okay, and that started with making sure the supernatural cat didn't get out of the bag.

"From what I've heard of the dragon shifters, Jet has overthrown his brother, Jin, and he's searching for the secrets of the Hugh Modali before he goes to Venice."

I raised an eyebrow. I hadn't told Pink about the strange pull I'd had to both Shanghai and Venice. At first I'd just thought it had something to do with Sonya, that I missed her, but there was something more. The mention of this dragon, this Jet, caught my interest. "What does that mean for my father?"

A gust of wind tackled her shield, breaking it for a moment and tousling her hair before she righted it again. This was clearly a topic she did not like discussing. I wondered what it was about my father that always had her so fidgety. I knew he had an effect on women, but witches could resist him, for the most part.

"Derek was after something in Shanghai," she said. "I heard rumor of another blood stone. It's why he was able to convince Apollo to finally attack his brother."

"But he didn't win," I finished for her. I knew Sonya was still alive. I felt her and every bone in my body begged me to drop whatever I was doing and get to her as fast as I could. The only thing that kept me in Detroit was knowing that I could make a difference for her here. The rebel coven of witches that supported me was part of a growing network of witches who didn't align themselves with the supernatural. Instead, they aligned themselves with mortals—with me.

"No," Pink confirmed and crunched her way through the snow. "He didn't win. In fact, one of our scrying attempts revealed that Hades is awake and has killed Apollo."

I stopped in my tracks and gaped at her. "And my father?" I wasn't sure how I'd feel if he was dead. Sure, we were trying to subdue him with the toxins, but I wasn't sure even that could kill him. I just wanted to protect Sonya.

She misinterpreted my shock and grabbed my hand, patting it and enveloping me with a moment of warmth as her shield partly covered me. "Your father is fine. Apollo must have boosted his power before he died, because there's no sign of deterioration from the toxins he's digested." She tilted her head. "Have you changed your mind? We don't have to go after him again. I'm sure that Hades has everything under control by now."

She didn't know my father very well if she thought he'd retreat to Seattle and pretend as if nothing had happened. No. He'd been planning this for hundreds of years. He'd fathered a demonspawn and laid the groundwork for some diabolical plan. No way this was it.

I growled with frustration, my anger taking over and helping me forget about the ruthless cold that made my nose go numb. "He'll go to one of his thrall houses, eventually. We'll just dose him again."

Her gaze flicked to me, and for once, she was unreadable. "You're okay with that? More girls will die."

"Of course I'm not fucking okay with that," I said, wanting to sound outraged, but then a sensation just above my heart made me clutch at my chest and buckle over.

The fuck was this?

"Nathanial?" Pink said, a bite of worry in her tone. When I didn't respond, she tried again. "Nate?"

I groaned as a searing pain stretched over my chest as if someone had stabbed me with a hot poker. I ripped away the layers of my coat, no longer able to feel the cold. I was hot. So fucking hot I was about to boil from the inside.

When I got down to my bare skin, I spotted the source of my agony. A blazing tattoo bled red light over my skin and smoke drifted into the air as it bored itself deeper into my body. "Pink?"

I cried. Whatever this was, it wasn't good, and it felt like I was fucking dying.

Her eyes went wide. "Nate, I—" She swallowed hard as her gaze flicked to mine. I'd never seen her look defeated before, but that's exactly what reflected back at me in her eyes. "Nate, listen to me. You're about to experience something very… unpleasant. Just remember the person who gave you this mark. Remember why you care for them."

I cried out as another stab of pain rippled through me. The world blurred and red-hot heat settled over me as I slipped through the ground. Yes, through the fucking ground into the earth.

There was only one place that was this hot… and down…

I reached for Pink, but she was already too far away. The ripples of a red breeze enclosed over me and then there was only darkness and screams.

ENVY

Sonya

"He's going to be okay, right?" I asked, hating how high-pitched my voice had gone. Nate was human. Even if my bond could keep him alive in Hell, he wasn't like Luke or Xavier. He didn't have supernatural powers to give him a boost.

Xavier settled the human onto the ground and backed away, giving him space.

Nate's clothes had barely survived the portal that had brought him here. In spite of the dire situation, I had to keep my eyes above the curve of his abdomen. I'd missed my human and even if he was mortal, he had a body that could compete with any incubus.

He groaned, but didn't wake up. The weak sound made my heart twist and reminded me where we were. We were in the third circle of Hell, the layer that identified with Nate and his ultimate sin.

Envy.

Statues circled us and stared down, each representing a different supernatural race.

The most prominent of course was Derek, the Incubus King, who loomed over us with his cock rigid and the white marble of his sculpture depicting him as the object of sex and desire. His power glowed in a crown atop his head and he stared down at us with a disapproving scowl, likely how Derek often looked at his human son.

There were so many statues. Aside Derek stood Nate's mother, Silvia, with her wings spread wide and her eyes made of lifeless stone that glowed with her silver power. She looked neither disapproving nor appeased, but rather just as inanimate as the stone that depicted her. This was how Nate saw his mother. She was dead to him, just as he was dead to her.

The statues weren't all people I recognized. One of the male muses garbed in traditional roman apparel stared down, Ares, and I only knew him by the iconic sword he wielded. It gleamed in the distant flares of hellfire and looked ready to strike us down if we made one wrong move.

The rest ranged from a mermaid, a siren with scales over her face, a dragon with the head of a human, a vampire with fangs bared, then it got weird. A panther. A wolf. Shifters, I guessed.

"Remember, this is the realm of envy," Xavier reminded me, bringing me out of my appraisal of the statues. If they were clues, then they weren't telling me anything I didn't already know. Nate hated his humanity. He hated that he was powerless and surrounded by so many reminders that he'd been born on the wrong side of the species. "You need to save Nate from himself. You need to prove to him his importance."

I blinked at him, then down at the unconscious form at my feet. Nate's rune glowed hot on his chest and the skin around it puffed with an angry red. "He's rejecting our bond," I whispered, more to myself than to anyone else. It stung that Nate would fight it. I knew that I'd left him on his own, but it wasn't because I'd wanted to.

Xavier and Luke gave me space as I knelt and stroked the hair from Nate's sweat-dampened forehead. "Nate, can you hear me?"

He stirred under my touch, but didn't wake up. I jerked when a howl sounded in the distance.

"Hellhounds," Xavier informed me.

My blood ran cold. "Excuse me?"

Luke stepped between us, his armor from the Arena having morphed into a more traditional shirt and pants that he so often wore. "You never said anything about hellhounds. If this circle of Hell is all about envy, what do hellhounds have to do with it?"

Xavier pressed his lips into a thin line before replying. "They're what Nate believes he deserves. Hellhounds feast on the weakest of souls. They are one of the few creatures capable of entirely erasing someone from existence. Instead of eternal damnation he'll just… cease to exist." He crossed his arms, his armor having morphed into a tailored Italian suit. It seemed once my guys overcame their sin, they had a measure of control when it came to Hell's tricks.

I whirled back to Nate and grabbed him by the shoulders, shaking him violently. "Nate! Snap out of it! You are not going to get eaten by hellhounds, you hear me? Not over my dead body!"

"Careful what you wish for," Nate murmured just before he opened his eyes. I'd forgotten how blue they were. Not like Luke's with an ethereal sky-blue that could be as translucent as ice. Nate's eyes were a deep, midnight blue that reminded me of an ocean during sunset.

I smiled and took his face in mine before giving him a deep kiss. Of course, my Nate wouldn't miss an opportunity to score, and forced my mouth open with his tongue and deepened the kiss, making heat flare at my core.

Breathless, I eased away from him. "If wishing you to remain in existence brings hellhounds to gobble me up, then it's worth it."

That seemed to trigger something in Nate and the mischief fled from his eyes, replaced with confusion and fear. He sat up and surveyed our surroundings. His eyes widened and he swallowed hard. "Sonya, where are we?"

Xavier answered, causing Nate to jolt. "Hell, and if you want to help us get on with it, then you'll stop feeling so sorry for yourself and realize being human isn't the end of the world."

Nate blinked at the vampire, his eyes growing wide as Xavier hissed at him—all vampire like—and his ruby eyes blazed with warning.

"That's not helping," I grumbled.

Nate's gaze swept to me, then past me and to Luke who leaned against one of the statues. "Hey. I know you."

Luke gave him a slow nod, even though his skin flushed. The last time the two had been in the same room had been when Luke had recharged my Blood Stone... "Yep, it's me. One of Sonya's bond, just like you." He indicated Nate's rune with his chin.

Nate's fingers explored the tattoo on his chest, wincing when he touched it.

This was a lot for him to take in. It took me a while to come to terms that Nate was in my bond, but he probably had no idea what that meant. His whole life supernaturals had dictated his life, and here I was, trapping him with yet another supernatural's destiny. "Hey, Nate?" I asked, kneeling and resting my hand on his arm. The hellhounds barked again, this time definitely closer. "When we made love in the library, do you remember what you told me?"

He blinked at me, his blue eyes glancing to Xavier and Luke. He wasn't an idiot. He knew what they meant to me, as well as what I might have done with them. Of course my guys would have known that I might have been intimate with Nate, so they didn't even flinch. "Uh, not really," Nate said, his words distant. The hellhounds yipped again, as if sensing Nate's distraction.

I grabbed his chin and forced him to look at me. His eyes were wild with fear, but also another emotion I recognized, only because I'd seen it a thousand times in the mirror.

Doubt.

Crippling self-doubt that he was worthy of my attention. Doubt that he deserved even a sliver of happiness. He wasn't what his father wanted him to be. He was mortal, which made him useless, or so he'd allowed himself to believe. There was a reason that Derek kept Nate around, why he'd tasked him over watching me. Nate had his own strengths and skills, ones that no one else had. I needed to remind him of that.

I eased in closer and lowered my voice, allowing seduction to seep into my words. "You told me that I was accustomed to being the seductress. You revealed to me my own desires, my desires to be taken, to be seduced." I grinned, my fangs slipping free of their sheath, making Nate's eyes go wide. "You gave me that, and now that I'm a vampire, you can give it to me as many times as you'd like."

I kissed him before he had a chance to protest. I wasn't as skilled as Xavier when it came to kissing with fangs, and I winced when I accidentally pricked him and the sweet, metallic tang of his blood blossomed in my mouth. My fangs were still wet with my poison, having subdued an entire army of fake-Lukes with it, and he moaned with pleasure. I grinned against his teeth.

The first of the statues cracked, sending the ground trembling beneath our feet. I snapped my gaze up just in time to see the statue of the vampire crumbling to dust.

"It's working," Luke said, surprise making his eyebrows raise.

I turned back to Nate and stroked his cheek. His eyelids fluttered open at my touch. "You see?" I asked. "You have power even over a vampire. I want you. I need you. You have seduced me and you have given me what no one else ever could."

He stroked my cheek in return, his thumb running down one of my fangs. He didn't ask me how I'd managed to become a vampire. Instead, he indulged me. "What have I given you that makes you look at me like that?" His gaze swept over me, mesmerized, as if what he was seeing was impossible. I realized that it had nothing to do with what I was, but that I adored him, that I spoke the truth when I said I needed him.

"You've given me what I desire most," I said. "You're a human who doesn't fear what I am. A mortal who can still want me, even after knowing exactly how deep my sins run." Wrapping my arms around his neck, I straddled him as desire thundered through me. The hardening arousal of him pressed at the thin layer of my underwear. Apparently, when my armor had transformed to clothing that represented how I felt most comfortable, it left me with revealing lingerie. Appropriate for a succubus turned vampire.

He kissed me and moaned into my mouth, careless of my fangs with his tongue. I forced myself to retract them as he kissed me again.

"Tell me more," he said between kisses and his hands ran over my thighs and under my thin gown, his thumbs rubbing circles dangerously close to where I wanted him to be.

"You're more intoxicating than a siren," I whispered. Shortly after I'd uttered the words the statue of a siren crumbled. "Stronger than anyone I know, even a dragon." In spirit, Nate could even put Jet to shame after all he'd endured and still survived. Another statue crumbled. He pressed a thumb hard over my clit and I tried to squeeze my legs closed, but he was in the way. He grinned against my teeth and drank in my moans. "I want you more than I want any supernatural, Nate." The other statues disintegrated, leaving only his father, Derek, looming over us. I blinked up at it and threaded my fingers through Nate's hair as I rolled my hips against his touch. "I want you more than the King of Sex."

Red eyes glowed in the distance and smoke drifted from nostrils, the multi-headed hellhounds having breached the fog. Derek's statue cracked and fell. The hellhounds barked their dismay before turning and tucking their tails between their legs.

Just as Nate was about to bring me to climax, the ground beneath us shifted, and then we fell.

Damn it.

SECRETS IN SHANGHAI

Jet

Taking Shanghai from my brother had been easy compared to what came next. Watching Sonya leave had destroyed a little piece of me, but I had to let her go. Derek had turned too many of the dragons to his cause and Shanghai had been brought to its knees by dragonfire. I trusted Sonya to be strong, to be able to withstand anything, but I wasn't going to topple a city down on her head. When Luke drew her away, I let him. I couldn't explain a little voice inside my head that told me I could trust Luke with everything, even Sonya's life... especially Sonya's life.

That same pull had split me in different directions, making me search the internet for Venice even before it'd become a war zone. The dragons loyal to me had sent scouts to investigate, telling me that one of the male muses was dead and that the vampires had a new queen.

From the sounds of it, that new queen was my Sonya.

I didn't like what they were calling her. Queen of the

Damned? Not sure what she'd done to earn that title. I was going to get to her as soon as things in Shanghai were settled. I had to trust that she could get through all of this without my help, but I hated that I couldn't even talk to her.

"My King," came a familiar voice, one of the older dragons who'd served my brother for hundreds of years bowed at the elevator's entrance. I hadn't even heard it ding. Showed how out of it I was.

I waved him in. "Come in, Vern, tell me what news you have for me."

He cleared his throat before reluctantly entering the room. He didn't like discussing matters in the suite. He much more preferred the library or the treasure room in Jin's old tower. Knowledge and wealth always made dragons more comfortable, but I preferred the penthouse suite where I'd cemented my bond with Sonya. Her scent still lingered in the room, although it grew fainter every day.

"There's been word from Venice, Majesty."

"Jet," I corrected him absentmindedly. I still wasn't used to being called "Majesty" and I wasn't going to start getting accustomed to it now. I'd dethroned my brother not because I wanted power, but because the old way of doing things needed to come to an end. Dynasties, rulers, segregation of the races, it all needed to stop.

The only thing that I agreed with was keeping the supernatural community a secret from the mortals. Ares had helped stabilize Shanghai, and was now hard at work minimizing the damage from the upheaval in Venice. Covering it up as an earthquake was a stretch, but a male muse was capable of impressive things.

"I've confirmed the identity of the vampires' new queen."

I froze. He didn't have to tell me who it was. I'd felt the shift in my soul only a few days ago. My pull towards Sonya had grown nearly unbearable and my tattoos had writhed across my skin, demanding that I go to her. She needed me now more than ever. Something bad was coming and she couldn't face it alone.

"Sonya," I whispered, and Vern nodded in confirmation.

"Do you wish me to make arrangements, Majesty?"

I glowered at him, but the stubborn old dragon wasn't about to change his ways now. I was his King, and as much as it irritated me to take up the title, I appreciated his loyalty.

"Not yet," I said with a sigh. I couldn't go to Sonya empty-handed. My mother had told me that the power of the Hugh Modali would mean the difference between life and death and I'd know when it would be time to seek it out. Now was that time, and from the rumors flying around dragon circles, my mother's words had been more literal than I'd ever realized.

My bond to Sonya grew stronger every day, but there was something else that plagued me. Nightmares of a dark sky descending on us kept me from sleeping. They didn't feel like dreams, more like a bad omen.

Death was coming for us, all of us, and I had to help Sonya stop it.

Upon Vern's insistence, I waited until nightfall to head out. Two dragons accompanied me and I left instructions behind for the rest to rebuild what Jin had been so keen to destroy. Our nation, our people, they were now divided. The power of the Hugh Modali could reunite us again, but if I didn't make it back, the dragons would have to use their own brains. We were a brutish race, but I liked to think it was possible for even reptiles to be civilized.

There was a power that was worth the risk, and necessary if I wanted to help my people. It was an orb called the Dragon's Eye.

With it in one's possession, a dragon shifter would be unstoppable. Only one of my line could wield it, and so it'd been locked away, the family line slain to prevent an uprising, except for me. My father thought he could one day use me to wield the power for himself. What a fool he'd been.

Flying in dragon form over my country was the most freeing feeling I'd had in a long time. Flanked by two dragons I'd grown up with, I was ready to take on the world.

It took two days of flying to get to the Hugh Modali ruins. The impact of its repel shield hit me deep in my stomach and made me dip out of the sky. My left wing crumpled first, sending me in an uncontrolled spiral to the ground.

Luckily, I'd been expecting it, and had already been flying low. I crashed hard into trees and dirt and flung debris in my wake.

My two friends, Bo and Yan, dove and met me on the ground, avoiding the worst of the magical field that kept dragons out. They hadn't felt the effects, but that was because they didn't have Hugh Modali blood. If they'd gone too far, their hearts would have just simply stopped. As a half-royal myself, at least I got a warning.

Yan shifted first, his gold scales flaking into ash, only his eyes retaining their metallic hue. "You okay?" he asked, his brow creased with worry.

I coughed up blood, but promptly wiped it on my arm. "Yeah, fine." He frowned at me.

His younger brother, Bo, shifted next. At only sixteen years of age, he had that stupid-bravado thing going on. He marched up to me and crossed his muscular arms, not quite shedding all of the golden scales that matched his family line. "You should have let me go first. I could have taken it."

Yan opened his mouth to tell him off, but I answered first. "Drink the potion, then you can take the lead, how about that?"

Bo straightened. The vial that would protect us hung low on his chest, the cord having been long enough for a dragon's neck. He popped it open and downed the contents without even a moment's hesitation. I smirked when he choked on it and buckled over as the magic took hold.

I waited for him to recover before taking my vial and downing it, and Yan followed suit.

Magic burned low in my stomach before spreading out to my extremities. It'd protect us from the curse put on the ruins, although we weren't sure for how long. The vial was water blessed by my mother from a stream not far from here. She hadn't told me that knowledge, more than implanted it in my genetic memory. I just somehow… *knew* what I needed to do in order to get back home. It's how I knew about the Dragon's Eye, and that it was waiting for me to claim my birthright.

"Come on," Yan said with a smile. "Let's get your heritage and get the hell out of here."

I couldn't have agreed more.

Moving into the ruins gave me unnatural chills up my spine, which was saying something. As a dragon shifter, there wasn't much that shook me, but the low howls of an unseen wind that swept through the underground tunnels made me quicken my pace. I didn't want to stay here any longer than I had to.

"Why do you think the Hugh Modali lived underground?" asked Bo.

His brother cuffed him on the back of the head. "Because they'd hear idiots like you from a mile away, now wouldn't they?"

I cracked a smile as we made our way deeper into the tunnels.

My eyes naturally shifted, using the dragonfire in my veins to allow me to see in the dark. My vision bled red, going into another spectrum, one of echoing sound waves, heat signatures, and something else. I realized the third layer coming into view was the ancient magic that had kept these ruins safe from my brother, my father, and all the dragons like him. It throttled at our necks, trying to strangle us, but the protection of the holy river kept us safe.

Bo and Yan didn't seem to be able to see it and kept going without stopping to grab at their necks to rid themselves of the strangling strands, so I resisted the urge to reach for my neck and swallowed hard. I didn't want to concern them.

The memories of my ancestors bubbled up inside my head, coming to life being so close to the land from which they were born. "The Hugh Modali were the original dragons," I said, keeping my voice low as I moved ahead of the brothers and allowed my instincts to show us the way. The tunnels parted into three directions and a natural pull took me left. I followed it without hesitation. "At the end of these tunnels are an array of traps, but if you know the correct path, you'll find the den."

Bo brightened at that. "A den of gold?" His scales gleamed in agreement with his excitement of the prospects.

I chuckled. "Yes, gold, but not just that." I paused, flaring dragonfire into my eyes for effect. "Magic. Ancient, forbidden magic that was used to create powerful artifacts like the Dragon's Eye."

Yan grinned and slapped his brother on the back. "Sounds like we're in for an adventure." He grinned at me. "Show us the way, fearless leader."

Satisfied that I'd eased their nerves, I carried on. We moved as quietly as a trio of naked dragon shifters could. Our bare feet slapped against dusty stones and ancient debris poked at my heels. I wanted to break into a run, but I was too pampered by my brother's old way of life. My feet ached and pinched at the few stones that had managed to get in my way. Luckily, the tunnels were primarily undisturbed, the magic applying to all animals as a means of defense against intrusion. Dragons weren't the only creatures that could shift.

After the better part of the evening I knew we were getting close. I smacked my lips against the dryness threatening to overtake my mouth and ignored the soreness building up my thighs, and even my back as we hunched our way through the smaller tunnels to our destination.

"How much further?" Bo prodded.

Yan hushed him immediately, but the ground rumbled in response to the disturbance.

We were there.

The end of the tunnel gleamed with light and I allowed my dragonfire to dim my vision into the human's spectrum. I squeezed through the opening and sucked in a breath when I found what was on the other side.

Gold. Magic in the form of dancing fire, and, unexpectedly, a sleeping dragon.

Yan and Bo bumped into me as they entered into the cavern, immediately crouching when they spotted the massive dragon and their smiles died on their faces.

"Holy shit!" Bo whisper-yelled.

Holy shit was right. The dragon stirred and my heart stopped as it rolled open its enormous eyes.

I saw now why the treasure I sought was called a "Dragon's Eye," because that's literally what it was.

The dragon had one normal reptilian eye that lazily stared at us, but the other, it was an inanimate object that rolled in its head, swirling with frightful blue power. Blue, the color of a flame at its hottest, and the birthplace of all dragonfire.

Who dares disturb my slumber? A voice asked, thundering in my skull.

I grabbed my head at the same time that Yan and Bo went for theirs. Apparently the dragon was speaking to all of us.

I stumbled forward and allowed my tattoos to writhe on my skin. I hadn't been inked with them by a machine. The tattoos were a natural part of my genetic makeup; a type of scar that marked my shifter abilities and gave me my power. No one could mistake what I was… one of the Hugh Modali. I couldn't hide it any more than I could hide my surprise that the ruins had not been completely abandoned.

The dragon yawned, sending the air wavering with heat as it opened its giant maw. I'd never seen a dragon so large as this one. Dragons were large, in general, but this one spanned the entire length of the cavern. Gold magic drifted over its scales and gleamed with ethereal light.

I grow impatient, young one. Why have you come here? The dragon narrowed its one good eye at us and the Dragon's Eye swirled in its head.

Yan gripped my arm hard. "We should leave."

I pulled from him and stepped onto the pile of treasure. My aching feet sank into the cool golden coins as I approached the dragon. "I apologize, ancient one. I came for my birthright, but I did not know that my lineage yet survived." The hairs on the back of my neck stood on end as the dragon appraised me, but I refused to show any fear or weakness. I kept walking towards it until I was within arms reach. The dragon lowered its head and its giant nostrils flared. A black tongue snaked out and tasted the air around me.

My blood memories didn't tell me about this dragon. I had no knowledge of who or what it was, or even if it was a shifter at all. Perhaps it didn't have a human form and this was some ancient relative… or conqueror of the Hugh Modali line.

I wouldn't expect you to know me, young one. I have been here so very long, without conversation, without servants. The dragon fluttered its eyes closed and released a heavy sigh, sending heat wafting over me. *I'm glad to finally have some. Do scratch my scales at my left elbow. They've been bothering me for centuries.*

I glanced at Yan and Bo, who mouthed at me to get the hell out of here, but I couldn't just leave. We'd come all this way and I was going to be damned if we were going to leave empty-handed.

I stepped around the dragon's large head, moving towards its elbow as it had asked. I walked slowly and deliberately, taking my time to appraise this creature and see if I could spot any weaknesses. The only benefit I had was this side was on the side of the Dragon's Eye, and if it really was an orb of magical power, perhaps the dragon couldn't use it to see out of.

"So, you know who I am?" I asked, hoping the dragon would give me more information I could use against it.

It growled at me until I stretched and reached for a scale that had flaked, not quite shedding its dead skin until I scratched at it, sending the old layers peeling off into ash.

The dragon sighed with relief. *Of course. Only one of the original line could come here. I thought them all dead. At the time, it seemed a good idea to undo my creations, but I've been so very bored. I do regret it.*

Blood hummed hot in my ears as adrenaline shot through my body. This wasn't just any dragon.

This was our god. The creator of all dragonkind called the Azure Dragon.

Before I had a chance to digest that, a searing pain speared through my chest and I buckled over. I bit my lip hard to stifle the cry that wanted to rip out of me. I couldn't do anything that would set the dragon off. Not when I knew what he was capable of. There was a reason I had no genetic memory of him. I wasn't related to this dragon. He'd created me, just like he'd created my parents and all the dragons who'd come before me.

The ground shifted and fresh heat spilled into the chamber, but I had a feeling this heat wasn't coming from the dragon.

The creature shifted, sending gold and magic swirling at my feet. Bo and Yan yelled for me, but I could barely hear them over the grumble of the dragon god. It opened its good eye to glare at me. *What is this? What magic do you bring with you, young one?*

I expected the dragon to snap at me and eat me whole. The pain that ransacked my body demanded a price. I fell to my knees and released the scream I'd been holding in just as the ground opened up and something drew me down into it.

The last thing I saw in the red haze of power was Bo and Yan running towards the dragon in mid-shift, scales sprouting across their skin as claws broke through their fingernails.

And then the portal closed, and I found myself trapped in my nightmares where the skies bled with smoke as if the entire world had burned to ash.

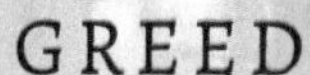

GREED

Sonya

"You know, this is the part where I ask if it hurt falling from heaven," Nate informed me with a grin.

I rubbed my ass, which I'd landed on very ungracefully. I gave Nate a glare before accepting Xavier's hand to get back on my feet. "Well, tough luck for you. I didn't fall from heaven. I fell from the third circle of Hell."

Nate shrugged and kicked one of the gold coins into the darkness. This layer of Hell was greed, and Jet's sin which I needed to help him overcome. I figured that would be easy, as I didn't see Jet as a particularly greedy person, but Hell didn't lie. An entire sea of gold glittered back at me as proof of what was in Jet's heart.

"Close enough," Nate said with a mischievous glint in his eye. "I've been waiting forever to use that pickup line."

I pinched him on the cheek. "You don't need any pickup lines with me."

He playfully snapped his teeth at my fingers as I pulled them away, and it won a smile out of me, but the good humor quickly faded from my mood.

Luke wandered through the coins. He stopped and stared, although I couldn't see anything in particular that might have gotten his attention. "What is it?" I asked and walked to his side. I looked down at the spot that he seemed so fascinated by, but all I could see was layer upon layer of gold coins.

"I sense Jet down there," Luke said, pitching his voice low as if he was afraid someone might hear us. He glanced at me, his eyes flaring with the silver magic of his angelic blood. "Don't you feel him?"

A cold sweat broke out over my body and I looked down at my runes. I still wore my lingerie, but the runes for Luke, Xavier, and Nate blazed with healthy magic. The rune for Jet, the one at the top of my navel, was cold and silent with only the faintest hum to assure me Jet was here, somewhere. I ran my fingers over my cold rune as panic threatened to take ahold of me.

"Jet? As in the dragon, Jet?" Nate asked, his voice painfully loud in the grim silence.

Xavier hissed at him. "Keep your voice down, mortal. We're not alone."

Goosebumps broke out over my skin. So, the creepy ominous sensation that there was a monster lurking in the distant fog wasn't just in my imagination. Great.

"Jet's a dragon shifter," I whispered as I knelt and ran my fingers over the coins. They were surprisingly warm to my touch. "He's one of our bond."

Luke knelt, his jaw flexing before he spoke. I was right to say that Jet was "our" bond, and not just a bond that belonged to me. Luke was the one who sensed him because all of my guys were bound to one another, even if that magic used me as its medium.

"Tell us about him," Luke offered. "If he's really under all of these coins, then he feels as if his greed has buried him alive. What did he crave most?"

I bit my lip as I thought about my brief time with the dragon shifter. I felt like there was so much more to him than a first impression. "He's part of the Hugh Modali, an ancient dragon lineage from his mother's side, but his brother was the one who inherited the throne. He challenged Jin, he won, but I don't think that's what Jet really wanted." He hadn't taken joy in killing his brother. Jet had done what was right, but I imagined his insecurity of his claim to the dragon's throne hadn't magically gone away.

Nate joined us and swept his hand over the coins, sending them shifting like sands. "A scorned bastard denied his birthright, huh? I can relate to that." Nate gave me a wink, but there wasn't much humor in his gaze. This particular suffering was a little too close to home. "I don't know the guy, but if I were him, I would want power. Those who had power over me wouldn't be able to tell me what to do anymore. I'd want something they'd respect." His gaze fell to the coins. "I suppose for dragons, that would be gold."

Xavier hummed his agreement. "The mortal's right. Jet's sin is that he covets a denied birthright, but it's for all the wrong reasons. That desire has devoured him from the inside for a long time; it's become his greatest sin." Xavier rested a cool hand on my shoulder that was protected only by the thin veil of my lingerie's fabric.

"So what do we do?" I asked just before thunder rolled over the landscape, sending the coins shifting and ringing their song through the endless sea of gold. Whatever we were going to do, we'd better do it fast.

Xavier released me. "I'm afraid it's both simple and arduous."

Luke breathed a long sigh. "We dig."

Jet

I couldn't breathe. Something cold and shifting crushed me from all directions. The cold tang of metal filled my mouth. My delicate sense of smell flared at the lack of oxygen and I suppressed the urge to thrash. Whatever was crushing me moved with me and if I moved, I'd only make it worse.

I'd recognize this sensation anywhere. This had been a reoccurring nightmare I'd never quite gotten over. Golden coins buried me alive. The very same measure of wealth of my race was what destroyed me. In some of my dreams I managed to dig myself out, only to be greeted by black fingers that stretched over the sky and devoured me all the same.

There was no digging out of this one. I couldn't move; couldn't expand my chest to take in needed breaths. I reduced myself to short, small hyperventilating puffs as I slowly suffocated. Panic threatened to take me under, but a distant sound gave me hope. Someone was digging from above.

I wasn't alone.

This wasn't like my nightmares. This was too vivid… and no one ever came to dig me out in my dreams. I instantly knew that Sonya was here and she was trying to get to me. That knowledge kept me alive. I fought for every small breath. I attempted to shift, forcing my muscles to contract and my tattoos to turn into scales, but I couldn't divert my mass into a dragon's body with this amount of weight crushing in on me.

Growling with frustration I was forced to stay still as coins shifted above. It wasn't enough to lessen the massive weight, but luckily I had my arms above me as if I'd fallen here. Warm air hit my fingers, the coins shifting to finally free them so that I could move the joints just above my wrist. A muffled voice came through as a hand gripped mine.

"Jet! Hang in there!"

I would have smiled, except that an unmistakable roar sounded in the distance and the coins shifted from low beneath my feet, pressing hard against my ankles as something surged *up*.

The Azure Dragon had followed me here. Shit.

Frantically I jostled my hand, hoping that was signal enough that I needed to get the hell out of here.

Sonya

Poor Jet was trapped under a massive pile of coins. He was lucky that he hadn't suffocated already, but the way his hand thrashed told me that we didn't have much more time. His tattoos swarmed over his knuckles and hardened into scales. He wanted to shift, but he couldn't with the coins pressing down on him.

I scooped handfuls of the coins and tossed them aside, but no matter how hard I dug the coins seemed to fall back in on my dragon shifter.

Luke, Xavier, and even Nate helped me as much as they could. Xavier blurred with his vampiric speed and ferried coins farther away from us than necessary. Clearly this layer of Hell had coins as far as we could see and I imagined it didn't matter how far the vampire might take away this pile. The coins shifted like a massive sea and seemed to undo our work as quickly as we cleared coins away.

"This is hopeless!" Nate growled as he took armfuls of coins and pushed them out of the way, only to find the coins shifting back and undoing his work.

I growled, because we'd managed to uncover Jet's hand, but we couldn't seem to get any further. Hell was doing some weird voodoo shit and working against us.

"Luke," I said, my voice taut as a plan formed.

He paused digging. The coins beneath his fingers glittered with his blood and his fingertips healed before my eyes. It pained me that he'd hurt himself trying to help us, but every bit helped right now and I appreciated his efforts. "If we just keep going we'll get to him," Luke insisted, but I heard the edge of panic in his voice. We'd managed to overcome each trial we'd faced so far, but maybe our luck had run out.

I shook my head and my hair stuck to my sweat-dampened forehead. "No. Every layer of Hell has had a trick to it so far, and this one can't be so simple as to dig Jet out of crushing greed." I bit my lip. "What overcomes greed? You can't just dig someone out of it, right? They need to change."

Luke frowned and stared down at his hands. The torn layer of skin stitched over itself as he healed.

"Do you suggest we allow him to dig himself out?" Xavier asked.

I backed away from the flailing hand, fighting all of my instincts to help my lover. "That's right."

Nate and the other guys gave me dubious looks, but they eventually backed away as well, leaving Jet's lonely hand flailing without anyone to hold it.

I hoped I was right, because if I wasn't, Jet would die alone and buried by his sin.

Jet

I sensed when Sonya left. I'd never felt so alone in all my life. Why would she abandon me? Had she given up? Had something happened to her?

A little voice rang inside my head and told me that I deserved this fate. I wasn't good enough. I was supposed to inherit my mother's honorable lineage, my father's throne, and neither of those had come to fruition. My father's throne was tainted with my brother's blood and my mother's lineage was guarded by a jealous dragon god that now stirred under my feet, ready to devour me.

This was the moment in my dreams where I either succumbed to hopelessness, or I dug myself free and faced what came next. I wasn't a quitter. There was no way I was just going to sit here and allow myself to get devoured by a scorned dragon god or suffocate to death under a sea of golden coins.

And so I shifted.

I knew it would hurt. I wasn't supposed to shift when there wasn't space to push out my bulky mass. My skin shred and hardened with scales. I pushed the coins away from me with a scream, using my own pain to power my shift.

My fingers turned into claws and wings pushed from my back. I didn't need to shift all the way. Just enough to get myself to the surface.

The breach of my wings to the warm air told me I was almost there. I speared my other hand up and found the surface, then I pulled myself free.

Cresting the sea of coins, I gulped in delicious air. Fangs kept my mouth ajar as my vision came into focus. I craned my neck up and faced the black scrawling fingers that raked across the sky. My stomach dropped because I'd hoped that I'd have been wrong about that part.

A voice is what brought my attention back to the landscape

that gleamed with gold. My eyes went wide when I saw her and my stomach pitched.

Sonya.

First there was elation, then panic as I remembered what was about to follow me out of the pit of coins. "Sonya! Stay back!" The words ripped out me half-human as I completed my shift and transformed to my dragon form.

Sonya

Luke yanked me back just in time as coins exploded everywhere and a second dragon burst from the pit.

"The fuck!" I screeched as I fell hard on my knees with Luke's body over me as a shield. Heat flared and I realized that we'd been hit by dragonfire.

I cursed and threw Luke off of me and he groaned. Dragonfire shouldn't be able to hurt me, and I expected that protection would expand to members in my bond as well, but Luke's left leg was fried to a crisp. His face went white as a sheet as he bit down a scream.

Nate ran up to us and tugged my arm. He eyes flicked as he searched the sky and a shadow passed over us. "Come on!" he hissed.

We crawled away just in time as another long streak of dragonfire burned the coins in the place we'd just been. Luke stumbled after us. His leg would heal, but he needed time.

I watched in both fascination and horror as a dragon with a rainbow of golds and blues shrieked and tore across the sky, snapping sharp teeth as he chased after Jet.

The dragon shifter streaked across the sky with brilliant emerald hues scattering across his scales. He couldn't adjust his position to breathe fire in return on his attacker. Every time he stooped to bank a sharp turn, claws and fire forced him to evade.

That's when I noticed something odd about the dragon that pursued him. "Look!" I shouted and pointed at the dragon's blue eye that swirled with power. It reminded me of the Blood Stone and I had no doubt that if we could remove it, we could stop the dragon's pursuit.

Xavier was the first to respond. He bared his fangs and tore into his wrist, then offered the bleeding wound to me. "Take what you need to get it done."

I didn't question him and took his wrist without hesitation and bit down. The power of the ancient vampire's life-force filled my body and made me dizzy with power.

Likewise Luke and Nate put their hands on me, sending my runes blazing to life.

I grinned as raw magic zapped at my fingers and took form of what I needed: a bow and arrow.

Not that I'd ever fired a bow and arrow in my life, but hey, this was magic doing my bidding. I didn't need to be trained. The power of my Blood Stone burned in my chest with approval and pride as I manipulated my bond and the willingness of my bond-mates to lend me their strength. I notched the arrow back, tracked the dragon as it completely ignored me as inconsequential, and then I aimed for its blue eye… and fired.

The streaking arrow that blazed with hellfire pierced its target and sent the blue orb free from the dragon it'd belonged to. The creature shrieked and bucked backwards. The dragon slammed to the ground and sent coins flying in all directions.

Giving Jet an opportunity, he whirled and his wide wings flared as he banked hard and landed on the ground. His swirling, emerald eyes appraised the situation and I held my breath as he weighed his options.

He glanced at the blue orb that rolled onto the coins. I knew that was something valuable to him. I sensed through our bond that this was the heaviest sin of all and with the power of that orb, he could obtain something he'd craved all his life. Respect from his people.

Then there was me. His reptilian eyes flashed at me with desire and recognition as his mate.

I recognized the trial now and knew that in this, there wasn't anything I could do to help Jet. I bit my lower lip that threatened to tremble and straightened. He had to choose me. He had to decide that I was worth all the gold in the world and every treasure that dragons held dear.

Jet's dragon diminished until he was a man walking towards me, all smiles as tattoos swirled over his skin as if dancing with the joy of his decision. Elation made me feel as if I could fly away.

He'd chosen me.

Jet crashed into me and engulfed me with his arms. I'd forgotten how huge he was and soon I was dwarfed by him and entangled in his grip. He wound his fingers through my hair and tilted my head back, his gaze lingering on my lips. "May I kiss you?" he asked.

I laughed and wrapped my fingers around his neck. "You better kiss me," I said.

He grinned and crushed his mouth to mine, filling me with his scent and his power. Red-hot heat scorched through me. I'd almost forgotten the delicious burn of his dragonfire.

A roar and then a rumble at our feet broke our kiss. Jet blinked at the members of my bond who surrounded us protectively and faced the dragon that still writhed in the coins. I balked as I realized that the landscape was devouring the creature.

There wasn't much time to consider what that meant, for as

soon as the coins and dragon disappeared into a void, the ground opened up beneath our feet and we dropped into darkness.

LIMBO

Sonya

Memories came back to me as we fell. I'd just managed to get through the first four rings of Hell, each one linked to a cardinal sin overcome by a member of my bond. However I knew that four was my magic number, my limit when it came to my power, even though there were seven cardinal sins.

A blurry nightmare struggled to take form in the darkness as I floated in nothingness. I knew I wasn't alone. Luke's hand found me first, and then his power slipped into me, securing itself in the rune that marked on my skin. Xavier was next, a red-hot bite that hit low on my abdomen, followed by Nate and Jet.

They joined me and their spirits wound into my runes. For the rest of my stay in Hell, they'd be with me, lending me their strength and their love. I knew I was going to need it.

Then the memory took hold and I watched a scene unfold that I'd relived a hundred times, but a witch's magic had ensured I'd forgotten the moment I woke up.

My mother had made a deal with a witch of the Shadow Coven, and now that I was lucid for this nightmare I could see past the wisps of shadow that swirled around the witch's face. To my surprise, she was young and beautiful, but I imagined anyone who sold their soul for power would be vain.

I settled onto my feet and faced her. My fingers shook and I curled them into fists. "You," I growled.

The witch turned and faced me, ripping free from the nightmare where she branded me with runes over and over again.

She snarled at me, her beautiful features twisting into wrinkles as she growled in return. "So, the bitch finally comes to allow me to finish the job." She pointed a glimmering ceremonial dagger at my face. "You should have died, child, all those years ago. Now, I'll make sure you die, slowly, painfully, and beg for mercy underneath my blade."

She slashed at me and I used my vampiric speed to avoid her strike, although her blade came dangerously close to my cheek. "So you picked up a few tricks before you died. That won't help you."

I grinned. The witch thought I was here because I was dead and had gone to Hell! That gave me an advantage. She didn't know that I had the power of four sins on my side and I was very much alive. "What have you done with my mother?" I spat and dodged her blow for a second time. I'd thought my mother dead and burned this whole time, but now that my memories had returned, I knew that she would be down here, somewhere, and that thought alone surged me with resolve to take this bitch out.

The witch snarled. She ignored me and instead her lips moved as she chanted a spell. I doubled over as my three runes of Pride, Sloth, and Lust burned hot. I didn't have mates to resolve those sins, and a witch of the Shadow Coven would be sure to sniff out my weaknesses. I cursed and whispered a chant of my own.

Nate. Luke. Xavier. Jet. Help me.

The ground beneath me immediately opened up, and then I was on my way to the fifth ring of Hell.

A MUSE TURNED MERMAID

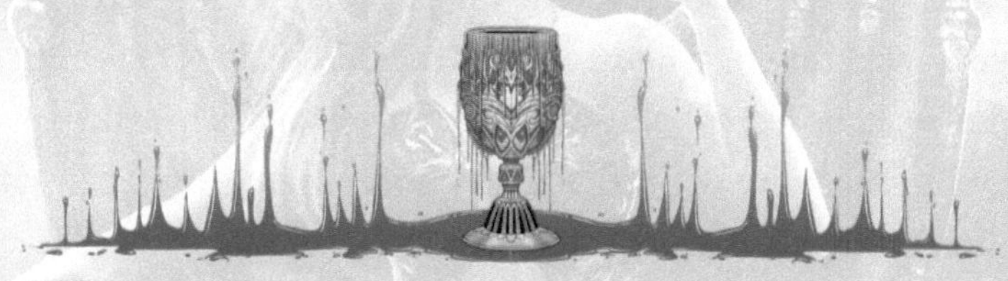

Sarah

It'd only been a few weeks since I'd become a mermaid, but it felt like a lifetime had passed by. I lazily swam through the undercurrents where my sisters didn't often go. I wasn't like them. I didn't participate in the mermaid orgies or gain a sense of peace that the sea was supposed to bring me. I'd given up everything of my past life, but something still tied me to land. Something kept me from enjoying what I was now and starting a new chapter.

It shouldn't have been possible, but that night when my father stole the Tear of the Sea and abandoned me, Vikki and the sirens had lifted me up in song, helping me to survive the transition as the mermaid my father had captured guided me home.

I didn't know her name, or perhaps she didn't have one, so I'd decided to call her Gem. It sounded appropriate to me. She was a hidden gem in the sea and glittered like one.

My mermaid savior followed me at a distance. She was always so worried about me. I glanced over my shoulder to find

Gem watching. Her eyes glowed with a soft golden hue of our kind and her irises watched me with their slitted stare. She was both beautiful and frightening. Her long tail glimmered with mystical scales that sent cloaking magic out in waves to keep us hidden from potential threats. The edges of her arms were rimmed with dangerous spikes that I'd discovered were also poisonous, after she'd fended off an arrogant shark that'd thought I was lunch. I hadn't quite mastered the cloaking spell yet. She was powerful both in her physical form and in our magic, which is why my father had chosen her. How he'd gotten her to the surface, I had no idea.

Turning away from her, I twisted my fin to propel me deeper. Usually I wandered around the lower ocean tunnels, looking for baubles or lost treasures. The urge to find something I had lost consumed me and so I searched, although for what, I still wasn't sure.

Do you think you'll find it tonight? Gem asked me, her voice ringing pleasantly inside my head.

She always asked if I'd find "it." We both knew my search was pointless, but she allowed it. She was powerful enough to restrain me back in the mermaid city if she wanted to, but she wouldn't do that to me. If anyone knew what it felt like to be caged, she did.

I hope so, I replied. The echo of my mind brushing hers was oddly comforting. Even though I hadn't fully accepted that I was a mermaid now—permanently. It just didn't feel like this life fit me very well.

Long rows of deep ocean kelp swayed and a crevice in the seafloor caught my eye. It was impossible to see anything this far down and my magic didn't work so well to give me vision in the dark. I worked better off echolocation and sensed my surroundings through the images that bounced back at me and faded until I sent the vibrations out again. I'd grown accustomed to the alternating view of my new world, but this time the crevice in the ocean floor remained constant. I realized that a red glow emanated from it and curiosity bloomed in me as I drifted closer.

I sensed Gem's apprehension before she spoke. *Dangerous,* she warned. The waters shifted as she shot through it and appeared at my side in a flurry of bubbles. She gripped my wrist and her eyes widened in warning.

Shrugging her off, I continued down into the red glow that called to me, making me feel more at home than I'd felt anywhere else on the ocean floor.

Once I passed the thin veil, I knew that I wasn't in the ocean anymore. The transition from the crushing depths to something more familiar was slow, but soon the waters drained and my own weight was what kept me down. I crawled on my elbows, dragging my massive fin that was now useless across whitewashed marble floors.

I should have been accustomed to magic portals by now, but my heart thundered in my chest as I coughed up water and forced myself to breathe oxygen again. I hadn't gone to the surface in so long that I'd almost forgotten how.

I blinked when I looked up and saw Vikki staring down at me, her hands propped on her hips and her small mouth twisted in a scowl.

"Well, it's about time," she said, then grinned and waved someone over. I balked when I saw the feminine form running towards us.

Sonya huffed and had the biggest smile on her face. She leaned on her knees as she gulped in air. "Hey, sexy." She winked at me. "Welcome to Hell."

PRIDE AND SLOTH

Sonya

I gave Vikki a raised brow. She'd said that we could lure Sarah to Hell with her pride. It didn't surprise me that "pride" was Sarah's cardinal sin. She was too proud to share me with anyone else. It was what made her unsuited to be my mate, but the magic between us had drawn us together anyway. She was doomed to be a sin that would never be forgiven. Pride was a failure on both our parts.

If she'd wronged me, she'd paid the price by everything that had happened to her. She was literally a fish out of water and it wouldn't do for a mermaid to be flopping around the flames of Hell, so there'd been one extra thing Vikki had to do for me.

The siren produced the Tear of the Sea, a ring that emanated with power, and handed it to Sarah. After Apollo's death, Vikki had tracked it down and then come to find me. She'd just been sitting here waiting for me in the fifth layer of Hell.

Sarah blinked at us, shock making her eyes go wide, which

only augmented the strange slitted irises of her new form. She accepted the ring and put it on, then clamped her jaw and suppressed a groan as bones crunched and her scales blistered off into ash.

Shaking, she stood on wobbly legs and reached out to Vikki for support. A jealous part of me flinched that she hadn't reached out to me, but I had to remember who Sarah was to me. She wasn't my mate. She was a sin bonded to me and if I didn't play my cards right, would be my downfall when I faced the witch who'd branded me with this curse again.

"Can you walk?" I asked, then grabbed my stomach and winced. During limbo I'd absorbed my mates' souls. Carrying them inside of me was the oddest sensation, but once I got out of Hell, everything would be all right. I had to accept their power and their gifts right now, no matter how much it terrified me.

Sarah leaned heavily on Vikki's arm, but gave me a raised brow. "Can *you?*"

I scoffed and limped my way down the sheet of white marble. It separated the two rings of Hell that seemed to have merged into one another. Sarah's pride glittered behind us with the crushing ocean full of mermaids who didn't care about anyone except themselves, and Vikki's sloth that waited before us. Vikki's sin didn't look so different than the depths of the oceans. A long stretch of shadows swirled with nothing for as far as I could see other than drifting fog and the scrawling fingers of my nightmares across the sky. The darkness was following us down into the depths of Hell and I wondered what it'd do when it caught up to me.

We walked on in silence until Vikki finally addressed the elephant in the room. "Okay, so, now that we're here, how do we get free?"

I glanced at her, taking note that her short hair stuck out at the ends as if she'd been pulling at it. She was scared. Fuck, I was too numb to even be scared. I wanted to have Nate, Xavier, Luke, and Jet out in the open and in my arms. I wanted their strength and their reassurance, but all I had with me was their power. The sooner we reached the lowest level of Hell, the sooner I could see them again.

"I don't want to get free," I told her as I continued through the drifting shadows. Black wisps wrapped around my ankles and a deep cold ran up my legs. The sensation of wanting to curl into a ball and fall asleep prickled at me the farther we walked into this domain, but I drew on the warmth of my Blood Stone and the power of my runes to fend it off. When Sarah staggered, I reached out to her and squeezed her hand, sending warmth up her arm in a flash of red. She blinked at me, then smiled.

"Don't tell me you like it here?" Sarah joked, her voice coming out scratchy. Her smile fell as quickly as it had appeared as she rubbed at her throat. She accepted Vikki's hand as we kept walking.

Jealousy surged in me again, not because I wanted Sarah all to myself. I had four amazing guys who loved me for exactly who and what I was. It was just that Sarah and I had so much history and pain. I hated that someone like Vikki was who she turned to. Her sin of sloth wasn't one of laziness, but of a siren's unwillingness to resolve pain. She wallowed in her misery and she always would. That was a siren's way, and she'd only bring Sarah down with her.

I felt those sins as if they were my own, a curse from my bond. The sooner we got to that witch, the better.

"We have one more sin to pick up," I reminded them as I continued to trek on through the shadows. It'd most definitely gotten darker the farther we'd gone. The sensation to stop and lie down made my eyelids feel heavy.

Vikki stifled a yawn, but she managed to keep up with me. "Right," she said. "What sin would that be, then?"

I paused, because I heard it before I saw it. Moans of women lost in the best sin of all. My lips ticked up in a grin.

"Lust, and I think we've found him."

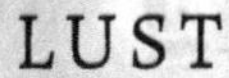

LUST

Sonya

It shouldn't have surprised me that Derek would be completely at home in Hell surrounded by his unforgivable sin. He pawed at a hoard of naked girls who draped over him, seemingly undisturbed by the slight horns that protruded from their foreheads. When he spotted me, his eyes lit up with ruby power and he grinned.

"Sonya, darling. You've come to join us?" He threaded his fingers behind his head and leaned back on the pile of cushions, sighing as women greedily bent down to stroke and lick. He didn't take his gaze off of me as they pleasured him.

Vikki and Sonya squeaked in shocked surprise behind me, but I wasn't put off by the display. I was a succubus and I knew lust better than anyone. I couldn't feed off of women, but Derek's lust scented the air and was more potent than a drug. Thankfully, the resistant his wife had given me kept its own and I was still under my own power, even under the full impact of the naked Incubus King.

I took a step closer and then stiffened when I realized that I, in fact, *could* feel the lust from the women. I'd heard that angels could take different forms, which included fallen angels. The girls giggling at me batted eyelashes over ruby-gleaming eyes. I buckled over when a fresh wave of their lust hit me.

Derek laughed with delight. "Dear, don't fight it." He sighed and leaned back further, stroking his fingers through a demon-girl's hair and lowered her mouth over his massive cock. "Just come and play," he added, his voice growling with need.

"You *cannot* go over there," Sarah hissed at me insistently.

Vikki nodded violently with her emphatic agreement. "You're a succubus. If you get all wrapped up in lust, you're never going to get out of here."

My eyelids drooped with the power that clawed through me. I'd never felt so much lust that was thick enough in the air to make my thighs clench. I curled my fingers over my stomach and drew on the heat from my runes, calling on my mates to push away the overpowering lust and remind me why I was here.

"Derek," I snapped, biting his name off my teeth like an unpleasant morsel. "I can't save you from your lust, but you can save me from an ancient curse that's gone on for too long." I pointed to a gleaming red staircase in the distance that spiraled down into the floor. Red light glowed from it in low, pulsing tones, leaving no doubt of where it led.

Derek rolled his head back and made a sound of complaint. "Sonya. I'm dead. Let me enjoy my eternal damnation in peace."

I blinked at him and staggered closer. He was right. He wasn't flesh and blood. He was a soul and he glittered with the telltale signs of the dead that was forever trapped in Hell. "Derek!" I shrieked. "How did you die? I saw Hades spare you."

Derek grinned, because I'd come too close, and grabbed my wrist. He yanked me down over him and spanked my ass. The pain zipped through me with malicious pleasure. Before he let me recover, he stroked his fingers over my thin underwear and lust wrapped around me until I found my mouth parting with a moan.

"Hades killed me when you weren't around to judge him," Derek said, his words growling low in his throat as he stroked me. He ran his thumb over my clit with violent pressure, punishing me for abandoning him to his fate. I moved to push off him, but he used his free hand to keep both wrists pinned to my back. He was so big that his one grip could hold me down while he relentlessly punished me. He pulled my underwear aside and slipped two fingers into me, making me cry out.

Just before the lust took me under and I would be beyond saving, Sarah pushed a demon-woman aside and cupped my face. "Sonya. Don't let him get to you. The bastard just wants you to stay with him. Don't give him the satisfaction."

My eyelids fluttered as I fought the lust that sank its teeth into me. Heat spiraled up my legs and my runes blazed as my mates sensed my distress, but it wasn't enough to fight what came so naturally to me. The demon-women kissed each other and added the crushing weight of sin to the symphony of pleasure.

Then Sarah did something unexpected. She brushed her lips over mine. I grazed my tongue over the sea salt that had dried on her plump lips before indulging in the kiss. She and I had never shared lust. It had always been something more that had drawn us together, and it was enough to bring me out of the Incubus King's control.

Freeing myself from Derek's grip, I twisted and kicked him in the balls. He might just be a spirit, but he could still feel that. He groaned and doubled over as he held himself. The demon-women eased away in a small semi-circle and giggled behind their hands.

"The fuck, Sonya," Derek complained as he gulped in fresh

breaths. "That seems uncalled for. I was just trying to give you a good time."

"No," I snapped and flared red heat through my body, burning the lust free of me with the power of my mate bonds. They were the ones who deserved my lust. Not this creep. "You were trying to trap me here," I said. "Now come on. Unless you want me to kick you in the balls again, you're going to do me one last favor."

He struggled to his feet, his perfect abs flexing as he stood and his midnight hair draping attractively over his forehead. He flashed me a grin as he recovered from the worst of the blow. "You were always full of surprises." He sighed and removed his hands, revealing his cock no worse for wear that stood at full attention.

It took all of my willpower not to admire him. "Right, and I'm also full of thoughts of my mates screaming in my head right now." It wasn't that I could actually hear them, but in particular I could *feel* Luke's rage, and now that I knew that was his cardinal sin, it made me crack a smile.

Derek gave me a raised brow, but instead of questioning me, his gaze fell to my runes that were glowing so hot they were visible through the sheer fabric of my lingerie. "Ah, well, I haven't seen a curse like that in a very long time." He sighed and adjusted his cock and pushed away a demon-woman who tried to stroke him. "Come on, then, succubus. I might be damned for eternity, but a mark like that means you have a chance at salvation. I won't begrudge you that." He waved me on as he approached the stairs. He snapped his fingers and black leather wrapped around his waist, forming the perfect pair of leather pants that made his ass look amazing. He paused and grinned over a muscled shoulder. "You going to gawk at me or are we going to go meet this witch of yours?"

Sarah broke from the shock first and curled her fingers into fists before she stormed past the Incubus King. Vikki trotted after her.

Right then. Off to the final layer of Hell and whatever damnation waited for me there.

HELL'S A WITCH

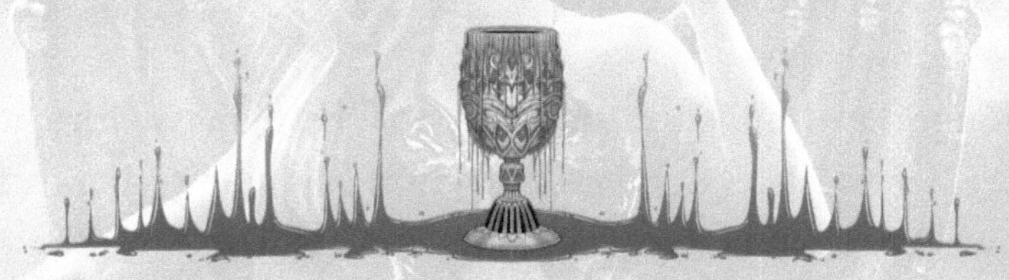

Sonya

I followed Derek into the pit, which is exactly where I imagined someone like him would end up if he ever died. I never in a million years would have thought I'd willingly follow him.

Sarah and Vikki held onto each other as they slipped into the bright flames of the lowest level of Hell. Derek, Vikki, and Sarah were my unresolved sins and they all played their part. Derek, his cock still rigid in his unseemly leather pants, took the lead and fearlessly walked through the flames. Vikki looked back at me, her eyes so dark they looked black, an endless void that represented her sin as a siren, forever consumed by her pain making her want to stand still and wallow in it. Sarah tugged her along, only giving me one dismissive glance. She resented me, her pride still biting at her heart that I'd required other lovers to survive. She'd never forgive me for that.

I stopped on the last step on the staircase to Hell and paused before the flames as I considered that. Forgiveness. That felt like it was important.

"Sonya?" a voice called me from beyond the flames and jolted me from my thoughts.

My eyes went wide and my breath caught in my throat. I scrambled into the wavering heat, because that voice had haunted my dreams all my life.

My mother.

I found her trapped in the worst of the flames with chains binding her wrists. Sarah was already at her side trying to free her, but hissed when the chains burned her. Vikki took a step back and called for Sarah to stop, that it was too dangerous. The way Sarah looked at me told me she knew what I was going through and she wanted to help. Panic colored her features and sweat gathered at her brow because she recognized the woman who looked so much like me right away. Long blonde hair, even if it was stuck to her face, framed her exquisite features. Pride swelled in my chest, an appropriate sin that I didn't deny myself.

"Mother!" I shrieked, but a witch's cackles kept me rooted to the ground.

The witch from my nightmares stepped through the flames and shadows swirled around her body like snakes, cutting through the bright red columns with ease. "Well, look at you, child. I underestimated you." Her dark eyes narrowed with malice and reflected the inferno that seemed to rage even harder around us. "It's time to end this."

Derek moved first. He'd been hiding in the flames, as if waiting for the evil he sensed to show itself. I never imagined that he loved me, or even really cared for me, but he launched for the witch and wrapped his fingers around her throat. "You don't belong here," he growled as he squeezed.

The witch's eyes bulged, but she flicked her wrist and the shadows sent Derek catapulting off of her. Embers flung into the air when he landed onto flames. They didn't consume him, though, only licked around his pants that wouldn't burn. He struggled to his feet and adjusted himself again, giving us a wicked smirk. Shadows coiled a line in front of him and barred his path.

"You'll get your turn," the witch promised with a sneer, then sent more shadows going after my mother.

Hearing her scream tore my heart into a thousand tiny pieces. I didn't care if the fires around her would burn me. I reached for her anyway, pushing Sarah and Vikki out of the way, and yanked on the chains. Pain shot up my arms, but I drew on the power of my runes, of my bondmates whose souls rested inside me, who would die for me if I asked for it. I had power over sin—four sins, at least, and that was a majority. It gave me enough strength to fend off the worst of the burn and unlatch the heavy buckles around my mother's wrists even as the witch's shadows writhed around us, blocking off Sarah and Vikki from any hope to assist me.

The witch shrieked with rage. "How can you break Hell's chains? You don't possess the power of shadow!"

No, I didn't, and my arms instantly sagged at my sides as invisible needles punished me for breaking the witch's spell.

My mother wrapped her arms around me and it all felt so surreal. How could she be here, in the bottom of Hell, trapped by a witch? How had she been here all this time?

"Daughter," she urged until she pulled away and I met her gaze. The power of Hell bled through her eyes with ruby brilliance, making her look even more breathtaking. She was like me. She was only strengthened here… the mother of the Queen of the Damned. "We don't have much time," she told me as she rubbed my arms, urging sensation back into them.

My vision blurred as tears threatened to overflow onto my cheeks. I couldn't remember the last time I'd cried. Probably the last time I'd seen my mother. "Time?" I echoed. We'd been robbed of time. I'd been denied a life with a mother and she'd been suffering down here all for what? To entertain a vile witch who'd tried to find a loophole to avoid Hell? Tough luck. I gritted my teeth together as feeling returned to my fingers and I made a fist. My gaze snapped to the witch who'd been busy chanting some new malicious spell to hit us with. "I need to kill her."

"No," my mother said and shook me so violently that my teeth clacked. "Hell doesn't work like that. If you disable her body, she'll just rise up again. You must defeat her the same way you have mastered your sins." She glanced down at my runes. Four of them burned hot. The three outliers had already begun to dim and fade. I was never meant to master them all. "Four," she murmured. "Four is enough."

I had to use my sins to my advantage. The most prominent of all burned through me and I recognized Luke's raw rage that made my chest expand, made an echo of wings ghost at my back. It should have frightened me to feel his power so thoroughly, but I felt his sin. I'd helped him overcome his anger, not destroy it, but use it for good. There was such a thing as righteous anger, I realized, and it empowered me instead of bringing me down. When painful slits sliced down my back, I buckled over with a cry.

"Yes," my mother cried. "You're doing it! Keep going!"

This was what she'd meant by mastering my sins. Each man's soul inside of me would feed me his power. Angel wings sprouted from my back and even in Hell, a coolness swept across the fresh appendages as they spread out into the open. Tingles ran through my body and new nerves flared to life.

I staggered past my mother, temporarily off-balance by my new wings, and approached the witch whose chants had only grown more frantic as her eyes bugged out when she saw me. I grinned, because a fucking Witch of the Shadow Coven was scared of *me.* A witch that had cursed me as a child, doomed my mother to years of imprisonment in Hell, and was about to become my bitch. This was going to be fun.

When I went to grab her, the next sin in my belly filled me with raw heat. Nate's envy. He'd overcome his helplessness and his envy had turned into strength. He knew now that his strengths were cunning, wit, and understanding of what made people tick. My world flashed as I saw right through the witch, her skin turning translucent and revealing the shadows that bound her black heart. This was Nate's power he offered me, to understand what fueled this witch. It was darkness, evil, and hatred, but there was something else there, something the witch had managed to keep alive and buried deep her in her heart. I paused as I stared at the tiny glimmering red gem.

A Blood Stone shard.

I reached for it, my hand going right through her chest and the witch screamed. She tried to move away from me but my vampiric speed easily kept up with her as I invaded her spirit. My mother was right. The physical body in this realm was just an illusion, one she could discard and reform. But her spirit, that's what I attacked now. I saw what kept her out of Hell's grasp and allowed her to create this realm where she kept my mother prisoner. A witch of her nature worshiped the power of the Blood Stone, so it made sense a shard would rest inside her soul protected by writhing shadows.

When I wrapped my fingers around the cold shadows that tried to resist me, my third sin kicked in. Greed. Jet's dragon wanted this power for us. Greed could be used to fuel ambition, and I let the power of dragonfire burn through my body, lighting up my skin like a beacon and disintegrating the witch's shadows under my fingertips.

Screams and shouts broke my concentration. Derek, Sarah,

and Vikki were all yelling at me and pointing at my feet, but I couldn't make out what they were saying. I was too immersed in sin and power.

Just when I was about to pluck the glittering red shard from the witch's soul, excruciating pain ran up my legs. I looked down to find myself trapped in a hellish device made of iron and fire. Giant jaws clamped around my thighs and dug into my flesh until it hit bone. My blood poured out over the infernal devices and made me dizzy.

I loosened my grip and the witch stumbled to the ground. She choked and ran her fingers over her chest, but I'd damaged her shadows.

The prison that had been keeping Derek blocked off from me disintegrated and he rushed forward just as stars sparked across my vision. He cupped my face and ran a finger over one of my fangs I didn't even realize I'd extended. They seemed to come out of their own accord. "Sonya. You need to overcome this witch." He leaned in close until the sweet musk of him wrapped around me. Even though I'd taken a resistant against his powers, the smooth perfection of his throat that throbbed with his pulse made my own heart quicken. "Drink," he commanded. "Take what you need to win." When I didn't bite, he glared at me with a gaze that said I'd better drink, and I'd better take every last drop. He had no intention of staying in Hell—and neither did I.

Fuck. The bastard wanted me to drink him dry? I was happy to grant his wish.

Without any further hesitation, I opened my mouth and sank my fangs into his glistening skin. The sweet burst of his life-force spilled down my throat and I sagged against him as the pain in my legs went numb. Xavier's sin of gluttony could come in handy when it came to blood. His approval swept through me, making my fangs seep magical pleasure into my victim. Derek was not one easily seduced, being the King of Sex and my very own unresolved sin of lust, but even his mouth parted and his pulse quickened under my tongue.

"Fuck," he whispered. "When I get out of this, I am hiring some vampires."

I twisted, biting down harder, making him groan as his pleasure mixed with pain. I wasn't going to forget who he was, and if I had anything to say about it, he was going to be staying right here in Hell where he belonged.

"Keep going, Sonya!" Sarah shouted from behind and I unlatched from Derek's throat and turned to find her and Vikki helping my mother. My eyes went wide when I spotted a rip in the veil back to the real world. A dark room with a pedestal with an open book atop it waited on the other side. I squinted at a woman who chanted, but she didn't look like a Witch of the Shadow Coven. After a moment recognition jolted me as Luke's soul told me who'd opened up a portal to Hell. This was Renee, Luke's mother, and a fucking powerful Seer. Damn.

"Get her through the portal!" I commanded and turned back to the witch who'd managed to amass a writhing ball of shadows.

She ignored me and continued her spell. Her lips moved but no sound came out. The flames all around us leapt higher and Derek started to crawl past me. I slammed my foot against his back and flared my new wings to keep my balance as he struggled under my weight. "You're not going anywhere," I told him. "I'll be back for you." When he growled, but flattened himself against the ground in submission, I used him as a stepping stool as I went towards the witch.

The ball looked like it was about ready to explode and I assessed the situation. Nate's power gave me a few options of what this could be. One: the witch was summoning something, but we were already in Hell, so I imagined if she could have summoned any demons to fight for her she'd have done that by now. No soul to bargain with… no demonic power. So that left option two: a self-destruction spirit bomb.

"Great," I muttered.

The witch stopped chanting and opened her eyes. Midnight shards swirled in place of her irises and she gave me a malicious grin of triumph. "It's over," she hissed. "If I'm going down, I'm taking you with me."

The Blood Stone I'd absorbed what seemed like eons ago finally broke its silence and spoke in my mind. *Sonya. This is it. This is what your nightmares have been preparing you for. If you fail now, the echoes of calamity won't be able to be contained. They'll spread across the skies with the black fingers of your terror and consume the world. You must cleanse Hell and take your place as its rightful ruler.*

I curled my fingers into fists. "How do I fight her?" I hissed under my breath.

A long sigh unfurled in my mind. *You don't.*

I shot up one eyebrow in surprise, but then I realized what my Blood Stone was talking about. What really resolved sin was painfully simple.

Forgiveness.

The witch's eyes widened just before I closed my own and spread my wings. I'd forgiven my four mates of their sins, but had I forgiven Sarah, Vikki, and Derek? Hardly. It wasn't easy, but if I wanted to make it out of this alive, that's what I had to do.

Sarah's pride had come between us, but could I really blame her for wanting me all to herself? Even if I wasn't built that way, she was loyal to a fault. I couldn't live in hatred for her being the way she was. I had to do what I'd always wanted her to do for me: accept. So I accepted Sarah in my heart, all her good and bad and felt the small rune on my left side twinge to life. Darkness seeped from it and swirled over the left side of my body, spreading tattoos over my skin.

It was working.

The witch lashed out at me as flickers of her spirit bomb sparked dangerous whips into the air, but magic had already enveloped me into a cocoon of safety. Vikki was next. I'd grown to feel compassion for her because she loved Sarah, even if Vikki was a siren and would always be married to her sorrow. It was in spite of her sin of sloth and languishing in her misery that she still found a way to stand up for Sarah and to protect her as best as she could. She even followed her all the way to Hell to make sure she was safe. I had to forgive her of her faults, just for that.

Her rune swept new power through my body, leaving fresh black spirals across my skin in its wake, and I readied myself for the last sin that would be the most difficult to forgive.

Derek, King of Sex, and mirror to my own faults. Lust had come close to destroying my life, but it'd also brought me closer to my four. Without lust, I wouldn't have bonded with them and I wouldn't have learned that lust could go hand-in-hand with love, make it stronger and impenetrable. Without Derek, I wouldn't have filled my Blood Stone with renewed power and I never would have bonded with my four. In spite of all the terrible things he'd done, I was truly grateful to him for that.

And so, my seven sins were complete, resolved, forgiven, and the witch screamed as the fires of forgiveness, hotter than hell-fire or dragonfire, poured from my body in merciless waves and turned my hair black as it flung about my face.

I opened my eyes as her shadows writhed and burned, taking the witch along with them until only the small shard of the Blood Stone she'd traded her soul for remained.

I plucked it off the ground that smoldered with embers, turned on my heel, and dragged Derek with me to the portal out of Hell.

EPILOGUE

Sonya

I couldn't just leave Derek there, not after I'd truly forgiven him. In his fucked up way, I think he tried to be a good guy. He'd only wanted to live out in the open instead of hiding in the shadows. I couldn't blame him for that, but I could never approve of his methods. I had to remember who he was and how long he'd been a part of this world. Living hundreds of years warped one's sense of morality, and perhaps I took it upon myself to remind him of his humanity. Or, at least, I knew the perfect person who could.

"No fucking way," Nate barked and crossed his broad arms over his chest.

I made sure to get alone time with all of my guys. This week was Nate's turn and I slipped my fingers over his arms, unfurling his defense, and slipped into his embrace. My lips teased against his and I pressed him against the wall of our oversized bedroom. A kingsized bed with tousled sheets invited us to delve into it again, but I wanted him on my terms. He wasn't going to bend me over and make me forget what I needed him to do, so I pinned him and ran my fingers over his chest as I breathed in his musk.

He strained against me, not able to get me off of him even if he actually wanted to. He knew he was mortal and I most certainly was not, but his eyes gleamed with delight and confidence. His gaze raked over me and the new tattoos that spread over my body. I was the Queen of Hell now, but I wasn't going to hurt him. I had added padding to this particular room for when Nate and I got together, just to make sure I didn't damage my favorite human when the fun got too rough. I didn't know how much control I had over my new powers.

Nate stiffened as my hips grated against his. "If you're trying to seduce me to get your way," he began as he eyes flared with mischief, "then show me you mean it."

He knew I was holding back. I trailed a finger up his neck and gazed longingly at his pulsing vein. Two tiny pink dots on his delicate skin showed where I'd marked him once already earlier today. My bite gave pleasure, and also healing. My other guys lost their marks in a matter of seconds, but Nate's body indulged my claim for at least a day. He was mine and his blood tasted more delicious than any I'd ever had, although I'd never admit that to anyone, and I'd especially never admit that to Nate. His ego was bad enough already now that he'd conquered his envy over supernatural races. "Your father can be redeemed; I'm sure of it," I murmured and then followed my tongue where my finger had been. When I got to the edge of his chin, I gave him a playful nip, not breaking the skin. I'd gotten better at controlling my vampiric urges and I strung out the promise of sex and the pleasure of my bite for hours. It drove Nate insane and I loved it.

Nate had been about to retort, but the sensual caresses made him growl and he shoved a leg between my thighs, spreading me open as he grabbed me with undeniable possession. Pressure radiated from my core as he rolled his fingers over my folds, the separation between us just a thin layer of my favorite lingerie. "The Queen of Hell," he teased as he nipped at my ear, "has a soft spot. Who would have thought?" He rubbed again, hard, winning a cry from me. Impatient, he ripped away the thin fabric and thrust two fingers inside of me.

"Not yet," I pleaded, but pleasure already swept through me and threatened to take me under.

"I've let you have your fun," he growled in my ear and ruthlessly thrust his fingers inside of me again. He used his free hand to hold my ass close to him as he pummeled me with pleasure. "Now it's time for mine."

My nails dug into his shoulders as the hardness of him pressed against my thigh. I wanted to reach for him and feel his supple skin across my fingertips. I moved a hand to his waistband but he squeezed me against him and kept my hand pinned on his chest. "I could overpower you," I threatened, but my words cut short when he rolled his thumb over the nub of my clit and made me gasp.

"What if I've been letting you think I'm weak?" he mused before pressing his lips to mine. He thrust his tongue into my mouth and I opened for him, wanting to taste him.

Pride, a sin I might have forgiven but never quite overcome, swelled in me and I did try to push him away then. I wanted to grab his cock and make him submit to me, but when I pushed against him, I realized… I couldn't move out of his grip.

He grinned against my mouth and resumed working his fingers inside of me, rolling pleasure with his strong strokes. "Had you fooled, didn't I?" he whispered, then took me by surprise as he rushed me across the room with undeniable *inhuman* speed and slammed me against the wall. The padding split against the blow at my back and I gasped. He ripped away my underwear and pulled out his cock before thrusting it inside of me. He didn't wait for my body to accept him. He pulled out and slammed in hard, taking me with the force and domination of a dragon.

That's when I spotted the dim red light behind his eyes. I'd recognize that power anywhere. "Are you… borrowing Jet's power?" I managed to gasp as he slammed into me again and choked off anything else I had to say.

He took my hand and ran it across the runes of my stomach, stopping when I reached Jet's. It blazed with heat. "Our bond has never been stronger," he told me. "I feel all of them." He grinned. "I hope Jet is alone right now, because he is feeling everything I am. You belong to us, Sonya, and we will share the pleasure you give us."

When he sucked one of my nipples into his mouth and rolled the other with his thumb, I relented and threw my head back, letting him take me.

I only felt a little guilty after the best night of sex with Nate I'd ever had. If Jet had really felt that pleasure, I most certainly hoped that he hadn't been doing anything important at the time.

Of course, he'd been in the middle of an elaborate meeting involving dragon politics and had been around some of the most esteemed and wealthy scaly shifters in China. Safely in our penthouse, his glare held so much venom and desire that I fidgeted. I never fidgeted.

"I said I was sorry," I offered as I crossed my leg over my knee, trying to look nonchalant and unapologetic. The façade might have held had I not just uncrossed and crossed my legs three times since I'd arrived.

I'd only just come through the portal that Xavier's witches

had set up for us. It glittered its ruby promises of refuge at the end of the long bedroom, but I glowered at the amused vampire who watched me through it, safe and sound in Venice. Xavier waited there until I finally huffed a sigh and marched over to it and drew the drapes from my side of the portal. Was a little privacy too much to ask? I knew Xavier worried about me. Jet could be dangerous, but I could take care of myself.

As much as Jet was angry with me, I was glad that I could see him again. My guys all had their own lives, but there was no way I could stay apart from any of them for long. The most sensible solution was to use magic, of course. Deep in the tunnels under Venice was the vampire stronghold, which I now commanded second to Hades. I was Xavier's bondmate and Queen of Hell, which gave me enough clout to use the power of the Blood Stone to make permanent portals to bedrooms across the world. Nate's room in Detroit. Luke's room in Seattle. And, of course, Jet's room in the penthouse at Shanghai where we'd first made love.

When I turned around, Jet had gotten closer. His heat radiated off his body and made the air twist around him. I rolled my eyes. "I'm getting a drink. Want one?" When he didn't reply, I shoved past him and poured myself a glass from the bar. I leaned back against it and swirled the ice cubes. I needed alcohol to handle Jet's amount of rage right now. His lust fogged the room and made me dizzy, but his tattoos swirled over his arms and told me that said I'd better not push him right now if I wanted to keep my head.

Jet narrowed his eyes as I took a delicate sip. "I went full-on erect in front of an entire room of dragon shifters and fucking *moaned.*"

I spit out my drink, successfully sending it everywhere. I should have apologized or tried to look a little bit sorry. Instead, I smothered a laugh behind my hand. "Holy shit," I muttered.

Jet glowered and wiped the whiskey I'd spit on him off his

face. He marched up to me and grabbed my hips, making me topple over my glass and it splashed onto the floor. He didn't bother to clean it up. Heat burned from his touch with the hottest dragonfire I'd ever felt from him and his eyes blazed with a familiar silver glow…

My eyes went wide. "Are you connecting with Luke?" His rage was a bit too potent—even for a dragon shifter.

He startled at that, then his gaze went distant as if he was sensing for the other male somewhere beyond my reach. He must have found something, because he cursed and shoved away from me. "I'm not going to do the same thing to Luke that Nate did to me. The poor bastard is probably having dinner with his mother."

I snickered. "Oh, come on. I'm sure it's fine." Instead of approaching him, I slipped the edge of my dress over my shoulder. It's not that I enjoyed dresses, but Xavier had stolen every piece of sensible clothing from my new room in the vampire den I'd managed to acquire and replaced them with stunning gowns. He'd promised all my jeans and tanks were getting washed, but had a malicious grin when I'd stepped through the portal. Now I understood why he'd dressed me up. Jet's gaze dipped to my breast that slipped free from the beaded fabric. I looked damn good, like a present being unwrapped. By the look in Jet's eyes, he wanted to unwrap me and ask questions later.

As if he couldn't resist, he reached up and ran one thumb over my hardening nipple, making me shiver. "You're going to damn me to Hell all over again," he said, but he had a glimmer of a smile playing across his lips. His teeth elongated into slight points and his eyes flashed with an eerie reptilian stare. He curled into my neck and gave me a playful bite. He knew I liked that. "I can't stay mad at you. Not when you're so willing to make amends."

"Yes," I promised and ran my fingers through his hair as he peeled away my dress. "Amends."

He lifted me and I wrapped my legs around his waist. Our kiss was surprisingly sweet and passionate. I loved Jet. I loved all my guys. I was so happy, so complete.

He pulled away and gazed at me with such hunger that I should have been terrified. His connection to Luke sent silver strands of power streaking across his tattoos. "I might hurt you," he admitted as he pressed me against the bar and the hard length of him caressed my most intimate areas, spreading fresh heat through my core.

"Never," I said, and parted my lips as my fangs came out of their own accord. I was about to lose control and if any of my guys could handle me right now, it would be my dragon. "But I might hurt you."

Jet growled and took out his cock, first rubbing it against me and making my threats diminish into whimpers.

He played with me until I writhed on top of him. I laced my fingers around his neck and squirmed, trying to get him to give me what I wanted. When he finally did, my skin burned as his power invaded my body and soul, making me explode with heat from the inside. When I threw my head back and cried out, flames licked across my skin and smoke drifted from my nostrils.

You'd think that I'd have learned from my first mistake, but of course, Luke was nice and pissed off. He actually *had* been having dinner with his mother when Jet had ravished the shit out of me.

Instead of repeating the mistake, all four of my guys gathered in a rare meeting. The best venue seemed to be Luke's house in

Seattle. He'd bought a place across from his mother's shop on Fortune Street. We all gathered into the cozy living room and nursed our drinks—except for Renee.

Renee didn't look old enough to be his mother. She looked even younger than me, but I suppose when one is an all-powerful Seer, age is not something you have to worry about. She finally huffed her annoyance and was the first to break the silence. "Well, I could cut the tension in this room with a knife," she declared as she shot to her feet.

My gaze fell to the deck of cards she continued to shuffle. Nate had been the one to free her from her false imprisonment. She'd been locked up for child abuse, having seen the terrible future where Luke needed a dark kind of training to prepare him for what Detective Anderson was going to do to him. It'd saved his life and his mind, but not before Luke had figured that out. Luckily, all it took was a little bit of witch magic to undo a court order, and she was a free woman. I didn't ask Nate what he traded to make a rebel coven of witches perform the spell, but I was grateful for it. It would have been difficult for me to convince enough witches to get to Seattle to do the spell. The portals they'd made only worked on me and those in my bond. They either would've needed to create new portals or taken flights to America, both options which would have drawn attention to them. Apparently witches were a rare and sought after commodity.

"It's fine," Nate said, leaning back in his chair and sprawling his legs. He winked at me when he caught me admiring the place where his shirt lifted up and revealed delicious curves disappearing into his waistband. "We'll get used to it."

Luke scoffed. "You weren't the one humiliated."

"Enough," Renee snapped. To my surprise, she didn't seem bothered that her son had probably had a psychic orgasm right in front of her. She lifted an eyebrow at me. "I'm not a prude, you know. I'm a mother. I've had sex, too, plenty of it, and am aware it's a natural part of life."

It was rare that a succubus blushed, but I felt its uncharacteristic heat sweep over my chest and up my neck. "Of course," I murmured, then stuck my face into my glass and knocked it back.

She smirked, then gave us each an appraisal. "Your bond is the first of many to come." She shuffled her cards again, then drew the top one and showed it to us. It displayed an elaborate rune, but I didn't recognize it. "The echoes of calamity have begun. You've stopped the worst of the first wave."

Intrigued, I leaned forward and cupped my glass. Alcohol buzzed through me before its effects were wiped out by my healing abilities. It was as close to drunk as I was going to get these days. "So, it wasn't a coincidence that my mother and I were targeted by a Shadow Witch?"

Renee nodded and it made me wish my mother was here. After all she'd been through she wanted some time alone with my grandmother. Nate had kept Grans safe in Detroit. I was looking forward to seeing them again.

Renee drew in a deep breath before speaking. "The Shadow Witch that trapped your mother would have broken a delicate balance. Shadow Witches sell their souls and go to Hell if and when they die. If she'd managed to find a loophole, Hell itself would have split in two and begun a series of events that would have brought death down on all of us. Because our worlds are closer than they should be, she was almost able to do it." She set the card on the ground and it glowed. "Our enemies will take many forms, as will the guardians who Fate chooses to rise up and stop the next threat." The rune's light died and Renee smirked. "Looks like our next guardians will be vampires, and their bondmate will be a mortal-born witch."

Xavier raised an eyebrow at that. "You're saying there will be another vampiric bond using the Blood Stone? Vampires can't mate with witches." He didn't seem very happy to hear that someone might challenge our rule in Venice, especially with a forbidden match.

Renee gave him the biggest grin I'd ever seen and her hand draped over Luke's shoulder. "You forget, Xavier, that my father was a vampire, and my mother was a Seer before me. That makes her a witch."

Xavier's gaze bounced between them, then went wide. "No, it can't be." He shot to his feet.

I'd never taken the time to see the similarities in Xavier and Luke, but the subtle signs were there. Same height. Same silky locks. Same lean frame that made my insides ignite.

Luke seemed just as surprised as the rest of us as realization dawned. "Are you saying that I have both angelic and vampiric blood?"

Renee nodded. "Yes, darling." She stroked his face as she beamed with sheer adoration and pride. "I don't know who your grandfather was, but I did enough research to find out that there are lost vampiric tribes. He came from one of them."

"There's a good reason those tribes were wiped out," Xavier hissed with menace that surprised me. "Mating with witches mixes magics and creates creatures with too much power." He appraised Luke's mother, as if seeing her in a new light. "Are you the instrument that fused our bond with Sonya?"

She went somber at the accusation. I approached her and rested a hand on her arm. Any trace of alcohol was now completely gone from my body and I felt entirely too sober to take in this new information. "You didn't just give Luke a vision, did you?"

Renee bit her lip before nodding. Her brown curls draped over her face, hiding her guilt from me, but I felt it. As Queen of Hell, I felt sin like a blade on my skin. "I knew the next calamity would come. I made the spell that triggered a balance in Fate." Her eyes shot up to meet mine, making me take a step back with the desperation and magic that sparked behind them. "Don't you see? I am the Keymaster of Heaven, Hell, and Earth. It's my job to make sure the realms are safe. If I had to trigger the spell of the guardians to fulfill my duties, then so be it."

Taking a moment to look at my guys—Nate with his hands folded as he watched the conversation grow tense, Jet with his tattoos sprawling over him in magical swirls and his eyes sliced with reptilian danger, Xavier with fangs bared and menace in his gaze, and finally Luke with hurt in his gaze—I knew I could never have lived a full life without them. I was complete, and because of Renee, I'd found my purpose. "No," I said, dropping my voice low, "I'm grateful for it."

The tension in the room eased and Renee's shoulders relaxed. "Then it's time for the next guardians to take the stage." Her gaze went distant. Darkness filtered over her irises and I knew she was looking into the future. "She'll meet them soon. She's a powerful witch. A coven lost, even more ancient than the vampires she will captivate."

I grinned. "May she have mercy on their souls."

THE END

Next in the Blood Stone Universe: The Vampire Curse: Royal Covens Books 1-3 (Complete Series)

ROYAL COVENS BOOKS 1-3
THE
VAMPIRE
CURSE
USA TODAY BESTSELLING AUTHOR
J.R. THORN

What does a fallen angel, a vampire, and a sexy bodyguard hav
the carriers of the seven deadly sins—and it's my job

I don't take shit from anybody, and that's what has g
so far. My mother's dead. My brother struck a deal
that gets me in all sorts of trouble, and my dream
fog of death that's determined to hu

Seems like destiny has finally caught up w

If I want to survive what's coming next, I'm
ness I've been running from all my life
dreams. It's real, and I'm going to need to
ing with the sin of l

Turns out be the long-lo

Seven Sins is a compi
devoured containin

THE BLO

SEVE

USA TODAY BES

J.R. T

9 781953 393012

Queen of Hell

Keep reading to enjoy this additional scene of Sonya and her mates that takes place after The Vampire Curse: Royal Covens Books 1-3 intended to read now. This is a thank-you for purchasing the Seven Sins Collection, so please enjoy!

YEARS LATER

"This isn't fair," I complained, languishing in Xavier's arms, naked, in bed, just like he preferred.

Luke ran his strong fingers over my legs, and I didn't protest when his touch ran higher, massaging me in more intimate places.

Jet paced the room, his rage evident that we had to leave Earth behind, but it had been his idea. "I've already made the arrangements," he said without looking up. His tattoos swirled over his skin, making him look like a living piece of art that I wanted to sink my teeth into. His reptilian eyes locked on me, full of passion, heat, and desire, but he put business first. And right now, he was determined that I would listen. "Bo and Yan are holding a vote right now to elect a new King to take my place in Shanghai."

"How democratic of you," Luke mused, grinning in a way that made me want to bite him."

I didn't tell Jet that I'd already been making arrangements for us to leave. When he'd begun telling me about the monster attacks, I knew. My role as Champion of the First Echo of

Calamity wasn't over. Something had happened and mortals were changing, converting into supernatural creatures that my fellow Champions didn't understand. Vampires, Succubi, Witches, among other creatures of the dark weren't welcome in Fortune Academy, a school founded by Renee and her new prodigy.

I'd made a school of my own, one that would give even the worst of the worst a chance. Hell needed a leader, one who could guide them against the tides of Calamity that threatened to take us all down a path of sin with no redemption.

Perhaps, one day, my daughter would find her way back to me as well. I had been too young to understand that there was good in all creatures, even monsters. A mistake I would mend in time.

Plus, if anyone understood sin and how to overcome it, it was me.

"You're just going to abandon your people and your home?" Xavier asked, running his fingers down my collarbone to glide over my breasts. All of us had become accustomed to mixing business and pleasure, especially with the developments as of late. With Hell threatening to merge with our world and infiltrating it with Demonspawn—and a few full-blooded demons—I couldn't justify staying above ground for much longer.

"If we don't stop what's happening then my people won't have a home still standing," Jet growled back, smoke drifting from his nostrils as he worked to contain his anger. This whole situation pissed him off and even if Xavier liked to prod at the dragon, all of my mates were at their breaking point.

"Don't antagonize him, Xavier," I chided my vampire, punishing him by getting up and crawling away, showing him my ass while I pushed Luke down onto the bed.

My angel allowed me to have my fun, enjoying my sense of domination as I bared my fangs. He leaned his head to the side, exposing his gorgeous neck and I bit down, indulging in his sweet blood that tasted of sunlight and ambrosia, a flower that only bloomed in the Heavens.

"The last time we were in Hell it was hot," Nate complained. "And we almost died." He crossed his arms and leaned against the wall, making a point not to join my oversized bed made to accommodate all my mates. He cocked his head, watching me grind my hips over Luke as I rubbed myself against his hardening cock. Feeding always made it difficult for me to think straight and all I wanted was blood and sex—both of which my mates gave me in ample supply.

"We won't be going to the sins layer," Xavier pointed out. I'd taken him to see our new home because I wanted him to see it first. The vampire understood politics and he understood my mates. I doubted I would be able to convince them that Hell could be our home, especially when I didn't want to go there myself, but I was its Queen and a demon named Lucifer was taking advantage of my absence. It was time to take my rightful place and stop Calamity's influence from destroying all the realms from the inside out.

"Okay, where would we be going then?" Nate asked, skepticism heavy in his voice. "The picnic in the park layer?"

Ignoring his snark, I took my fill of Luke's blood and unlatched from him as the hot, sticky essence trailed down my throat. Nate watched me, his humor fading as his eyes burned with desire because he liked it when I fed. I positioned Luke's dick and the angel grabbed onto my hips, lowering me onto him as I began a slow, delicious joining of our bodies.

"A palace," I promised as I offered him a hand to join us. "A place where you will become something more than you are now." As my sin of envy, Nate would be drawn by that promise, one I fully intended to fulfill. He had supernatural blood in him, dormant and untapped. With my help, he would become something *more.*

I glanced at my dragon who prowled closer to me, drawn by my lust. Sensing my need, my vampire approached me from behind, his fingers exploring my body as his fangs grazed my throat.

"All of you will," I vowed.

The succubus side of my powers had dampened over the years to make way for my growth as the Queen of Hell, and an immortal vampire, but I kept the best parts of me that had once been succubus. I enthralled my mates, calling them to join me in our pleasure as we celebrated this change and said goodbye to our mortal lives.

Heat billowed into the room as my mates all put their hands on me, their mouths tasting me and I lost myself to their oblivion. Hell opened up around us, swallowing us whole and a transformation of my form took hold.

Long, bat-like wings spread from my back and horns protruded from my head. A ring of fire ran around my hair, forming a crown as I lost myself to ecstasy.

This had happened a few times before, ever since I'd started making trips to the Hell Realm, and only lasted for the duration of my union with my mates. It was when I let go of control and allowed something deeper within me to take over that I embraced what I really was.

I was the Queen of Hell, and it was time to take my throne.

THE END

Next in the Blood Stone Universe: The Vampire Curse: Royal Covens Books 1-3 (Complete Series)

ROYAL COVENS BOOKS 1-3
THE VAMPIRE CURSE
USA TODAY BESTSELLING AUTHOR
J.R. THORN

NOTE FROM THE AUTHOR

Thank you for reading all the way to the end of Sonya's story! I hope you enjoyed it and will leave a review!

Sonya's story has been far more popular than I could have hoped. Thank you all who have enjoyed her story.

While this is the end of Sonya's story, the Blood Stone Series in an ongoing world, she makes reappearances in every new series I write within the Blood Stone Universe. The next trilogy is called "Royal Covens" and continues where Vampire Sins left off. You won't want to miss it!

Next in the Blood Stone Series: Royal Covens (Book 1 in The Vampire Curse collection)

ROYAL
COVENS
BOOK ONE
HER
VAMPIRE
MENTORS
USA TODAY BESTSELLING AUTHOR
J.R. THORN

RECOMMENDED READING ORDER

All Books are Standalone Series listed by their sequential order of events

Standalone Stories

Taste Me

Their Blood Queen

Dragonrider Academy

Elemental Fae Universe Reading List

Elemental Fae Academy: Books 1-3

Midnight Fae Academy

Fortune Fae Academy

Fortune Fae M/M Steamy Episodes

Candela

Winter Fae Queen

Hell Fae

Blood Stone Series Universe Reading List

Recommended Reading Order is Below

Seven Sins (Books 1-3)

Book 1: Succubus Sins

Book 2: Siren Sins

Book 3: Vampire Sins

The Vampire Curse: Royal Covens (Books 1-3)

Book 1: Her Vampire Mentors

Book 2: Her Vampire Mentors

Book 3: Her Vampire Mentors

Fortune Academy (Part I)

Year One

Year Two

Year Three

Fortune Academy Underworld (Part II)

Book 3.5: Burn in Hell

Book Four

Book 4.5: Burn in Rage

Book Five

Book Six

Book 6.5: Burn in Brilliance

Fortune Academy Underworld (Part III)

Book Seven

Book Eight

Book 8.5: Burn in Ruin

Book 8.666: Burn in Darkness

Book Nine

Book Ten

Crescent Five

(Rejected Mate Wolf Shifter RH)

Book One: Moon Guardian

Book Two: Moon Cursed

Book Three: Moon Queen

Book Four: Moon Kissed

Dark Arts Academy (Vella)

Ongoing serial

Book One (KU)

Book Two (KU)

Unicorn Shifter Academy

- *Book One*
- *Book Two*
- *Book Three*

Non-RH Books (J.R. Thorn writing as Jennifer Thorn)

Noir Reformatory Universe Reading List

Noir Reformatory: The Beginning (Standalone)

Noir Reformatory: First Offense

Noir Reformatory: Second Offense

Noir Reformatory Turns RH from this point with the addition of a third mate

Noir Reformatory: Third Offense

Sins of the Fae King Universe Reading List

(Book 1) Captured by the Fae King

(Book 2) Betrayed by the Fae King

Learn More at www.AuthorJRThorn.com

The Blood Stone Series Interior Art

JET

SARAH &
VIKKI

XAVIER

QUEEN OF HELL

This concludes Sonya's Story, but she will make brief appearances in future Blood Stone Series Books, so be sure to be on the lookout! If you'd like to see what happened to her daughter Lily, start reading Fortune Academy! Turn the page for the first chapter!

Fortune Academy

Chapter One

It all started with a severed hand and a hot bounty hunter. For the record, I would never chop off the hand of a hot guy... unless he was being a total douchebag—which he was. Plus, it grew back, so it doesn't even really count... not that I was aware bounty hunters could regrow appendages, but hey, no harm no foul.

Right, I tend to blather on without context so let me start from the beginning, right around the time when my memories restarted in the middle of the street with no idea who I was. Boy, was I in for a surprise when I figured that one out.

The first thing I remember from that point on was my clothes sticking to my skin and my hair plastered to my cheeks from the freezing rain. Everything was sore as if I'd been run over by a bulldozer. I wandered, drawn by a pull that promised refuge until I found myself in a dark alley facing the back entrance of a bar. Raindrops hit my face like irritating little insects, but I couldn't seem to find the strength to leave this particular doorstep. Something bad had happened to me and I must have run until I couldn't run anymore. My legs trembled underneath me like jello and my heart wouldn't stop thundering in my ears. All I could do was gulp in breaths of air and wait for someone to open that dull, red door lined with scratches.

The moonlight was too bright, but I peered up at the sky and pleaded for mercy anyway. I didn't know what I needed mercy for, or why I was paralyzed in the freezing rain at this grimy doorstep, but I just knew that this was my last hope. I had to stay here until that door opened.

The streetlights blasted on and made me flinch, but I stared at the door until it opened and a woman in her late forties peered down at me with a disgusted scowl. She stared at me for a long time before she stepped aside. "Come on," she said, then turned around and left the entranceway free.

That's how I became Cindy's newest waitress. Waiting like a drowned rat at the back of her bar to what was supposed to be her secret entrance reserved for smoke breaks. Well, that's how all supernaturals found Cindy. Now when I walked outside I could spot the little ugly engraving in the corner of the doorway that drew people like me to the place. A little tiny skull etched there with a dumb grin on its face like it knew how many headaches it would bring Cindy. This was her punishment... to help people like me who had no memory of who they were or what they'd done. Ever since the Second Echo of Calamity apparently the world had gone to all sorts of shit and supernaturals had to start over with clean slates, memories included. What Cindy had done to deserve her fostering of looney supernaturals, I had no idea and she wasn't about to admit it to me.

The thing was, Cindy attracted just that, supernaturals. Sure, something was off about me, but even I felt like I didn't quite fit in with the supernatural crowd of misfits. I had a feeling that my memory loss didn't have much to do with the whacky weirdness that was going on with the world. It was something more personal... but Cindy didn't have to know that.

I liked Cindy. She never asked questions or gave me a hard time when I didn't seem to know basic things. It felt like I had to learn how to live life all over again. Something fundamental had changed in me and I couldn't put my finger on what. Without having any memory of my past, I wasn't even going to try and figure it out. Let it come naturally, that's what Cindy always said.

We had this weird kind of understanding that made our relationship work. I'd shown up on her doorstep in the middle of the night covered in blood and soaked with rain and she'd taken me in just like she'd done with so many before me.

That's what the mother of monsters always did.

"Guy at table three has been ogling you for an hour," Jess told me as she balanced a tray on her hip.

Jess was the closest thing I had to a friend in the same way that Cindy was the closest thing I had to a mother. Jess had arrived only a few weeks before I did, but she was already well on her way to recovery. Cindy had set up a few interviews for Jess at various escort gigs. Normally I'd disapprove, but Jess seemed to love the attention, so I hoped she would be happy when it was time for her to go.

"Don't be a bimbo," I said, making a point to ignore the guy she'd pointed out. "No way he's looking at me when you're standing right here." I gave her short skirt and halter top a raised brow. She already had voluptuous boobs and a rounded ass big enough to make a guy stop in his tracks, and that outfit made everything pop in just the right way. "I'm not a succubus like you."

She grinned, showing off her pearly white teeth. "I'm serious, Lily, he's checking you out!"

Dread washed over me. I had the good looks, sure. Long, blonde hair, legs that could kill in some heels and plump lips that would be perfect for pouting... if I ever pouted, which I didn't. I desperately hoped that I wasn't a succubus.

I still didn't know what I was yet, which was frustrating, but since being a succubus was still on the table I scanned the bar just for good measure. Every guy in the place was drooling over Jess and making a fool of themselves... every guy except for the one at table three.

Our gazes matched long enough for a jolt of familiar awareness to slam through me.

Okay, that was weird.

I tried to pretend I was fascinated with my phone. "I'm off duty, Jess," I reminded her as I scrolled through a mindless social media thread. "Go give the guy a new beer. The one you gave him an hour ago looks flat and he's probably just thirsty."

"Yeah," she snickered and waggled her eyebrows, "thirsty for some of your lo-ove," she said, making sure to sing-song the last word.

Ignoring her, I continued to scroll through my phone. It wasn't hard to pretend my fascination when the damn thing was so addictive. Cindy allowed me to use it as long as it was only for "research," as she called it. I never called anyone or posted anything online. I loved to read about humans and see what kinds of things they shared with each other. Most of it involved vague statements I didn't understand, pictures of kittens—which I always approved of—and snaps of perfectly arranged meals. Then there was the occasional political post about the emergence of supernaturals. Everyone had an opinion, especially when it came to Fortune Academy. *A Place Where Supernaturals Belong*. That was their slogan.

When I'd asked Cindy about it, she'd sneered and told me that if I was smart, I'd steer clear of anything related to that place.

Not that I was going to tell Cindy my opinion, but she had to be wrong. An entire organization dedicated to helping lost supernaturals? While I appreciated all that Cindy did for me, she didn't have answers. Fortune Academy would give me a fighting chance at figuring out what the hell I was.

One slight problem… the academy had stringent prerequisites to join, one of which is demonstrating a supernatural ability —which I hadn't been able to do yet. I only knew I was supernatural because I'd lost my memories and Cindy's door rune had called me to her.

I'd figure out what I was… but it wasn't going to be easy.

Jess elbowed me in the ribs. "Hey, are you listening to me?"

I rolled my eyes. "You're still here? I said I was busy."

She leaned in and lowered her voice, not taking her eyes off the stranger. "I really think you should go talk to him, Lils. I can tell when a guy has the hots, and while he definitely has the hots for you, something is off about him that I can't really figure out. I don't like it."

I chuckled. "I'll tell you what's off about him. There's a gorgeous succubus in the room and he's staring at me. Clearly the guy's missing some marbles." And of course she didn't like it. Jess needed to get all of the male attention—which was fine with me.

"Hey, sweet cheeks!" A guy from across the bar yelled at Jess. "You bringing me those beers, or what?"

Jess waved at him and giggled, which just pissed me off. "You should go kick that guy in the balls."

Jess huffed and readjusted her tray. "That's not how I get the good tips. Now go talk to the hottie at table three or I will." She pursed her lips and gave me a you-better-go-talk-to-him-or-else look and then marched over to deliver the impatient human his beers.

I turned my attention back to the topic of our discussion. The stranger hunched into himself, hiding his face in the shadow of his cowl. I frowned.

That either meant he was shy, or he was hiding something.

Someone who could resist a succubus' charms wasn't the shy type, so I stuffed my phone in the back of my jeans pocket and marched over to his table. I crossed my arms until he grunted at me.

"Oh, so you can talk?" I snapped. Irritation put me on edge. I was standing right in front of him and he wouldn't look up at me. "What, you can stare at me all night when I'm halfway across the room but when I come to your table you've got nothing to say?"

He twisted the untouched beer that Jess had delivered to him an hour ago, leaving a ring of condensation on the table. "So, you don't remember me." His voice came out husky and low… and apparently he knew who I was.

My entire body froze and a cold sweat broke out on my face. I'd harbored the secret hope that someone might recognize me in a popular bar, but I'd also feared the day someone who knew me might show up. I'd arrived at a monster's orphanage... and I'd been soaked in more than icy rain that night I'd shown up at Cindy's doorstep.

Yes I'd been covered in blood—but it was blood that wasn't my own. By the time I got my clothes off that night and slipped into a borrowed set of pajamas, I discovered I didn't have a single scratch on me.

I somehow managed to swallow the bitter fear that crawled up my throat. Letting out a nervous laugh, I flipped my hair over my shoulder. Guys always reacted better when they thought I was a dumb blonde. "Sorry. Maybe if you weren't hiding behind your cowl I could actually see your face, you know? Hard to jostle the memory with just a broody voice."

He hesitated and then shifted so that his cowl moved just enough for me to see the hard ridge of his chin. "I don't brood," he growled.

It was almost cute how he immediately retorted the insult. I was about to make it worse, but then he pulled back his hood all the way and hot damn, the guy was smoking.

And, well, his eyes glowed with a metallic orange magic that marked him as a supernatural bounty hunter… but yeah, details.

I shouldn't have been surprised that a bounty hunter would show up at Cindy's bar, but he still managed to take me off guard. While my mind was mush, my body reacted to the deadly flash of silver that was his blade. The world around me stilled with a magical lock. I didn't know if it was something I'd done or if it had been the bar's defenses. Taking advantage of the moment, I twisted to put as much distance as possible between me and the hunter.

Except… he tracked my movements with ease, his eyes locked onto mine as I moved. When I flinched, he flicked the blade and its merciless silver etched across my vision. I knew it would be sharp enough to cut my head clean off my body, but I realized a half-second too late that he hadn't been aiming for me.

Jess cried out and clutched at the embedded hilt, crumpling to the floor as time unlocked from its slowed momentum.

"Jess!" I screamed and lurched to her aid, but the hunter had me by the arm with a vice grip.

"You're welcome," he growled and tugged me into his chest. "She was about to kill you."

Flattened against his hard abs, I curled my fingers into the thick layers of his coat and peered up at him, taking in the full brutal force of his hard edges and glowing eyes. Everything about him screamed danger, but the way he held me was protective... almost gentle.

A clatter of metal hit the floor and broke a silence that I realize didn't make any sense in a crowded bar. No one seemed to notice that Jess had been stabbed, or that a hunter with glowing eyes was holding me.

That was because time was frozen... but not Jess.

Jess... who now had a dagger plunged in her chest.

Even a succubus should have died from a mortal wound like that, but she snarled as if irritated by the blade and launched for me. The hunter reacted before I did and held out his hand to defend me, which would have been sweet, except the weapon struck clean through flesh and bone, severing his hand and sending it flopping to the floor like a lump of meat.

"Oh dear..." I murmured.

He cursed and wrapped the stumped remains of his hand in his cloak. When Jess cried out and collapsed to her knees, I realized that he hadn't cursed under his breath, but rather cast a spell.

So, my bounty hunter had some magical mojo.

"You bastard!" Jess screamed. "She's mine!"

My brain couldn't process Jess screaming at the hunter, so my gaze wandered throughout the bar that was like a snapshot in time.

A group three tables down held up their beers in celebration and one sloshed his contents into the air, the foam and droplets making a perfect arc over his friend's head.

Cars outside that should have been speeding down the dark alleyway were now stopped. The one closest to the window featured a woman with her hair fanned out behind her as if she was trapped in a photoshoot.

Then I spotted Cindy watching from the back with the door

cracked open. Even she was trapped in the moment. Whatever had frozen time, only the hunter, Jess, and I were able to move. It bothered me more that Cindy was just back there... watching... as if waiting for something to happen. If she knew who the hunter was, why wouldn't she have stopped me from talking to him?

The hunter shook me with his remaining hand. He should have been buckled over in pain, but I didn't know much about bounty hunters. Maybe he could shut his pain off. "You need to stop daydreaming," he snapped. "Look." He pointed and my gaze obeyed even though my brain didn't want to process what was going on.

A knife rested on the ground just inches from Jess's hand, but not the one the hunter had stabbed her with. That one was still lodged in her chest and blood pooled around the wound and seeped into her clothing.

"Jess?" I asked, my voice cracking when I finally realized that she'd been coming at us with a knife. Not just any knife, but a blade etched with runes that glowed red.

I considered Jess my friend, even though I'd only been here a few weeks and was still trying to remember who I was. Cindy told me that I shouldn't rush it. Just take as much time as I needed. Jess had always been supportive in her own way, but this wasn't the Jess who talked to me about guys or stole a shot with me from behind the bar. She gripped the hilt of the dagger still embedded in her chest and glared at me. I'd never seen anyone look at me with such hatred, much less someone I thought was my friend.

"You're a monster," she said, almost like it was something she'd kept in for far too long. "You're supposed to work for us. No one else can have you!" She lurched for the dagger she'd dropped, but cried out in pain and slapped her hand on the floor.

If it hadn't been for the hunter who still held me with one

strong arm, I would have gone ice cold. I hadn't been in many situations where I was this stressed, but sometimes when a customer got rowdy or Cindy raised her voice my fingertips would go so cold that they'd feel numb until I grabbed onto someone. Now the urge to touch devoured me worse than I'd ever felt it and I crawled my hands up the hunter's clothes until I reached a patch of skin exposed at his neck. He flinched the moment my icy fingers met his, but he didn't stop me. Instead he stroked my hair out of my eyes and gave me a sobering look.

"It's Lily, right?"

Hearing my name jolted me into awareness and I looked into his eyes that still glowed with that fascinating metallic golden gleam. "Uh, yeah." How did he know my name?

He surveyed the bar and frowned. "I can't hold the time lock once we step outside of this bar. We're lucky that the monster mother was on the other side of the door when I initiated it." He glanced down at the dagger still in Jess's chest. I noticed one gem on the end of the hilt glowing green, but that light was starting to fade. "We don't have much longer. Do you think you can move?"

The shock of what he was proposing made all the heat I'd gathered into my fingertips surge straight through my whole body. He jerked away from me and cursed.

"You can't mean that I'd go somewhere with you?" I asked.

"Yes," he growled, transforming from the kind and patient stranger I'd been clinging to back into the hunter that had come to... what had he come here to do? "If you stay here you'll be killed... or worse. You have to come with me."

Sense came back to me as I bristled. No one told me what to do. "I can take care of myself, thank you very much."

"You better listen to him," Jess drawled, grinning manically as her eyelids drooped and blood tinted her teeth pink. It was the most terrifying sight I'd ever seen, especially since one side of her face was starting to droop and one of her eyes was turning black. "I'm not really a succubus, you know. I'm something else... something even better. I wasn't ready to show you, but looks like I don't have a choice. You lost your memory because you weren't ready to learn what you are, but I've embraced it."

"You shut your mouth," the hunter snapped and produced a second blade. "Lily is nothing like you."

She gurgled on another laugh. "Oh, protective, are you? Didn't come to kill her... but to collect her for your little academy? How quaint."

I dug my fingernails into my palm. The air around us started to tremble as if the whole world was about to fall apart. I couldn't leave Jess here, dying, even if she was frightening me. I didn't care what she was, I needed to give her a chance to explain. Maybe if she thought I wouldn't go with him she'd stop trying to attack me.

She gave me a look of pity. Which was incredulous. Jess, the one with the knife in her chest and her face falling apart, gave *me* a look of pity. "Such a sweet thing. You still want to help me, don't you?" She sighed. "Tricky blood you have. Two-thirds of you is perfect for Monster Academy, but there's that nasty little extra third that shows its ugly head. I see it right now in your eyes. No proper monster would look at me like that." Her face twisted with rage. "Mother will burn it out of you. Then you can join us and Monster Academy will finally have its star pupil." She chuckled. "Or failed experiment. Either way, I will be getting some major extra credit for this."

"Monster Academy?" I shrieked. "Jess, what the hell are you talking about?"

She opened her mouth to answer me, but a loud crack reverberated through the room and time unlocked from its latch.

"Time to go," the hunter said and took me by the arm again.

Everything happened all at once. The serene silence dropped into a clatter of noise typical of a busy bar. Startled, I ducked as if the bombardment of sounds was an object hurled at my head, and good thing, too. Cindy burst through the door and launched fire—fucking fire!—from her hand.

I'd never seen anything like it. The flames were so hot that they melted straight through a pair of guests and sent their corpses disintegrating to the floorboards. The bar exploded and the scent of fear hit me like a wall.

"Come on!" the hunter shouted and tugged at me, but I was rooted to the spot. He gave me a look of surprise.

That's right. I was supernatural. No fucking idea what I was, but he wasn't going to move me unless I agreed to it.

Which, going with him was starting to feel like a good idea. Jess was talking about hooking me up with Monster Academy—no idea what that was but it didn't sound good—and Cindy was throwing fire around and killing people.

I had a decision to make and not much time to make it. One quick glance at Jess gave me mixed feelings. She clearly wasn't a succubus. Jess's beauty melted off of her as if the dagger in her chest drained her of her outer skin. I wasn't sure if it had been a spell or some elaborate magical sleeve, but whatever this creature was before me now with black eyes and wrinkled skin was the real Jess.

Strangely, I wanted to get to know her. Those black eyes still had Jess inside of them. There was more darkness and pain, but still the friend that I'd come to care for.

Yet, when she went for the cool blade again on the floor, I knew that she would rather kill me than let the hunter have me. Perhaps I was naive, just like she always told me I was.

Closing my eyes with resignation, I let the hunter haul me out of the bar and into the cold night.

Of course, it was fucking raining, and the blood on me wasn't my own.

Keep Reading in Fortune Academy!

www.ingramcontent.com/pod-product-compliance
Lightning Source LLC
Chambersburg PA
CBHW020533310726
48979CB00014B/2312/J

* 9 7 8 1 9 5 3 3 9 3 0 1 2 *